PENGUIN CLASSICS

THE SAGA OF GRETTIR THE STRONG

ÖRNÓLFUR THORSSON studied Icelandic literature at the University of Iceland, specializing in medieval literature. He was a lecturer at the Icelandic University College of Education for eight years and has also taught at the University of Iceland and the University of Leeds. His published work includes annotated Icelandic editions of *The Saga of Grettir the Strong*, *The Saga of the Volsungs* and *Sturlunga Saga* and, in collaboration, a complete edition of the Sagas and Tales of Icelanders, Snorri Sturluson's *Heimskringla*, the *Collected Works* of Snorri Sturluson and the only dictionary of Icelandic slang. He has written, lectured and broadcast extensively on medieval and modern literature and served on the boards of publishing houses and cultural bodies, including the Reykjavík Literature Festival. Örnólfur Thorsson is now the Director of the Office of the President of Iceland.

BERNARD SCUDDER was born in Canterbury, Kent, and studied English at the University of York and Icelandic at the University of Iceland. Since 1977 he has lived in Reykjavík, where he is a full-time translator. Including more than a dozen published works, his translations from Icelandic encompass sagas, ancient and modern poetry, and leading contemporary novels and plays. He translated two major sagas for the *Complete Sagas of Icelanders* (1997) and edited most of the poetry in that collection. In 1998 two novels in his translation were shortlisted for the European Union's Aristeon Literary Prize.

The Saga of Grettir the Strong

Translated by BERNARD SCUDDER

Edited with an Introduction and Notes by
ÖRNÓLFUR THORSSON

PENGUIN BOOKS

PENGUIN BOOKS

Published by the Penguin Group
Penguin Books Ltd, 80 Strand, London WC2R ORL, England
Penguin Group (USA) Inc., 375 Hudson Street, New York, New York 10014, USA
Penguin Books Australia Ltd, 250 Camberwell Road, Camberwell, Victoria 3124, Australia
Penguin Books Canada Ltd, 10 Alcorn Avenue, Toronto, Ontario, Canada M4V 3B2
Penguin Books India (P) Ltd, 11 Community Centre, Panchsheel Park, New Delhi – 110 017, India
Penguin Group (NZ), Cnr Airborne and Rosedale Roads, Albany, Auckland 1310, New Zealand
Penguin Books (South Africa) (Pty) Ltd, 24 Sturdee Avenue, Rosebank 2196, South Africa

Penguin Books Ltd, Registered Offices: 80 Strand, London WC2R ORL, England

www.penguin.com

First published 2005

022

Translation copyright © Leifur Eiríksson Publishing Ltd, 2005
Introduction and Notes copyright © Örnólfur Thorsson and Bernard Scudder, 2005
All rights reserved

Leifur Eiríksson Publishing Ltd gratefully acknowledges the support of the
Nordic Cultural Fund, Ariane Programme of the European Union, UNESCO,
Icelandair and others

Set in 10.25/12.25 pt PostScript Adobe Sabon
Typeset by Rowland Phototypesetting Ltd, Bury St Edmunds, Suffolk
Printed and bound in Great Britain by Clays Ltd, Elcograf S.p.A.

www.greenpenguin.co.uk

Contents

Contents

Acknowledgements

Bernard Scudder's translation of *The Saga of Grettir the Strong* was originally published in volume two of *The Complete Sagas of Icelanders*, Reykjavík, 1997.

Help and advice from all the individuals, too numerous to mention in full, who were involved in the long genesis of the translation and this edition is gratefully acknowledged. Bernard Scudder would particularly like to thank Fredric Heinemann for his critical reading of the original translation and Don Brandt for his proofreading. Örnólfur Thorsson is especially grateful to Guðmundur Andri Thorsson, Halldór Guðmunds-son and Sverrir Tómasson for their useful and constructive advice.

The editor and translator jointly thank Jóhann Sigurðsson, publisher of the *Complete Sagas*, Viðar Hreinsson, editor, and Gísli Sigurðsson for their advice, encouragement and patience throughout this long process, and likewise Alastair Rolfe, Hilary Laurie, Lindeth Vasey, Margaret Bartley, Emma Horton, Laura Barber and others at Penguin for displaying the same virtues in bringing this volume to fruition.

Introduction

The Sagas of Icelanders

Composed in the vernacular by anonymous authors in the thirteenth to the fifteenth centuries, the Sagas of Icelanders refer to events several centuries before, from the birth of a nation with the settlement of Iceland in the ninth century and through to its consolidation in the second half of the eleventh century.

Most scholars date the Golden Age of saga writing to the second half of the thirteenth century, when the unique society of the Commonwealth, which had neither king nor central executive power but enforced law and order through blood vengeance, was dissolving in civil war that would culminate in Iceland's subjugation to the Norwegian crown. In this respect *The Saga of Grettir the Strong*, with its late date of composition (late fourteenth century or around the year 1400) is a misfit. It represents a kind of interface where the Icelandic Middle Ages and the Renaissance meet and it is also a swansong in which the author pays tribute, with a hint of nostalgia, to a narrative tradition that he knows by heart. A world was passing, never to return.

The Saga of Grettir was composed at the dawn of a new era and much of its style, form and narrative technique, characterization and attitude to literary tradition prefigure the birth of the novel. Nowhere else in saga writing do we have such a clear sense of an author with an overview of the tradition he is at once drawing from and contributing to, piecing together and reworking his narrative with the same conscious purpose as a modern novelist.

Christianity, which was adopted in 1000, introduced the art of writing to Iceland and ushered in organized contact with educational and cultural centres on the European continent. Icelanders studied in Germany, France and Britain, and were influenced by these countries on their return. Some brought books which were translated into Icelandic: hagiographies, accounts of Christian martyrs and other literature that might help eradicate the vestiges of paganism from the Icelanders' minds.

But in their narrative art the Icelanders soon diverged from their European contemporaries in their relish of the vernacular. After the Age of Learning in the twelfth century, when they concentrated on translating and writing works of scholarship, they turned their attention to their own origins, to cherished oral traditions describing the settlement of Iceland and the foundation of the Commonwealth, which became the foundation for works which were based on historical fact but obeyed artistic laws of characterization and plot.

The Sagas of Icelanders – forty in all – depict many lives from more than one generation, generally opening in Norway with a brief account of the reasons that many men of noble birth fled the tyrannical rule of King Harald Fair-hair to begin new lives for themselves in Iceland. Subsequently, the sagas focus on their descendants, especially the third and fourth generations. Many deal with conflicts sparked by disputes which are not always lofty. Once a conflict begins its escalation seems unstoppable and the plot is swept along by the fates guiding the characters, while in their attitude towards these events the saga heroes reveal their true characters: confronted by two bad choices, they invariably opt for the one that will preserve their honour and reputation for posterity.

On the basis of their heroes and geographical settings, the Sagas of Icelanders may be classified into two main groups. One is the *Biographies*, focusing on a single character who dominates the stage from childhood to death. An elaboration upon the biographical format portrays the lives of several generations of the same family but devotes the most detail to a single main hero. For example, Egil Skallagrimsson and Grettir the Strong dominate the action of the sagas named after them, even

though their forebears' adventures are related in the opening
sections.

The other class is the *Sagas of Feuds*, which tend to depict
events over a delimited period of time (such as *The Saga of
Havard from Isafjord*, *The Saga of the Confederates*, *Hen-
Thorir's Saga*) or in a narrow geographical setting (e.g. *The
Saga of the People of Ljosavatn*, *Valla-Ljot's Saga*, *The Saga
of the People of Vopnafjord*), mainly set in a specific district
although the action may spill over to other localities, even
abroad, as in the case of *Njal's Saga*.[1] While this class of sagas
certainly contains many memorable characters, these heroes are
only depicted at the more momentous periods in their lives; in
Njal's Saga, for example, we are only introduced to Njal and
Gunnar as grown men and know nothing of their childhood
and youth.

Iceland is the focal point of the Sagas of Icelanders, but the
action of many of them is prefigured with accounts of varying
detail about the exodus from Norway. After the settlement,
dealings between Icelanders and kings of Norway are a recurrent theme, not least when, before assuming control of their
families' farms, aspiring young heroes set out into the world to
prove their manhood and qualities – as warriors and poets –
and to demonstrate they are a match for the royalty of mainland
Scandinavia. In its broadest sense the setting of the sagas spans
the whole known western hemisphere, with Iceland at the
centre. In their quests to test their strength and explore, the
heroes range to Greenland and Vinland (North America) in
the west, Russia in the east, Lapland in the north and Constantinople and Jerusalem in the south. Icelanders and their forebears
from Scandinavia raided the shores of Ireland, sailed to Rouen
and London and made war on the peoples of the Baltic. Wherever they go, they are portrayed in the sagas as prized by earls
and kings, they lead armies into battle and are unmatched as
warriors, the most elegant and desirable of all men in the eyes
of the women of the Norwegian royal courts, undaunted by
nobility and authority. More often than not they are described
as the equals of kings, if not their kinsmen; Grettir Asmundarson and King Olaf of Norway are related through the same

forebear five generations back, as stated in the opening chapter. However, the typical hero relinquishes fame abroad to return to Iceland, settle down and farm. The centre of these people's existence is Iceland, on a modest farm shelter by towering mountains.

Back home in Iceland they have returned to a realistic and routine world in which all the chieftains, farmers and farm labourers go about the daily business society has assigned them. Young people in the same district fall in love, often spawning a long sequence of events; boys fight, young men play ball games, farmers amuse themselves at wrestling and horse-fights. People busy themselves with everyday chores and tasks in a closed world which is diametrically opposed to the splendour that the heroes always enter abroad. To avenge a slight in their youthful games (chapter 15), Grettir ambushes Audun (chapter 28) when the latter is carrying curds back to his farm, and similarly avenges the death of his brother Atli by killing Thorbjorn Ox and his son Arnor (chapter 48) when they are baling hay in the meadows. The earthly business of life is intertwined with accounts of heroic deeds in a way that would be unthinkable in the continental genre of chivalric literature. When they occur, magic and sorcery, portents and visions give the impression of being an integral component of the saga world, part of daily life and not a threat from a world beyond.

The Sagas of Icelanders draw on stories passed down from one generation to the next, consciously reworking their action and character portraits into literary creations, and are influenced in various ways by contemporary historical events, by native and foreign literature, written and oral, and by native and foreign learning. But while the existence of such a productive melting pot seems beyond dispute, our knowledge of the precise ingredients that went into it is piecemeal and to a large extent conjectural. The forty sagas we have today – and many have probably been lost – have been preserved in copies made over the centuries both by professional scribes and amateur scribes or ordinary farmers who admired these works of literature and sought to preserve and share them.

We know nothing about the original authors, when and

where they lived, their background and motivation, their audience or readership; wide divergences in the extant versions mean that we cannot even establish an original or prototype for any of the sagas. In *The Saga of Grettir the Strong*, we sense a strong authorial presence in the conscious marshalling of material into an artistic whole, but we are none the closer for that to knowing his identity, nor whether he assembled from scratch the saga that we have today or merely reworked earlier disparate elements from a kind of Grettir 'cycle'. Whoever it was who composed *The Saga of Grettir* in the fourteenth century leaves no question as to his firm grounding in familiar and now lost literature, Icelandic and foreign, ancient and contemporary, and he seems to be jousting or in dialogue with a whole literary corpus, playing with concepts and motifs and implicitly or explicitly introducing familiar figures from other sagas into the outlaw's story, in particular from older works such as *Egil's Saga*, *The Saga of the People of Eyri*, *The Saga of the Sworn Brothers* and *The Saga of the People of Laxardal*. Like Grettir's own life, the saga that bears his name can be seen as a defiant and glorious last stand, before the dawn of the Renaissance.

2
Grettir: Outlaw, Poet and Tragic Hero

The Saga of Grettir the Strong charts the life of an exceptional man who spent most of his life on the periphery of civilization, condemned to loneliness by a curse from a ghost and persecuted by his enemies. This is the saga of a strongman and a poet, a traveller, a killer and a slayer of monsters and, in the unusual tasks he performs, he calls to mind characters as disparate as Beowulf and the mighty god Thor, who in the pagan pantheon championed the war against the giants that continuously threatened to disrupt and destabilize.

Grettir was a 'problem child', which is not uncommon for saga heroes. He resembles the 'coal-biter' or 'male Cinderella', a stock figure who seems unpromising, lazy, obstinate and taciturn in youth, but flourishes into strength and prowess in manhood; in fact, this similarity is so striking that the author feels compelled to make clear that Grettir 'did not lounge around in the fire hall'.

Grettir is a complex character from the moment he is introduced in chapter 14, for it is difficult to explain his nasty streak in terms of a lack of other qualities. The cruel tricks he plays on animals and on his father to avoid work often involve considerable ingenuity and effort. Also, his taciturnity does not spring from an inability to use words, but rather from a gift for using them sparingly and sharply, as in his pithy exchanges with his father.

Both the time frame and the geographical setting of the saga are unusually broad. The action shifts from Norway via the British Isles (chapters 1–13) to Iceland, where the main drama takes place (chapters 14–85, interspersed with a couple of journeys to Norway), and ends in Constantinople and Rome. Like many other sagas, it begins in Norway when Harald Tangle-hair (later King Harald Fair-hair) forcibly unites the country into a single realm, culminating in the battle of Havsfjord around 885. Typically in the sagas, an individual of noble birth refuses to submit to Harald's authority and leaves Norway to make a new life in the virgin territory of Iceland – in *The Saga of Grettir*, it is the hero's great-grandfather Onund Tree-leg.

The Saga of Grettir the Strong ends close to the middle of the eleventh century, when Thorstein Dromund and his wife Spes become hermits in Rome. It therefore has the formal structure of a *family saga*, describing the lives of four generations: Onund Tree-leg and his descendants. Although some account is given of several family members, Grettir and his brothers are cast in the main roles, and this is effectively Grettir's biography, since he occupies centre stage most of the time.

The Saga of Grettir the Strong shares strong structural characteristics with *the sagas of outlaws*: *Gisli Sursson's Saga*[2] (written c.1270–1320) and *The Saga of Hord and the People of Holm* (1340–80). At the centre of the narrative is an outlaw in the wild, exiled from human society, pursued by farmers who resent his overbearing attitude and relentlessly persecuted by a leader of the community (in Grettir's case, Thorir from

Gard, who blames the outlaw for the death of his two sons). While outlaws and outcasts are found in other sagas – for example Hrapp in *Njal's Saga* (1270–90) and Ospak in *The Saga of the Confederates* (1270–1300)[3] – their tales are generally told only for as long as they remain part of the community. Once they have gone into the wild they drop out of the story, but in the outlaw sagas the viewpoint and the narrative follow them into exile and look back at society with the outlaw's lonely but defiant eyes.

'No man is an island,' said John Donne, but these saga outlaws are. Thrown on the mercy of nature, in a symbolic way they find temporary sanctuary on islands: Gisli on Hergilsey, Hord on the Holm in Hvalfjord, and Grettir on Drangey. All three of these outlaws are noble-born individuals at odds with their society who clash with both their communities and families, although family divisions are less prominent in *The Saga of Grettir*.

Each of their lives follows a course dominated by ill fate and prophecies of doom, but Grettir is the least fortunate of them all – his every step is opposed by Providence. Gisli and Grettir share a fear of the dark and a strong sense of loneliness in their exile, sometimes appearing more like wild animals than human beings. Gisli digs a lair like a fox and is in fact rescued in one memorable episode by a man called Ref ('Fox'). Grettir makes himself a den like a bear and in Norway he kills a bear and a man called Bjorn ('Bear'), who had provoked him into doing so. Both outlaws have evil spirits and sorcerers for antagonists and both lose their lives through evil prophecies or spells. Gisli is sapped of his strength by the heathen dream woman who persecutes him with increasing force throughout his exile. Grettir is fatally weakened by Thurid, who 'had been well versed in magic and knew many secret arts when she was young and people were heathen'.

But Grettir and Gisli differ in character, probably reflecting the way social attitudes have changed over the fifty years separating their deaths. Gisli places ideals above life itself, stubbornly sacrificing personal happiness for his own sense of honour. He loses his peace of mind, but keeps his physical strength. Grettir, on the other hand, gradually sheds the impetuousness that drove him into outlawry in the first place and learns the virtue of patience. But it is too late. His society has lost patience and passed sentence on him.

Grettir learns to rein in his anger. In Norway he kills Bjorn, but he only flogs Gisli Thorsteinsson, and merely has a peaceful chat with Thorodd the son of Snorri the Godi. In his years of exile Grettir thus gains increasing peace of mind, but it is his body that betrays him in the end.

On another level, *The Saga of Grettir* is a study of the poetic temperament and might also be classified among the *sagas of poets*. Forty-six of the verses in this saga are attributed to its hero, and some are known from other sources such as Snorri Sturluson's *Prose Edda*. For sheer poetic volume *The Saga of Grettir* ranks alongside *The Saga of Bjorn, Champion of the People of Hitardal* (written c.1280–1320)[4] and *The Saga of the Sworn Brothers* (1270–1300). As it happens, Grettir spends a considerable amount of time with the heroes of both these sagas on his travels. But unlike the heroes of most sagas of poets, he does not fight another poet for a woman's love. Instead, Grettir uses language to confront society. Some of his most memorable battles are fought with words rather than weapons. Physically unmatched, in the end he is beaten by language in the form of the evil prophecies of Glam and the runes and curses of Thurid.

One poet invites particularly close comparison with Grettir: Egil Skallagrimsson, the hero of *Egil's Saga* (1220–40).[5] The descriptions of their childhood and youth are similar: both are unruly lads and difficult for their parents to handle, almost to the extent of being troublemakers, while their brothers are model figures whom their parents adore. They quarrel with their fathers, who envisage unremarkable roles for them and refuse to support them when they leave home, and both are the favourites of their mothers, who protect them in childhood and encourage them to perform brave deeds. From an early age they both display a gift for poetry, although Egil is by far the better poet.

For all their physical strength, they are men of words and

suffer some rough treatment from older boys. Egil, aged seven, kills his adversary immediately, while Grettir savours his revenge in adulthood when he returns from Norway. Both warrior poets commit their first slayings when young and for little reason: Egil kills his opponent at games and, for good measure, the man who ran his father's farm; Grettir kills Skeggi after a quarrel over a bag of food.

In the end, however, Egil settles down as a worthy farmer in Iceland, whereas Grettir remains an outlaw with no way back into society. This difference might reflect the fact that Egil lived in pagan times, when slayers of men were shown more tolerance than in the Christian epoch in which Grettir lived. Most of the action of his saga takes place after 1000, the period when the pioneer society had largely become institutionalized, and old-fashioned heroic warriors like Grettir were increasingly regarded as social misfits. Christian nominal humility and forgiveness had supplanted the ethic of personal valour and vengeance.

Many readers will naturally see Grettir as a tragic hero, though he is not a plaything of Fate on the scale of, say, Gunnar and Njal in *Njal's Saga* or Gudrun Osvifsdottir in *The Saga of the People of Laxardal* (written c.1250–70).[6] Despite his pronouncement that 'No man is his own creator', Grettir tends to take his fate in his own hands and he cannot resist the challenge when Providence invites him to assert himself even further. He ignores warnings and premonitions, loses his temper at critical moments (for example when he strikes the urchin who insults him in church, instead of concentrating on the task in hand: proving his innocence before the king), and displays a total lack of the medieval virtue of humility, which is his brother Thorstein's hallmark at the end of the story.

Psychologically, Grettir is the product of two opposing influences. Asmund, his father, wants him to be a worthy citizen in a community of hard-working farmers. Asdis, his mother, looks back to her heroic forebears in the Vatnsdal family and urges Grettir to noble deeds, giving him a sword, which is an heirloom, and even sending his younger brother Illugi to join him in exile to make his last years bearable.

These polarities persist throughout the saga: Grettir repeatedly strives to 'test his strength' and play the hero in a society that has outgrown the ancient warrior ethic. He is not merely a nuisance, but an outright threat to society's values and his tragedy is that of a man born after his time.

It is not until his ill-judged fight with the ghost Glam that Grettir discovers his mission as a vanquisher of supernatural beings that live, as he does, on the fringes of society. The scourge of both honest men and evil monsters, Grettir is condemned to loneliness, plagued by fear of the dark, but unable to show himself in the light. At this level, The Saga of Grettir certainly ranks among the greatest tragedies. Strangely enough, the only serious threats to this anti-social character's life occur when he is living outside society in the wild, at the mercy of outlaws like himself; when he is in hiding almost on his enemies' doorstep, he repeatedly evades capture.

The author of The Saga of Grettir borrows motifs and influences from both Icelandic and Continental Romance and fantasy literature from the twelfth to fourteenth centuries, particularly in the closing six chapters, when Grettir's death is avenged in Constantinople, but also in the 'ghostbusting' that marks a turning point in his life. The sagas generally depict the supernatural realm in rather matter-of-fact terms, but the exceptional elements of folklore that surround Grettir suggest that the realist focus of classical tradition had changed by the time the saga was composed.

Finally, The Saga of Grettir the Strong is a moral story, preaching the flaws of self-assertion and the virtues of repentance. In fact, the saga incorporates so many types of literature it is tempting to regard it as a commentary on them all.

3
A Literary Odyssey

Grettir's voyages around Iceland include a 'literary tour' of the settings of other sagas and encounters with main characters from them. Direct allusions are made to three known sagas: The People of Laxardal (chapter 10), The Confederates (chapter 14) and *Bjorn, the Champion of the People of Hitardal* (chapter 58), which had almost certainly been committed to vellum when *The Saga of Grettir the Strong* was composed. Reference is also made to the elegy in *The Saga of the Sworn Brothers* (chapter 25) and a verse is quoted from it (chapter 27), while two other sagas – *Bodmod, Grimolf and Gerpir* (chapter 12) and *Earl Eirik* (chapter 19) – are named which are now lost or perhaps only existed in oral versions.

Intertextual links are a fairly common feature of the sagas. Some works show similarities in wording and occasionally identical passages, particularly when describing settlements. Whether this points to the existence of written sources or merely a common oral stock is not certain. *The Saga of Grettir* incorporates external material to a far greater extent than any other, quoting literary sources and imitating the stylistic features of different genres. The author slots his hero into the overlapping cycles from which the entire saga corpus is composed – to make Grettir somehow synonymous with the overall achievement of the saga tradition.

To some extent we can even imagine our unknown author's library. It probably included the sagas named above, plus at least nine others identified by scholars, which are not named directly but either supply passages – such as the long-winded oath in chapter 72, also found in *The Saga of the Slayings on the Heath* (written *c*.1250–70) and in the thirteenth-century legal code known as 'Grey Goose' (*Grágás*) – or motifs like the ancestral sword that the young Grettir is given by his mother – from *The Saga of the People of Vatnsdal* (1270–1320)[7] – and even the image of the rebellious son (*Egil's Saga*). Implicit references are made to shorter tales about men of legendary strength (such as Orm Storolfsson and Thoralf Skolmsson in chapter 58). *The Book of Settlements* probably supplied some historical material and the narrative for the early sections of *The Saga of Grettir*. There are also links with the sagas of the kings of Norway in the prelude to Onund Tree-leg's settlement in Iceland, as well as Grettir's own visits to Norway and the episode in Constantinople, which draws on *The Saga of King Harald the Stern*.

The closing chapters about Thorstein Dromund and Spes contain obvious borrowings from Continental Romance literature. Spes's ambiguous oath is very similar to one found in the Icelandic version of *The Saga of Tristram and Isond*, and the relish of intrigue – with cuckolded husbands and shrewd women who take lovers – is a familiar Continental theme. Grettir's rape of the servant-woman has a close parallel with a tale in Boccaccio's *Decameron* (1349–51), while his love of trickery and disguise calls to mind late-medieval rogue literature.

Grettir and his adventures are mentioned in a number of other medieval Icelandic writings, albeit usually in passing. Nevertheless, these fragmentary references tend to corroborate the saga narrative. They tell us that Grettir was a poet, known as the Strong, and an outlaw for longer than any other man in Iceland; that he killed Thorbjorn Ox to avenge his brother Atli's slaying, vied with Bjorn the Champion in trials of strength, stayed in 'Grettir's lair', spent an uneasy time with the sworn brothers Thormod and Thorgeir, and was saved by Thorbjorg from being hanged.

The author was also alert to a large body of material that had not been written down, such as oral traditions about Grettir himself, picaresque escapades in which he could cast his hero, old verses and later ones to attribute to him, as well as many proverbs. Proverbs are used on a scale unparalleled in the saga tradition. It contains almost 180 proverbial sayings and more than 80 proverbs; half of them are not found in any of the other Sagas of Icelanders, and *The Saga of Grettir* is, in fact, the oldest source for many common sayings in modern Icelandic. While many of the proverbs in the later part of the saga pronounce on Fate and Fortune, as befits an epic, others appear in a far more ironic context. For instance, when Grettir enters the story as a ten-year-old prankster who shirks his chores on the farm, the author makes him speak entirely in pithy sayings and proverbs which embody classical ethical teachings: 'A true friend spares others from evil,' 'The more you try, the more you learn,' 'It's a bad thing to goad the obstinate,' 'The foreseeable happens, and the unforeseeable too,' 'Wisdom falls short where it is most expected' (chapter 14). Fired off almost mechanically by a rebellious child, their effect is not only to undermine his father's authority, but also to mock the conventions of the genre.

Folklore elements are particularly strong in *The Saga of Grettir*. They were presumably borrowed from oral tradition, although they also demonstrate that by the time the saga was written classical realism was in irreversible decline. Ghosts were considered a part of the everyday world of the sagas, but hardly to the extent that a hero would stake his reputation on putting them to rest. There are intriguing parallels between the episode in which Grettir slays the giant in the underwater cave in Bardardal (chapters 64–7) and the Old English epic *Beowulf*, not only in the narrative, but also in the pike 'known as a shafted sword' (*heftisax*, a term unique to this saga) and the weapon named *hæftmece* in *Beowulf*. *Beowulf* is thought to have been composed around 800, but is preserved in manuscript from the time of the action of *The Saga of Grettir*. Scholars now believe, however, that the echoes are coincidental.

A direct borrowing from a folktale might account for the fact that the Grettir who performs brave deeds in Bardardal is curiously out of character from the rest of the saga – gone is his fear of the dark and he settles down to a life of almost domesticated bliss, even fathering a son, before setting off on his way again. A similar incongruity occurs in another archetypal folktale setting: the concealed, remote valley of Thorisdal (chapter 61), where outlaws could stay under the protection of giants. Ideal as this hiding place might seem, the author relegates it to a strangely insignificant place in his narrative, and again Grettir is different. Glam's curse that Grettir will always be afraid of the dark seems not to work in Thorisdal and for the only time in his life our hero regrets killing – a lamb, because the pining ewe keeps him awake with her bleating. Another peculiar feature of this episode is that the author abandons the objective, third-person narrative which is the hallmark of saga writing and Grettir himself is said to be the source for the description of the valley.

4
Narrative Structure

In its structure (see diagram on p. 220), *The Saga of Grettir the Strong* calls to mind a triptych with two wings that illuminate and enhance the magnificent centrepiece, but which may be removed without damaging it. The central section, in turn, can be divided into five 'acts', of which the final and longest can be represented as six separate episodes in a grand tour of Iceland. Although differing in length, the three main sections of the saga are closely interrelated. They present three very different kinds of hero: first Onund Tree-leg, then Grettir on his odyssey through the worlds of men and monsters, and finally his half-brother, Thorstein Dromund.

In many ways the two 'wings' of the triptych resemble each other, providing a contrast to Grettir's story. They both take place outside Iceland: Onund's tale set in Norway and Britain, and Thorstein's in Norway, Constantinople and Rome. Also, both these secondary male heroes emerge safely from difficult journeys and overcome adversity – when Onund loses a leg, he simply props himself up on a stump in order to fight (he is 'the bravest and nimblest one-legged man ever to live in Iceland', as the saga so memorably puts it). Favoured by fortune, Onund found rest in old age beneath a 'cold-backed mountain'. In contrast, we gain the impression that Grettir was born too late, his heroism is out of date. Thorstein Dromund is the hero of the new era, singing his way out of a dungeon in Constantinople, employing cunning rather than brute strength to effect revenge and win love, and eventually finding peace of mind and forgiveness in a stone cell in Rome. We are no doubt expected to take Onund and Thorstein into account while reading about Grettir – they are everything he is not.

The three-part structure also represents a journey through time, from the rocky pagan heroic age of Onund to the monastic cells of Rome, and important milestones on this route are indicated in the style and atmosphere. For instance, Onund's tale is remote and terse, with short sentences and brief dialogue. It is only when Grettir enters the narrative as a ten-year-old boy that the dialogue comes alive and assumes a more prominent place in the text, mixing proverbs, idioms and metaphors. With Grettir's entrance the text becomes much more ambiguous and ironic. In the account of the berserks arriving on Haramsoy, for example, the author deftly keeps up the suspense by changing the point of view, as elsewhere in Grettir's struggle with Glam and the fights with trolls in Bardardal. In these episodes the author borrows prototypes and motifs from other sagas of Icelanders, while also introducing narrative characteristics more familiar today from folktales and legends.

The third section of the saga has a very different atmosphere: a more complex style, longer sentences, an abundance of late loan-words and a heightened emphasis on the characters' rhetorical skills. This reaches its climax at the end of the story when with a learned disquisition Spes encourages Thorstein to take up the monastic life. Were we to set up stylistic signposts on this literary voyage, we could say the author travels from *The Book of Settlements* via the Sagas of Icelanders and folktales through to chivalric adventures and the then more fashionable Continental Romance; that is, from history to fable, from fact to fiction.

However, in one way or another Grettir leaves his mark on all three sections. The first depicts the world of the Vikings on land and at sea, where he would have been in his element, peopled by weather-beaten and brazen warriors who fought berserks before settling down in Iceland. In the second, Grettir is the main character, while the third section tells how his death was avenged in Constantinople. Good fortune is restored to the family and the saga ends with the redemption of all past sins.

The central section of the saga – the life and death of Grettir – falls into five 'acts' with several common features. They all begin in a situation of relative calm, but there is a progression, a set pattern of related events, until they end in legal or figurative outlawry for Grettir (for the different types of outlawry, see Social, Political and Legal Structure). At the end of the first act he is outlawed from Iceland and at the end of the second from Norway. The third ends with Glam's curse, which can be said to banish him from the society of ordinary people. After an unsuccessful attempt to find his feet again in Norway, he is expelled by King Olaf Haraldsson, then declared an outlaw in Iceland and condemned to death – although the death-struggle takes up the greater part of the story.

These five acts are linked in various ways. There are obvious parallels between the two voyages to Norway. On the first, Grettir wants to 'prove himself' abroad, as his father had done before him, although Grettir is forced to leave, having been exiled for murder at the age of fifteen. In contrast to the familiar saga motif of earning renown and wealth abroad, Grettir's reputation is built neither in the service of kings nor in battle, but in low-life, 'fringe' heroics. He first demonstrates that he is capable of using his strength to work and save others when, in a curiously theatrical scene, he bails out Haflidi's ship. In Norway he earns fame by laying to rest the ghost in Kar's mound on Haramsoy, where he earns a sword, and plays the 'knight in shining armour' by rescuing Thorfinn's wife and daughters from the clutches of evil berserks – but only after giving them a mighty scare by pretending that he was on the other side (chapter 19). He crowns these achievements by wrestling a bear in Salten, but he soon loses his temper again and ends up killing three brothers to avenge slights to his honour. No longer safe in Norway, he returns to Iceland, his three-year exile at an end.

On Grettir's second trip to Norway, Glam's curse is beginning to have an effect: the voyage is an ill-fated counterpoint to the glorious one he made earlier. Again he rescues his sailing companions from disaster, but this time, when he swims off to fetch fire, he accidentally kills the sons of Thorir from Gard by setting fire to their house. His attempt to prove his innocence fails dismally when he loses his temper at a fateful moment and appears to kill a boy who insults him in church; thereupon Grettir is banished by the king.

By this stage we know the character of Grettir and the saga well enough to feel something tragically inevitable about it all. Grettir's temper, his pride and his hot-headedness will surely get the better of him. A final moving scene with Thorstein suggests that Grettir's magnificent but unfortunate life will be avenged, albeit through cunning, wisdom and devotion rather than brute force.

In the same way there are links between the first, third and fifth acts. In the first, Grettir shows he is overbearing and rash, and in the third his violence and arrogance bring him face-to-face with evil in the form of Glam. After this there is no going back. Grettir's fight with Glam is his last 'trial of luck' and, even though he decapitates the ghost, he emerges as the real loser, because he has to live for the rest of his life under a curse, terrified of the dark. In the build-up to this episode, he is increasingly impatient and rash, deliberately provoking quarrels and eager to test his strength against anything. Grettir appears to be compelled by some kind of self-destructive force.

His chance to be a hero comes when the focus shifts to those evil beings that prey on the people of Forsaeludal. The only character capable of ridding the valley of a menacing troll is the Swedish heathen shepherd Glam. However, he dies in the attempt and his ghost haunts the farm at Thorhallsstadir far more menacingly than any troll.

At this stage, a distinct Christian element is introduced: Glam is portrayed as arrogant in his praise of heathen beliefs and his refusal to fast on Christmas Eve, and in a sense he is punished for obstinately clinging to the old faith. He is killed at Christmas – the first instance in which the Icelandic word *jól* can definitely be translated as such (in earlier episodes 'Yuletide' is more appropriate). The turning point in the saga has been reached and in Glam Grettir has found a worthy opponent, although he has already been warned by his maternal uncle Jokul that 'fate and fortune do not always go hand-in-hand' (chapter 34). After a tense build-up when Glam twice seems too intimidated to appear, they finally do battle in an encounter abounding in minute detail and slick, almost cinematic scene changes. Grettir wins the fight, but loses his good fortune. Glam's dying curse deprives Grettir of any future strength he could have hoped to gain, but also instils in him a fear of the dark – a horrible prospect for a man who will spend the rest of his life as an outlaw. Grettir essentially lives by his strength and wits and cannot be defeated by human means – but he is made vulnerable

xxvi   INTRODUCTION

by Glam's curse and is eventually overcome in battle after being
weakened by magic.

In act five Glam's fateful prophecy is played out with increasing momentum. This section is the longest and the most complicated. Its structure appears to be loose and disjointed as we
read about Grettir's adventures in the settled and uninhabited
parts of Iceland, among men and monsters in an ever-increasing
state of loneliness. Comic and serious chapters alternate and
Grettir's theatricals lighten the tone of this part of the saga.
They include his encounters with the sworn brothers, skir-
mishes with petty farmers in the West Fjords, raids on other
farmers in Myrar, the tricks he plays on his main adversary,
Thorir from Gard, and his assertion of his manhood to counter
the maid's taunts – although this assumes a more sinister tone
as, apparently, the only rape described in the sagas. Nevertheless, a strong tragic undercurrent develops, a 'thickening atmosphere of doom' as his ill-fortune intensifies, his supporters drop
away and his loneliness becomes increasingly unbearable until
at last he is forced into his island stronghold in Skagafjord.
Unlike many sagas, the action in this part of the story is not
confined to one or two regions of Iceland, with a few excursions
abroad. Like the hero of a picaresque novel, Grettir travels all
around the country and into the highland interior as well. He
even makes completely uneventful trips to the southern districts
and the East Fjords for no other apparent purpose than to be
able to say that he has been there.

Grettir's journey around Iceland is a kind of literary journey
as well, as he visits the settings of several other sagas and
their main characters. However, the author's references are not
limited to the sagas, for he introduces motifs, material and
techniques from contemporary European fiction (*fabliaux*, for
example) and from folklore and popular belief, presumably
drawing on oral traditions. These scenes give us some idea of
the way in which pagan beliefs were sidelined with the advent
of Christianity, where once giants and strange beings lived in
some ill-defined border between the worlds of man and nature.

Larger than life himself, Grettir feels quite at home with
giants such as Thorir from Thorisdal, and he often stays with

the cave-dweller Hallmund; both have daughters whose company he enjoys (though he gets bored eventually and returns to the world of men). And when a worthy trial of strength is at hand he is eager to rid the community of scourges and plagues, as in the episode with the giant in Bardardal. Another type of cultural input is provided with the scene at the Hegranes Assembly which contains one of the most detailed descriptions in saga literature of traditional wrestling or *glíma*. It also includes a beautiful if somewhat drawn-out formulaic oath invoking all the forces of heaven and earth.

Grettir spends the last three years of his life in self-imposed exile for his own safety on the island of Drangey, a barely scaleable rock stack in Skagafjord, in northern Iceland. His only company is that of his faithful younger brother Illugi, who will die a classical hero's death with him rather than accept dishonourable clemency, and the slave Glaum, whose laziness leaves their fortress open to assault. Grettir, suffering from a malignant leg wound brought on by the dark arts of a heathen crone, ceases to be the hunter and becomes the hunted. It is no coincidence that his killer, Thorbjorn Hook, has only one eye, like the god Odin, and has to seek advice from his sorceress foster-mother. But heathendom does not triumph in the end. The society that passes judgement on the morality of Grettir's death is avowedly Christian. Magic is equated with deception and Hook is condemned rather than celebrated.

The moral criticism that clings to Hook following Grettir's murder becomes even more marked in the third main section of the saga, the episode of Thorstein Dromund and Spes. It has a different tone to the others: we are in a new and exotic world as the action moves from Drangey in the north to Constantinople in the east, from one end of the known world to the other. The narrative technique changes accordingly to assume the character of a chivalric Romance with its labyrinthine architecture, exotic city and social theatricals. The author adopts a more complex style and indulges in displays of rhetorical dexterity and learning. There are obvious parallels with the sagas of the kings of Norway and the motifs of Romance literature such as the story of Tristan, and this section has a distinctly Continental feel to it. Dromund, exacting the belated revenge he had prophesied when Grettir mocked his skinny arms, is the hero – but Spes is also the first true heroine in this saga. Thorstein and Spes use their wits rather than brute force to legalize a love affair that is untenable from a strictly moral point of view. After a long and happy sixteen-year relationship, they try to repent for their sins by forsaking worldly wealth, seeking pardon and devoting themselves to the spiritual life.

5
Themes, Motifs and Echoes

Like many other works in this genre *The Saga of Grettir the Strong* is systematically structured with prophecies, parallels and thematic echoes (see pp. 236–7). The narrative races along towards the first climax when Grettir wrestles with Glam, then slows down towards the second climax as Thorbjorn Hook closes in on him. Grettir often does the same thing twice, but usually in different ways, inviting us to draw a comparison. Twice he fights Audun, wins hoards of treasure from monsters (on Haramsoy and in Bardardal), travels to Norway, battles with berserks and swims to fetch fire.

Sometimes we are presented with the same scenario three times, as if to underscore the sense of history repeating itself and the inevitability of Fate. The number three seems to dominate Grettir's life. He grapples with three heavy rocks to test his strength. He has three main dwelling places far from the world of men – Arnarvatn moor, Thorisdal and Drangey – and he spends three years in three places. Three valleys feature prominently in the events of his life and he has three enemies who are all named Thorbjorn (Ox, the Traveller and Hook). The number three especially recurs in the events on Drangey: the trio of Grettir, Illugi and Glaum spend three years on their rocky outpost; Hook makes three attempts to assail it; the crone Thurid puts a curse on a tree when three weeks remain until winter; the tree washes up on the shores of Drangey three times; Glaum has three 'accidents' that threaten their survival: he lets their fire go out, brings the cursed tree back and forgets to pull up the ladder to the top of the island.

Fraternal differences are a common theme in the sagas (Egil Skallagrimsson's jealous rivalry with his 'mainstream' brother Thorolf is a classic example) and Grettir is contrasted with both his brother Atli and half-brother Thorstein Dromund, while his younger brother Illugi appears to be the pure hero that Grettir aspires to be, without his unlucky streak and personality flaws. In particular, the author gives a strange echo to the different destinies of the two brothers, the peaceful farmer Atli and the outlaw Grettir. Atli kills two sons of Thorir from Skard, is killed by Thorbjorn Ox and avenged by Grettir, his brother; Grettir accidentally burns to death two sons of Thorir from Gard, is killed by Thorbjorn Hook and avenged by Thorstein Dromund, his half-brother.

Grettir's struggle with animals, evil spirits and monsters is repeated and developed with an almost fugal structure. Grettir wrestles with the mound-dweller in Haramsoy and acquires the magnificent short-sword; he kills a bear in Salten; then he fights with Glam and is subjected to his curse; and finally he purges Bardardal of the giants that terrorize the valley. A fifth encounter is with Thorbjorn Hook's foster-mother, the sorceress who learnt her trade before the coming of Christianity, and here the situation is reversed: Grettir is no longer the ghostbuster, but the ghost; the monster rather than the monster-slayer, a terrible scourge and a scavenger, as the people of Skagafjord call him; and Thorbjorn has taken on the purgative role which Grettir himself had played earlier. The reader senses that there is no way out for Grettir: the tables have turned.

Subtle echoing devices underpin the narrative structure, many of them verging on the bizarre. In particular, there are several 'limb' motifs. Feet and legs constitute an important theme. Grettir's great-grandfather, the warrior Onund (and son of Ofeig Hobbler), loses a leg in battle and earns the nickname 'Tree-leg', but Fortune does not desert him. Grettir, by contrast, accidentally inflicts on himself the leg wound that festers and leads to his death. Arms play a parallel thematic role, in the comparison between Grettir and his brother Thorstein (chapter

41). Phallic endowments complete the use of 'limb' motifs: in chapter 75 the servant-woman mocks Grettir for being 'short-sworded', while Onund's grandfather Ivar Horse-cock appears to have been at the opposite end of the spectrum.

Ivar's nickname, in turn, links up in an obtuse way with 'Handing Grettir Around', a poem about Grettir's dealings with the lowly farmers of the West Fjords, 'which witty men composed and embellished with humorous phrases for people's amusement' (chapter 52). Ólafur Halldórsson has published what has survived of this poem, which is preserved in the oldest, though hardly the best, manuscript of *The Saga of Grettir*. He maintains that the poem was originally used for after-dinner entertainment of a carnivalesque type that possibly had its ultimate origins in fertility rites. The Grettir in the poem refers to an animal's penis that is 'handed round from one bench to another while the poem is sung or recited' – the object is to pass it on to one's neighbour at the feast and not be left holding it. Halldórsson suggests that 'Handing Grettir Around' was included with the first version of the saga, and believes that the description of the farmers who try to get Grettir off their hands by passing him on to their neighbours derives from a game of this sort. Perhaps there are parallels not only with the farmers in Langidal, but also between this game and Grettir's own trials and tribulations as he travels all over Iceland, visiting a succession of important chieftains who all receive him well but do not want 'to be left holding him'. A reference to 'being rid of Grettir' in *The Tale of Helgi Thorisson* in the Flateyjarbok manuscript suggests that the subtext would have been obvious to a medieval audience.

Not all the motifs in the saga are so rooted in local tradition. Despite his aggressive and arrogant nature, Grettir subscribes to Christian rather than heathen values, as when he tries to fast while staying with the giant Thorir in Thorisdal. The only major saga hero not to witness the transition from paganism to Christianity (he was four years old at the time of the conversion), Grettir campaigns in his own way for the newly established faith: Christians must take on the evil spirits, trolls and berserks that are the last vestiges of heathendom. Although his heroics might appear anachronistic, in his role of ghostbuster Grettir acts in a sense as a standardbearer of the new Christian faith. He has something in common with another great traveller and folktale favourite, Bishop Gudmund Arason, who roamed Iceland with his band of followers in defiance of the authorities in the first decades of the thirteenth century, consecrating springs, fighting trolls and laying ghosts to rest. Both the Bishop and Grettir are associated with Drangey and they are also important champions of Christianity: the Bishop as a model of faith and piety, Grettir as a liberating force who dispatches heathen presences. It is surely no coincidence that his main battles with supernatural beings are all fought at Christmas.

Having travelled around Iceland fighting these beings, Grettir is eventually destroyed by magic. Nonetheless, he is far too human and complex to be a Christian martyr. 'The strongest man ever to have lived in Iceland' proudly clings to the values of the heroic age that has been eclipsed, although, when all is said and done, he is his own worst enemy.

Nevertheless, an underlying Christian symbolism can be identified in the recurrent stones and rocks. Grettir's forebears move from the cold and rocky home that Onund Tree-leg founded on Strandir and establish themselves at Bjarg ('Rock'), which might be regarded as the fundamental symbol of 'stead-fast Christian faith'. This was the material rock on which Asmund's family should have built its status as leading citizens in a community of farmers – and probably would have done had Atli not been swept into a feud. Grettir's sanctuary, the sheer and uninhabited rock stack of Drangey, might have been an ideal home for an anchorite, but in the saga it becomes a kind of fortress of anachronistic heroic values. And finally the rock comes to serve its true Christian purpose when Thorstein and Spes retire to contemplate life in their stone cells at the end of the saga, thereby demonstrating the proper, Christian way to isolate oneself from society.

6
Characters

The Saga of Grettir the Strong broadly resembles the mainstream saga tradition in its characterization. Main characters are introduced with a concise description of their physical qualities and a few well-chosen words about their temperament and personality, and this portrait is fleshed out by their words and actions, the treatment they receive from others and their reputation before and after death.

However, in *The Saga of Grettir* there is probably a more moralizing undertone to the characterization. Grettir's brother Atli, for example, plays a fairly important part in the action of the first half of the saga, especially in his dealings with Thorbjorn Ox. His popularity is mentioned twice and his good qualities are repeatedly underlined, presumably to sharpen the contrast with Grettir. We have a closer picture of the two adversaries most fateful to Grettir, Glam and Thorbjorn Hook, and in some respects Grettir and Hook are compared rather than contrasted. They are both short-tempered and, in an interlude more reminiscent of a morality play than a classical saga, Hook and his stepmother clash and he loses an eye while she loses her life. The scene recalls Grettir's own unruly childhood, taken to its logical extreme.

Another stock character in the Icelandic sagas is the strong and steadfast woman. Relatively few women appear in *The Saga of Grettir*, and most are mere foils to Grettir's manhood, although the more complex female characters are sharply delineated. Grettir's mother Asdis is a strong character as she urges her sons to adhere to the ancient heroic values (chapter 69); so too is Thorbjorg the Stout, who manages her husband's affairs in his absence and overrules the farmers to save Grettir from being hanged (chapter 52). Grettir's final and most dangerous opponent, the old crone Thurid, is also carefully delineated. Her sorcery represents a lost age in much the same way as Grettir's heroism, and she is the only character in the saga capable of bringing about his downfall. Finally, the Byzantine noblewoman Spes repeatedly outwits her husband to win the man she loves. The author even puts the stock phrase of sworn brothers from the heroic age in her mouth, when she tells Thorstein Dromund that she wants them to 'meet the same fate' (chapter 91).

Grettir the Strong is undoubtedly a hero, though hardly a traditional one. His tragedy is not so much that Providence forsakes him, but that society no longer needs heroes. His is not the only saga of Icelanders to explore the dilemma of what to do with a hero in peacetime. Many of the accounts of poets, outlaws and champions emphasize their increasing rootlessness and the dwindling tolerance shown by the community towards their violence and overbearing behaviour. They are forced to move from one district to another or to spend long periods of time on voyages abroad, where they merge seamlessly into the world of folklore and legend.

Thus the hero is an ambiguous figure in the sagas. His natural home is abroad, where he is in his element killing his own and others' enemies, doling out a brutal summary justice to gloating Vikings and berserks, and winning the favours of the good and the great. In Iceland, however, heroism is a kind of safety-valve for society. It is used to implement sentences passed at assemblies, to seek out guilty men and to defend honest farmers. But it is unwelcome when there is no need for it, all the more so when the hero, like Grettir, can find no outlet for his energy and strength and even provokes hostility. Sometimes it is far from certain whether the reader is expected to sympathize with him or not. Grettir's difficulty in finding a role for himself in society is seen most clearly when he tries by all possible means to become enrolled among Bardi's followers (whose adventures are recounted in *The Saga of the Slayings on the Heath*) and when he attacks Audun, a peaceful, good-natured and admirable farmer, to avenge a childhood fight.

Grettir's fierce individualism is opposed to society's typical family structure; his trials and tribulations take place on the borders of the civilized world; his actions are barely within the realm of the human. He doesn't fit in to this society of hard-working farmers, deprives them of their possessions and slaughters their sheep, just as he robs peaceful travellers on the highland routes across Iceland. Grettir's sin is arrogance. Once he has glimpsed another world in his fight with Glam the ghost, he can never return to the world of men except as a kind of spirit himself. Towards the end, at least in the eyes of his enemies, Grettir resembles the evil visitations he has spent his life fighting.

Unruly and impetuous, when he loses his temper Grettir often does as much harm to himself as to others – as when he slaps the boy in the church in Norway or throws the stone at Thurid, or when he impetuously chops the log on Drangey and wounds himself. Grettir lacks the humility and moderation that a good Christian should strive for and Glam's prophecy condemning Grettir to loneliness might simply be a shrewd insight as to where his character flaws are leading him.

More than once Grettir is advised to be wary of company, a lesson he ought to have learned after he took in the two outlaws on Arnarvatn moor. But at Drangey he has grown so afraid of the dark that he cannot remain alone, so he takes his brother with him. On their way they meet a strange man: 'He had a large head and was tall, slim and poorly dressed [...] he said he was named Thorbjorn. He was a vagrant who could not be bothered to work, and very boastful; people made great fun of him and some even played tricks on him' (chapter 69). Thorbjorn has the same name as Grettir's three other main adversaries, but his nickname is Glaum, meaning something like 'merrymaking'. In Glaum we have, in some way, a symbol of the community. Grettir takes him with him to Drangey and it is Glaum who prepares the way for Grettir's death. Glaum seems to be a free man when he meets the brothers, but in Drangey he is always called a slave. He is a comic figure, similar to Don Quixote's Sancho Panza. Glaum is the last mirror held up to Grettir's face and he exposes the futility of heroism perhaps better than any other character in the saga.

Although he represents a bygone era, Grettir is far from being a mere stereotype. He has a gift for the well-turned phrase and displays great presence of mind and resourcefulness when the occasion demands. As an outlaw, too, he is a born survivor and after Glam's curse seems to meet his inevitable fate with increasing self-control.

At the end of the saga, Fortune returns to the family and Thorstein Dromund becomes a new type of hero. Certainly he is a brave warrior, but his strengths are patience, resourcefulness, a desire for solitude (not the loneliness that Grettir reluctantly suffers) and self-imposed seclusion (not outlawry).

7
The Survival of *Grettir*

The Saga of Grettir the Strong features prominently in debates about the origins and dating of the sagas. In the early days of Old Icelandic scholarship, it was widely believed to be the product of two eras. The original version was supposed to have been composed in the 'classical vein' in the latter half of the thirteenth century by a gifted author (perhaps even Sturla Thordarson the Lawspeaker, who is four times quoted or referred to in the text), then 'corrupted' by a lesser author to produce the extant version, which was regarded as rather disjointed in terms of subject matter, form and style. Later it was considered to be the work of a single author, composed in the first decades of the fourteenth century. Most recently it has been argued that the saga was probably not written before 1400. This would make its author a contemporary of Geoffrey Chaucer (*c.*1345–1400) and other authors at the dawn of the Renaissance.

The main arguments for a more recent dating of *The Saga of Grettir*, in the form we know it, are (1) *Manuscript evidence*: The dating of the four oldest manuscripts, around 1500 and showing little textual difference between them, suggests a late date of composition. So does the fact that the poem 'Handing Grettir Around' is preserved in the oldest of them. (2) *Internal evidence*: Historical information about individuals, genealogies, artefacts, customs and habits is common in the sagas, but is not always reliable because of the whims of textual preservation. We do not know the origin of this material, which may have been supplied by authors or scribes with a special interest in and knowledge of the past, or may be simply a fabrication or fiction added to lend the story authenticity. Nothing of this kind in the saga invites an early dating – several references to Sturla Thordarson and his time are probably better explained as *topoi* or narrative devices used by the storyteller to give an impression that his story is older, based on *auctores* or authorities – a stock medieval device. (3) *External evidence*: Grettir appears in several other sources. What is said of him there does not contradict *The Saga of Grettir the Strong*, but neither does it include significant parts of the story. It seems that, while the character of Grettir was familiar to other saga writers, details or passages from the plot were not. (4) *Literary relations or intertextuality*: As has been argued above, this saga is almost unique in the genre for its conscious dialogues and close literary engagement with other sagas, which must have been written down and in circulation by the time of its composition. The late- or post-medieval character of the closing six chapters of *The Saga of Grettir* must also invite a later dating.

In terms of style, structure, narrative technique and point of view, *The Saga of Grettir the Strong* has moved on from the distinctly Icelandic genre of the classical saga and seems to align itself with the literary redefinition that was taking place elsewhere in Europe at the intersection between the Middle Ages and the Renaissance.

8

The Saga of Grettir the Strong is a complex and tightly woven voyage from pagan times to the monastic cells of Christianity, through medieval Icelandic literature – recorded and unrecorded – from Norway to Iceland and on to Constantinople, and a tour of the whole of Iceland. Grettir the traveller has been called an anachronism, a champion born too late for the age he lived in to relate to him, inhabiting a lost heroic world. In the same way the saga looks back with some nostalgia to the literature that pays homage to that world's values. His saga is a vision of two worlds, at once a farewell to the world of the hero and a greeting to a new age, a new hero and new literature.

NOTES

1. *Njal's Saga*, trans. with an Introduction by Robert Cook (London: Penguin, 2001).
2. *Gisli Sursson's Saga and The Saga of the People of Eyri*, trans. Martin S. Regal and Judy Quinn with an Introduction by Vésteinn Ólason (London: Penguin, 2003).
3. *The Saga of the Confederates*, trans. Ruth C. Ellison, will be published in *Five Comic Sagas* (forthcoming from Penguin). It also appears in *The Sagas of Icelanders* (London: Penguin, 2000).
4. *The Saga of Bjorn, Champion of the People of Hitardal*, trans. Alison Finlay in *Sagas of Warrior-Poets*, ed. with an Introduction by Diana Whaley (London: Penguin, 2002). *The Saga of the Sworn Brothers*, trans. Martin S. Regal, will be published in *Five Comic Sagas*.
5. *Egil's Saga*, trans. Bernard Scudder with an Introduction by Svanhildur Óskarsdóttir (London: Penguin, 2004). Also in *The Sagas of Icelanders*.
6. *The Saga of the People of Laxardal*, trans. Keneva Kunz with an Introduction by Bergljót Kristjánsdóttir (forthcoming from Penguin). Also in *The Sagas of Icelanders*.
7. *The Saga of the People of Vatnsdal*, trans. Andrew Wawn, in *The Sagas of Icelanders*.

All of the Icelandic sagas referred to in the Introduction can be found in *The Complete Sagas of Icelanders* (Reykjavík: Leifur Eiríksson Publishing, 1997). For other works referred to see Further Reading.

NOTES

1. Nick Squre, trans., with an introduction by Herock Gherk (London: Penguin, 2001).

2. Gith Bequeits Eurp and Zen Ovn of the Courts of Turi, trans. M. ... ... Regel and ... ... (London ...) ... Introduced in ... ... (London: Penguin, 2001).

3. The ... of the Prophecies ..., trans. Regis ... ... , will be published in ... ... Seq... the hermen... from Penguin. See also The Stone of the modern (London: Penguin, 2000).

4. The Stone of Barse Sharestan of the People of Tirazia, trans. Albert ... also Mrs. Al... (London) ... ... , is an introduction by Diana Whaley (London: Penguin, 2002). The Stone of the Superb Remers... (London: Murray, 1993), with the introduction (London ...).

5. Egil's Saga, trans. Bernard Scudder, with an introduction by Svaud bit (Harmondsworth: Penguin, Penguin 2004). Also in The Sagas of the makers.

6. The Sagas of the People ... makind, might known R.M. with an introduction by Bernard Rebbas, also at (Harmondsworth: Penguin) ... , Ga... ... ... (London: Penguin, 2002), is included in ... ...

7. The Saga of ... Epople in Wildleb ... trans. Robert ... ... , in the Sagas of Icelande.

8. Most of the titles of sagas referred to in these notes can be found in The Complete Sagas of Icelanders (five vols). Leifur Eiríksson Publishing, 1997). For other works referred to see 'Further Reading'.

Further Reading

The Sagas of Icelanders

The Complete Sagas of Icelanders (Including 49 Tales), 5 volumes, ed. Viðar Hreinsson (Reykjavík, 1997)

The Story of Grettir the Strong, trans. Eiríkr Magnússon and William Morris (London: 1896; repr. 1901)

The Saga of Grettir the Strong: A Story from the Eleventh Century, trans. George Ainslie Hight (London: 1915). Reprinted with an Introduction by Peter Foote (London, 1968)

Grettir's Saga, trans. Denton Fox and Hermann Pálsson (Toronto, 1974)

The Sagas of Icelanders: A Selection, ed. Örnólfur Thorsson (London, 2000)

Selected Bibliography

Amory, Frederic, 'The Medieval Icelandic Outlaw: Life-style, Saga and Legend' in *From Saga to Society*, ed. Gísli Pálsson (Enfield Lock, 1992), pp. 189–203

Arent, Margaret, 'The Heroic Pattern: Old Germanic Helmets, Beowulf and Grettis Saga' in *Old Norse Literature and Mythology: A Symposium*, ed. Edgar C. Polomé (Austin and London, 1969), pp. 130–99

Blaney, Benjamin, 'The Berserk Suitor: the Literary Application of a Stereotyped Theme' in *Scandinavian Studies* 4, 4 (1982), pp. 279–94

Chambers, Raymond W., 'Beowulf's Fight with Grendel and Its Scandinavian Parallels' in *English Studies* 11 (1929), pp. 432–35

——*Beowulf: An Introduction to the Study of the Poem* (Cambridge, 1959)

Cook, Robert G., 'The Reader in Grettis Saga' in *Saga-Book* XXI, 3–4 (1984–5), pp. 133–54

——'Reading for Character in Grettis Saga' in *Sagas of the Icelanders: A Book of Essays*, ed. John Tucker (New York and London, 1989), pp. 226–40

Damico, Helen, 'Dystopic Conditions of the Mind: Toward a Study of Landscape in Grettissaga' in *In Geardagum VII: Essays on Old English Language and Literature* (1986), pp. 1–15

Ellis Davidson, Hilda R., 'Folklore and Literature' in *Folklore* 86 (1975), pp. 73–93

Fjalldal, Magnús, *The Long Arm of Coincidence: The Frustrated Connection between Beowulf and Grettis Saga* (Toronto, Buffalo and London, 1998)

Glendinning, Robert J., 'Grettis Saga and European Literature in the Late Middle Ages' in *Mosaic* 4 (1970), pp. 49–61

Harris, Joseph, 'Saga as historical novel' in *Structure and Meaning in Old Norse Literature: New Approaches to Textual Analysis and Literary Criticism*, ed. John Lindow et al. (Odense, 1986), pp. 187–219

Harris, Richard L., 'The Deaths of Grettir and Grendel: A New Parallel' in *Scripta Islandica* 24 (1973), pp. 25–53

Hume, Kathryn, 'The Thematic Design of Grettis Saga' in *Journal of English and Germanic Philology* 73 (1974), pp. 469–86

——'From Saga to Romance: The Use of Monsters in Old Norse Literature' in *Studies in Philology* 77 (1980), pp. 1–25

Jorgensen, Peter, 'Grendel, Grettir and Two Scaldic Stanzas' in *Scripta Islandica* 24 (1973), pp. 54–61

Liberman, Anatoly, 'Beowulf – Grettir' in *Germanic Dialects: Linguistics and Philological Investigations*, ed. B. Brogyanyi and T. Krömmelbein (Amsterdam and Philadelphia, 1986), pp. 353–401

Pálsson, Hermann, 'Icelandic Sagas and Medieval Ethics' in *Medieval Scandinavia* 7 (1974), pp. 61–75

Turville-Petre, Joan, 'Beowulf and Grettis Saga: an Excursion' in *Saga-Book of the Viking Society* 19 (1977), pp. 347–57

General

Andersson, Theodore M., *The Problem of Icelandic Saga Origins: A Historical Survey* (New Haven, London, 1964)
——*The Icelandic Family Saga: An Analytic Reading* (Cambridge, Mass., 1967)
'The Book of Icelanders' in *The Norse Atlantic Saga*, trans. Gwyn Jones (Oxford, 1964)
The Book of Settlements (Landnámabók), trans. Hermann Pálsson and Paul Edwards (Winnipeg, 1972)
Byock, Jesse L., *Feud in the Icelandic Saga* (Berkeley, 1982)
——*Medieval Iceland: Society, Sagas and Power* (Berkeley, 1988)
——*Viking Age Iceland* (New York, 2001)
Clover, Carol J., *The Medieval Saga* (Ithaca and London, 1982)
Hallberg, Peter, *The Icelandic Saga*, trans. Paul Schach (Lincoln, 1962)
Hastrup, Kirsten, *Culture and History in Medieval Iceland: An Anthropological Analysis of Structure and Change* (Oxford, 1985)
Íslendingabók (The Book of Icelanders), trans. Halldór Hermannsson (Ithaca, 1930)
Jesch, Judith, *Women in the Viking Age* (Woodbridge, 1992)
Jochens, Jenny, *Women in Old Norse Society* (Ithaca, 1995)
——*Old Norse Images of Women* (Philadelphia, 1996)
Kellogg, Robert, and Robert Scholes, *The Nature of Narrative* (Oxford, 1966)
Ker, W. P., 'Epic and Romance' in *Essays on Medieval Literature*, second edn (London, 1908; repr. New York, 1957)
Kristjánsson, Jónas, *Eddas and Sagas: Iceland's Medieval Literature*, trans. Peter Foote (Reykjavík, 1997)
Meulengracht Sørensen, Preben, *Saga and Society: An Introduction to Old Norse Literature*, trans. John Tucker (Odense, 1993)

Lindow, John, and Carol J. Clover, *Old Norse-Icelandic Litera-
  ture: A Critical Guide* in *Islandica* 45 (Ithaca, London, 1985)
Lönnroth, Lars, *Njáls Saga: A Critical Introduction* (California,
  1976)
Miller, William Ian, *Bloodtaking and Peacemaking: Feud, Law
  and Society in Saga Iceland* (Chicago and London, 1990)
Nordal, Sigurður, *Icelandic Culture*, trans. Vilhjálmur T.
  Bjarnar (Ithaca, 1990)
Ólason, Vésteinn, *Dialogues with the Viking Age: Narration
  and Representation in the Sagas of Icelanders*, trans. Andrew
  Wawn (Reykjavík, 1997)
Pulsiano, Phillip, and Kirsten Wolf (eds.), *Medieval Scandina-
  via: An Encyclopedia* (New York and London, 1993)
Ryding, William W., *Structure in Medieval Narrative* (The
  Hague, 1971)
Schach, Paul, *Icelandic Sagas* (Boston, 1984)
Sigurðsson, Gísli, *The Medieval Icelandic Saga and Oral
  Tradition: A Discourse on Method*, trans. Nicholas Jones
  (Cambridge, Mass., 2004)
Steblin-Kamenskij, M. I., *The Saga Mind*, trans. Kenneth H.
  Ober (Odense, 1973)
Tucker, John (ed.), *Sagas of Icelanders* (New York, 1989)

A Note on the Translation

The text in this edition is reprinted with minor revisions from Bernard Scudder's translation in the *Complete Sagas of Icelanders* (Leifur Eiríksson Publishing, 1997). The saga is translated from Örnólfur Thorsson's Icelandic edition (*Grettis saga með formála, viðbæti, skýringum og skrám*, Sígildar sögur 4, Reykjavík, 1994), which largely follows the text in AM 551 4to, one of the four main vellum manuscripts dating from the end of the fifteenth century at the earliest. Bernard Scudder also translated the Introduction and notes, and, together with Gísli Sigurðsson, made some contributions to it in collaboration with Örnólfur Thorsson.

As the swansong of the classical epic saga, interleaved with elements of folktale, picaresque and Romance, *The Saga of Grettir the Strong* is no less of a troublemaker for the translator than its hero was to his contemporaries. Its strong literary subtext and dialogues with tradition inevitably lose some of their depth when transplanted into a culture where the allusions are unfamiliar. The problem extends beyond pure stylistic features to the very nature of the text itself, since no author of any saga of Icelanders has a larger vocabulary, and none uses more *hapax legomena*, i.e. words that do not occur elsewhere in the genre. *Grettir* employs, for example, considerably more lexemes than *Njal's Saga*, which is longer by a third. The author consciously and dexterously tailored his style to the different times and settings he describes, spanning the spectrum from the economical and 'primitivist' opening in the Age of Settlements to the loan words and more convoluted constructions in the 'Romance' scenes in Constantinople. Its range of voice and timbre, spanning from the objective heroic to the moralizing, from the ironic to the evocation of public reprobation, is unparalleled within the saga tradition.

Against this monstrous qualification, the translator's aim, like that of everyone engaged in the *Complete Sagas of Icelanders* project, has been above all to strike a balance between faithfulness to the original text and appeal to the modern reader. The *Complete Sagas* project also seeks to reflect the homogeneity of the world of the sagas of Icelanders, by aiming for consistency in the translation of certain essential vocabulary, for instance terms relating to legal practices, social and religious practices, farm layouts or types of ships.

As is common in translations from Old Icelandic, the spelling of proper nouns has been simplified, both by the elimination of non-English letters and by the reduction of inflections. Thus 'Þorsteinn' becomes 'Thorstein' and 'Önundur' becomes 'Onund'. The reader will soon grasp that '-dóttir' means 'daughter of' and '-son' means 'son of'. Place names have been rendered in a similar way, often with an English identifier of the landscape feature in question (e.g. 'Hvítá river', in which 'Hvít-' means 'white' and '-á' means 'river'). A translation is given in parentheses at the first occurrence of place names when the context requires this, such as Spjotsmyri (Spear-mire). For place names outside Scandinavia, the common English equivalent is used if such exists; otherwise the Icelandic form has been transliterated. Nicknames are translated where their meanings are reasonably certain.

The translation of the poetry is particularly challenging, both because of obscurities and corruptions in the texts and because its intricate metre, flexible word order and compressed and often riddling diction do not transpose well into English. Grettir was not one of the greatest saga poets, although one would hardly have dared to say this to his face. As in his dealings with men and monsters, he tended to apply brute strength to force his metres and meanings into submission, and his love of riddles and dissembling often leads him (or those who passed on his verse from one generation to the next) into excruciating obscurity. While the present translation attempts to render something of the meaning and style of the original – and opts to emphasize the fluidity of content at the expense of rigid form – the over-riding aim has been to produce English verses that are comprehensible and poetically satisfying.

THE SAGA OF
GRETTIR THE STRONG

1 | There was a man named Onund. He was the son of Ofeig
Hobbler,[1] whose father was Ivar Horse-cock. Onund's
sister Gudbjorg was the mother of Gudbrand Lump, whose
daughter Asta was the mother of King Olaf the Holy. On his
mother's side Onund was from Oppland, while his father's
family mainly came from Rogaland and Hordaland.

Onund was a great Viking and raided in the countries west
of Norway. Balki Blaengsson from Sotanes and Orm the
Wealthy went with him on his raids. Their third companion
was named Hallvard. They had five ships, all well manned.
They went raiding in the Hebrides and when they reached the
Barra Isles, they came across a king named Kjarval[2] who also
had five ships. They launched an attack on him and a heavy
battle ensued. Onund's men fought fiercely. Many men were
killed on both sides and in the end the king fled on one of his
ships. Onund's men seized the ships and a great amount of
wealth as well, and set up winter quarters there. For three
summers they went raiding in Ireland and Scotland, then they
went to Norway.

2 | In those days there was great turmoil in Norway. Harald
Tangle-hair, son of Halfdan the Black, had been the king
of Oppland and fought his way to control of the realm. After
that he set off for the north and fought many battles, all of
which he won. Then he headed south, making war and con-
quering every territory wherever he went. When he reached
Hordaland, a massive band turned out to face him, led by

Kjotvi the Wealthy, Thorir Long-chin, the people of South Rogaland and King Sulki.

Geirmund Dark-skin was in the British Isles then and did not take part in that battle, even though he had land in Hordaland.

That autumn Onund and his companions sailed back from the west. When Thorir Long-chin and King Kjotvi heard this news they sent men to meet them and ask them to join their forces, promising them worthy rewards. They joined forces with Thorir and the others, because they were eager to put their strength to the test, and said they wanted to be in the thick of the battle.

They clashed with King Harald in Rogaland, by the fjord named Havsfjord. Both sides had great armies, and the battle[3] was one of the greatest ever fought in Norway. Most sagas refer to it, because it is such matters that sagas usually relate. Troops arrived from all over Norway and many other countries, and a large number of Vikings.

Onund drew up his ship alongside Thorir Long-chin's, in the midst of the fray. King Harald sailed up to Thorir's ship, because Thorir was a great berserk and brave fighter. Both sides fought fiercely. Then the king urged his berserks on. They were called Wolf-skins;[4] iron weapons would not bite on them and when they charged they were unstoppable. Thorir fought valiantly, but was killed on his ship after a brave stand. Then the attackers cleared the ship from stem to stern and chopped through the ropes that tied it to the others; it drifted back from between the other two ships. After that the king's men attacked Onund's ship. Onund was at the bow and fought bravely.

Then the king's men said, 'That man in the gunwale is putting up a tough fight. Let's leave him with some reminders that he has been in a battle.'

Onund was standing with one foot on the gunwale, striking a blow, when someone lunged at him, and as he warded off the attack he buckled at the knees. At that moment one of the men in the prow of the king's ship struck at him, hitting him just below the knee and chopping off his leg. Onund was put out of action immediately and most of his men were killed.

Onund was carried to the ship owned by a man named

Thrand, who was the son of Bjorn and the brother of Eyvind the Norwegian. He was on the side fighting against King Harald and had drawn up his ship alongside Onund's.

After this, the main fleet split up. Thrand and the other Vikings got away as best they could and sailed off west. Onund went with him, and so did Balki and Hallvard Surf.

Onund's wound healed, but he wore a wooden leg for the rest of his life, and so he was nicknamed Onund Tree-leg as long as he lived.

3 | Many excellent men were in Britain at that time; they had fled their lands in Norway because King Harald outlawed all those who had fought against him and seized their property.

When Onund's wounds had healed, he and Thrand and eight others went to see Geirmund Dark-skin, since he was then the most renowned Viking in the territory west of Norway, and asked him if he wanted to try to recover the land he had ruled in Hordaland, offering him their support. They thought that they would come to regret the loss of their property sorely, for Onund came from a great family and was a wealthy man. Geirmund replied that, since King Harald had grown so strong, he thought there was little hope of their recovering much by force now, because others had suffered defeat when almost the whole country had opposed him. He had no intention of becoming the king's slave, he said, by begging for what he had previously owned, but would rather find another place to establish himself. By then he was also past his prime. So Onund and the others went back to the Hebrides where they joined many of their friends.

There was a man named Ofeig, whose nickname was Grettir (Snake). He was the son of Einar, whose father was Olvir the Child-sparer.[5] Ofeig's brother was Oleif the Broad, whose son was Thormod Skafti. Another of Olvir's sons was Steinolf, whose daughter Una married Thorbjorn Salmon-catcher. Steinmod was yet another of Olvir's sons. He was the father of Konal, whose daughter was Alfdis from Barra. Konal's son Steinmod was the father of Halldora, who married Eilif, the son of Ketil the One-handed. Ofeig Grettir's wife was Asny, the daughter of Vestar Haengsson. Ofeig's sons were Asmund the Beardless and Asbjorn, and his daughters were named Aldis, Aesa and Asvor.

Ofeig had fled west across the sea from King Harald's oppression and so had his kinsman Thormod Skafti, with all the people from their households. They raided many parts of the British Isles.

Thrand and Onund Tree-leg intended to go westwards to Ireland to meet Eyvind the Norwegian, Thrand's brother, who was in charge of defending the Irish realm. Eyvind's mother was Hlif, the daughter of Hrolf Ingjaldsson, whose grandfather was King Frodi, while Thrand's mother was Helga, the daughter of Ondott Crow.

Bjorn, Thrand and Eyvind's father, was the son of Hrolf from Ar. He had fled from Gotland after he burned to death King Solvi's brother-in-law Sigfast in his house. He went to Norway that same summer and stayed the winter with Grim the Hersir, the son of Kollbjorn Scurrilous. Grim tried to murder Bjorn for his money. From there, Bjorn went to Ondott Crow, who lived in Kvinesfjord in Agder province. Ondott welcomed Bjorn warmly and he stayed there for the winter, but went raiding every summer until his wife Hlif died. Afterwards, Ondott married his daughter Helga to Bjorn, who then gave up raiding.

Eyvind had taken charge of his father's warships and grown to be an important chieftain in Britain. His wife was Rafarta, daughter of King Kjarval of Ireland. Their sons were Helgi the Lean and Snaebjorn.

When Thrand and Onund reached the Hebrides, they met Ofeig Grettir and Thormod Skafti, and a close friendship developed among them, because all the people who met up again after being in Norway at the height of the warfare there felt as though they had rescued each other from the dead.

Once, when Onund grew very quiet, Thrand asked him what was on his mind.

Onund replied with a verse:

1.

I am not happy after facing
the arrow-hail pounding on shields.
Much happens too early; we flinched
at the ogresses' howling.   *ogresses' howling*: axe
Most men, I feel, doubtless
deem me of little mettle;
this is what most has deprived
me of my delights.

Thrand told Onund that he would always be thought a brave
man: 'You should settle down and marry. I will support you in
word and deed if you let me know whom you have in mind.'

Onund said this was a noble gesture, but that he once had
better prospects of making a good marriage.

'Ofeig has a daughter named Aesa,' Thrand replied. 'We can
approach her if you wish.'

Onund said he would like that.

Then they raised the matter with Ofeig. He responded favourably and said he was aware that Onund was of great family and
a wealthy man – 'but I value his land little. And he's only half
the man that he was, while my daughter is still a child.'

Thrand said Onund was in finer fettle than many men with
both legs. And with Thrand's support the matter was settled
and Ofeig made over her dowry in the form of possessions,
because neither of them was prepared to accept farms in
Norway as being of any value.[6]

Shortly afterwards, Thrand was betrothed to Thormod
Skafti's daughter. Both women were to remain pledged to be
married for three years afterwards. The men went raiding
during the summers, but spent the winters on Barra.

4 | There were two Vikings named Vigbjod and Vestmar.
| They came from the Hebrides and were at sea in both
summer and winter. They had eight ships and raided in Ireland,
doing many evil deeds there until Eyvind the Norwegian took
charge of defending the realm. Then they shifted to the Hebrides

and raided there and all the way down to the firths of Scotland.

Onund and Thrand went off to seek them out and were told that they had sailed to the island named Bute.

Then Onund and Thrand went there with seven ships. When the Vikings saw how many ships the others had, they felt they had sufficient forces, so they took their weapons and sailed off to face them. Onund ordered his men to position the ships in a narrow, deep channel between two cliffs, which could only be attacked from one end, and then by no more than five ships at once. Being a clever man, Onund took five ships into the channel, but left them scope to retreat when they wished, since there was open sea behind them. There was also an islet on one side of them where he positioned one of his ships, and they brought many rocks to the edge of the cliff there, out of sight of the ships below.

The Vikings advanced boldly, thinking the ships were caught in a trap. Vigbjod asked who these people were that had been penned in.

Thrand told them he was the brother of Eyvind the Norwegian – 'And this is my companion, Onund Tree-leg.'

The Vikings laughed and said:

2.
May the trolls swallow you whole, Tree-leg,
may the trolls topple you all.

'It's not often we see men go into battle who can't even stand up for themselves.'

Onund said that there was no telling until it was put to the test.

After that, they lined up their ships and a great battle ensued. Both sides advanced resolutely, and when the battle reached full pitch Onund let his ship drift towards the cliff. When the Vikings saw that, they thought he was trying to escape, so they pursued him under the cliff as fast as possible. At that moment, the men who had been placed on the cliff moved out to the edge and launched such huge rocks on to the Vikings that they were unable to withstand the onslaught. A large number of Vikings were killed, and others were put out of action by their

THE SAGA OF GRETTIR THE STRONG

injuries. Then the Vikings tried to sail away, but they could not, because by that time their ships had been driven by both the fleet and the current into the narrowest part of the channel. Onund and his men made a vigorous attack on Vigbjod, while Thrand took on Vestmar, but he made little progress.

When Vigbjod's crew began to thin out, Onund and his men boarded the ship. Vigbjod noticed this and urged his men forward, while he turned to face Onund. Most of Onund's men yielded their ground, but he told them to wait and see the outcome of his encounter with Vigbjod, because Onund was a very strong fighter. They wedged a log under Onund's knee so that he would stand quite firmly. The Viking moved along the ship from the aft until he reached Onund, and struck at him with his sword, hacking his shield away where the blow struck. His sword rebounded into the log below Onund's knee and stuck there. As Vigbjod leaned over to jerk the sword back, Onund aimed a blow at his shoulder, cutting off his arm and putting him out of action. Once Vestmar knew that his companion was felled, he rushed for the outermost ship and fled, as did all his men who could make their way there. Afterwards, Onund and his crew examined the casualties.

Vigbjod was on the verge of death by then.

Onund went up to him and spoke a verse:

3.
See if your wounds bleed.
Did you see me flinch?
You did not deal a scratch to me,
the one-legged slinger of riches.   *slinger of riches*: noble (generous) man
Many breakers of battle-axes   *breakers of battle-axes*: good fighters
are more brag than brains.
That man was not generous   *generous with his strength*: i.e. did not
with his strength when challenged.   put up a good fight

They seized a great amount of booty and returned to Barra in the autumn.

5 | The following summer they made preparations to sail
west to Ireland. Balki and Hallvard set off across the
ocean and went to Iceland, where there was said to be plenty
of good land available. Balki then took land in Hrutafjord and
lived at two farms, both named Balkastadir. Hallvard took
land in Sugandafjord (Surf fjord) and Skalavik as far as Stigi,
and settled there.

Thrand and Onund went to see Eyvind the Norwegian. He
welcomed his brother warmly, but when he found out that
Onund was with him, he became angry and wanted to attack
him. Thrand asked him not to, saying there was no justification for aggression against Norsemen, especially if they were
not causing any trouble. Eyvind replied that Onund had shown
aggression towards King Kjarval in the past and would pay for
it now. The two brothers talked the matter over at length until
Thrand said that he and Onund would share the same fate, and
Eyvind backed down. They spent a long time there that summer
and went raiding with Eyvind, who considered Onund a very
courageous man. They went to the Hebrides in the autumn.
Eyvind bestowed all their inheritance on his brother, if Bjorn,
their father, were to die before Thrand. Then they stayed in the
Hebrides until they married their brides, and for several winters
afterwards.

6 | The next thing that happened was that Bjorn, Thrand's
father, died. When Grim the Hersir heard this he went
to see Ondott Crow and claimed the inheritance left by Bjorn,
but Ondott said Thrand was his father's heir. Grim pointed
out that Thrand had gone west to Britain, and Bjorn was from
Gotland; the king was entitled to inherit from all foreigners.
Ondott said he planned to keep the inheritance for his grandson
Thrand, so Grim left without gaining anything from his claim.

Thrand heard the news of his father's death and set off from
the Hebrides at once, along with Onund Tree-leg. At the same
time, Ofeig Grettir and Thormod Skafti left for Iceland with
the people from their households, and landed at Eyrar in the

south, where they spent their first winter with Thorbjorn
Salmon-catcher. After that they took land in Gnupverjahrepp.
Ofeig settled on the western side, between the rivers Thvera
and Kalfa, and lived at Ofeigsstadir near Steinsholt. Thormod
settled on the eastern side and lived in Skaftaholt. Thormod
had two daughters: Thorvor, whose son was Thorodd the Godi
from Hjalli, and Thorve, the mother of Thorstein the Godi, who
was the father of Bjarni the Wise.

To return to Thrand and Onund, they sailed over to Norway
with such a strong wind behind them that their voyage went
unreported until they reached Ondott Crow.

He welcomed Thrand warmly and told him about the claim
Grim the Hersir had made to inherit from Bjorn: 'It seems more
proper to me for you rather than the king's slaves to inherit from
your father. You have also had the good fortune to manage to
come here without anyone knowing about your voyage. But I
suspect that Grim will make a move against either of us if he
can. I want you to take the inheritance for yourself and go
abroad.'

Thrand said that he would do so. He then took the inheritance and made preparations to leave Norway at once.

Before he put out to sea, Thrand asked Onund Tree-leg
whether he wanted to go to Iceland. Onund said that first he
would see his kinsmen and friends in the south of Norway.

'Then we will part now,' said Thrand. 'I would like you
to support my kinsmen, because they will be the victims of revenge if I escape. I will go to Iceland and would like you to go
there too.'

Onund promised he would do so and they parted in great
friendship. Thrand went to Iceland, where Ofeig and Thormod
gave him a warm welcome. Thrand lived at Thrandarholt, west
of the river Thjorsa.

7 | Onund went south to Rogaland and met many of his
  | kinsmen and friends there. He stayed there in secret with
a man named Kolbein. He heard that King Harald had seized
his property and entrusted it to a man named Harek, who was

the king's agent. One night, Onund went to his house and made a surprise attack on him. Harek was led out to be executed. Onund took all the possessions that he and his men could find, then burned the house. He stayed in various places that winter.

That autumn, Grim the Hersir killed Ondott Crow for refusing him the inheritance in the king's name. Signy, Ondott's wife, carried all their valuables out to a ship that same night and left with her sons, Asmund and Asgrim, to stay with her father Sighvat. Shortly afterwards she sent her sons to her foster-father Hedin in Sokndal, but they were not happy there for long and wanted to go back to their mother. They went to stay at Kvinesdal for Yule with Ingjald the Loyal. He took them in on the insistence of his wife Gyda, and they remained there for the winter.

In the spring, Onund went north to Agder, for he had heard of Ondott's death, and that he had been slain. When he met Signy he asked her what assistance they would accept from him. She told him they were eager to take vengeance upon Grim the Hersir for killing Ondott. Ondott's sons were sent for and when they met Onund Tree-leg they joined forces and kept a watch on Grim's activities.

Grim brewed a great deal of ale that summer, because he had invited Earl Audun to stay with him. When Onund and Ondott's sons heard of this, they went to Grim's farm and set fire to the houses, taking them by surprise, and burned Grim the Hersir to death inside along with some thirty men. They took many valuables away with them. Onund went and hid in the woods, while the brothers took their foster-father Ingjald's boat and rowed off to stay in hiding close to the farm.

Earl Audun arrived for the feast as planned, but his friend was nowhere to be found. He gathered men and stayed there several nights without finding a trace of Onund and his companions. The earl slept in a loft with two other men.

Onund knew about everything that was happening at the farm and sent for the brothers. When they arrived, Onund gave them the choice of keeping guard over the farm or attacking the earl, and they chose to attack him. They broke down the door of the loft with a battering ram and Asmund grabbed the earl's two companions and dashed them down so hard that he almost killed them. Asgrim ran at the earl and demanded compensation for his father's death, because Audun had plotted with Grim the Hersir and joined in the attack when Ondott was killed. The earl said he had no money with him and asked to be able to pay later. Then Asgrim pressed the point of his spear against the earl's chest and told him to pay up at once. The earl took off his necklace, three gold rings and a velvet cloak. Asgrim took these valuables and gave him the nickname Audun Chicken.

When the farmers and local people became aware of the assault, they came out to try to help the earl. A fierce battle followed, because Onund had a large party with him, and many worthy farmers and earl's men were killed. Then the brothers went and reported to Onund what they had done with the earl.

Onund said it was unfortunate that the earl had not been killed – 'That would be some sort of revenge upon King Harald for the losses we have suffered on his account.'

They said that this was a greater disgrace for the earl, and then they left for Surendal to see Eirik Ale-eager, who was a landholder. He took them all in for the winter.

That Yule they had drinking feasts with a man named Hallstein Horse. Eirik played host first, and served them well and honestly. When it was Hallstein's turn to be host, a disagreement occurred and Hallstein struck Eirik with a drinking-horn. Eirik was unable to take revenge, and went home.

Ondott's sons were furious at this, and soon afterwards Asgrim went to Hallstein's farm, walked in alone and dealt him a mighty wound. The people indoors leapt to their feet and attacked Asgrim, but he fought them off and escaped from their clutches out into the dark. They thought they had killed him.

Onund and Asmund heard about the incident. They assumed that Asgrim was dead and there was nothing for them to do about it. Eirik advised them to go to Iceland and said that they would not stand a chance in Norway once the king got round to dealing with them. They took his advice and made preparations to sail to Iceland, taking a ship each. Hallstein was laid up with his wounds and died before Onund and his men sailed off. Kolbein, who was mentioned earlier, joined Onund's ship.

8 | Onund and Asmund put to sea when they were ready and sailed together.

Then Onund spoke a verse:

4.
Once I was thought fit to brave
the howling winds of swords;
when the piercing shower of spears
roared down – and Hallvard too.
Now with one leg I must mount
my steed of the waves,
bound for Iceland's shores.
This poet is past his prime.

They had a rough time at sea, and the strong southerly wind drove them north off their course. They reached Iceland, and were north of Langanes when they got their bearings. Their ships were so close together that they could call out to each other. Asmund said they ought to sail to Eyjafjord, and they agreed to, but when they tacked towards land, a storm blew up from the south-east. Onund's crew tried to sail close-hauled, but their sailyard tore loose, so they lowered sail and were driven out to sea. Asmund reached shelter by Hrisey Island and waited there for a favourable wind into Eyjafjord. Helgi the Lean gave him the whole of Kraeklingahlid to settle in, and he lived at southern Glera.

His brother Asgrim went to Iceland several years later and lived at northern Glera. He was the father of Ellida-Grim, whose son was named Asgrim.

9 | To return to Onund Tree-leg. He and his men drifted for several days until a north wind blew up and they could sail to land. Those who had been to Iceland before recognized that they were west of Skagi. They sailed into Strandafloi bay

and when they made land at South Strandir, six men rowed out
towards them on a ten-oared boat and asked who was in charge
of the ship. Onund told them his name and asked them where
they were from. They told him they were members of Thorvald
from Drangar's[7] household.

Then Onund asked whether all the land had been taken along
Strandir, and they told him that there was little left to settle[8] in
the inner part of Strandir, and none on the way north there.
Onund asked his crew if they wanted to go and look in the west
or take what was given to them there. They chose to take a
look at the land first, sailed into the bay and anchored in the
creek by Arnes, put out a boat and rowed to land.

A wealthy man named Eirik Snare was living there and had
taken the land between Ingolfsfjord and Ofaera in Veidilausa.
When Eirik heard that Onund had arrived, he invited him to
accept anything he wanted, but said there was little land left
that had not been settled already. Onund said he would like to
see what there was first.

They went across the fjords and when they reached Ofaera
Eirik said, 'Look at this place. None of the land here is settled,
all the way to Bjorn's settlement.'

A large mountain jutted out on that side of the fjords, and
snow had fallen on it.

Onund looked at the mountain and spoke a verse:

5.
This spear-shooter's life wavers
a course from right to left,
leaving lands and rights: my ribbed ship
roams the seas like a tame horse.
I have left behind many kinsmen
and lands to reach this pass:
I have struck a harsh bargain, swapped
my fields for the cold-backed mountain.   *cold-backed mountain*:
                                                              i.e. Kaldbak

'Many people have lost so much in Norway,' Eirik replied, 'that
will never be made good. I think almost all the land has been
settled in the main districts, so I would not encourage you to

leave this place. I will keep my word and you can have whatever of my land that you like.'

Onund said he would accept the offer and took the land from Ofaera and the three bays of Byrgisvik, Kolbeinsvik and Kaldbaksvik, all the way to the cliffs at Kaldbakskleif. Then Eirik gave him the whole of Veidilausa and Reykjarfjord and the part of Reykjanes that was on his side. No agreement was made about harvesting the beach, because so much drifted in that everyone could take what he wanted.

Onund made a farmstead in Kaldbak and kept a large household. When his livestock began to increase, he set up another farm in Reykjarfjord.

Kolbein lived in Kolbeinsvik and Onund stayed there peacefully for several years.

10 | Onund was so brave that few men were a match for him, even if they were completely able-bodied. He was well known all over Iceland because of his ancestry.

The next thing that happened was the quarrel between Ofeig Grettir and Thorbjorn the Champion of Earls, which ended with Thorbjorn killing Ofeig at Grettisgeil near Hael. Ofeig's sons gathered a large party to bring the case against his slayer. They sent for Onund Tree-leg, who rode south in the spring and stayed at Hvamm with Aud the Deep-minded.[9] She welcomed him warmly, since he had stayed with her in Britain.

Her grandson Olaf Feilan was a grown man by this time and Aud was old and frail. She mentioned to Onund that she wanted her kinsman Olaf married and wanted him to ask for the hand of Alfdis from Barra, a cousin of Onund's wife Aesa. Onund thought this a good match and Olaf rode south with him.

When Onund met his friends and kinsmen they invited him to stay with them. They discussed the case of Ofeig's killing and brought it before the Kjalarnes Assembly,[10] because the Althing had still not been established at this time. The case was settled and heavy compensation was paid for Ofeig's killing, while Thorbjorn the Champion of Earls was sentenced to outlawry. His son was Solmund, the father of Kari the Singed.[11] They lived outside Iceland for a long time afterwards.

Thrand invited Onund and his party to stay with him, along with Olaf and Thormod Skafti. They presented Olaf's proposal of marriage, which was readily accepted, because everyone knew Aud was a generous woman. The bargain was settled and Onund and his men rode home afterwards. Aud thanked Onund for supporting Olaf.

The same autumn, Olaf Feilan married Alfdis from Barra, and Aud the Deep-minded died, as is related in *The Saga of the People of Laxardal*.

11 | Onund and Aesa had two sons. The elder one was named Thorgeir and the younger one Ofeig Grettir. Aesa died soon after this episode and Onund married a woman named Thordis. She was the daughter of Thorgrim from Gnup in Midfjord and was related to Skeggi from Midfjord. Onund had a son by her named Thorgrim. He soon grew up to be tall and strong, a dedicated farmer and a wise man.

Onund lived at Kaldbak into his old age. He died of illness and is buried in Tree-leg's Mound. He was the bravest and nimblest one-legged man ever to live in Iceland.

Thorgrim was the most prominent of Onund's sons, even though the others were older. By the time he was twenty-five his hair was streaked with grey, so he was nicknamed Grey-head. His mother Thordis got married again, to Audun Shaft from Vididal in the north, and their son was Asgeir who lived by the river Asgeirsa. Thorgrim Grey-head and his brothers owned a great amount of property together and never divided it out themselves.

Eirik Snare lived at Arnes, as was related earlier. His wife was Olof, the daughter of Ingolf from Ingolfsfjord. Their son Flosi was a promising man who had many friends. Three brothers, Ingolf, Ofeig and Eyvind, had come to Iceland and taken the three fjords named after them, and lived there afterwards. Eyvind's son Olaf lived in Eyvindarfjord at first, then moved to Drangar. He was a powerful man.

No quarrels occurred while the older men lived, but after Eirik died Flosi claimed that the people from Kaldbak had no legal right to the lands that Eirik had given to Onund. A serious dispute developed among them, but Thorgrim and his brothers remained there as before. The local people could not hold games together after that.

Thorgeir was in charge of the brothers' farm in Reykjarfjord and was in the habit of rowing out to fish, because the fjords were full of fish then.

Then the people in Vik made a plan. There was a man named Thorfinn who was one of Flosi's farmhands at Arnes. Flosi sent him to kill Thorgeir and he hid in the boat-shed. That morning, Thorgeir prepared to put out to sea and go fishing, taking two men with him, one named Hamund and the other Brand. Thorgeir led the way. He had a leather flask full of drink on his back. It was very dark and as he was walking down from the boat-shed Thorfinn ran up to him and struck him between the shoulderblades with an axe, which sunk in with a squelch. Thorfinn let go of the axe, because he assumed there would be no point in dressing the wound, and he wanted to escape at once.

So Thorfinn ran off to Arnes and arrived there before it was completely daylight. He announced that Thorgeir had been killed and said he would need Flosi's protection.

The only action they could take would be to offer a settlement, he said, 'And that will make our case look a little more favourable, considering how serious it is.'

Flosi said he would wait to hear what had happened first, 'And I can see you're pretty scared by your mighty deed.'

To return to Thorgeir. He had spun round when the blow struck him, so that the axe went into the leather flask without wounding him. Because it was dark they did not search for the attacker, but rowed out along the fjords to Kaldbak, where they told what had happened.

They made great fun of the incident and called him Thorgeir Bottle-back, and the nickname stuck with him. This verse was made about the attack:

6.

In the old days, heroes would bathe
shield-biters like shimmering fish   *shield-biters*: swords
in a sea of blood flowing from wounds
deep as sharp-pointed roofs.
Now the weakling who never won
renown far and wide has smeared,
from sheer cowardice, both sides
of his axe with curdled whey.

12 | At this time a great famine occurred in Iceland the like of
     | which has never been seen since. Almost no fish were
caught and nothing drifted ashore either. It lasted for many
years.

One autumn some merchants on a trading-ship were driven
off course and shipwrecked in Vik. Flosi took four or five
of them into his house; their leader was named Stein. They
stayed in various places around Vik and planned to rebuild
their ship from the wreckage, but it proved too much for them.
The ship was too narrow at the stem and stern and too wide-
beamed.

That spring, a mighty northerly gale set in, lasting for almost
a week. After it died down everyone went out to see what had
been brought ashore.

There was a man named Thorstein who lived at Reykjanes.
He found a whale beached[12] on the inner side of the promon-
tory, at a place named Rifsker (Reef skerry or Rib skerry). It
was a huge finback whale. He sent a messenger off to Vik at
once to tell Flosi, and then to the neighbouring farms.

There was a man named Einar who lived at Gjogur. He was
a tenant of the people from Kaldbak and was supposed to keep
track of everything that drifted ashore on their side of the fjord.
He saw that the whale had beached and set off in his boat at
once and rowed across the fjord to Byrgisvik. From there he
sent a messenger to Kaldbak. When Thorgrim and his brothers
heard the news, they made ready to leave as quickly as they
could and set off in a ten-oared boat, twelve of them in all.

Kolbein's sons Ivar and Leif went with them too, in a party of six, and every other farmer who could make it went out to the whale.

To return to Flosi. He sent for his kinsmen from Ingolfsfjord and Ofeigsfjord to the north, and for Olaf Eyvindarson, who was living at Drangar then. Flosi and the people from Vik arrived first. They began flensing the whale straight away and hauling the pieces up on to land. There were almost twenty of them to begin with and their numbers soon grew.

Then the people from Kaldbak turned up in four boats. Thorgrim claimed the whale as his own and forbade the people from Vik from cutting up the whale, sharing it out or taking it away. Flosi asked him to prove that Eirik had specifically granted Onund Tree-leg the right to everything that drifted ashore there, otherwise he would defend it by force. Thorgrim thought he had too few men, so he did not mount an attack.

Then some men in a boat came rowing furiously over to that side of the fjord. They soon came ashore; it was Svan from Hol in Bjarnarfjord and his farmhands. When he joined Thorgrim he told him not to let himself be robbed. They were already close friends and Svan offered his support, which the brothers accepted. Then they launched a fierce attack. Thorgeir Bottle-back jumped up on the whale first and went for Flosi's farm-hands. Thorfinn, who was mentioned before, was flensing the whale, standing just down from the head in a foothold he had cut for himself.

'I'm returning your axe,' said Thorgeir.

Then he struck a blow at Thorfinn's neck, chopping off his head.

Flosi was standing on the beach when he saw this and urged his men to fight back. They fought for a good while and the people from Kaldbak came off better. Hardly anyone had any weapons apart from the axes and knives they were using to cut up the whale. The people from Vik were driven away from the whale and on to the beach, but the Norwegian merchants were armed and dangerous. Stein, their skipper, chopped off Ivar Kolbeinsson's leg, but Ivar's brother Leif clubbed one of Stein's companions to death with a whale rib. They fought with everything they could lay their hands on and men were killed on both sides.

After this, Olaf from Drangar arrived with several boatloads of men who joined Flosi's side. The people from Kaldbak were outnumbered then, but had already loaded their boats, and Svan ordered them aboard. They made their way towards the boats, with the people from Vik pursuing them. When Svan reached the sea he struck out at Stein the merchant, inflicting a bloody wound on him, then leapt on to his boat. Thorgrim dealt Flosi a heavy wound and managed to get away. Olaf struck at Ofeig Grettir, dealing him a fatal wound. Thorgeir snatched Ofeig up in his arms and leapt aboard the boat with him. The people from Kaldbak rowed back across the fjord and the two sides parted.

This verse was made about the incident:

7.
I heard they were rather hard,
the weapons wielded at Rifsker:
many men struck out, armed
only with strips of whalemeat.
The metal-Goths gave   *metal-Goths*: (legendary) warriors
as good as they got:
they lobbed lumps of blubber.
That was a brawl, not a battle.

Afterwards a truce was arranged between them and they presented the case to the Althing. Thorodd the Godi, Skeggi from Midfjord and many men from south Iceland supported the people from Kaldbak. Flosi was outlawed along with many others who had been with him. The case impoverished him, because he insisted on paying all the compensation by himself. Thorgrim and his brother were unable to prove that they had paid for the lands and drift rights which Flosi had laid claim to.

Thorkel Moon was the Lawspeaker then and was asked to rule on the matter.

He said that in a legal sense some payment appeared to have been made, although not the full price – 'because Steinunn the

Old and my grandfather Ingolf[13] did likewise when she accepted
the whole of Rosmhvalanes from him in return for a coloured
hooded cloak. That settlement has never been invalidated, even
though it is a much weightier case. I propose,' he said, 'that the
disputed land should be shared out equally between the two
parties. Then it will be agreed as law that each will have the
right to whatever drifts ashore on his own land.'

This was done and the land was divided up. Thorgrim and
his brother handed over Reykjarfjord and all the land on the
far side of it, but kept Kamb. A large amount of compensation
was paid for Ofeig, but Thorfinn had forfeited his right to
compensation. Thorgeir received compensation for the plot to
kill him. After this they were reconciled.

Flosi set off for Norway with Stein the merchant and sold his
lands in Vik to Geirmund Wobbler, who lived there afterwards.
The ship built by the merchants bulged out wide and was
nicknamed Trekylli (Pouch of wood). Trekyllisvik bay is named
after it. Flosi set off abroad on it, but was driven back into
Oxarfjord. What happened after that is told in *The Saga of
Bodmod, Grimolf and Gerpir.*

13 | After this, Thorgrim and Thorgeir divided up all they
     | owned: Thorgrim received all the money and possessions,
and Thorgeir the land. Then Thorgrim moved to Midfjord and
bought land at Bjarg with Skeggi's support. Thorgrim married
Thordis, the daughter of Asmund from Asmundargnup who
had taken land in Thingeyri.

Thorgrim and Thordis had a son named Asmund. He was
tall, strong and wise, and had a fine head of hair, although he
went grey at an early age. Because of this, he was nicknamed
Grey-locks or Grey-fluff.

Thorgrim turned out to be a dedicated farmer and made all
his men work very hard. Asmund was reluctant to work and
the father and son did not get on well together. This continued
until Asmund was grown up, when he asked his father for
the means to travel abroad.[14] Thorgrim replied that he would
not give him very much, but let him have a few goods to

trade. Asmund went abroad and soon started acquiring much wealth. He sailed to a number of countries and was an outstanding merchant, becoming very rich. He was a popular and trustworthy man, and had many kinsmen of high standing in Norway.

One autumn, Asmund was staying in Vik in Norway with a man of high standing named Thorstein, who was from Oppland and had a sister named Rannveig. She was a very good match, so Asmund asked to marry her, which was arranged with Thorstein's support. Asmund settled there for some while and became highly respected.

He and Rannveig had a son named Thorstein who was very handsome and strong with a powerful voice, tall but rather ponderous in his movements. Because of this he was nicknamed Dromund (Galleon).[15]

While Thorstein was still a young boy his mother fell ill and died. After her death, Asmund grew restless in Norway, so Rannveig's family looked after Thorstein and his possessions, while Asmund set off sailing again and became a man of renown.

Asmund landed in Hunavatn when Thorkel Scratcher was the chieftain in Vatnsdal. When he heard of Asmund's arrival, Thorkel rode out to his ship and invited him home to Masstadir in Vatnsdal. Asmund went there to stay. Thorkel was the son of Thorgrim, the Godi of Karnsa, and was a man of great wisdom.

All this took place after Bishop Fridrek and Thorvald Kodransson had arrived in Iceland. They were living at Laekjamot at this time and were the first Christian missionaries in the north of Iceland. Thorkel and many others took the sign of the Cross. Many incidents occurred between the bishop's men and the people of the north which are not part of this saga.

There was a woman named Asdis who was brought up in Thorkel's household. She was the daughter of Bard, the son of Jokul, whose father was Ingimund the Old. Ingimund was the son of Thorstein and grandson of Ketil the Large. Asdis's mother was Aldis, who was the daughter of Ofeig Grettir, as mentioned earlier. She was unmarried and considered an outstanding match on account of both her family and her wealth.

Asmund had grown bored with sailing and wanted to settle in Iceland, so he asked for Asdis's hand in marriage. Thorkel was well aware of Asmund's background and knew him to be both wealthy and clever with his money, so it was arranged that he would marry Asdis. Asmund became a close friend of Thorkel's and a good farmer, well versed in law and ambitious.

Shortly after this, Thorgrim Grey-head died and Asmund inherited the farm at Bjarg.

14 | Asmund Grey-locks set up a farm at Bjarg, a large and impressive place with many people in the household. He was a popular man.

These were the children he had with Asdis: Atli was the oldest, a straightforward and gentle man, quiet and unassuming. Everyone liked him. Grettir was their second son. He was very overbearing as a child, taciturn and rough, and mischievous in both word and deed. His father Asmund showed him little affection, but his mother loved him dearly. Grettir Asmundarson was handsome, with a broad, short face, red-haired[16] and fairly freckled, and as a child he was slow to develop. Asmund had a daughter named Thordis who later married Glum, the son of Ospak Kjallaksson from Skridinsenni. His second daughter, Rannveig, married Gamli, the son of Thorhall the Vinlander.[17] They lived at Melar in Hrutafjord and had a son named Grim. Glum and Asmund's daughter Thordis had a son named Ospak, who quarrelled with Odd Ofeigsson, as is told in *The Saga of the Confederates*.

Grettir grew up at Bjarg to the age of ten. He began to develop then and Asmund told him he would have to do some work on the farm. Grettir answered that he was not suited for it, but asked all the same what he was supposed to do.

Asmund said, 'You will look after the geese I am rearing.'

'A trifling job for weaklings,' Grettir replied.

'Do the job well,' said Asmund, 'and we'll get on better.'

Grettir took charge of the geese. There were fifty of them and many goslings as well. Before long he began to have trouble rounding them up and thought the goslings were tedious, which infuriated him because he had a fairly short temper. A little while later some vagrants passing by found the goslings dead outside; the geese's wings were broken. This was in the autumn. Asmund was furious and asked Grettir if he had killed the birds.

Grettir grinned and answered:

8.
When winter comes around I wring
the goslings' necks for certain;
and if older ones are there as well
I can deal with them single-handed.

'You won't deal with them any more,' said Asmund.

'A true friend spares others from evil,' Grettir replied.

'You will be given another job,' said Asmund.

'The more you try, the more you learn,' Grettir replied. 'What am I supposed to do now?'

'I always have my back rubbed by the fireside, you will do that,' said Asmund.

'That will be warm for my hands,' said Grettir, 'but it's still a job for weaklings.'

Grettir did this job for some time, but as autumn went on Asmund began to relish sitting inside in the warmth and urged Grettir to scratch his back harder.

In those days it was the custom on farms to have big fire halls where everyone sat beside the long fire in the evenings. Tables were set up there and everyone slept alongside the fire in the evening. Women would comb wool there during the day.

One evening when Grettir had to scratch Asmund's back, the old man said to him: 'You ought to shake off that laziness of yours for once, you layabout.'

'It's a bad thing to goad the obstinate,' said Grettir.

'You're good for nothing,' Asmund replied.

Seeing the wool-combs lying on the bench, Grettir picked one up and ran it along Asmund's back. Asmund leapt to his feet in a rage and struck at Grettir with his stick, but he dodged the blow. Then Grettir's mother came in and asked what they were fighting about.

Grettir spoke a verse:

9.

He should ward off harm from me,
but wants me to burn my hands;
I feel it sorely, bearer of gold;   *bearer of gold*: woman
we both suffer for this plan.
Goddess of cloth, I go to work   *goddess of cloth*: woman
on the spreader of treasure   *spreader of treasure*: noble man
thoroughly with uncut nails:
I see beaks pecking at deep wounds.

Grettir's mother disliked this trick he had played and said he would not turn out to be a heedful sort of person. Relations between Asmund and Grettir did not improve after this incident.

Some time later, Asmund told Grettir to look after his horses. Grettir said he liked that idea more than rubbing his father's back by the fire.

'Now you will do exactly as I tell you,' said Asmund. 'I have a fawn mare with a dark stripe down her back; I call her Kengala (Back-stripe). She is so acute about the weather and the water-level in the rivers that a snowstorm never fails to materialize if she refuses to graze. In that case you should keep the horses in the stable, but take them north to the ridge when winter sets in. It seems to me that you need to make a better job of this task than the other two I gave you.'

Grettir replied, 'That's a cold and manly job. But I'm wary of trusting the mare, because I've never heard about anyone who has before now.'

Then Grettir took over looking after the horses and Yule came and went. Then it turned very cold and snowed, making the ground difficult for them to graze. Grettir had thin clothes on and was still fairly tender. He began to feel the cold, while Kengala always stood out in the most exposed places every time there was a storm. She never entered the meadow early enough to be able to return to the stable before nightfall. Grettir thought he would play a trick on her to pay her back for staying out all the time.

Early one morning, Grettir went to the stable and opened it. Kengala was standing at the trough, because even when the other horses were given fodder she would eat it all herself. Grettir climbed on her back with a sharp knife in his hand and slashed her across the shoulders with it and down her back on either side of her spine. The mare was fat and shied from humans and she reacted violently, rearing up and hammering the walls with her hooves. Grettir fell off her back and when he got to his feet he tried to mount her again. After a sharp struggle, he ended by flaying all the hide off her back right down to the flanks, then drove the horses out to the pasture. The only thing Kengala bit at was her own back and just after midday she started up and ran back to the stable.

Grettir closed up the stable and went home. Asmund asked him where the horses were and Grettir said he had put them inside the stable as usual. Asmund said there must be a snow-storm in the offing, when the horses refused to stay outside in such weather.

'Wisdom falls short where it is most expected,' said Grettir.

The night passed and the snowstorm did not materialize. Grettir drove the horses outside and Kengala could not stand being out in the pasture. Asmund thought it was peculiar that the weather did not change.

On the third morning, Asmund went to see the horses.

He went up to Kengala and said, 'I think the horses have had little benefit from such a good winter, but your back will be as firm as ever, Kengala.'

'The foreseeable happens, and the unforeseeable too,' said Grettir.

Asmund rubbed the mare's back and its hide came off with his hand. He was puzzled by the state she was in and said Grettir must be responsible. Grettir grinned and said nothing.

Asmund went home ranting.

He went into the fire hall and heard his wife say, 'Surely my son looked after the horses well.'

Asmund spoke a verse:

10.

First of all, he has flayed
my trusty Kengala. Fair women
mostly go too far with their words:
Grettir tricked me.
That lad is certainly wise enough
to teach me not to entrust him
with orders. May the goddess   *goddess of the ring*: woman (Asdis)
of the ring take in my words.

Asdis answered, 'I do not know which I object to more: that
you keep giving him jobs or that he does them all the same
way.'

'This will be the end of that now,' Asmund said. 'But he'll be
treated all the worse for it.'

'Then neither of us should accuse the other,' said Grettir, and
the matter rested there for a while.

Asmund had Kengala put to death.

Grettir played many more pranks in his youth which are not
recounted in his saga. He grew very big, but no one knew how
strong he was, because he was not a wrestler. He often made
verses and ditties that tended to be scornful. He did not lounge
around in the fire hall,[18] and he was taciturn most of the time.

15 | There were many young men growing up in Midfjord at
      | this time. Torfa the Poetess, who lived at Torfustadir, had
a son named Bersi, an accomplished young man and fine poet.
The brothers Kormak and Thorgils[19] lived at Mel, and a lad
named Odd was brought up with them. He was a dependant
living on their farm, so he was nicknamed Odd the Pauper-poet.
There was a man named Audun who grew up at Audunarstadir
in Vididal, a straightforward and kind person and the strongest
lad for his age in that area. Kalf, Asgeir's son, lived at Asgeirsa
with his brother Thorvald. Grettir's brother Atli had also grown
very manly by this time and was an exceptionally peaceful
character who was liked by everybody.

All these youths used to play ball games at Lake Midfjardarvatn. People would go there from Midfjord and Vididal, along with many others from Vesturhop and Vatnsnes and from Hrutafjord, too. Those who came from farthest away used to stay overnight there. Players of equal strength were matched against each other and it was generally an enjoyable event every autumn.

When Grettir was fourteen he went to the games at the insistence of his brother Atli. Players were lined up to face each other and Grettir was pitted against Audun, who was mentioned before. Audun was several years their elder. He hit the ball over Grettir's head so that he could not catch it, and it bounced far away over the ice. Grettir lost his temper at this, thinking that Audun had done it to make fun of him, but fetched the ball all the same, came back and, when he was within reach, hurled it at Audun's forehead, making it bleed. Audun struck out at Grettir with the bat he was holding, but it only glanced off him, because Grettir dodged the blow.

Then they grappled with each other and started wrestling, and everyone could tell Grettir was stronger than they had thought, because Audun was very powerful. After they had fought for a long time, Grettir lost his balance in the end and Audun jumped on him and kneed him in the groin. Atli, Bersi and many others ran over and broke up the fight.

Grettir said there was no need to hold him like a mad dog: 'Only a slave takes vengeance at once, and a coward never.'[20]

No one allowed the incident to develop into a quarrel, because the brothers Kalf and Thorvald wanted them to make up afterwards. Moreover, Grettir and Audun were distant relatives. The game went on as before and nothing else caused any friction.

16 | Thorkel Scratcher was very old by now. He was the godi of the people from Vatnsdal and a great chieftain. As befits relatives by marriage, he and Asmund Grey-locks were close friends and Thorkel made a habit of riding to Bjarg every spring to visit everyone there. In the spring after this incident he went to Bjarg as usual.

Asmund and Asdis welcomed him with open arms. He spent three nights there and the two kinsmen talked together about many things. Thorkel asked Asmund how capable he imagined his sons would turn out to be. Asmund said he expected Atli to become a good farmer, prudent and wise.

'A useful man, just like you,' said Thorkel. 'But what do you say about Grettir?'

'He will be a strong and unruly man,' said Asmund. 'He has been obstinate and caused me trouble.'

'That does not bode well, kinsman,' Thorkel replied. 'Anyway, what arrangements will we make for riding to the Althing this summer?'

'I'm starting to have trouble moving about, and I'd prefer to stay at home,' said Asmund.

'Do you want Atli to go instead of you?' asked Thorkel.

'I don't think I can spare him, because of all the work on the farm and all the provisions he has to get,' said Asmund. 'Grettir refuses to do any work here and he is clever enough to handle my legal duties[21] at the Thing under your guidance.'

'It's up to you to decide, kinsman,' said Thorkel.

When he was ready to leave, Thorkel rode off home and Asmund sent him on his way with fine gifts.

Some time later, Thorkel made preparations to go to the Thing. He rode there taking sixty men with him, all the men who supported his authority as a godi. He arrived at Bjarg and Grettir rode from there with him. They rode south over the moor called Tvidaegra (Two days' journey). Since there were few places to rest the horses in the highland, they rode fast for the settled district. When they reached Fljotstunga they decided it was time to sleep, so they unbridled their horses and let them loose with their saddles on. The men slept there until late and when they woke up they looked around for their horses, which had strayed off in all directions and some had been rolling on the ground. Grettir was the last to find his horse.

In those days it was the custom for people to take their own provisions to the Thing with them and most people rode with a bag of food across their saddle. The saddle had moved under the belly of Grettir's horse, but his bag was missing, so he went to look for it, but could not find it anywhere. He noticed a man walking around at a brisk pace and asked him who he was. The man said his name was Skeggi and that he was a farmhand from As in Vatnsdal.

'I'm with Thorkel's party,' he added, 'and I've been careless and lost my bag of food.'

'Misfortunes are better shared than single,' said Grettir. 'I've lost the bag I had with me too. Let's look for them together.'

Skeggi thought this was a good idea and the two of them roamed the area for a while. All of a sudden Skeggi darted across the moorland and snatched up a bag there. Grettir had seen him bend down and asked what he had picked up.

'My bag of food,' said Skeggi.

'Who says it's yours?' asked Grettir. 'Let me have a look. One thing may look like another.'

Skeggi said no one was going to take his belongings from him. Grettir grabbed at the bag and they tugged at it, both insisting they were right.

'It's strange of you to suppose,' said the farmhand, 'that just because not all the people in Vatnsdal are as rich as you, they wouldn't dare to keep hold of what's theirs against you.'

Grettir said people should have what was theirs, whatever their status.

Skeggi said, 'What a pity Audun's too far away to throttle you like he did at the ball game.'

'Be that as it may,' said Grettir. 'You certainly won't throttle me, whatever happened then.'

Skeggi seized his axe and struck at Grettir. Seeing this, Grettir grabbed the shaft of the axe with his left hand, above where Skeggi was holding it, and wrenched it free in an instant. Grettir struck him with the same axe right through to his brain. The farmhand dropped down dead on the spot.

Grettir took the bag of food and threw it across his saddle, then rode off to join his companions. Thorkel was riding in front, unaware of what had happened. People had noticed that Skeggi was missing from the party and when Grettir reached them they asked him what he knew of his whereabouts.

Grettir spoke a verse:

11.

I imagine a cleft-dwelling troll   *cleft-dwelling troll*: ogress living in
made a wild rush for Skeggi,   the cliffs; also an axe
that battle-axe was thirsty   *battle-axe*: hag, also axe
to taste blood just now.
Not sparing her fangs, she stretched
her harsh mouth over his head,
split his forehead in two:
I was there when they fought.

Thorkel's men ran up then and said a troll would never have
taken him in broad daylight.

Thorkel kept quiet, then said, 'There's more to it than that.
Grettir must have killed him. So how did it happen?'

Grettir told him all about their quarrel.

'Things have taken a bad turn,' said Thorkel. 'Skeggi was
sent to accompany me. He was from a good family and I
will accept responsibility by paying whatever compensation is
decided, but I have no control over whether a sentence of
outlawry is passed. You have two options, Grettir: either go to
the Thing and take the chance of what is decided there or turn
back now.'

Grettir chose to go to the Thing and went on with them. The
case was brought by the slain man's heirs. Thorkel undertook
to pay compensation, but Grettir was sentenced to lesser outlawry and was banished from Iceland for three years.

When they rode back from the Thing, the chieftains rested
their horses at Sledaas before going their separate ways. Grettir
lifted up a boulder lying in the grass there, which is now called
Grettishaf (Grettir's Lift).[22] Many people went up to look at it
and were astonished that such a young man could lift such a
huge rock.

Grettir rode home to Bjarg and told his father what had
happened. Asmund showed little reaction to the news and said
Grettir would turn out to be a troublemaker.

17 | There was a man named Haflidi who lived at Reydarfell in the Hvitarsida district. He was a merchant and owned a trading ship which had been hauled up on the River Hvita. One member of his crew was a man named Bard, who had a young and pretty wife.

Asmund sent a messenger to Haflidi asking him to take Grettir on and look after him. Haflidi said he had been told Grettir was an unruly character, but for the sake of his friendship with Asmund he agreed to take him along, and made preparations to sail abroad. Asmund refused to give Grettir anything for the journey except provisions and a little homespun cloth. Grettir asked his father to give him a weapon.

'You've never done anything I've told you. And I don't know what useful thing you would do with weapons, so I won't give you any.'

'Then there's no need to reward a favour that isn't done,' said Grettir.

The father and son parted with little love lost between them. Many people wished Grettir a safe journey, but few a safe return.

His mother accompanied him on his way.

'You haven't been sent on your way as well equipped as I would like to see someone of your standing, my son,' she told him before they parted. 'What I think you lack most is a useful weapon. Something tells me you will be needing one.'

Then she took an inlaid sword from under her cloak, a fine piece of workmanship.

'This sword belonged to my grandfather Jokul and the most prominent people of the Vatnsdal clan[23] and it brought them many triumphs. I want to give you this sword. Make good use of it.'

Grettir thanked her kindly for the gift, saying he thought it was better than any other gift, even much more valuable ones. Then he went on his way and Asdis wished him many good things.

Grettir rode south over the moor, not stopping until he had

crossed it and reached the ship. Haflidi welcomed him warmly
and asked him what he was equipped with for the journey.

Grettir spoke a verse:

12.

Rider of the cloak that clothes the wind!   *cloak that clothes the wind*:
I think that rich man has given me   sail; its *rider*: seafarer
a poor start from home. I hoped
for gold from the dragon's lair.
For her gift of a wound-maker
a woman of calibre proved
the truth of the ancient saying:
The mother is best to the child.

Haflidi said it was obvious that she cared the most for him.

They put to sea when they were ready to sail and the wind
was favourable, and when they were clear of all the shallows
they hoisted sail. Grettir made himself a place to sleep under
the ship's boat and refused to leave it, neither to bail out the
ship nor turn the sails, nor do any of the tasks on board he was
supposed to share with the rest of the crew. Nor would he pay
them to be relieved of his duties.

They sailed south around Reykjanes and then along the south
of Iceland and when they lost sight of land they ran into strong
breaking waves. The ship tended to leak and could hardly stand
up to the breakers and the crew were drenched. Grettir kept
making lampoons about them, which infuriated them.

One day when it was both windy and cold, the crew called
out to Grettir and told him to pull his weight – 'Our fingers are
frozen to the bone!'

Grettir looked up and said:

13.

What luck if every layabout's fingers
would shrivel up and drop off.

They could not get him to work, but disliked his behaviour all
the more and said they would make him pay for all the lampoons and offences he had made.

'You'd much rather stroke Bard's wife's belly with your

hands than do your duties on board,' they said. 'We won't stand for it.'

The weather grew steadily worse and the crew had to bail out the ship day and night and they started threatening Grettir.

When Haflidi heard this, he went over to where Grettir was lying and said to him, 'I don't like the way you and the crew have been getting on. You refuse to do your duties and you lampoon them into the bargain and now they're threatening to throw you overboard. This is no way to behave.'

'Why can't they get on with their own business?' Grettir asked. 'But I'd like to leave a couple of them lying around before I disappear overboard.'

'That is impossible,' said Haflidi. 'Things won't turn out well for us if this is the way you and the crew are going to behave. I want to suggest a plan to you.'

'What is it?' asked Grettir.

'They complain about you making lampoons about them,' said Haflidi. 'I suggest that you make a lampoon about me and then maybe they'll put up with you better.'

'The only verse I would ever make about you would be praise,' said Grettir. 'I would never compare you with those layabouts.'

Then Haflidi said, 'You could make a verse that sounds better if you look closely at it, but is none too pretty on first impression.'

'I can manage that,' said Grettir.

So Haflidi went up to the crew and said, 'You're toiling away so hard, it's no surprise that you disapprove of Grettir.'

'His lampoons annoy us more than anything else,' they said.

Then Haflidi said in a loud voice, 'He'll certainly pay for it in the end, too.'

Hearing Haflidi criticizing him, Grettir spoke a verse:

14.
Life has changed for loud-mouthed
Haflidi since he supped
on curds at Reydarfell;
he felt at home then.

See the proud spearhead   *breakfast*: or, read as *break fast* for a
of battle breakfast now   battle image
day and night on the elk   *elk that rides the . . . seas*: ship
that rides the land-hugging seas.[24]

The merchants disliked the verse intensely and said that Grettir
would not get away with heaping abuse on Haflidi.

Then Haflidi said, 'Grettir deserves to be humiliated by you,
but I don't want to stake my honour against his spite and
heedlessness. We will not take revenge on him while we are in
such peril, but you can remember it when you reach land if you
wish.'

'Why can't we put up with it like you?' said the merchants.
'Why should lampoons hurt us more than you?'

Haflidi told them to try and afterwards they took far less
offence at his lampoons. They had a long, rough passage and
the ship began leaking in several places. The crew toiled so hard
that they began to flag.

Bard's young wife made a habit of sewing up Grettir's shirt-
sleeves[25] for him and the crew made fun of him for it.

Haflidi went over to where Grettir lay and spoke a verse:

15.
Stand up from where you're buried, Grettir,
the ship is furrowing the waves deep
while you chatter cheerfully
with that glad-hearted woman.
She has rolled up your sleeves, sewn them
tight around your arms, that woman,
she wants you to respect
your companions who are working below.

Grettir stood up at once and spoke a verse:

16.
I stand up, how much beneath me
the ship is heaving and pitching.
I know the woman will frown
on me for slouching on board.

That maid of fair spirit and face
is sure to disapprove
if I let others here
always do my work for me.

Then he ran to the men who were bailing water at the aft of
the ship and asked what they wanted him to do. They said he
would not do much good.

'Many hands make light work,' said Grettir.

Haflidi told them not to refuse his assistance – 'Maybe he
thinks he can get all this business off his hands by offering to
help.'

In those days there were no bilge troughs on ships, but the
bailing was done using buckets or tubs, which was a wet and
tiring job. Two buckets were used and one was carried down
while the other went up. The bailers told Grettir to dip the
buckets in the water, saying this would show them what he was
capable of. He answered back that this would not take much
effort to show them and he went down and filled the buckets
with water, while two men emptied them. Before long they
were exhausted. Four others took over from them and the same
thing happened. Some claim there were eight men emptying the
buckets for him by the end when the ship was completely bailed
out. After this, the merchants spoke very differently about
Grettir, because they saw what he could accomplish on account
of his great strength. He also turned out to be very energetic in
helping them afterwards with whatever was needed.

They were carried eastwards across the ocean and a heavy
fog descended. The next thing they knew was that one night
their ship sailed into a skerry, ripping a hole in the keel under
the prow. The ship's boat was put out with all the women and
goods on board. There was an islet nearby and they took as
much of their belongings to it as they could manage that night.

When day broke they discussed where they had landed. Some
of them who had sailed abroad before recognized that they had
reached South More in Norway. There was an island named
Haramsoy a short way off towards the mainland, where a lot
of people lived and the local landholder had his home.

18 | The landholder who lived on the island was named Thor-
finn. He was an important chieftain, the son of Kar the
Old, who had lived there for a long time.

When it was fully light, people on the island could see the
merchants in trouble. Thorfinn was told and reacted at once by
sending out a large warship[26] that he owned, with sixteen oars
on either side. Almost thirty men were on board and they rowed
with all their might and saved the merchants' belongings, but
the ship sank and many valuables were lost with it. Thorfinn
had all the people from the ship taken to his house, where they
stayed for a week, drying out their goods. Then the merchants
left for the south – and have left the saga.

Grettir remained behind with Thorfinn and kept a low profile. Mostly, he said very little and Thorfinn fed him, but did
not pay much attention to him. Grettir was unsociable towards
him and refused to go outside with him during the day. Thorfinn
disapproved, but could not bring himself to refuse him food.
Thorfinn was a very houseproud and cheerful host and liked
everyone else to be happy too.

Grettir went visiting a lot, often to the other farms on the
island. There was a man named Audun who lived at a place
called Vindheim. Grettir went there every day and struck up a
friendship with him and would sit there late into the day.

Late one evening, Grettir was about to walk back to
Thorfinn's when he saw a great fire flare up on the headland down from Audun's farm. Grettir asked what strange
thing was happening there. Audun said he had no need to find
out.

'Where I come from,' said Grettir, 'people who saw that
would say it was the glow of a treasure hoard.'[27]

'The keeper of that fire,' answered the farmer, 'is someone
we are better off not trying to find out about.'

'I'd like to find out,' said Grettir.

'There's a mound on the headland,' said Audun, 'where Kar
the Old, Thorfinn's father, was buried. At first they owned a
single farm on the island, but since Kar died he has haunted the
island and frightened away all the farmers who owned land

here. Now Thorfinn owns the entire island and no one who is under his protection is harmed by Kar.'

Grettir said he had done well to tell him this and added, 'I'll come back tomorrow. Have some tools ready for me to dig with.'

'I advise you not to get involved in this,' said Audun, 'because I know Thorfinn will hate you for it.'

Grettir said he was prepared to take that risk.

The night passed and Grettir came back early in the morning. The tools were ready for him and the farmer accompanied him to the mound.

Grettir broke open the mound and worked furiously, not stopping until he had reached the timber props, by which time it was very late in the day. Then he tore away the props. Audun discouraged him as best he could from entering the mound.

Grettir told him to watch over the rope – 'because I want to find out what's in there.'

Then Grettir went inside the mound. It was dark and smelled unpleasant. He explored the mound to see how it was laid out. He found some horse bones, then he rubbed against the carved back of a chair and could tell there was a man sitting in it. A huge amount of gold and silver had been piled up there and the man's feet were resting on a chest full of silver. Grettir took all the treasure and carried it over to the rope. And when he was walking back inside the mound, something grabbed him tight. He dropped the treasure and fought back, and the two of them grappled violently, knocking everything over that was in their way. The mound-dweller went for him ferociously and Grettir backed off for a long time, until he realized that he would need all his strength. They both fought with all their might and struggled towards where the horse bones were. They grappled for a long while there and both of them were brought to their knees at different times, until in the end the mound-dweller toppled over backwards with a mighty crash. Audun ran away from the rope, thinking that Grettir must have been killed. Then Grettir drew his sword, Jokul's Gift, swung at the mound-dweller's neck and chopped off his head. He placed the head up against the mound-dweller's buttocks[28] and took all the treasure over to the rope. Audun was nowhere around, so he had to clamber up the rope himself and then pull up the treasure, which he had tied to the end of it.

Grettir was feeling very stiff after his fight with Kar and went back to Thorfinn's farm with the treasure. Everyone there was seated at the table. Thorfinn glared at Grettir when he entered the hall and asked him what he needed to do that was so important he couldn't keep the same hours as other people.

'Many little things happen at night,' Grettir said.

Then he spread out on the table all the treasure he had taken from the mound. Grettir had his eye on one piece of the treasure in particular, a fine short-sword. He said he had never seen such a good weapon before and handed it over last of all. Thorfinn's eyebrows lifted when he saw the treasure and the short-sword, because it was an heirloom that had never left his family.

'Where did you get this treasure from?' Thorfinn asked.

Grettir spoke a verse:

17.

Spreader of gold that glitters on waves,	*spreader of gold*: generous man
my hopes of winning treasure	*hopes ... dashed*: i.e. he perhaps
from the mound are clearly dashed:	realizes Thorfinn will take the
men will soon hear of this.	treasure himself
Yet I see too that few makers	*makers of sword-blizzards*: warriors
of sword-blizzards will earn	
much joy when they seek	*dragon's mire*: treasure where
the dragon's mire of gold there.	dragons lie

Thorfinn answered, 'You are not a man of faint heart. No one until now has ever been keen to break into that mound. I know that it is a waste of treasure to bury it in the ground or a mound, so I cannot say you have done wrong, because after all you brought it to me. And where did you find that fine short-sword?'

Grettir answered with a verse:

18.

Spreader of gold that burns on waves,
in a murky mound I gained hold
of the sword that stretches wounds:
a ghost was felled then.
Were it mine, that scourge of men,
that precious flash of flame   *flash of flame*: i.e. sword
clashing down on helmets,
would never leave my hand.

'You state your case well,' said Thorfinn, 'but you must prove your prowess before I give you the sword, because my father never gave it to me while he was alive.'

'There's no telling whom it will serve the best in the end,' Grettir answered.

Thorfinn took the treasure and kept the sword by his bedside. The winter passed and Yule came around, and nothing else eventful happened.

19 | Earl Eirik, Hakon's son, had left for England the previous summer to see his brother-in-law, King Canute the Great. He had appointed his son, Earl Hakon, as ruler of Norway, but had entrusted his brother Earl Svein with governing the realm and taking care of Hakon, who was still only a boy.

Before leaving Norway, Earl Eirik had summoned the landholders and powerful farmers to him. They discussed many aspects of the law and government of the country, because Eirik was a firm ruler. People there thought it was a disgraceful practice to allow robbers and berserks to challenge men of high standing to duels for their money or wives, without compensation being paid for the one who was slain. Many had suffered disgrace and lost their money and some had even lost their lives, so Earl Eirik banned all duels in Norway. He also outlawed all robbers and berserks who caused any trouble. Thorfinn Karsson from Haramsoy was involved in planning this measure, because he was a wise man and a close friend of the earl.

The worst troublemakers were said to be two brothers called Thorir Paunch and Ogmund the Evil. They came from Halogaland and were bigger and stronger than anybody else. They would go berserk and spare nothing when they flew into a rage. They used to take away men's wives and daughters and keep them for a week or two, then return them. Wherever they went, they used to plunder and cause other trouble. Earl Eirik outlawed them throughout Norway. Thorfinn was the most avid campaigner to have them banished and they felt that he deserved to be paid back with all the hatred they could show. Then the earl went abroad, as described in his saga,[29] and Earl Svein ruled and governed Norway.

Thorfinn went home to his farm and stayed there most of the time until Yule, as mentioned above. Towards Yule he made preparations to go to another of his farms, in a place named Slysfjord on the mainland. He had invited many of his friends there, but his wife was unable to go with him, because their grown-up daughter was ill, so the two women stayed behind at home. Thorfinn took thirty freed slaves with him to the Yule feast, which was a joyful and merry occasion.

On Yule Eve the weather was bright and calm. Grettir spent most of his time outdoors during the day, and saw ships sailing north and south along the shore, because everybody was on the way to feasts. The farmer's daughter had recovered by then and could walk about with her mother. The day passed.

Then Grettir saw a boat being rowed up to the island. It was not large, but had overlapping shields arranged from stem to stern and was painted above the waterline. The men on board were rowing vigorously, heading for Thorfinn's boat-shed. When the boat touched ground the crew leapt ashore; Grettir counted them and there were twelve in all. They did not seem to have come in peace. After they had hauled their boat ashore on to dry land, they ran over to Thorfinn's boat-shed. Inside was Thorfinn's huge warship which had always needed thirty men to launch, but the twelve of them tugged it straight out on to the gravelly beach, lifted up their own boat and put it in the boat-shed.

Grettir could tell they were not going to wait for an invitation, so he went up to them and greeted them warmly, asking who they were and the name of their leader.

The one he had asked answered back at once that he was named Thorir and nicknamed Thorir Paunch. Then he mentioned his brother Ogmund's name and those of the rest of their companions.

'I expect your master Thorfinn has heard about us,' he said. 'Would he happen to be at home?'

'You're in luck,' said Grettir, 'because you've arrived at a very good time, if you are the men I think you are. The master of the house is away and all the free-born men in the household have gone with him and they aren't planning to return until after Yule. His wife and daughter are at home. If I had any score to settle, this is exactly the time I would have wanted to arrive, because everything you need is to be had here, ale and other pleasures.'

Thorir kept quiet while Grettir talked away, then he said to Ogmund, 'Things have not gone the way I predicted and I have a mind to repay Thorfinn for having us outlawed. This man tells us just what we wanted to hear and we don't need to force the words out of him.'

'Every man is the master of his own words,' said Grettir. 'I'll look after you in every way I can. Come home with me.'

They thanked him and said they would accept his offer. When they reached the farmhouse, Grettir took Thorir by the arm and led him into the main room. Grettir was very talkative then. Thorfinn's wife was in the main room hanging up tapestries and making it ready for Yule. Hearing Grettir talking to someone, she stopped where she was on the floor and asked who it was that he was welcoming so openly.

'It is the right thing to do, to give guests a kind welcome, my good lady,' said Grettir. 'Master Thorir Paunch has arrived with eleven companions and they intend to stay here for Yule. That's a fine thing, because we were rather short of company before.'

'I don't rank them with masters or fine men,' she replied, 'because they are the worst robbers and evil-doers around. I would gladly have given almost anything I own for them not to have come here at this time. And you're repaying Thorfinn badly for rescuing you from a shipwreck without a penny to your name and keeping you all winter as a free man.'

'You would do better to help the guests out of their wet clothes than to criticize me. You'll have plenty of chance to do that later.'

Then Thorir said, 'Don't be surly, my good lady. You won't lack anything though your husband is away from home, for you'll have a man in his place, and so will your daughter and all the women of the household.'

'That's spoken like a true man,' said Grettir. 'They won't be able to complain about being neglected.'

All the women rushed out of the room and were seized with fear and fits of weeping.

'Hand over anything you want me to look after,' Grettir told the berserks, 'your weapons and wet clothes, because the women will be easier to handle when they are not scared.'

Thorir said he did not care how much the women bickered, 'but you deserve to be treated completely differently from the rest of the people here. I think we can make a true friend of you.'

'That is up to you,' said Grettir. 'I for one don't treat all men alike.'

Then they put down most of their weapons.

Afterwards, Grettir said, 'I think you had better go over to the table and have something to drink, because all that rowing must have made you thirsty.'

They said they were quite ready to do that, but did not know where the cellar was, so when Grettir asked whether they would leave everything to him, the berserks readily agreed. Grettir went off, fetched the ale and served it up. They were very tired and gulped it down in great draughts. He kept plying them with the strongest ale there was for a long time and told them many amusing tales. It was a very noisy gathering and the people of the household had no wish to join them.

Then Thorir said, 'I have never met a stranger who has treated us as well as this man. How would you like us to reward you for your service?'

'I don't want any reward for the time being, but if we're still as good friends when you leave as we seem to be now, then I'll join your band. Even though I may be a lesser man than some of you, I won't get in the way of your doing great deeds.'

They were delighted at his words and wanted to make a firm pledge of companionship at once.

Grettir declined, saying, 'There's truth in the old saying that "Ale makes another man." Let's not rush into doing any more than I have said already. We are all rather impetuous characters.'

They said they would not take the promise back. As the evening wore on and it grew very dark, Grettir noticed that they were becoming worn out by all the drinking.

'Don't you think it's time for bed now?' he said.

Thorir said it was – 'and I'll keep my promise to the lady of the house.'

Grettir left the room and called out in a loud voice, 'Get into bed, ladies! Master Thorir wants you there!'

They shouted curses back at him, howling and screaming, just as the berserks left the room.

'Let us go outside,' Grettir said to them. 'I'll show you where Thorfinn keeps his clothes.'

They agreed and they went out to a huge, solid-built outhouse with a big lock on the door. Beside it, joined by a single boarded wall, stood a big, solid privy. They were quite tall buildings, with some steps leading up to them. The berserks became rather unruly and started pushing Grettir about and he dodged out of their way, then when they least expected it he dashed out of the building, grabbed the latch, slammed the door and locked it. Thinking at first that the door must have swung shut by itself, Thorir and his companions did not pay any attention to it. They had a light with them, because Grettir had been showing them many of Thorfinn's belongings, and they went on looking around inside for a while. Grettir rushed back to the farmhouse and, reaching the doorway, he called out in a loud voice to ask where the farmer's wife was. She was too scared to reply.

'There's a fine catch here for the taking,' he said. 'Are there any suitable weapons around?'

'There are plenty of weapons, but I don't know what use they'll be to you,' she replied.

'We'll talk about that later,' he said. 'Now it's everyone for himself. It's now or never.'

'It would surely be a godsend if anything could improve our lot now,' said the farmer's wife. 'Old Kar's barbed spear is hanging above Thorfinn's bed. A helmet, coat of mail and that fine sword are there too, weapons that will not fail you as long as your courage holds up.'

Grettir snatched up the helmet and spear and girded on the sword, and went straight out again. The woman called out to the farmhands, telling them to go with this good, brave man. Four of them ran for their weapons, but four others did not dare to approach.

To return to the berserks, they felt Grettir was taking a long time about coming back and began to suspect a trick. They ran for the door and discovered it was locked, then pushed against the timber wall so hard that every board in it creaked. Eventually they managed to break down the boarding into the privy, and from there they headed down the steps. They went berserk and began howling like dogs.

Just at that moment, Grettir turned up. Using both hands, he thrust the spear at Thorir's stomach just as he was on his way down the steps and it went straight through him. The spear was fitted with a long, thin blade; Ogmund the Evil was behind Thorir and bumped against him so that the spear pierced him right up to the barbs, out between his shoulderblades and into Ogmund's chest. Both of them tumbled down dead from the spear.

All the men who had come out ran down the steps. Grettir attacked each one in turn, slashing at them with his sword or lunging with his spear, while they fought back with logs that were lying out on the field or anything else they could find. They were deadly characters to deal with even when they had no weapons, because of their mighty strength. Grettir killed two of the Halogalanders in the hayfield. The four farmhands came out then; they had been bickering over who should have which weapon. They advanced when the berserks were on the retreat anyway, but when the berserks fought back they scampered off to the buildings again.

Six Vikings fell there and Grettir was the slayer of them all. The other six fled; they made their way down to the boat-shed and went inside. They defended themselves with oars and dealt Grettir such fierce blows that he almost sustained serious injuries.

The farmhands went back, boasting of their prowess. The farmer's wife ordered them to go and find out what had happened to Grettir, but they would not.

Grettir killed two men in the boat-shed, but four escaped from him. They ran off in pairs in different directions and Grettir chased the two who were closer to him. It was pitch black by now. They ran into a barn on the farm named Vindheim that was mentioned earlier, and after a long struggle Grettir killed both of them. He was feeling very stiff and exhausted by then and the night was almost over. When the weather turned cold with drifting snow he did not feel like looking for the two remaining Vikings, so he went back home to the farm.

The farmer's wife lit a light at the windows of the top rooms to guide him on his way and by following the light he eventually made his way home.

When he reached the door, the farmer's wife went up to him and welcomed him in.

'You have won great renown for this,' she said, 'and delivered me and my household from a shameful fate which we would never have recovered from, if you had not rescued us.'

'I think I'm much the same person you were heaping abuse on earlier this evening,' said Grettir.

'We didn't know you were the mighty warrior that you have proved yourself to be,' she said. 'Feel free to take anything you want in this house that is fitting for us to give and an honour for you to accept. And I have a feeling Thorfinn will reward you even more handsomely when he comes home.'

'There is little need for rewards for the time being, but I'll accept your offer until your husband comes home. And I trust you will be able to sleep in peace from berserks.'

Grettir had not had much to drink that evening and lay down

with his weapons beside him during the night. At daylight the next morning people were summoned from around the island and they set out to find the berserks who had escaped the night before. They were discovered towards the end of the day, lying up against a rock, dead from the cold and their wounds. Their bodies were carried off to the shoreline and buried there in a shallow grave.[30] After that the islanders went home, certain that peace had been brought to them.

When he went back to the farmer's wife, Grettir spoke this verse:

19.

Twelve wielders of battle-flame	*battle-flame*: sword
I sent to a sea-lapped grave,	
alone and undaunted I brought	
swift death upon them all.	
Woman, high-born tree of gold,	*tree of gold*: woman
what deed that one man does	
will ever be worthy of praise	
if this one counts for little?	

'There are certainly few men like you around these days,' said the farmer's wife.

She made him sit in the high seat and treated him well in every respect. Time passed until Thorfinn was due home.

20 | After Yule, Thorfinn made preparations to go back home and gave many of the people he had invited to the feast fine gifts when they parted. Then he set off with his band of men until he drew close to his boat-shed. They noticed a ship lying on the sand and soon recognized that it was his big warship. Thorfinn had not yet heard anything about the Vikings.

He ordered them to hurry for land – 'For I suspect that this is not the work of any friends of mine,' he said.

Thorfinn led his men ashore and went straight over to the boat-shed. He saw a boat inside it which he recognized as belonging to the berserks.

Then he said to his men, 'I suspect that such events have happened here that I would have given the island and everything on it to have been able to avert.'

They asked him why.

Then he said, 'The Vikings have been here, the worst men I know about in the whole of Norway: Thorir Paunch and Ogmund the Evil. They won't have done us any favours here, and I don't trust that Icelander very much.'

He spoke at length to his companions about this.

Grettir was at home and delayed the people on the farm from going down to the beach, saying that he did not care if the man of the house was nervous about what might have happened. Then the wife asked his permission to leave and he said she was free to go where she pleased, but he showed no signs of going himself.

She rushed off to see Thorfinn and welcomed him warmly.

He was happy to see her and said, 'Praise God that I see you and my daughter safe and happy. So what has happened to you since I left?'

'Things have turned out well in the end,' she said, 'but we came very close to suffering a shameful fate that we would never have recovered from if your winter guest had not helped us.'

'Let's sit down now and you tell me all that happened,' said Thorfinn.

She told him in detail about everything that had happened, praising Grettir's courage and action.

Thorfinn remained silent until she had finished the story, then said, 'The old saying is true, that it takes time to know people. So where is Grettir now?'

'He's in the main room of the farm,' she replied.

Then they went back to the farmhouse. Thorfinn went up to Grettir, embraced him and thanked him eloquently for the integrity he had displayed.

'Now I will say something to you that few men say to their friends,' Thorfinn said. 'I hope you need help some time and then you would really see whether I could prove useful to you or not. I will never really be able to repay your good deeds unless you end up in trouble. But my hospitality is open to you for as long as you need to accept it and I will treat you the best of all my men.'

Grettir thanked him kindly and said, 'I would have accepted your offer earlier too.'

Grettir spent the winter there on the best of terms with Thorfinn. He became renowned for this deed all over Norway, especially in places where berserks had been causing the most trouble.

In the spring, Thorfinn asked Grettir what he was planning to do and Grettir replied that he wanted to go north to the market in Vagen. Thorfinn told him that as much money as he wanted was there for the taking, but Grettir said all he needed was a little cash. Thorfinn said this was only a matter of course and he accompanied him to his ship. Then he gave Grettir the fine short-sword which Grettir carried for the rest of his life and was a precious piece of work. Thorfinn also invited him back whenever he needed any help.

Grettir went north to Vagen where a large crowd had assembled. Many people whom he had never met before welcomed him warmly on account of the great deed he had done in killing the Vikings. Many leading men invited him to stay with them, but he preferred to go back to his friend Thorfinn. He took a passage on a trading ship owned by a man named Thorkel, who lived at Salten in Halogaland and was from an important family there. Thorkel welcomed Grettir warmly when he arrived at his farm and made an eloquent invitation to him to stay for the winter. Grettir accepted the offer, stayed with Thorkel that winter and was very well looked after.

21 | There was a man named Bjorn who was staying with Thorkel, a distant relative of his and from a good family, but rather short-tempered. He was not popular with the ordinary people, because he spread stories about the men who stayed with Thorkel and drove many of them away. He and Grettir hardly got on at all. Bjorn looked down on him, while Grettir was stubborn, and friction developed between them.

Since Bjorn was a boisterous and swaggering character, many young men used to seek his company and loiter with him in the evenings.

Early in the winter, it happened that a savage bear left its den and was so ferocious that it spared neither men nor animals. Everyone assumed it must have been woken from hibernation by the noise that Bjorn and his companions were always making. The animal grew so troublesome that it would prey on the farmers' livestock and since Thorkel was the wealthiest farmer in the district, he suffered the greatest losses.

One day Thorkel summoned his men to join him and find out where the bear's den was. They discovered it in the cliffs overlooking the sea: there was a single cliff with a cave in it and a narrow track leading up to it. There was a sheer drop below the cave down to boulders on the shore, which would have spelled certain death. The bear lay in its den by day, but usually came outside at night. No pens could protect the sheep from the bear, and dogs shied from it. Everyone thought it was a terrible situation.

Thorkel's kinsman Bjorn said that the most difficult task was over once the den had been found.

'I will now put to the test,' he said, 'who will come off the better in this game, my namesake[31] or me.'

Grettir acted as though he did not know about Bjorn's boasts.

Bjorn started going out every night when everyone else went to bed. One night he went to the den and heard the bear inside roaring ferociously. Bjorn lay down on the path with his shield over him, planning to wait until it came outside as usual. The bear got wind of him and stayed inside. Bjorn grew very sleepy lying there and could not keep awake. Suddenly the animal came out of its den, saw him lying there, clawed at him with its paw and pulled the shield off him, then tossed it over the edge of the cliff. Bjorn woke up with a start, took to his heels and ran home. The bear came close to catching him. His companions knew this, for they had been spying on him; they found the shield the following morning and made great fun of him for it.

At Yuletide, Thorkel went to the den for himself, with seven other men – Bjorn and Grettir and other followers of his. Grettir was wearing a fur cloak which he took off while they moved in on the bear. It was difficult to attack, because they could only prod it with spears which it warded off with its mouth. Bjorn eagerly urged them to attack it, but never went close enough that he was in any danger. When no one was watching he took Grettir's cloak and threw it into the bear's den. They were unable to make any progress and turned back home towards the end of the day. When Grettir was making ready to go home he noticed his cloak was missing and could see that the bear was lying down on it.

'Which of you lads has played a trick on me and thrown my cloak into the den?' he asked.

'Someone did it who dares to admit it,' said Bjorn.

'I won't make a big fuss about that,' said Grettir.

Then they turned back home. After they had gone some way, the thong on Grettir's leggings broke. Thorkel told the others to wait for him, but Grettir said there was no need.

'Don't imagine Grettir will run off and leave his cloak behind,' said Bjorn. 'He wants to win fame by killing the bear single-handed after the eight of us have given up on it. Then he would live up to his reputation, but he has put up a poor show today.'

'I don't know how this will turn out for you,' said Thorkel, 'but you are no match for him, so leave him alone.'

Bjorn said neither of them had the right to put words into his mouth.

A ridge was blocking their view of each other and Grettir turned back to the path. This time there was no one to vie with about making the attack. He drew the sword Jokul's Gift and had a strap on the hilt of his short-sword which he slipped around his wrist, because he felt he had more scope to act with his hand free.

He went straight along the path and when the bear saw him it ran at him ferociously and lashed at him with the paw that was farther away from the cliff. Grettir struck with his sword, hit the paw above the claws and chopped it off. Then the bear tried to strike him with its good paw and shifted its weight to the stump; because that paw was shorter than it had expected, the bear toppled into Grettir's arms. Grettir grabbed the bear by the ears and held it at arm's length to prevent it from biting him. He said later[32] that holding off that bear was his greatest feat of strength. Because the bear thrashed about and the path was so narrow, they both toppled over the edge of the cliff. The bear was heavier than Grettir, so it hit the boulders first, with him on top of it, and was badly injured by the fall. Grettir grabbed his short-sword, drove it through the bear's heart and killed it. Then he went home, taking his cloak with him, which was ripped to shreds. He also took the piece of the paw that he had cut off.[33]

Thorkel was sitting drinking in the main room when Grettir walked in. Everyone laughed at Grettir in his tattered cloak. He produced the piece he had cut off the bear's paw and put it on the table.

'Where is my kinsman Bjorn now?' said Thorkel. 'I have never seen your weapons bite so sharp. I want you to make redress to Grettir for the dishonour you have done him.'

Bjorn said that he would take his time about doing that – 'and I don't care whether he likes it or not.'

Then Grettir spoke a verse:

20.

That murderous weasel often returned	*murderous weasel*: i.e. Bjorn
dripping sweat of fear, not blood,	
in the twilight after he visited	
his winter-clad foe.	*winter-clad foe*: i.e. the bear
No one saw me sitting	
by the bear's den late at night,	
yet I brought that furry beast	
out from the cave's mouth.	

'You have certainly done well,' said Bjorn, 'and you tell a different story about me, too. You must think your barbs have struck home.'

'Grettir, I do not want you to take vengeance on Bjorn,' said

Thorkel. 'I will pay you the full compensation due for a man's life, if you two are reconciled.'

Bjorn said he had better things to spend his money on than paying compensation for that – 'I think you should leave each man to himself when Grettir and I clash.'

Grettir said he liked the idea.

'For my sake at least, Grettir,' Thorkel said, 'you must not impose on Bjorn while the two of you are staying with me.'

'So be it,' said Grettir.

Bjorn said he would not go around in fear of Grettir, wherever they met. Grettir grinned and refused to accept any compensation on Bjorn's behalf, and they remained there for the rest of the winter.

22 | In the spring Grettir went back north to Vagen with the merchants. He and Thorkel parted in friendship, while Bjorn set off for England at the helm of a ship that Thorkel sent there. Bjorn spent the summer there and bought all the goods Thorkel had told him to. Then he sailed back to Norway as the autumn drew on.

Grettir stayed in Vagen until the fleet put out and sailed north with some merchants as far as the port named Garten, which is on the estuary where Trondheim stands, and they put the awnings up. When they had finished, they saw a ship approaching from the south. They recognized at once that this was one of the ships that sailed to England, and when it landed just down the coast from them, the crew went ashore.

Grettir and his companions went over to them.

When they met he saw that Bjorn was one of the crew and said to him, 'It's a good thing that we should meet here, because we still have an old score to settle. I want to put our strength to the test now.'

Bjorn said the argument was a thing of the past to him, 'But if any wrong was done, let me pay you any compensation for it that you would feel honoured to accept.'

Then Grettir spoke a verse:

21.

I beat the spiky-fanged bear,
word of that deed spread far;
that harsh-hearted beast ripped
the warrior's long pelt.
The devious guardian of rings   *guardian of rings*: man, i.e. Bjorn
whose work that was shall pay.
I do not think I am one
to outbid others in boasts.

Bjorn said money had been paid to settle greater wrongs than this.

Grettir replied that there were not many people around who had played malicious tricks on him, and that he had never accepted compensation and would not this time either – 'We will not both walk away from here in one piece if I have any say in the matter. I declare you a coward if you dare not fight.'

Bjorn could see that he had no hope of talking his way out of this situation, so he took his weapons and went ashore. Then they rushed at each other and fought, and before long Bjorn was wounded and fell down dead to the ground. Seeing this, Bjorn's companions went to their ship, sailed north to call on Thorkel and told him about the incident. He said this had not happened any sooner than was to be expected.

Shortly afterwards Thorkel went to Trondheim, where he went to see Earl Svein.

After he had killed Bjorn, Grettir went south to More to see his friend Thorfinn, and told him what had happened.

Thorfinn welcomed him warmly.

'And it's a good thing that you need a friend,' he said. 'Stay with me until this business is over.'

Grettir thanked him for his offer and said he would accept it this time.

Earl Svein was staying at Steinkjer in Trondheim when he heard news of Bjorn's killing. One of the earl's men, whose name was Hjarrandi, was Bjorn's brother. He was furious when he heard about Bjorn being killed and asked the earl for his support in this matter. The earl promised it, then sent a

messenger to summon both Thorfinn and Grettir to appear
before him. They prepared to leave as soon as they heard
the earl's order, and went to Trondheim. The earl arranged a
meeting with them to discuss the matter and asked Hjarrandi
to attend it as well.

Hjarrandi announced he would never carry his brother's life
around in his purse.[34]

'I will either meet the same fate as he did or take vengeance
for him,' he said.

When the case was examined, the earl felt that Bjorn had
done Grettir much wrong. Thorfinn offered to pay such an
amount of compensation that the earl considered would honour
his heirs and gave a long speech about the freedom that Grettir
had brought to people in the north when he killed the berserks,
as described earlier.

'That is quite true, Thorfinn,' said the earl. 'He purged the
country of a great scourge. I am honoured to accept compensation on your recommendation. In addition, Grettir is
renowned for his strength and courage.'

Hjarrandi did not want to accept this settlement, so they
all left the meeting. Thorfinn appointed one of his kinsmen, Arnbjorn, to be with Grettir every day, because he knew
Hjarrandi was waiting for a chance to kill him.

23 | One day when Grettir and Arnbjorn were walking around
     | the streets of the town to keep themselves amused, they
went past a gate and a man suddenly rushed out brandishing
an axe with both hands and aimed a blow at Grettir. Not
expecting the attack, Grettir was slow to react. Arnbjorn saw
the assailant, grabbed hold of Grettir and pushed him so hard
that he fell to his knees. The axe struck him on the shoulder
blade, ran down it and out under his armpit, causing a
deep wound. Grettir swung round, drawing his short-sword,
and recognized Hjarrandi. The axe had stuck in the ground,
Hjarrandi was slow in pulling it back out, and Grettir struck
at him, slicing off his arm at the shoulder. Then Hjarrandi's
companions ran up, five of them in all, and a fight ensued.

Grettir and Arnbjorn made short work of it: they killed Hjarrandi's five men, while one escaped[35] and went straight to see the earl and tell him the news.

The earl was furious when he heard this and called an assembly for the following day. Thorfinn attended it.

The earl charged Grettir with the killings and he admitted them, saying they had been in self-defence.

'I have a wound to prove it,' said Grettir. 'I would have been killed if Arnbjorn had not saved me.'

The earl replied that it was a shame he had not been killed – 'You will be the death of many men if you remain alive.'

Grettir's friend and companion Bersi, the son of Torfa the Poetess, was with the earl at that time. He and Thorfinn went before the earl and asked for Grettir to be spared, and suggested that the earl himself judge the case so long as Grettir were granted his life and the right to stay in Norway. The earl was reluctant to make any settlement, but eventually he gave in to their entreaties. A truce was made allowing Grettir to remain in peace until the spring, although the earl refused to make a binding settlement until Gunnar, the brother of Bjorn and Hjarrandi, was present. Gunnar had a house in the town of Tunsberg.

In the spring the earl summoned Grettir and Thorfinn to Tunsberg, where he planned to stay himself when most of the ships were calling there. Grettir and Thorfinn went there and the earl was already in town when they arrived.

Grettir met his brother Thorstein Dromund there. He welcomed Grettir warmly and invited him to stay, since he had a house in the town. Grettir told him about the case he had become involved in and Thorstein was sympathetic, but warned him to be on his guard against Gunnar. Spring drew on.

24 | Gunnar was in town, waiting for a chance to attack Grettir.

One day Grettir happened to be drinking in a tavern to avoid running into Gunnar, when the door was rammed so hard it broke into pieces. Four men ran in, fully armed: Gunnar and his men had come and they attacked Grettir. He grabbed his weapons, which were hanging above him, and retreated into the corner to defend himself. He held his shield in front of him and wielded his short-sword, and they made little headway against him. He struck a blow at one of Gunnar's men – and that was all it took. Then Grettir cleared a space for himself on the floor and his assailants backed off to the far side of the tavern. Then another of Gunnar's men was killed. Gunnar tried to escape with his remaining companion, who reached the door but tripped on the threshold, fell to the ground and was slow to get back to his feet. Guarding himself with his shield, Gunnar backed away from Grettir, who attacked him vigorously and jumped up on to the cross-bench nearest the door. Gunnar's hands, holding the shield, were still inside the door, so Grettir hacked down between his body and the shield, chopping off both his hands at the wrist. Gunnar tumbled over backwards through the door and Grettir dealt him a death blow. Gunnar's companion made it back to his feet at that moment and ran straight off to the earl to tell him the news.

Earl Svein was furious when he heard this account and summoned an assembly in the town immediately. When Thorfinn and Thorstein Dromund found out they mustered all their kinsmen and friends and turned up for the assembly in a very large band. The earl was very surly and would hardly listen to anyone.

Thorfinn went up to the earl first and said, 'I have come here to offer you a settlement with honour for the killings that Grettir has committed. You alone will shape and set the terms, if his life is spared.'

'You never seem to tire of asking for Grettir's life to be spared,' the earl answered angrily. 'But I don't think that you have a good case. He has killed three brothers now, one after the other, all of them so brave that none of them would carry another in his purse. There is no point in pleading for Grettir's life, Thorfinn, because I will not perpetrate injustice in this country by accepting compensation for such atrocities.'

Then Bersi, Torfa the Poetess's son, stepped forward and asked the earl to accept a settlement.

'I implore you with the offer of all I own, because Grettir is a man of great family and a good friend of mine, my lord. You must see that it is better to spare one man's life and win the gratitude of many men, and decide for yourself the amount of compensation to be paid, than to reject an honourable gesture and risk not being able to capture the man anyway.'

The earl replied, 'That is an honourable attitude, Bersi. You always show what a noble man you are. Nonetheless I have no intention of breaking the laws of this land by sparing the lives of men who deserve to die.'

Then Thorstein Dromund stepped forward, greeted the earl and made an offer on Grettir's behalf with an eloquent speech. The earl asked him what his motivation was in making an offer on behalf of such a man. Thorstein told him they were brothers.

The earl said he had not been aware of that – 'It is noble of you to want to help him. But since I have ruled that no compensation will be paid in this case, I will treat you all in the same way. I will have Grettir's life, whatever the cost, as soon as I can arrange it.'

Then the earl leapt to his feet and refused to consider their offers of a settlement any longer. Thorstein and the others went back to his house and prepared to defend themselves. When the earl realized this, he had all his men arm themselves and marched there in procession. Before they arrived, Thorstein and the others mounted a guard at the gate. Thorfinn, Thorstein, Grettir and Bersi stood at the front and each of them had a large band of men with him.

The earl told them to hand over Grettir and not push themselves to the brink. They all repeated their earlier offers, but the earl refused to listen to them.

Thorfinn and Thorstein said the earl had more work on his hands than simply taking Grettir's life – 'for we will all meet the same fate and it will be said that you have gone to great lengths to take one man's life when we are all slain with him.'

The earl replied that he would spare none of them. Battle seemed to be on the point of breaking out. Then many fair-minded men approached the earl and pleaded with him not to be the cause of such a disaster, saying that he would suffer heavy losses before his opponents were killed. The earl realized the wisdom of this advice; he calmed down somewhat. A settlement was drawn up, which Thorfinn and Thorstein were eager to accept provided Grettir's life was spared.

'You will understand,' said the earl, 'that although I am making a great compromise over these killings, I do not call this a settlement of any kind. I do not care to fight my own men, even though this whole matter has shown how little you respect me.'

Then Thorfinn said, 'This is a much greater honour for you, because you alone will set the amount of compensation to be paid.'

The earl said that he would allow Grettir to leave in peace for Iceland as soon as ships began sailing there, if they wished, and they said they would accept that offer. Then they paid the earl the compensation he wanted, and there was no love lost between them when they parted. Grettir went off with Thorfinn, and he parted with his brother Thorstein in great friendship. Thorfinn won renown for the support he had given to Grettir in the face of overwhelming odds. None of Grettir's supporters enjoyed the earl's friendship after that, with the single exception of Bersi.

Grettir made this verse:

22.

Thorfinn, partner
of the thunderer's elite   *thunderer's elite*: chosen warriors in Valhalla
was destined
to give me help
when the woman   *woman who reigns in the realm of the dead*:
who reigns entombed   Hel, goddess of the dead
in the realm of the dead
laid claim to my life.

23.

Of all men most,
the cliff-giants' killer   *cliff-giants' killer*: the god Thor
and dwarf's abode,   *dwarf's abode*: stone (Icel. *steinn*);
                                   Thor + stone = the name Thorstein

mighty ship	*mighty ship*: dromond
of the distant seas,	(Icel. *dromundr*), a medieval galleon
kept evil Loki's	(i.e. Thorstein Dromund)
deathly daughter	*Loki's daughter*: the goddess Hel
at bay from me.	

24.

None of the men	
of the thing-leader	*thing-leader*: king (i.e. Earl Svein)
had any heart	
to tackle us	
when the leopard	*leopard*: i.e. Bersi (Icel. = '*bear*')
wished to smite	
their forts of thought	*forts of thought*: heads or breasts
with his shield-fire.	*shield-fire*: sword

Grettir went back north with Thorfinn and stayed with him until he arranged a passage for him with some merchants who were sailing to Iceland. Thorfinn gave him many fine garments and a painted saddle and a bridle. They parted in friendship and Thorfinn told him to visit him if he ever returned to Norway.

25 | While Grettir was abroad Asmund Grey-locks lived at Bjarg and was considered one of the leading men in Midfjord. Thorkel Scratcher died at the time when Grettir was not in Iceland. Thorvald Asgeirsson lived at As in Vatnsdal then and became a great chieftain. He was the father of Dalla; she was married to Isleif, who later became bishop of Skalholt.[36] Asmund enjoyed much support from Thorvald in presenting law cases and many other matters.

There was a man named Thorgils who was brought up at Asmund's farm. He was known as Thorgils Masson[37] and was a close relative of Asmund's. Thorgils was a strong man and earned much wealth with guidance from Asmund, who bought him land at Laekjamot, where he went to live. Thorgils kept his household well provided for and went to Strandir every year where he took whales and other provisions. He was an intrepid character, venturing as far as the outer Almenningar.[38]

In those days the sworn brothers Thorgeir Havarsson and Thormod Kolbrun's Poet[39] were in their prime. They owned a ferry, raided where they pleased and were very overbearing.

One summer, Thorgils Masson chanced upon a beached whale at Almenningar and started flensing it with his companions. When the sworn brothers heard of this, they went there and at first everyone seemed to be on good terms. Thorgils offered them half of the uncut part of the whale, but they insisted on being given all that had not yet been cut, unless they divided all the meat, cut and uncut, equally between them. Thorgils firmly refused to hand over any of the meat he had already cut. Tempers flared, both sides seized their weapons, and a battle ensued. Thorgeir and Thorgils duelled fiercely for a long time without any of the others intervening. In the end, after a long, hard fight, Thorgils was killed by Thorgeir. Thormod fought the rest of Thorgils' men somewhere else, and he emerged as victor, killing three of them.

After Thorgils' death, his companions returned to Midfjord, taking his body with them. He was greatly mourned. The sworn brothers kept the entire whale for themselves. Thormod refers to this encounter in the drapa he made in memory of Thorgeir.

Asmund Grey-locks learned of the killing of his kinsman Thorgils. He was responsible for pursuing the case for it. He examined the body, named witnesses to the wounds and brought the case before the Althing, which was considered the correct procedure for a killing that took place in another quarter. And time passed.

26 | There was a man named Thorstein Kuggason, the son of Thorkel the Squat and grandson of Thord Bellower. Thord was the son of Olaf Feilan, whose father Thorstein Red was the son of Aud the Deep-minded. Thorstein Kuggason's mother, Thurid, was the daughter of Asgeir Scatter-brain, who was Asmund Grey-locks' uncle on his father's side.[40]

Thorstein Kuggason took charge of the case for the killing of Thorgils Masson, together with Asmund Grey-locks. Asmund

sent a message to Thorstein to call on him. Thorstein was a
good fighter and very aggressive. He set off to see Asmund at
once and they discussed the case. Thorstein was vehement and
insisted that no compensation would be accepted, saying that
they had enough support from kinsmen to punish the killings
either with outlawry or revenge. Asmund replied that he would
follow any course he wanted to take. They rode north to see
their kinsman Thorvald to ask him for his support and he
agreed at once. Then they prepared the case against Thorgeir
and Thormod. Thorstein rode back to his farm at Ljarskogar
in the district of Hvamm.

There was a man named Skeggi who lived at the nearby farm
of Hvamm, and he took Thorstein's side in the case. Skeggi
was the son of Thorarin Foal's-brow, whose father was Thord
Bellower. Skeggi's mother, Fridgerd, was the daughter of Thord
from Hofdi.

They mustered a large band to ride to the Althing and pursued the case vigorously. Asmund and Thorvald rode down
from the north with sixty men and spent several nights at
Ljarskogar.

27 | There was a man named Thorgils who lived at Reykja-
   | holar at that time, the son of Ari Masson. His grandfather,
Atli the Red, was the son of Ulf the Squinter, who took land
in Reykjanes. Thorgils Arason's mother, Thorgerd, was the
daughter of Alf from Dalir. Alf had another daughter named
Thorelf, who was the mother of Thorgeir Havarsson. Because
of their kinship, Thorgeir could count on the support of Thorgils, who was the leading man in the West Fjords Quarter.
Thorgils was so charitable that he would give food to all free-
born men for as long as they cared to accept it, so there was
always a large number of people with him at Reykjaholar.
Thorgils enjoyed great honour for his generosity and was a
kind and wise man. Thorgeir used to stay with him for the
winter and go to Strandir in summer.

After Thorgils Masson had been killed, Thorgeir went to
Reykjaholar to tell Thorgils Arason the news.

Thorgils offered him a place to stay there.

'But I imagine they will be difficult about the case,' he said, 'and I am reluctant to make matters any worse. I will send someone to Thorstein to offer him compensation for the killing of Thorgils. If he refuses a settlement, I will not make a firm stand in your defence.'

Thorgeir said he would abide by what Thorgils saw as best.

In the autumn, Thorgils Arason sent a messenger to Thorstein Kuggason to approach him about a settlement. Thorstein was absolutely against accepting any compensation for the killing of Thorgils Masson, but said he would settle the other killings as wise men suggested. When Thorgils heard this, he called Thorgeir over and asked what he thought would be the most useful support to provide. Thorgeir said he would prefer to leave the country if he were outlawed and Thorgils replied that he would try to arrange that.

A ship had been laid up in the river Nordura in Borgarfjord and Thorgils secretly paid for a passage on it for the two sworn brothers. The winter passed by.

Thorgils heard that Thorstein had gathered a large band of men to go to the Althing and that they were all staying at Ljarskogar then, so he put off his departure, wanting them to be on their way south before he set off, and that is what happened. When Thorgils rode south, the sworn brothers went with him and on the way Thorgeir killed Bundle-Torfi at Maskelda and Skuf and Bjarni in Hundadal valley.

In his drapa about Thorgeir, Thormod said:

25.
Fate favoured the warrior
when the swords rained down:
Mar's son paid for his pride,
ravens tore at raw flesh.
Then the rider of the waves,   *rider of the waves*: seafarer, i.e. Thorgeir
the skilled battle-worker,
gladly lent his hand
to kill Skuf and Bjarni.

Thorgils made an immediate settlement for the killings of Skuf and Bjarni in the valley, which kept him there for longer than he had planned. Thorgeir headed for the ship, but Thorgils went to the Thing and did not arrive before the court had convened.

Then Asmund Grey-locks invited a defence for the killing of Thorgils Masson. Thorgils Arason approached the court and offered to pay compensation provided that Thorgeir was acquitted. He sought a defence in the question whether the common land was not free for anyone to harvest. The Lawspeaker was asked if these were legal grounds for a defence. Skafti,[41] who was the Lawspeaker at that time and supported Asmund because of their kinship, answered that this law only applied to people of equal standing and that farmers enjoyed preference over single men. Asmund said that Thorgils Masson had offered the sworn brothers an equal share of the uncut part of the whale when they arrived, and this refuted the defence. Thorstein and his kinsmen pursued the case vigorously and refused to approve of anything less than a sentence of outlawry on Thorgeir. Thorgils realized he had to choose between mustering his men for an attack, without being sure how that would turn out, or letting them have their way. Since Thorgeir was already on board the ship, Thorgils let the case take its course. Thorgeir was outlawed, while compensation was paid for the people Thormod had killed, and he was free.

Asmund and Thorstein gained much stature from this case. Everyone went home from the Thing afterwards. Some claimed Thorgils had not put much effort into pursuing the case, but he paid little attention and let people say what they pleased.

But when Thorgeir heard he had been outlawed, he said, 'I want everyone who has had me declared an outlaw to pay the full price for it in the end, if I have any say in the matter.'

There was a man known as Gaut Sleituson, the son of Sleitu-Helgi (Helgi the Cheat) and a kinsman of Thorgils Masson. He was one of the crew on board the same ship that Thorgeir was sailing on. He made snarling remarks to Thorgeir and threatened him, and seeing this, the merchants thought it was

obvious they should not travel on the same ship. Although
Thorgeir said he did not care how much Gaut scowled at him,
they opted to make Gaut leave the ship and he went back up
north to the countryside. Thorgeir and Gaut did not clash for
the time being, but the incident led to a quarrel between them,
as would emerge later.

28 | Grettir Asmundarson went back to Iceland that summer
     | and landed in Skagafjord. By then he was so renowned
for his strength and vigour that no young man was considered
his equal. He rode home to Bjarg at once and Asmund gave
him a warm welcome. Atli was running the farm then and the
two brothers got on well together. At this stage, Grettir had
grown so overbearing that he felt nothing was beyond him.

Most of the boys whom Grettir had played games with on
Midfjardarvatn before he went abroad were grown men by this
time. One of them was Audun, who lived at Audunarstadir in
Vididal, the son of Asgeir and grandson of Audun. His great-
grandfather was Asgeir Scatter-brain. Audun from Audunarstadir was a good farmer and a worthy man. He was stronger
than anyone else in the north of Iceland, but was considered a
very peaceful man in his district.

Grettir remembered the humiliation he felt he had suffered
from Audun at the ball game described earlier and he wanted
to put to the test which of them had grown stronger since then.
So he set off for Audunarstadir in the beginning of hay-time.
Grettir dressed extravagantly and rode off in the finely wrought
painted saddle that Thorfinn had given him. He had a good
horse and took his finest weapons with him.

Grettir arrived at Audunarstadir early in the morning and
knocked on the door. Few people were at home. Grettir asked
whether Audun was in. He was told that he had gone to the
shieling to fetch food. Grettir unbridled his horse, and because
the hayfields had not been mown it headed for the grassiest
part. Then Grettir went into the hall, sat down on the bench
and fell asleep.

A little later Audun returned home and noticed a horse with

a painted saddle in the hayfields. He had two horses to carry
the food and one of them was carrying curds in skins with the
necks tied up, called curd pouches. Audun unloaded the horses
and carried the curds indoors in his arms. His eyes had not
adjusted to the darkness and Grettir stuck out his foot from the
edge of the bench, tripping him over. He landed on the curd
pouch and the band it was tied with came undone. Audun leapt
to his feet and asked what trickster was there. Grettir said his
name.

Audun said, 'That was a stupid thing to do. What are you
here for?'

'I want to fight you,' Grettir replied.

'I have to see to the food first,' said Audun.

'As you please,' said Grettir, 'if you don't have anyone else
to do it for you.'

Audun bent down to pick up the curd pouch, slung it into
Grettir's arms and told him to take what he was given. Grettir
was covered with curds, which he considered a greater insult
than if Audun had given him a bloody wound. Then they
went for each other and grappled fiercely. Grettir attacked him
furiously and Audun yielded his ground, realizing that Grettir
had grown stronger than him. Everything in their way was
knocked over and they tumbled all over the hall. Both of them
exerted themselves to the full, but Grettir got the upper hand
and eventually he brought Audun to the ground, after he had
torn off all Grettir's weapons. They were struggling hard and
crashing about when the ground began shaking too. Grettir
heard someone ride up to the farm, dismount and hurry indoors. He saw a smartly dressed man enter, wearing a red cloak
with a helmet on his head. The man had come over to the
longhouse because he could hear the noise of their brawling.
He asked what was going on in there.

Grettir said his name. 'And who's asking?' he added.

'My name is Bardi,'[42] said the newcomer.

'Are you Bardi Gudmundarson from Asbjarnarnes?'

'The very same,' said Bardi. 'And what are you up to here?'

'Audun and I are playing a little game,' replied Grettir.

'I'm not sure how much of a game it is,' said Bardi. 'And you don't make a good pair either. You are an unjust and overbearing man, Grettir, while Audun is gentle and kind. Let him get up at once.'

'Never reach around a door for the handle,' Grettir answered back. 'I think you'd do better to avenge your brother Hall than to interfere in what Audun and I get up to.'

'I'm always being told that,' said Bardi, 'but I'm not sure whether he ever will be avenged. All the same, I want you to leave Audun alone, because he's a gentle man.'

Grettir did as Bardi suggested, although he was not happy about it. Bardi asked what they were quarrelling about.

Then Grettir spoke a verse:

26.

Odin here, for all I know,	*Odin:* i.e. Audun (one of Odin's aliases)
might reward you for your pains,	
pay back your strivings	
with a swollen neck.	
That's how the gold-watcher's god	*gold-watcher's god:*
choked my words long ago,	Odin (i.e. Audun)
before the snake that coils	*snake:* i.e. Grettir (also a name given to
around mountains left home.	snakes, lit. 'frowner', 'face-puller')

Bardi said it was not surprising if he sought revenge.

'Now I will make a settlement between you,' he said. 'I want you to leave the matter as it stands and put an end to it.'

They let the agreement stand because they were kinsmen, but Grettir did not like Bardi and his brothers much. Then they rode off together.

On the way, Grettir said to Bardi: 'I have heard that you plan to ride to Borgarfjord this summer. I propose that I should join you when you go there, which I think is a better offer than you deserve.'

Bardi was pleased with the proposal, thanked him and accepted it at once. Then they parted.

Bardi turned round and called back to Grettir.

'I want to make a condition,' he said. 'You can't come along without my foster-father Thorarin's consent, because he is in charge of the expedition.'

'You ought to be capable of making your own plans,' Grettir replied. 'I don't leave other people to decide where I go. But I'll be annoyed if you leave me out of the band.'

Then they went their separate ways and Bardi said he would send word to Grettir, 'if Thorarin wants you to go'. Otherwise he was to stay at home.

Grettir rode home to Bjarg, and Bardi to his farm.

29 | That summer a big horse-fight was held at Langafit down from Reykir, which was well attended. Atli from Bjarg had a fine stallion from the same stock as Kengala, grey with a black mane and a stripe down its back, and he and his father prized it highly. The brothers Kormak and Thorgils from Mel had a brown stallion, which was reliable for fighting and was pitted against Atli's. Many other good horses were there.

Odd the Pauper-poet, Kormak's kinsman, was supposed to lead their horse to the fight later in the day. Odd had grown into a strong, swaggering man, overbearing and reckless. Grettir asked Atli who was supposed to lead his horse to the fight.

'I'm not exactly sure,' Atli replied.

'Do you want me to be your second?' Grettir asked him.

'Only if you restrain yourself,' said Atli. 'There are some very pushy characters here.'

'Let them pay the price for their impetuousness if they can't control themselves,' said Grettir.

Then the stallions were brought out; the horses were kept tied together at the edge of the riverbank, just above a deep pool. The horses fought well and it was a good show. Odd goaded his horse on vigorously, while Grettir kept his horse back, holding its tail with one hand and the stick he used to goad it on with the other. Odd was standing close to the front of his horse and it was difficult to be sure that he was not prodding Atli's horse with his stick to drive it back. Grettir showed no sign that he noticed this. As the horses moved towards the river, Odd jabbed at Grettir with his stick and hit him on the shoulder blade, as Grettir had his back turned to

him. It was a hard enough blow to cause a swelling, although
it did not bleed. At that moment the horses reared, Grettir
ducked under the haunches of his stallion and jabbed Odd so
hard in the side with his stick that it broke three of his ribs and
sent him flying into the pool, taking his horse with him and the
other horses which were tethered together. People dived in and
dragged him back out of the river.

A great clamour followed. Kormak and his men went for
their weapons, and so did the people from Bjarg. When the
people from Hrutafjord and Vatnsnes saw this, they intervened
and separated them. They all went home after that, amid threats
from either side, but everything remained quiet for a while. Atli
did not say much about the incident, but Grettir was more
brash about it and said they would meet again later if he had
any say in the matter.

30 | There was a man named Thorbjorn who lived at Thor-
    | oddsstadir in Hrutafjord. He was the son of Arnor Hairy-
nose, whose father Thorodd had taken land on that side of
Hrutafjord all the way to Bakki. Thorbjorn was an exceptionally strong man and was nicknamed the Ox. He had a brother
named Thorodd who was called Half-poem. Their mother was
Gerd, the daughter of Bodvar from Bodvarsholar.

Thorbjorn was a brave fighter and always had plenty of
men with him. He was noted for having more trouble in
obtaining farmhands than other farmers did, and he paid hardly
any of them for their work. He was not thought easy to deal
with.

One of his kinsmen was named Thorbjorn, too, and called
Traveller. He was a merchant and shared everything with his
namesake. Most of the time he stayed at Thoroddsstadir and
was not thought to bring out the best in Thorbjorn Ox. He was
a disdainful character and liked to mock people.

There was a man named Thorir, the son of Thorkel from
Bordeyri. His daughter Helga married Sleitu-Helgi. Thorir
lived at Melar in Hrutafjord at first, but after the killings at
Fagrabrekka[43] he sold the land to Thorhall the Vinlander, the

son of Gamli, and moved south to live at Skard in Haukadal. His son was Gamli, who married Rannveig, Asmund Grey-locks' daughter. At this time they were living at Melar and lived together well.

Thorir from Skard had two sons, Gunnar and Thorgeir. They were promising men who had taken over their father's farm, but spent most of their time with Thorbjorn Ox and became excessively overbearing.

In the summer in which all this took place, Kormak and Thorgils rode south with their kinsman Narfi to Nordurardal on some business. Odd the Pauper-poet was with them and had recovered from the bruising he received at the horse-fight. While they were south of the moor, Grettir left Bjarg with two of Atli's farmhands. They rode over to Burfell and continued over the ridge into Hrutafjord until they reached Melar in the evening. They spent three nights there. Rannveig and Gamli welcomed Grettir warmly and invited him to stay longer with them, but he wanted to ride back home. Grettir then heard that Kormak and his men had returned from the south and spent the night at Tunga.

Grettir prepared to make an early start from Melar. Gamli told him to be on his guard and offered to let him have some men to accompany him. Grim, who was Gamli's brother and an outstandingly vigorous man, went with him together with another man, and the five of them rode off until they reached Hrutafjord ridge, west of Burfell. There is a big boulder there called Grettishaf (Grettir's Lift). Grettir spent much of the day trying to lift it and stayed there so long that Kormak's men arrived. He went up to them and they all dismounted. Grettir said it was more in the spirit of free-born men to strike the mightiest blows they could, instead of fighting with sticks like vagrants. Kormak told his men to take up the challenge like men and fight for all they were worth.

Then the two bands of men ran for each other and fought. Grettir led his men forward and told them to make sure no one attacked him from behind. They fought for some time and people from both parties were wounded.

The same day, Thorbjorn Ox had ridden over the ridge to

Burfell and saw the encounter when he and his men were riding
back. Thorbjorn Traveller was with him, together with Thorir's
sons Gunnar and Thorgeir and Thorodd Half-poem. When
they reached the fight, Thorbjorn told his men to try to break
it up, but the fighting was so fierce they could do nothing to stop
it. Grettir stormed around and when he confronted Thorir's two
sons he knocked them both off their feet. They flew into a
rage and Gunnar dealt Atli's farmhand a mortal blow. When
Thorbjorn saw this he told them to separate, promising his
support to the side that obeyed him. Two of Kormak's farmhands had been killed by then. Grettir, realizing that he could
not prevail if Thorbjorn's men joined the other side, called an
end to the fight. Everyone who had taken part was wounded
and Grettir was annoyed that they had been separated. Afterwards they all went home and never reached a settlement over
the incident.

Thorbjorn Traveller made many jibes about it and relations
between the people from Bjarg and Thorbjorn Ox deteriorated
into total hostility, as emerged later. Atli was not offered any
compensation for his farmhand, but he gave the impression
that he was unaware of this. Grettir stayed at Bjarg until hay-
time. There is no account or mention that he and Kormak ever
encountered each other again.

31 | After Bardi Gudmundarson and his brothers parted with
     | Grettir, they rode home to Asbjarnarnes. They were the
sons of Gudmund, the son of Solmund. Solmund's mother,
Thorlaug, was the daughter of Saemund the Hebridean, who
was the foster-brother of Ingimund the Old. Bardi was a very
distinguished man. He soon set off to see his foster-father,
Thorarin the Wise, who welcomed him warmly and asked him
what he had achieved in mustering forces for the expedition
they had planned. Bardi replied that he had enlisted a man
whose assistance was worth twice that of anyone else.

Thorarin paused for a while, then said, 'That must be Grettir
Asmundarson.'

'A wise man can guess the future,' said Bardi. 'That's the very man, foster-father.'

Thorarin replied, 'It is true that Grettir is the greatest of all men now living in our country, and for as long as he keeps his health it will be a long time before he is beaten with weapons. But he is a man of unbridled temper and I doubt how much good fortune he will enjoy. You will need to make sure that not everyone on your expedition is a man of ill-fortune – there will be plenty of those even if he does not go along. He will not be going anywhere, if I have any say in the matter.'

'I never expected you to grudge me the bravest man, whatever happens, foster-father,' said Bardi. 'No one in my straits can provide for everything.'

'You will succeed, even if I provide for things,' replied Thorarin.

The matter was settled as Thorarin wished and no message was sent to Grettir. Bardi went south to Borgarfjord and the Slayings on the Heath[44] took place.

Grettir was at Bjarg when he heard that Bardi had ridden south. He grew angry about not having been told and said that this was not the end of the matter. He received word when they were expected from the south and rode down to the farm at Thoreyjargnup, planning to ambush Bardi and his men when they rode back. He set off from the farm for the hillside and waited there.

That same day Bardi and his men rode back from the south over Tvidaegra, after the Slayings on the Heath. There were six of them and they were all severely wounded.

When they came up alongside the farm Bardi said, 'There's a big man up on the hillside, fully armed. Do you recognize him?'

They said they did not know who it was.

Bardi said, 'I believe Grettir Asmundarson is there, and if that is so he will be looking for us. I imagine he took offence at not being with us and I don't think we are at all prepared if he makes any trouble. I will send for help from Thoreyjargnup, since I don't want to stake everything against someone as over-bearing as him.'

His men agreed that this was a wise course of action and did as he said. Bardi and the others rode on their way and when Grettir saw them he came down in front of them. They exchanged greetings and Grettir asked if there was any news. Bardi told him everything that had happened, without flinching. Grettir asked who were the men with him and Bardi told him they were his brothers and his brother-in-law Eyjolf.

'You have cleared your name at last,' said Grettir, 'so the next thing to do is to find out which of us is the stronger.'

'I have other fish to fry than having a pointless fight with you,' said Bardi. 'I think I have done enough to be free of that.'

'You must be losing your nerve then, Bardi,' said Grettir, 'if you don't dare to fight with me.'

'Call it what you want,' Bardi replied. 'If you want to push people around you should pick on someone other than me. And you quite probably will, because your overbearing knows no bounds now.'

Disturbed by Bardi's prediction, Grettir began to wonder whether to attack one of them, but thought this would be a rash idea, since they were six and he was alone. At that moment a party arrived from Thoreyjargnup to join Bardi. Grettir backed off and went over to his horse, while Bardi and his men rode away. They did not bother to wish each other farewell. There is no mention of any further encounters between Bardi and Grettir.

Grettir himself has said that he felt confident about fighting any three men at once, nor would he flee from four without putting it to the test, but would only fight more men than that if his life was at stake, as this verse says:

27.

Versed in valkyries' arts, I trust	*valkyries' arts*: warfare
myself to tackle three men	
wherever the war-goddesses' storm	*war-goddesses' storm*: battle
demands memorable deeds.	
But if the choice is mine	
I will not meet more	
than four ship-stormers	*ship-stormers*: Vikings
when killers roar for blood.	

After parting with Bardi, Grettir went to Bjarg. He sorely regretted not having anything to test his strength against and asked around for a challenge to take up.

32 | There was a man named Thorhall who lived at Thorhallsstadir in Forsaeludal,[45] inland from Vatnsdal. He was the son of Grim, whose father was Thorhall, son of Fridmund, the first settler of Forsaeludal. Thorhall's wife was Gudrun and they had a son named Grim and a grown-up daughter named Thurid. Thorhall was a man of wealth, which was mostly in livestock; no man owned as much farm stock as he did. Although he was not a chieftain, he was a capable farmer.

His farm was badly haunted and he hardly ever managed to find shepherds whom he thought capable. He consulted many wise men about what to do, but no one could give any advice that worked.

Thorhall rode to the Thing every summer. He owned fine horses. One summer at the Althing, Thorhall went to the booth of Skafti Thoroddsson the Lawspeaker. Skafti was exceptionally wise and gave good advice when asked. He and his father differed in that Thorodd could see into the future and was called devious by some people, while Skafti suggested to anyone what he considered to be the right course, if it were followed. For this reason, he was called his father's better.

Thorhall entered Skafti's booth. He welcomed Thorhall warmly, knowing him to be a wealthy man, and asked what news there was.

Thorhall said, 'I would like to ask you for some advice.'

'I am little capable of that,' Skafti replied, 'but what is your problem?'

Thorhall said, 'The situation is that I have trouble keeping my shepherds. Some of them are treated roughly, while others leave before their time is up. No one who knows what the job involves is prepared to take it on.'

Skafti answered, 'There must be an evil being at work if people are more reluctant to look after your sheep than their own. But since you have approached me for advice I will provide you with a shepherd by the name of Glam. He hails from Sylgsdalir in Sweden[46] and came to Iceland last summer; a big, strong man but not really the type that ordinary people welcome.'

Thorhall said he did not mind, as long as he looked after the sheep well enough.

Skafti said that no one else would stand much chance if Glam could not look after them with all his strength and courage. Thorhall left then; this was at the end of the Thing.

Thorhall noticed that two of his fawn horses had gone missing and went to look for them himself. This was seen as proof that he was not a man of great standing. He went up to the foot of Sledaas ridge and southwards around the mountain known as Armannsfell.

Then he saw a man coming down from Godaskog wood with some brushwood loaded on a horse. They soon met. Thorhall asked him his name and he said he was called Glam. He was a well-built man and very strange-looking, with wide blue eyes and wolf-grey hair. Thorhall was quite taken aback when he saw this man, but realized he had been sent.

'What work are you best at?' asked Thorhall.

Glam said he was easily capable of looking after the sheep in winter.

'Will you look after my sheep?' Thorhall asked. 'Skafti put you into my charge.'

'I'll be most useful to you if I am left to do as I please, because I have a bad temper when I don't like something.'

'I won't suffer for that,' said Thorhall, 'and I want you to come to me.'

'I can do that,' said Glam. 'Are there any problems?'

'It is supposed to be haunted,' said Thorhall.

'I'm not afraid of ghouls,' said Glam. 'It makes it more interesting.'

'Those are qualities you'll need,' said Thorhall, 'and it helps if you're not exactly puny, either.'

Afterwards they made an agreement that Glam would arrive at the Winter Nights. Then they parted and Thorhall found his horses where he had just been looking for them before. Thorhall rode home and thanked Skafti for the favour he had done him.

The summer passed and Thorhall heard nothing of his shepherd. No one knew about him, but at the appointed time he turned up at Thorhallsstadir. The farmer welcomed him warmly, but the other people on the farm did not take a shine to him, least of all the farmer's wife. Glam took charge of watching the sheep and it was little effort for him. He had a deep, booming voice and the sheep flocked together when he called to them. There was a church at Thorhallsstadir, but Glam would not go near it. He was not given to worship and had no faith, but was peevish and rude. Everyone found him obnoxious.

Time went by until Christmas Eve. Glam got up that day and called out for his food.

The farmer's wife answered, 'It is not the Christian custom to eat on this day, because tomorrow is the first day of Christmas. It is our duty to fast today.'

Glam replied, 'You have all sorts of superstitions that I dismiss as worthless. People don't strike me as being any better off now than they were in the days when they didn't practise such things. I preferred the way people were when they were called heathens. I want my food and don't try any tricks.'

The farmer's wife said, 'I know that you'll suffer for it today if you go ahead with this evil act.'

Glam told her to bring some food immediately, otherwise she would be the worse off. She did not dare to disobey and when he had eaten his fill he went outside in a rather stormy mood. It was dark and snow was falling. The weather was stormy and grew much worse as the day progressed. People heard the shepherd early in the day, but less as the day wore on. Then the snow began to drift and in the evening there was a blizzard. Everyone went to Mass and night fell, but Glam did not return home. The idea of going out to look for him was suggested, but because of the raging blizzard and pitch darkness, no search was made. He did not return on Christmas Eve, and everyone waited until the Mass was over.

When it was fully daylight the people set off to make a search and found sheep scattered among the snowdrifts, thrown

around by the storm; some had fled to the mountains. Then
they found a huge trampled area towards the head of the valley,
which looked as if a mighty skirmish had taken place there,
because rocks and soil had been torn up in many places. They
looked more closely and saw Glam lying a short distance away.
He was dead, black as hell and bloated to the size of a bull.[47]
Although they were repulsed and shuddered at the sight of him,
they tried to carry him to the church, but could only manage
to move him as far as the edge of a chasm a short way above
them. Having done this, they went home and told the farmer
about the incident.

Thorhall asked what could have caused Glam's death and
they said they had traced some footprints which were as large
as if a barrel had been slammed down in the snow, and they
led up from the trampled ground to the crag at the head of the
valley – splashes of blood ran alongside them. They concluded
that the evil being, which was there before, had killed Glam,
but that he must have dealt it a mighty, fatal wound, because
no one has ever been aware of it since.

On the second day of Christmas, another attempt was made
to take Glam's body to the church. Oxen and horses were
tethered to it, but could not budge it on flat ground, where
there was no slope to go down. After that, the body was left
there. On the third day a priest went with them and they
searched all day, but could not find Glam. The priest did not
want to search again and the shepherd was found when the
priest was not with them. They gave up trying to take him to
the church and buried him in a shallow grave where he was.

Shortly afterwards, people became aware that Glam was not
resting in peace. He wrought such havoc that some people
fainted at the sight of him, while others went out of their minds.
Immediately after Christmas, people thought they saw him at
the farm and were so terrified that many of them fled. After
that, Glam started straddling the roof[48] at night until it was
nearly smashed to pieces. Then his ghost roamed around by
day and night. Even people with ample reason for going into
the valley hardly dared to venture there. The local people
thought this was a terrible plague.

33 | In the spring Thorhall took on some new farmhands and began farming again. The hauntings waned when the days were at their longest and time passed until midsummer.

A ship arrived in Hunavatn that summer. There was a man named Thorgaut on board, a big and powerful foreigner with the strength of two men. He was on his own and had not tied himself down anywhere, but wanted to find some kind of work because he had no money.

Thorhall rode down to the ship and met Thorgaut and asked if he wanted to go and work for him. Thorgaut said he might well do so, adding that he was not particular about what he did.

'You ought to prepare yourself for something that's not fit for weaklings to do,' Thorhall said, 'because of the ghosts that have been haunting the place. I don't want to deceive you about that.'

Thorgaut answered, 'I won't be giving up just because I see a little ghoul. No one else will be comfortable there if it scares me. I won't leave the job on account of that.'

They struck a bargain and Thorgaut was appointed to watch over the sheep during the winter. The summer passed and Thorgaut took charge of the sheep during the Winter Nights. Everybody liked him. Glam kept coming to the house and straddled the roof.

Thorgaut was quite amused at this and said that the wretch would have to come closer 'before I get scared of him'.

Thorhall told him to keep that to himself: 'It's better if you two don't put your strength to the test.'

Thorgaut answered, 'You've definitely had the courage shaken out of you, but stories like that won't finish me off overnight.'

Winter passed and Christmas came around. On Christmas Eve, the shepherd went to tend to the sheep.

The farmer's wife said, 'It would be better if the old story did not repeat itself, I feel.'

'Don't worry about that, lady,' he replied. 'Something worth telling will have to happen if I don't come back.'

Then he went back to tend to the sheep. The weather was fairly cold and the snow was drifting heavily. Thorgaut was accustomed to come back at twilight, but on this occasion he did not return at that time. People returned from the Mass as usual and thought events were following a familiar pattern. The farmer wanted to mount a search for his shepherd, but the people who had returned from Mass argued against it, saying they would not risk being snatched away by trolls at night. The farmer did not have the resolve to go alone, so nothing came of it.

After they had eaten on Christmas Day, they went out to search for the shepherd. They went to Glam's grave first, expecting him to be responsible for the shepherd's disappearance. A terrible sight greeted them when they approached the grave, for they found the shepherd there, his neck broken and every bone in his body crushed. They took him to the church and Thorgaut caused no one harm afterwards.[49] Glam, however, redoubled his efforts and caused so much trouble that everyone fled from Thorhallsstadir, apart from the farmer and his wife.

The same cowherd had been there for a long time. Thorhall did not want him to leave, because he was a kindly man who looked after the cattle well. He was very advanced in years and reluctant to go, for he realized that all the farmer's livestock would be ruined if no one tended to it.

One morning after midwinter the farmer's wife went to the milking shed to milk the cows as usual. It was fully daylight then, for no one dared go outside before then apart from the cowherd, who would go out as soon as it started to grow light. She could hear a great crashing noise inside the shed and mighty bellowing and ran back indoors screaming that she had no idea what awful deeds were being done in there. The farmer went out and when he came to the bulls they were butting each other. He was disturbed by this sight and went into the barn. There he saw his cowherd lying on his back with his head in one stall and his feet in another. The farmer went up to him and felt him and realized at once that he was dead; his back had been broken over the stone wall dividing the stalls.

Thorhall thought it was not safe to stay there any longer and left the farm, taking with him everything he could. Glam killed all the livestock that was left behind, then went all over the valley and laid waste all the farms inland from Tunga.

Thorhall stayed with friends for the rest of the winter. No one could venture into the valley with horses or dogs, because the animals were killed on the spot.

When spring arrived and the days were at their longest, the hauntings waned somewhat and Thorhall wanted to return to his land. Although it was not easy for him to find farmhands, he started farming at Thorhallsstadir again. But the same thing happened again: when autumn came around the hauntings increased. The farmer's daughter was the main victim and in the end it led to her death. They tried everything imaginable to stop the hauntings, but nothing worked. Everyone thought the whole of Vatnsdal valley would be left uninhabited if nothing were done.

34 | To return to Grettir Asmundarson. He stayed at home at Bjarg the autumn after he had left Killer-Bardi at Thoreyjargnup. Just before the Winter Nights, Grettir rode north over the ridges to Vididal and stayed at Audunarstadir. He and Audun made a full reconciliation. Grettir gave him a fine axe and they pledged each other their friendship. Audun lived at Audunarstadir for a long time and had many descendants. His son was Egil, who married Ulfheid, the daughter of Eyjolf Gudmundarson. Their son Eyjolf, who was killed at the Althing, was the father of Orm, chaplain to Bishop Thorlak.

Grettir rode north to Vatnsdal and paid a visit to Tunga. Jokul Bardarson, his maternal uncle, was living there at that time. Jokul was a big, strong man and exceptionally arrogant. He was a merchant and was very overbearing, but a man of many gifts. He welcomed Grettir, who stayed with him for three nights.

Glam's hauntings had become so notorious that people hardly talked about anything else. Grettir asked in detail about all the incidents that had taken place.

Jokul said the stories were no exaggeration – 'Would you be curious about looking in there, kinsman?'

Grettir said he would.

Jokul told him not to – 'for this is a great test of fortune and you are an important man in your family. We do not consider any other young man a match for you, but evil begets evil as far as Glam is concerned. And it's much better to tackle human beings than such evil beings.'

Grettir said he was interested in calling at Thorhallsstadir and seeing how things were there.

Jokul said, 'I can see there's no point in trying to dissuade you, but the saying is true that fate and fortune do not always go hand-in-hand.'

'Peril waits at a man's door, though another goes in before,' said Grettir. 'You should consider what fate you yourself will meet in the end.'

Jokul replied, 'We both may have some insight into the future, but neither of us can prevent it happening.'

After that they parted ways and neither was pleased with the other's predictions.

35 | Grettir rode to Thorhallsstadir and the farmer welcomed him warmly. He asked Grettir where he was heading and the farmer was pleased when he replied that he wanted to stay there for the night.

Thorhall said he was grateful that Grettir had come, 'For there aren't many people who feel they stand to gain from staying here at present. You must have heard of the tricks being played here and I wouldn't like you to have any trouble on my account. Even if you leave here in one piece, I'm certain that you will lose your horse, because no one who comes here manages to keep his horse unhurt.'

Grettir said that horses were easy to come by, whatever might happen to this one.

Thorhall was pleased that Grettir wanted to stay and welcomed him with open arms. Grettir's horse was firmly locked indoors, then they went to sleep and the night passed without Glam turning up.

Then Thorhall said, 'Things have changed for the better since you arrived, because Glam usually rises every night and plays havoc on the roof or breaks down the doors, as you can see for yourself.'

Grettir said, 'Either he will not bide his time much longer or will give up for more than a single night. I'll stay another night and see what happens.'

Then they went to inspect Grettir's horse, which had not been touched. The farmer thought everything was pointing in the same direction.

Grettir stayed a second night. The wretch did not return and the farmer thought the outlook was much more promising. Then he went to inspect Grettir's horse. The stable had been broken into when he arrived and the horse had been dragged outdoors and every bone in its body broken.

Thorhall told Grettir what the situation was and told him to leave – 'because you're a dead man if you wait for Glam.'

Grettir answered, 'A glimpse of that wretch is the least I can ask in return for my horse.'

The farmer said he would gain nothing by seeing Glam – 'for he is different from any human form.[50] But I feel better for every hour you are willing to stay here.'

The day passed and at bedtime Grettir did not get undressed, but lay down on the bench facing the farmer's bed closet. He covered himself with a shaggy fur cloak, tucking one end under his feet and the other behind his head, so that he could see out through the opening at the neck. In front of the seat was a very strong bed-frame and he braced his feet against it. The frame had been smashed right away from the door to the house and some makeshift boards had been put in its place. The partition which had separated the hall from the entrance way had been broken away, too, both above and below the crossbeam. All the beds had been shifted and the place was hardly fit for habitation. A light was left burning in the living-room that night.

About a third of the way through the night, Grettir heard a
great din outside. Something had climbed up on to the house
and sat astride the roof of the hall, kicking against it with its
heels so that every piece of timber in the house creaked. This
went on for a long time. Then it climbed down from the roof
and went to the door. When the door opened, Grettir watched
the wretch stick its head inside, which looked hideously big
with grotesque features. Glam moved slowly and stood up
straight once he was through the door. He towered up to the
rafters, turned to the hall, rested his arm on the crossbeam and
glowered inside. The farmer did not make a sound, for he had
already had quite enough just hearing what went on outside.
Grettir lay there, completely still.

When Glam noticed something lying in a heap on the seat,
he moved along inside the hall and gave the cloak a sharp tug.
Grettir braced his feet against the bed-frame and did not yield.
Glam yanked at it again, much harder, yet the cloak still would
not budge. The third time he tugged so hard with both hands
that he sat Grettir up on the bench and they ripped the cloak
in two between them. Glam looked at the strip he was left
holding, astonished that someone could tug so hard against
him. At that moment Grettir ducked under Glam's arms and
clutched him around the waist, squeezing against his backbone
with all his might in the hope of toppling him. But the wretch
gripped Grettir's arms so tightly that he was forced to yield
his grip. Grettir backed away into one seat after another. All
the benches were torn loose and everything in their way was
smashed. Glam tried to make it to the door, while Grettir
struggled for a foothold. Eventually Glam managed to drag
him out of the hall. A mighty fight ensued, because the wretch
intended to take him outside the farmhouse. But difficult as
Glam was to deal with indoors, Grettir saw he would be even
harder to handle outdoors, so he struggled with all his might to
stay inside. Glam's strength redoubled and he clutched Grettir
towards him when they reached the entrance hall. When Grettir
realized he could not hold him back, in a single move he suddenly thrust himself as hard as he could into the wretch's arms
and pressed both feet against a rock that was buried in the

ground at the doorway. The wretch was caught unawares and, as he had been straining to pull Grettir towards him, Glam tumbled over backwards and crashed through the door. His shoulders took the door-frame with him and the rafters were torn apart, the wooden roofing and the frozen turf on it, and Glam fell out of the house on to his back, face upwards, with Grettir on top of him. The moon was shining strongly, but thick patches of clouds covered and uncovered it in turns.

Just as Glam fell, the clouds drifted away from the moon and Glam glared up at it. Grettir himself has said that this was the only sight that ever unnerved him. Suddenly Grettir's strength deserted him, from exhaustion and also because of the fierce way Glam was rolling his eyes and, unable to draw his sword, he lay there on the brink of death.

Glam was endowed with more evil force than most other ghosts[51] as he spoke these words: 'You have gone to great lengths to confront me, Grettir,' he said, 'and it won't seem surprising if you do not earn much good fortune from me. I can tell you that you have attained half the strength and manhood allotted to you had you not encountered me. I cannot take away from you the strength you have already achieved, but I can ordain that you will never become any stronger than you are now, strong enough as you may be, as many people will find out to their cost. You have become renowned until now for your deeds, but henceforth outlawry and killings will fall to your lot and most of your deeds will bring you misfortune and improvidence. You will be made an outlaw and be forced to live alone and outdoors. And this curse I lay on you: my eyes will always be before your sight and this will make you find it difficult to be alone. And this will lead to your death.'

As the wretch finished saying this, the helplessness that had come upon Grettir wore off. He drew his short-sword, chopped off Glam's head and placed it against the buttocks. Then the farmer came outside, having dressed while Glam delivered his speech. He had not dared to approach until Glam had been felled. Thorhall praised God and thanked Grettir kindly for having overcome this evil spirit. They set to and burnt Glam to ashes, then carried them in a skin bag and buried them as far away as possible from grazing land or paths. After that they went back home; it was close to dawn by then. Grettir lay down, for he was very stiff.

Thorhall had people sent for from the neighbouring farms in order to show them and tell them what had happened. Everyone who heard of this exploit was greatly impressed by it and said that in all of Iceland no man was a match for Grettir Asmundarson in strength, courage and all accomplishments.

Thorhall sent Grettir on his way with generous gifts, giving him a good horse and splendid clothes, because those he had been wearing were all ripped to shreds. They parted in friendship. Grettir rode off to As in Vatnsdal where Thorvald welcomed him warmly and asked in detail about his encounter with Glam. Grettir told him about their dealings and said that he had never before been through such a test of strength, so long had they grappled together.

Thorvald told him to keep his temper in check – 'and everything will turn out well. Otherwise, you will be prone to misfortune.'

Grettir said that his temperament had not improved and that he had much more trouble restraining himself and was much quicker to take offence than before. He noticed a marked difference in that he had grown so afraid of the dark that he did not dare to go anywhere alone after nightfall – he thought he could see all kinds of phantoms. It has since become a saying about people who suffer hallucinations that Glam lends them his eyes or they see things with Glam's eyes.

Grettir rode home to Bjarg when he had finished his business and stayed there for the rest of the winter.

36 | In the autumn when Grettir went north to Vatnsdal, Thorbjorn Ox held a great feast which many people attended.

Thorbjorn Traveller was at the feast. The guests talked about many things and the people of Hrutafjord asked about the clash with Grettir by the ridge that summer. Thorbjorn Ox gave a good account of Grettir and said Kormak would have come off the worse if no one had intervened to separate them.

Then Thorbjorn Traveller said, 'There were two things: I didn't see Grettir perform any brave deeds and, if anything, I think it gave him a shock when we arrived and he was quite happy to have the quarrel broken up. Nor did I see him try to take vengeance when Atli's farmhand was killed. I don't think Grettir has any courage if he lacks the force of numbers.'

Thorbjorn was very sarcastic about all this.

Many people there said these were empty jibes that Grettir certainly would not stand for if he heard about them. Nothing else noteworthy happened at the feast and everyone went home. There was a lot of friction between the two sides that winter, but neither attacked the other. Nothing else noteworthy happened that winter.

37 | Early the following spring, before the assembly, a ship arrived from Norway. The people on board brought plenty of news. First of all, the Norwegian crown had changed hands. King Olaf Haraldsson had taken power and Earl Svein had fled the country that spring after the battle of Nes.[52] Many remarkable tales were told about King Olaf, including the fact that he gave the warmest welcome of all to men who were accomplished in some way and took them into his service. This news delighted many young men and made them eager to go abroad.

When Grettir heard this news he became interested in sailing to Norway, hoping to receive honour from the king there like everyone else. A ship was moored at Gasar in Eyjafjord and Grettir took himself a passage on it. At this time he still did not have much to take with him on the voyage.

Asmund was growing very frail with age by now and hardly ever left his bed. He and Asdis had an exceptionally promising young son named Illugi. Atli took complete charge of running the farm and all the husbandry, which made a great improvement, because he was both prudent and clever.

Grettir went to the ship. Thorbjorn Traveller had secured a passage on it too, before anyone knew Grettir would be on board. Many people tried to dissuade Thorbjorn from sailing on the same ship as Grettir, but he said he would go all the same. He made his preparations to leave and was rather late about it. He did not make it north to Gasar until the ship was ready to sail.

Before Thorbjorn set off from the west Asmund Grey-locks fell ill and was bedridden.

Thorbjorn Traveller turned up at Gasar late in the afternoon as the crew were washing their hands in the booths before sitting down to their meal. People greeted Thorbjorn when he rode between the booths and they asked him the news.

He said he had nothing to tell them – 'except that I reckon that Asmund the warrior from Bjarg must be dead by now.'

Most of them agreed that a worthy man had left the world.

'How did it happen?' they asked.

Thorbjorn replied, 'That warrior did not meet a great end. He suffocated in the smoke of his own fireplace, like a dog. But it was no loss, he'd gone senile anyway.'

They answered, 'What a strange way to talk of such a man. Grettir wouldn't be pleased if he heard that.'

'I can endure that,' said Thorbjorn. 'Grettir will need to raise his short-sword higher than he did by the ridge in Hrutafjord last summer before I am frightened of him.'

Grettir heard quite clearly what Thorbjorn was saying, but did not interrupt him while he was telling his story.

When Thorbjorn finished, Grettir said, 'I predict that you won't suffocate in the smoke of your fireplace, Traveller, but you might not die of old age either. What a strange thing to do, talking so scornfully about innocent people.'

Thorbjorn said, 'I don't plan to retract anything. And I didn't think you put on a very brave show when we saved you from the people from Melar who were pummelling you like a bull's head.'

Then Grettir spoke a verse:

28.

| The bow-slinger's tongue | *bow-slinger*: warrior |

The bow-slinger's tongue   *bow-slinger*: warrior
is always too long with its words;
some will incur
sore revenge for that.
Many who call for shields   *many who call for shields*:
to parry the sword's biting wounds   i.e. many warriors
have paid with their lives, Traveller,
for less wrong than you have done.

Thorbjorn said, 'The day I will die is the same as ever, however much you babble.'

Grettir replied, 'My predictions have never died of old age until now and nor will this one. Defend yourself if you want. You won't have a better chance later.'

Then Grettir struck a blow at Thorbjorn, who put out his hand intending to parry it. But the blow struck his arm above the wrist and then his neck, chopping his head clean off. The merchants said that he had struck hard, like a true king's man, adding that it was no loss when a quarrelsome and venomous man like Thorbjorn was killed.

Shortly afterwards they put out to sea and reached Norway late in the summer, landing just south of Hordaland. Then they heard that King Olaf was staying in Trondheim. Grettir secured himself a passage to the north with some traders, because he wanted to go and see the king.

38 | There was a man named Thorir[53] who lived at Gard in Adaldal, the son of Skeggi Bodolfsson. Skeggi had taken land in Kelda district, all the way to Keldunes, and was married to Helga, the daughter of Thorgeir from Fiskilaek. Skeggi's son Thorir was a man of great standing and a seafarer. He had two sons, Thorgeir and Skeggi. They were both promising men and grown-up at this time.

Thorir had been in Norway the summer that King Olaf arrived from England. He struck up a close friendship with the king and with Bishop Sigurd, as shown by the fact that Thorir had a large knorr built in the woods and asked Bishop Sigurd to consecrate it, which he did. Afterwards, Thorir sailed to Iceland and when he grew tired of travelling he had the knorr dismantled. He had the beaks of the prow set up above the door to his house where they remained for a long time afterwards. They were so sensitive to the weather that one of them would whistle when a southerly wind was in the offing and the other before a northerly wind.

When Thorir heard that King Olaf had become sole ruler of Norway he felt he had something to claim there for the sake of their friendship. Thorir sent his sons out to Norway to meet the king and intended them to enter his service. They arrived in the south of the country late in the autumn and took a boat northwards along the coast to meet the king. They reached harbour just south of Stad and moored there for several nights. With plenty to eat and drink on board, they did not venture outside because the weather was so bad.

To return to Grettir and his men. They were making their way north along the coast and often ran into rough weather, since winter had started. And when they headed north for Stad they ran into a mighty storm with blizzards and frost and just managed to get ashore one night. Everyone was exhausted by the cold and they moored beside a grassy bank where they managed to carry their goods and provisions to safety. The merchants complained bitterly about not being able to take the fire with them, claiming that their health and very lives were at stake. They spent the evening there, all in a very sorry state.

As the evening wore on they saw a great fire blazing on the other side of the channel they had entered. When Grettir's shipmates saw the fire they said it would be a fortunate man who could have some of it, but doubted whether they ought to unmoor the ship, since that seemed too risky to everyone. Then they discussed at great length whether anyone would be capable of going to fetch the fire. Grettir made little contribution to their conversation, but said that once there had been men who would not have flinched at doing so.

The merchants said they were no better off now if such men could not be found any longer – 'But would you feel up to it, Grettir?' they asked. 'You are said to be the most accomplished man in Iceland and you definitely know how much we need it.'

'It doesn't strike me as much of a feat to fetch the fire,' Grettir said, 'but I don't know whether you'll offer a greater reward than the person who does it will ask for.'

'Why should you think we are so dishonourable that we would not make proper reward for such a deed?' they said.

'I will try if you think there is such a pressing need, but I have a premonition that I will gain no credit from it.'

They assured him this would never happen and said he spoke like a man of true integrity.

After that Grettir prepared for his swim. He took off his clothes and put on nothing but a cowl with breeches of homespun cloth underneath. He tucked up the cowl and tied a bast rope around his waist, and took a cask with him. Then he dived overboard. He headed straight across the channel and went ashore. He saw a house and heard voices and great merriment. Grettir went up to it.

The people inside were the sons of Thorir who were mentioned earlier. They had been staying there for several nights, waiting for the weather to die down so that they could sail on north beyond Stad. They had sat down to drink; there were twelve of them. Their boat was moored in the main harbour where a hut had been built for people to stay in who were travelling along the coast. A great quantity of straw had been carried inside and there was a huge fire on the floor.

Grettir burst into the house, unaware who was inside. By the time he reached land his cowl was frozen stiff and he looked frighteningly huge, like a troll. The people inside were startled and took him to be an evil creature. They struck at him with everything they could lay their hands on. A great scuffle ensued and Grettir warded off the blows with his arms. Some of the men struck him with blazing logs and the fire spread all over the house. Then he managed to leave with the fire and returned to his companions. They lavished praise on his exploit and his bravery and said no man was a match for him.

The night passed and the crew felt they had been saved when

they had the fire. The weather was fine the next morning and
the merchants woke up early and made ready to sail away,
saying that they would go and find the people who had made
the fire, to find out who they were. They unmoored the ship
and sailed across the channel, but instead of finding the hut
they saw a great pile of ashes with human bones inside and felt
certain that it must have burned down along with everyone
inside it. They asked Grettir whether he had caused this mishap
and called it a pernicious crime. Grettir said what he had suspected had come true, that they would reward him badly for
fetching the fire and said it was a bad thing to help dishonourable men. Grettir suffered greatly for this incident, because
wherever the merchants went they said that he had burnt those
men in their house.

Word soon spread that Thorir from Gard's sons had died
there, with their companions, and the merchants drove Grettir
off their ship and refused to have him with them. He became
so despised that no one wanted to have anything to do with
him. Grettir thought the outlook was bad, but wanted to go
and see the king at any cost, so he headed north for Trondheim
where the king was staying. Before Grettir arrived, the king had
heard all about the matter and was given a very slanderous
impression of him. Grettir stayed in town for a few days before
he managed to see the king.

39 | One day when the king was sitting in conference, Grettir
   | went in and greeted him respectfully.

The king looked at him and said, 'Are you Grettir the Strong?'

'I have been called that,' he replied, 'and I am here in the
hope of gaining from you some respite from the slanders that
have been made against me, for an incident which I say was not
my doing.'

'You are certainly a big enough man,' said King Olaf, 'but I
do not know if you will have the good fortune to clear your
name of this charge. However, it does seem more likely than
not that you did not burn the men inside deliberately.'

Grettir said he would welcome the chance to be cleared of

the accusation, if the king considered it possible, and the king told him to give a true account of what had happened between them.

Grettir related the episode described earlier, adding that everyone was still alive when he left carrying the fire – 'and to prove it I will undertake any ordeal that you consider within the law.'

King Olaf replied, 'We will grant you leave to carry hot iron[54] to prove your case, if Providence deems it so.'

Grettir was pleased with the idea. He started fasting to prepare himself to carry the iron and the day of the ordeal arrived. The king went to church with the bishop and a large gathering, because many were curious to see Grettir, after all that had been told about him. Then Grettir was brought to the church and when he entered many of the people there looked at him and said he was exceptional in strength and build.

As Grettir was walking down the aisle a young and quite ugly boy ran up to him and said, 'What a strange custom in this country that calls itself Christian, to allow evil-doers and bandits and thieves to go about in peace and undergo ordeals. What would an evil man do except try to save his own life for as long as he can? Here now is a criminal who has been proven responsible for evil deeds and burning innocent people alive in their houses, and he is being given the chance of an ordeal. This is an outrage.'

He went up to Grettir and gave him the finger, pulled faces and called him the son of a sea-troll and other rude names. Grettir flew into a rage, lost control of himself, raised his fist and boxed the boy on the ear, knocking him out cold; some people claim he was killed on the spot. Nobody seemed to know where the boy came from or what became of him, but the most common explanation is that he was an evil spirit sent to bring Grettir bad luck.

A great rumpus broke out in the church and the king was told that the man who was to carry the hot iron had started a brawl.

King Olaf went farther inside the church, saw what was going on and said, 'You are an ill-fated man, Grettir. The ordeal that everything was ready for cannot take place now. Nothing can be done about your ill-fortune.'

Grettir answered, 'For the sake of my family I had expected greater honour from you than I look set to earn, lord,' and recounted his kinship with King Olaf,[55] which was described earlier. 'I should very much like you to take me into your service,' Grettir continued. 'Many of the men you have with you are not considered better fighters than I am.'

'I can see there are few men to match you in strength and valour,' said the king, 'but you are far too ill-fated to be with us. You may go in peace as far as I am concerned and spend the winter wherever you want, but in the summer you will go to Iceland, because it is there that you are ordained to rest your bones.'

'First I would like to undertake the ordeal for the burning,' answered Grettir, 'because I did not do it deliberately.'

'That is very likely,' said the king, 'but since you ruined your chance of an ordeal through your impetuousness, you will never clear yourself of this accusation any better than you have managed so far. Rashness always breeds trouble. If any man has ever been accursed, it must surely be you.'

Afterwards, Grettir stayed in town for a while and received nothing more from King Olaf. Then he went south, planning to go east to meet his brother Thorstein Dromund in Tunsberg. Nothing is told of his journey until he arrived in Jaeren in the east.

40 | At Yuletide Grettir arrived at the house of a farmer named Einar. He was a wealthy married man with an unmarried daughter named Gyrid, a beautiful woman who was considered a fine match. Einar invited Grettir to stay with him over Yule and he accepted.

In many parts of Norway at this time, outlaws and criminals would suddenly appear from the woods and challenge men to duels for their women, seizing their possessions where there was little resistance.

It happened one day over Yule that a large band of criminals

called on Einar. Their leader was a huge berserk named
Snaekoll. He challenged Einar either to hand over his daughter or defend her if he was man enough. But the farmer was no
longer a young man, nor was he a warrior.

He thought he had a big problem on his hands and asked
Grettir secretly what action he could suggest, 'Because you are
called a man of renown.'

Grettir told him not to agree to anything that he considered
a disgrace. The berserk was sitting on a horse and wearing a
helmet with the cheek-guards undone. He was holding out a
shield rimmed with iron and acted very menacingly.

The berserk said to the farmer, 'Make your choice at once.
What does that great lout standing beside you suggest? Maybe
he would fancy playing a game with me?'

Grettir said, 'The farmer and I are two of a kind, because
neither of us is given to fighting.'

Snaekoll said, 'It would give you a fright having to face me
if I lose my temper.'

'What is tested is known,' replied Grettir.

The berserk thought that Grettir and the farmer were stalling.
He started to howl loudly and bite the edge of his shield. He
put his shield in his mouth, spread his lips over the corner of it
and acted like a savage. Grettir strode over to him and when
he came alongside the berserk's horse he kicked the bottom of
the shield up into his mouth so hard that his face ripped open
and his jaws fell down to his chest. In a single action he grabbed
the berserk's helmet with his left hand and dashed him from
his horse, and with his right hand he drew the short-sword he
was wearing and struck him on the neck, chopping off his
head. When Snaekoll's companions saw this, they fled in all
directions. Grettir could not be bothered to chase them, for he
could tell they were not at all brave. The farmer and many other
people thanked him kindly for this bold and resolute deed.

Grettir stayed there over Yule and was well provided for, and
the farmer sent him on his way with generous gifts. Then Grettir
headed east to Tunsberg to see his brother, who welcomed
him kindly and asked about his journey and the slaying of the
berserk.

Grettir spoke a verse:

29.

With a mighty kick from my ankle's thorn,	*ankle's thorn*: foot
Snaekoll, the tender of battle-din,	*tender of battle-din*: warrior
felt his bossed battle-shield	
smash on his dinner's door.	*dinner's door*: mouth
So hard did the iron-plated wall	
that guards the barbs' walkway	*barbs' walkway*: battle; its *wall*: shield
batter the house where his teeth are stacked	*house*: i.e. mouth
that his jaws split down to his chest.	

Thorstein said, 'You would do well in many ways, kinsman, if you were not dogged by misfortune.'

'What is done will be told all the same,' answered Grettir.

41 | Grettir stayed with Thorstein for the rest of the winter and into spring.

One morning when the two brothers were lying in the attic where they slept, Thorstein woke up and saw that Grettir had stretched his arms out on top of his bedclothes. Grettir woke up shortly afterwards.

Then Thorstein said, 'I've been looking at your arms, kinsman, and I'm certainly not surprised at the strong blows they have delivered to so many men, because I have never seen any man with such arms.'

'You should have known,' said Grettir, 'that I would never have accomplished the deeds I have done if I weren't stoutly built.'

'I would have preferred less muscle and more good fortune,' said Thorstein.

Then Grettir said, 'The saying is true: no man is his own creator. Show me your arms then.'

Thorstein showed him: he was exceptionally skinny.

With a smile, Grettir said, 'I've seen quite enough. Your ribs look like hooks and I don't think I've ever seen another pair of tongs like those arms of yours. I can't imagine you even have the strength of a woman.'

'That may be true,' said Thorstein, 'but you should know that if these skinny arms don't avenge your death, nothing ever will.'

'How can we tell what will happen in the end?' said Grettir. 'But it strikes me as pretty unlikely.'

Nothing else is mentioned about their conversation. Spring passed and Grettir found a passage on a ship and went to Iceland in the summer. He and his brother parted in friendship and never met again.

42 | To return to the killing of Thorbjorn Traveller. Thorbjorn Ox heard about it, as described earlier. He flew into a rage at the news and said many people had scores to settle.

Asmund Grey-locks had lain ill for a long time that summer and when he felt his strength waning he called for his kinsmen and said he wanted Atli to take over the farm after his death.

'But I do fear,' said Asmund, 'that you can hardly expect any peace for troublemakers. I want all my relatives to take the most care of him. I have nothing to propose about Grettir, for all his doings seem at the mercy of the wheel of Fortune. Strong as he might be, I am afraid he will have more trouble of his own to deal with than to give support to his kinsmen. But even though Illugi is young, he'll grow into a brave man if he can keep out of harm's way.'

When Asmund had made the arrangements he wanted with his sons, his illness intensified. He died shortly afterwards and was buried at the church he had built at Bjarg. His death was mourned as a great loss by people in the district.

Atli became an eminent farmer and kept a large, well-provided household. Towards the end of summer he went out to Snjofellsnes to get some stockfish. He took a large number of horses with him and rode from home to Melar in Hrutafjord to visit his brother-in-law Gamli. Atli was joined on the journey by Gamli's brother Grim and another man. They rode west through Haukadalsskard pass and followed the route out to Nes. There they bought plenty of stockfish, which they loaded on to seven horses, and went home when they were ready.

43 | Thorbjorn Ox heard that Atli and Grim were away from
     | home. The brothers Gunnar and Thorgeir, the sons of
Thorir from Skard, were staying with him. Thorbjorn felt jealous of Atli's popularity and urged the brothers to ambush him
on his way back from Nes. So they rode home to Skard and
waited for Atli and the others to pass by there with their horses.
As they reached the farm at Skard they could see Atli and his
men riding past and the brothers set off at once with their
farmhands in pursuit.

When Atli saw them coming he ordered the others to unload
the packs from the horses.

'They must be coming to offer me compensation for the
farmhand of mine that Gunnar killed last summer. We will not
make the first move, but defend ourselves if they attack us.'

Thorir's sons reached them and dismounted at once. Atli
welcomed them and asked if there was any news – 'Or were
you going to grant me compensation for my farmhand,
Gunnar?'

'You people from Bjarg do not deserve decent compensation
from me,' Gunnar replied. 'The slaying of Thorbjorn, whom
Grettir killed, is more deserving of compensation.'

'I don't have to answer for that,' said Atli. 'And you're not
responsible for that case anyway.'

Gunnar said that was not the point – 'Let's attack them now
and take advantage of the fact that Grettir isn't around.'

Then they went for Atli. There were eight of them in all,
while Atli and his men numbered only six. Atli moved in front
of his men and drew the sword Jokul's Gift, which Grettir had
given him.

Then Thorgeir said, 'They are both too proud for their
own good. Grettir held his short-sword high at the ridge in
Hrutafjord last summer, too.'

Atli replied, 'He is more used to mighty deeds than I am.'

Then they fought. Gunnar attacked Atli furiously, as if in a
frenzy.

After they had fought for a while, Atli said, 'We will earn no
prestige from killing each other's farmhands. There would be

more point if we were to fight together by ourselves, for I have never killed a man before.'

Gunnar refused his offer.

Atli told his farmhands to guard the pack-horses, 'And I will find out how they respond.'

Then he advanced so vigorously that Gunnar and his men were driven back. Atli killed two of the brothers' companions. After that he turned to face Gunnar and struck a blow that sliced through his shield below the handle and struck him in the leg below the knee. He dealt another blow at once that proved fatal.

Meanwhile Grim Thorhallsson attacked Thorgeir and they fought for a long time, because they were both stalwart men. When Thorgeir saw his brother Gunnar killed, he tried to flee, but Grim ran after him and chased him until he tripped and fell on to his face. Grim swung his axe and buried it between his shoulder blades. They spared the lives of the four remaining men, tended to their wounds, loaded the packs back on the horses and went home to announce the killings.

Atli stayed at home with a large band of men that autumn. Thorbjorn Ox was furious, but was unable to act because Atli was so popular. Grim stayed the winter with him, and so did his brother-in-law Gamli. Another of his brothers-in-law, Glum Ospaksson from Eyri in Bitra, was there too. There was a large band of men at Bjarg and much celebration throughout the winter.

44 | Thorbjorn Ox took charge of the case for the slaying of Thorir's sons. He brought charges against Grim and Atli, who defended themselves on the grounds that the brothers' unlawful assault had led them to forfeit their immunity. The case was presented to the Hunavatn Assembly and both sides were there with large numbers of men. Atli had plenty of supporters, because of his many kinsmen. Friends of both sides tried to mediate and discuss a settlement and everyone agreed Atli was a man of good character, peaceful yet resolute in the face of a challenge. Thorbjorn realized there was no more

honourable course than to accept a settlement. Atli made a condition that he would not agree to banishment from his district or exile abroad.

Two men were appointed to arbitrate the settlement: Thorvald Asgeirsson on behalf of Atli and to represent Thorbjorn, Solvi the Elegant. Solvi's father was Asbrand Thorbrandsson, whose grandfather, Harald Ring, had taken land in Vatnsnes all the way to the River Ambattara in the west and the River Thvera in the east and right across to the Bjargaos estuary, with all the land on that side of Bjorg down to the sea. Solvi was a boisterous person, but wise as well, so Thorbjorn chose him to make a settlement on his behalf.

Then they announced the settlement they had decided, whereby half compensation would be paid for Thorir's sons and the other half waived because of their unlawful assault and plot to kill Atli. The slaying of Atli's farmhand at the Hrutafjord ridge and the two who were killed with Thorir's sons cancelled each other out. Grim Thorhallsson was forced to leave the district and Atli wanted to pay the compensation by himself.

Atli was very pleased with the settlement, but Thorbjorn was displeased by it. They were nominally reconciled when they parted, but Thorbjorn was heard to comment that their dealings were not yet over if he had his way. Atli rode home from the assembly and thanked Thorvald for his support. Grim Thorhallsson moved south to Borgarfjord to live at Gilsbakki, where he became an eminent farmer.

45 | There was a farmhand named Ali who lived on Thorbjorn's farm; a man of little fortune and lazy too. Thorbjorn told him he would beat him if he did not work harder, but Ali said he had no urge to do so and answered him back insolently. Thorbjorn said he should not dare to disobey, but Ali answered him with words just as strong, until Thorbjorn could not stand it any more, knocked him to the ground and treated him roughly.

After that, Ali fled from the farm and headed over the ridge to Midfjord, not stopping until he reached Bjarg. Atli was at

home and asked him where he was heading. Ali said he was
looking for a place to work.

'Aren't you Thorbjorn's farmhand?' asked Atli.

'We weren't on such good terms,' Ali said. 'I didn't stay there
long, but it was bad while it lasted. When I left, I had grown
tired of the tunes he was always squeezing out of my throat. I
will never go back there, whatever happens to me. And it is
true that you two are very different in the way you treat your
workers. I would very much like to work for you if there is any
chance.'

Atli answered, 'I have plenty of farmhands without having
to deprive Thorbjorn of the ones he has taken on. You strike
me as a weakling. Go back to him.'

Ali said, 'I'll never go there of my own free will.'

Ali stayed there for a while. One morning he went off with
Atli's farmhands and worked like a man with a thousand hands.
Ali kept this up through the summer. Atli ignored him, but had
him fed because he approved of the work he was doing.

Then Thorbjorn heard that Ali was at Bjarg. He rode over to
Bjarg with two other men and called Atli out to talk to him.
Atli went outside and greeted them.

Thorbjorn said, 'You are trying to start yet another confron-
tation and quarrel with me, Atli. Why did you take my farmhand – did you have any right to do so without permission?'

'I can't see any proof that he's your farmhand,' Atli replied.
'I don't want to keep him if you have proof that he is. But I
don't want to have to drag him out, either.'

'You can have your way for now,' Thorbjorn said. 'But I
demand that man back and forbid him to work for you.[56] I will
come back once more and it's not certain that we'll part on
better terms then than now.'

Atli replied, 'I'll be here waiting and take whatever comes.'

Then Thorbjorn rode home. When the farmhands came back
to the farm that evening, Atli told Ali about his conversation
with Thorbjorn. He ordered him to be on his way and said he
did not want him to stay there any longer.

Ali replied, 'The old saying is true, that men who are praised
most betray worst. I did not imagine that you would send me

away now, after I have worked my fingers to the bone for you this summer in the hope that you would look after me. Yet this is what you all do, for all the good impression you make. Now I will be beaten before your very eyes if you refuse to give me any protection or help.'

Atli changed his mind on hearing this speech and did not feel inclined to send him away. Time passed until hay-time came around.

One day just before midsummer, Thorbjorn Ox rode over to Bjarg. He was wearing a helmet, with a sword girded around him and a spear in his hand. It was a broad spear with a very broad blade. That day it was wet outside. Atli had sent his farmhands out to cut hay and some of his men had gone north to Horn to catch fish. There were few other men at home with Atli.

Thorbjorn arrived around noon. He was alone and rode up to the door. It was shut, but no one was outside. Thorbjorn knocked on the door, then hid behind the house so that no one would see him from the door. A knock was heard and a woman answered the door. Thorbjorn caught a glimpse of the woman, but kept himself hidden, since he had something else in mind. She returned to the main room. Atli asked who was there and she replied that she could not see anyone outside. While they were talking about this Thorbjorn knocked loudly on the door.

'That person wants to see me,' said Atli. 'He must have some business with me, whether it proves beneficial or not.'

Then he left the room and went to the door. He could see nobody outside. Since it was raining heavily, he did not go out, but held on to a doorpost with each hand and looked around.

All of a sudden Thorbjorn rushed up to the door holding his spear in both hands and lunged at Atli's stomach, piercing him right through.

When Atli took the blow he said, 'Broad spears are the fashion these days.'

Then he fell forward on to the threshold. The women who had been in the room came out and saw that Atli was dead. Thorbjorn had already mounted his horse by then. He announced that he was responsible for the killing and rode home afterwards.

Atli's mother Asdis sent for people to help. Atli's body was dressed and buried beside his father.

Atli's death was deeply mourned, for he had been both wise and popular. No compensation was produced for the killing of Atli and no claim was made, because it was Grettir's duty to follow up the case if he came back to Iceland. The matter was left to rest that summer. Thorbjorn incurred little approval for this deed, but stayed where he was on his farm.

46 | Just before the Althing met that summer, a ship arrived at Gasar. The crew brought news of Grettir's travels, including the burning. Thorir from Gard was furious and felt obliged to take vengeance on Grettir for the death of his sons. He rode off with a large party and raised the matter of the burning at the Althing, but people were reluctant to discuss it while there was no one to answer for it. Thorir said he would not settle for less than seeing Grettir outlawed throughout Iceland for such an ignominious act.

Skafti the Lawspeaker answered him: 'Certainly this is an evil deed, if the account of it is correct. But one man only tells half a tale and most people prefer the worse side of a story with two sides. Under the present circumstances I will not declare Grettir an outlaw for this deed.'

Thorir was a powerful figure in his district, a great chieftain and popular among many great men. He pursued the matter so hard that there was no chance for Grettir to be cleared. Thorir then declared Grettir an outlaw throughout Iceland and proved to be his fiercest enemy, as was often shown afterwards. He put an outlaw's price on Grettir's head, then rode home. Many people said that Thorir had acted more from anger than respect for the law, but the declaration remained in force. Nothing else of note happened until after midsummer.

47 | Towards the end of summer Grettir Asmundarson landed
     | in the River Hvita in Borgarfjord. People from the district
went down to the ship and Grettir heard all the news at once:
first his father's death, then his brother's slaying and thirdly his
own outlawry throughout Iceland.

Then Grettir spoke a verse:

30.
In one fell swoop it befell
the wise verse-gatherer: outlawry,
my father's death to bear nobly
in silence, and my brother's.
But on other mornings, many
shoots of the Valkyrie's war-tree   *Valkyrie's war-tree*: battle;
will be the sadder for my sorrows,   its *shoots*: warriors
breaker of swords in battle.   *breaker of swords*: warrior

People say that Grettir's mood did not change in the slightest
when he heard this news and he remained as cheerful as before.
Grettir stayed on his ship for a while, because he could not find
a horse to his liking.

There was a man named Svein who lived at Bakki, inland
from Thingnes. He was a good farmer and a cheerful character
and often made humorous poems. He owned an exceptionally
swift brown mare that he called Saddle-head.

Grettir left Vellir one night, because he did not want the
merchants to find out. He took a black cowl which he wore
over his clothes as a disguise, then set off past Thingnes and
up to Bakki. It was daylight by this time. He saw a brown
horse in the hayfields, went over to it and bridled it, then
mounted it and rode inland along the bank of the Hvita,
below Baer to the River Flokadalsa and up on to the track
above Kalfanes. The farmhands at Bakki were getting up
around that time and told the farmer someone had taken his
horse.

Svein got up, smiled and spoke this verse:

31.
Away he rode, the helmet-tree,   *helmet-tree*: warrior
the rider of the prow;   *rider of the prow*: seafarer
by the farm he swept away
Saddle-head in his hands.
This tricky character,
holder of the shield that blocks
the battle's sun, will do deeds
more dangerous than this.

Then he took his horse and set off in pursuit. Grettir rode on
until he reached the land above the farm at Kropp, where he
met a man named Halli who said he was on his way down to
the ship at Vellir.

Grettir spoke a verse:

32.
Bowman, tree with boughs of elm,   *elm*: bow; its *tree*: bowman
spread word far and wide
that you have found Saddle-head
all the way up at Kropp.
On a mare's back there was a man
who plays for high stakes,
wearing a black cowl:
Halli, speed on your way!

They went their separate ways and Halli headed down the
track, but had not reached Kalfanes by the time Svein came
riding towards him. They exchanged a quick greeting.

Then Svein spoke a verse:

33.
Did you see where he rode,
that prankster, that cunning slob,
on a horse from the next farm?
Great is our loss.
We here shall demand
vengeance upon that thief;
whatever happens, he'll be left
black and blue if I catch him.

'You will manage that, then,' said Halli, 'for I saw that man who said he was riding Saddle-head and told me to spread the word far and wide. He was very large and wearing a black cowl.'

'He must have a high opinion of himself,' said Svein, 'and I'll find out who he is.'

Then he rode off after him.

Grettir arrived in Deildartunga. A woman was standing outdoors. Grettir started talking to her, and spoke this verse:

34.

Noble guardian of gold,	*guardian of gold*: woman
tell this ditty to whom it behoof:	*behoof*: i.e. a pun on the horse's
The snake in its lair	owner
has snatched his horse away.	*snake*: Grettir (which means 'snake')
I, the bold-worded server	
of Odin's ale will ride	*Odin's ale*: poetry; its *server*: poet
that mare in fury, not resting	
before I reach Gilsbakki.	

The woman memorized the verse and he rode on his way.

Svein rode up soon afterwards, before the woman went indoors. When he arrived, he spoke this verse:

35.

What swinger of swishing swords
rode in a swirling storm
hard on a dark-hided horse
here a few steps ahead?
That bold man will surely
wear a sheepish look
and pine for his lost glory,
flee me for long today.

She told him the verse that she had been taught.

He pondered over it, then said, 'That man is likely to prove more than a match for me, but I'll find him all the same.'

Then he rode through the district, and he and Grettir were always within sight of each other. The weather was windy and raining. Grettir arrived at Gilsbakki by daylight and when Grim Thorhallsson learned of his arrival he gave him a very warm welcome, inviting him to stay. Grettir accepted the offer. He freed Saddle-head and told Grim how he had come by the horse.

Then Svein arrived, dismounted and saw his horse there. He spoke this verse:

36.
Who has been riding my mare?
What will I earn for the favour?
Who has seen a greater thief?
What has the cowl-wearer staked?

Grettir had taken off his wet clothes and when he heard the verse he answered:

37.
I rode the mare to Grim's.
He's more a man than a crofter.
I have little favour to pay you.
But let us settle in friendship.

'A settlement will certainly be made,' said Svein, 'and you have paid for your horse ride in full.'

After that they took turns speaking verses and Grettir said he could not find fault with him for wanting to look after his property. Svein spent the night there, just like Grettir, and they both made many humorous verses about the incident, which they called the Saddle-head Verses.[57] The next morning Svein rode home and he and Grettir parted on good terms.

Grim told Grettir about many things which had happened in Midfjord while he was abroad, adding that no compensation had been made for Atli and that Thorbjorn Ox was in such a powerful position that if the situation continued Asdis might not be able to go on living at Bjarg.

Grettir spent only a few nights with Grim, because he did not want news of his arrival to reach the north before he got there himself.

Grim told him to call on him if he needed any assistance, 'But I want to avoid breaking the law and being sentenced to outlawry for harbouring you.'

Grettir bade him farewell, saying, 'It is likely that I will need your help more later.'

Then Grettir rode north across Tvidaegra heath and on to Bjarg, arriving at night. Everyone was asleep, apart from his mother. He went round the back of the house to the door there where he knew there was a passage, then found his way into the main room and up to his mother's bed. He shook her. She asked who was there and Grettir said his name.

She sat up, kissed him, heaved a sigh and said, 'Welcome home, kinsman. But what short-lived benefit I have had from my sons! The one I depended on most has been killed, you have been declared an outlaw and a criminal, and the third is too young to act.'

'It is an old saying,' said Grettir, 'that one misfortune is overcome by suffering a greater one. There is greater consolation than money and I expect Atli to be avenged. As for me, many people will be pleased to escape from me in one piece.'

She said this did not seem unlikely. Grettir stayed there for some while, his whereabouts known only to a few, and he tried to find out what the people in the district were doing. No one had heard that Grettir had arrived in Midfjord. He found out that Thorbjorn Ox was staying on his farm and had only a few men with him. This was after hay-time.

48 | Grettir rode west over the ridges one fine day and arrived at Thoroddsstadir just before noon. He knocked on the door and some women went out and greeted him. They did not recognize him. He asked for Thorbjorn and they said he had gone to the meadows to bind the hay, taking his sixteen-year-old son, Arnor; Thorbjorn was a very energetic worker and hardly ever idle. When Grettir heard about him he wished them well and rode away to the path towards Reykir.

There was some grassy marshland below the ridge where Thorbjorn had cut a great amount of hay, which was now completely dry. He intended to bind it and take it back to the farm with his son, while a woman was there raking it together into little stacks. Grettir rode along the lowest part of the land, while Thorbjorn and his son were higher up. Having bound one bundle, they were starting on the next. Thorbjorn had put down his shield and sword by the bundle, but his son had a hand-axe with him.

Seeing someone arriving, Thorbjorn said to his son: 'There's a man riding up to us. Let's stop binding the hay and find out what he wants.'

They did so.

Grettir dismounted. He was wearing a helmet and was girded with a short-sword, and he was carrying a great spear in his hand, with no barbs on it but a silver-laid socket. He sat down and removed the rivet from the shaft, to prevent Thorbjorn from throwing the spear back at him.

Then Thorbjorn said, 'He's a big man and I'll never recognize anybody if that isn't Grettir Asmundarson, who has a great score to settle with us. We must face him bravely and not show any signs of fear. Let's follow a plan: I will face him and see how we get on together, because I feel confident about taking on any man single-handed. You creep up behind him and drive your axe between his shoulder blades with both hands. You won't need to be careful about him harming you when his back is turned.'

Neither Thorbjorn nor his son was wearing a helmet. Grettir entered the marshland and when he was within range he threw his spear at Thorbjorn, but since the shaft was looser than he had expected it flew off course, the head came loose and it stuck in the ground. Thorbjorn picked up his shield and brandished it, then drew his sword and turned to face Grettir when he was sure who he was. Grettir drew his short-sword and when he swung it around he noticed the boy standing behind him, so he kept on the move. When he saw the boy was within striking distance he raised his sword aloft, then swung the back of the blade at Arnor's head so hard that it broke his skull and killed him. Thorbjorn rushed forwards and swung a blow at Grettir, who drew his buckler with his left hand to parry it, then thrust out with his sword, splitting Thorbjorn's shield and striking him such a blow on the head that his brains spilled out and he fell down dead on the spot. Grettir did not deal them any more wounds. He searched for his spear, but when he could not find it he went over to his horse and rode out to Reykir where he announced the killings.

The woman who was working on the meadow saw the killings and ran home in a panic to say that Thorbjorn and his son had been killed. Everyone at the farm was very surprised, because none of them knew about Grettir's movements. They sent for people from the next farm and a large band soon arrived and took the bodies to church. Thorodd Half-poem took charge of prosecuting for the killings and mustered a band of men at once.

Grettir rode back to Bjarg, saw his mother and told her about the incident.

She was pleased at the news and said that now he had shown the Vatnsdal family traits.

'But this will mark the start and the cause of your outlawry,' she said. 'I know for a fact that you will never stay here very long on account of Thorbjorn's kinsmen, but at least they know now that you are capable of anger.'

Then Grettir spoke a verse:

38.

In wether fjord Odin's weapons	*wether fjord*: Hrutafjord (= Rams' fjord)
stormed the bear-hugging	*Odin's storm of weapons*: battle
giant's adversary, the ox	*giant's adversary*: Thor; Thor + bjorn
mustered its full force.	(bear): Thorbjorn

Now for Atli's slaying, long
unavenged after he slumped
to the fair earth,
he is repaid in kind.

Asdis said this was true, 'But I do not know what action you can take now.'

Grettir said he would seek out his friends and kinsmen in the west.

'I won't be causing you any trouble,' he told her.

He made ready to leave and he and his mother parted with affection. He went to Melar in Hrutafjord first and told his brother-in-law Gamli all about the killing of Thorbjorn.

Gamli told him to hurry out of Hrutafjord – 'while Thorbjorn's kinsmen still have their band of men together. We'll give you as much support as we can in the settlement for Atli's killing.'

After that, Grettir rode westwards over Laxardal moor, not stopping until he reached Thorstein Kuggason's farm at Ljarskogar, where he stayed for much of the autumn.

49 | Thorodd Half-poem asked around to find out who had killed Thorbjorn and his son. When he and his men came to Reykir, they were told that Grettir had turned up there and announced that he was responsible for the killings. Thorodd thought he could tell what had happened and went to Bjarg. A large number of people were gathered there and he asked whether Grettir was among them.

Asdis said he had ridden away and that she would not hide him 'if he were here anyway. You ought to be pleased to drop the matter. But what happened was not too heavy a vengeance for Atli's death. You never asked whether I suffered for that. Now it is fitting to let things stand as they are.'

Then they rode back home, unable to see what more could be done.

The spear that Grettir had lost was not found for a long time, until the days that people still alive today can remember. It was found towards the end of Sturla Thordarson the Lawspeaker's life, in the marshland where Thorbjorn was killed, which is now known as Spjotsmyri (Spear-mire). This is taken as proof that Thorbjorn was killed there, although some accounts say that he was killed in Midfitjar.[58]

Thorbjorn's kinsmen received word that Grettir was at Ljarskogar, then gathered forces and set off there. But Gamli noticed them from Melar and tipped off Thorstein and Grettir about the party that was leaving Hrutafjord.

When Thorstein heard this he sent Grettir to Tunga to stay with Snorri the Godi,[59] because they were on speaking terms at the time.

He told Grettir he should ask Snorri for help, but go west to

Thorgils Arason at Reykjaholar if he refused: 'He'll take you in for the winter. Stay in the West Fjords until these matters are settled.'

Grettir said he would follow his advice. He rode over to Tunga, met Snorri the Godi and asked him to take him in.

'I am growing old now and have no inclination to take in outlaws if I am not compelled to,' Snorri answered. 'Why did that noble man turn you away, anyway?'

Grettir said that Thorstein had often treated him kindly, 'But it will take more people than just him to sort this matter out.'

Snorri said, 'I can speak in your favour if that will be of any help, but you should look for somewhere else to stay.'

They parted after these words and Grettir headed west to Reykjanes. The party from Hrutafjord arrived at Samsstadir, where they heard that Grettir had left Ljarskogar, so they turned back.

50 | Grettir arrived at Reykjaholar just before the Winter Nights and asked Thorgils for winter lodgings.

Thorgils said that Grettir was welcome to food, like any free-born man, 'But this is not a particularly comfortable place to stay.'

Grettir said he was not choosy.

'Then there's another problem,' Thorgils added. 'There are two very unruly men staying here, the sworn brothers Thorgeir and Thormod. I don't know how you'll get on together, but I always let them stay here for as long as they like. You can stay here if you want,[60] too, but none of you will be allowed to pick quarrels with each other.'

Grettir said he would not start trouble with anyone, especially if this was his host's wish.

Soon afterwards the sworn brothers came back. There was some friction between Thorgeir and Grettir, but Thormod got on well with him. Thorgils told the sworn brothers everything he had told Grettir and they held him in such esteem that none of them said a word out of place to the others, even though they were not always of like mind. The first part of winter passed in this way.

People say that Thorgils owned the islands named Olafseyjar, about six miles out into the fjord off Reykjanes. Thorgils owned a fine ox, which had not been brought back in the autumn. He kept on mentioning that he wanted it back before Yuletide.

One day the sworn brothers made ready to go and fetch the ox, if a third man could be found to join them. Grettir offered to do so and they welcomed the idea, so the three of them set off in a ten-oared boat. It was a cold day with a northerly wind. Their boat was kept in Hvalshausholm and when they put out the wind got up. They landed on the islands and caught the ox.

Then Grettir asked whether they would prefer to carry the ox aboard or hold the boat still, since there were quite powerful waves breaking on the islands. They told him to hold the boat, so he stood half-way along it on the seaward side, up to his shoulderblades in the sea, and held it so firmly that it did not move an inch. Thorgeir took hold of the rear of the ox and Thormod the front, and they lifted it out to the boat and sat down to row away. Thormod rowed at the prow, Thorgeir amidships and Grettir at the stern, and they headed into the bay. When they rounded the cliff at Hafraklett they ran into a gale.

Then Thorgeir said, 'The stern is holding us back.'

Grettir said, 'The stern will keep up if there are decent rowers in front.'

Thorgeir pulled on the oars so hard that both the rowlocks broke and he said to Grettir, 'You row harder while I mend the rowlocks.'

Grettir rowed hard while Thorgeir mended the rowlocks. But when Thorgeir started rowing, Grettir's oars had become so worn that he snapped them in half against the side of the boat. Thormod said they ought to row more gently and not break anything. Grettir snatched up two wooden shafts that were lying in the boat, punched a couple of holes in the side of the boat and rowed so furiously that every beam in the boat creaked with the strain. But since it was a sturdy boat with rather brawny men on board, they made it to Hvalshausholm.

Grettir asked whether they would prefer to take the ox back
to the farm or beach the boat. They chose to beach the boat
and pulled it up on land with all the water that was in it, and
the thick ice on it too. Grettir led the ox, which walked very
stiffly because it was tethered and rather fat. The ox grew
exhausted and when it got as far as Tittlingsstadir it could go
no farther.

The sworn brothers went back to the farm, because none of
them would help the others do their jobs. Thorgils asked about
Grettir and they told him where they had left him behind. He
sent men off to find him and when they got as far as Hellisholar
they saw a man walking towards them with an ox on his back:
it was Grettir carrying the ox. Everyone was astonished at what
he was capable of. Thorgeir was especially jealous of Grettir's
strength.

One day just after Yule, Grettir went by himself to bathe in
the pool.

Thorgeir knew this and said to Thormod, 'Let's go up to
Grettir and see how he reacts if I jump on him when he leaves
the pool.'

'I don't like the idea,' said Thormod, 'and he won't treat you
kindly for it either.'

'I'm going to anyway,' said Thorgeir.

Then he went down the slope, holding his axe high.

Grettir was walking away from the pool then and when they
met, Thorgeir said, 'Is it true, Grettir, that you have said you
would never run away from a man on his own?'

'I'm not sure about that,' Grettir replied, 'but I've never run
very far away from you.'

Then Thorgeir raised his axe. Grettir ducked the blow,
tackled Thorgeir and brought him down hard.

Thorgeir said to Thormod, 'Are you going to stand around
watching while this madman flattens me?'

Thormod grabbed Grettir by the feet, intending to pull him
off Thorgeir, but could not budge him. He was girded with a
short-sword and made to draw it, but just then Thorgils came
up and told them to calm down and stop pitting themselves
against Grettir. They did as he said and turned the episode into

a joke. There are no accounts of any other clashes between them. Thorgils was thought to have been a man of good fortune for being able to restrain such violent characters. In the spring they all departed.

Grettir went in to Thorskafjord and was asked how he had liked his food and winter lodgings at Reykjaholar.

He replied, 'When I was there the most enjoyable part of my meal was being around to eat it in the first place.'

Then he set off west over the moors.

51 | Thorgils Arason rode to the Althing with a large band of men. All the men of distinction from all over Iceland attended it. He soon met Skafti the Lawspeaker and they had a talk.

'Is it true, Thorgils,' Skafti said, 'that this winter you harboured the three most difficult men in the country, all of them outlaws, yet you managed to prevent them from doing each other harm?'

Thorgils said this was true.

'That is the mark of great leadership,' said Skafti. 'But what do you think of their characters and how brave is each one of them?'

'I consider them all unusually brave of heart,' Thorgils said, 'but I think two of them know the meaning of fear. Yet they differ, for Thormod is a god-fearing man and very religious, while Grettir is so afraid of the dark that he wouldn't dare go anywhere after dark if he could choose. But I don't think my kinsman Thorgeir knows what fear means.'

'Their characters must be just as you say,' said Skafti and they parted with these words.

At this Althing, Thorodd Half-poem brought charges for the killing of Thorbjorn Ox, which Atli's kinsmen had prevented him from presenting at the Hunavatn Assembly. Here he felt there was less likelihood of the matter being quashed.

Atli's kinsmen consulted Skafti about the charges and he told them that he thought he could see a legally valid defence which should earn them full compensation.

The cases were referred for settlement and the majority
agreed that the killings of Atli and Thorbjorn would cancel
each other out. When Skafti learned this he went to the men
who had considered the settlement and asked on what grounds
they had arrived at their decision. They stated that the men
who had been killed were of equal status.

'Which happened first,' asked Skafti, 'Grettir's outlawry or
Atli's death?'

They worked out that there was a week's interval between
Grettir being declared an outlaw at the Althing and Atli's killing, which happened immediately after the Althing.

Skafti said, 'I suspected that you would overlook this point
in bringing the action. You regarded someone as responsible
for prosecuting the case who had already been outlawed and
therefore could not defend himself or prosecute it. I declare that
Grettir is ineligible in this case and that by law the next of kin
must be responsible for following it through.'

Then Thorodd Half-poem said, 'Who will answer for killing
my brother Thorbjorn, then?'

'That's for you to determine for yourselves,' said Skafti, 'but
Grettir's kinsmen will not pay out any money for him or his
actions if they cannot pay for his freedom.'

When Thorvald Asgeirsson discovered that Grettir had been
ruled out as a party to the case, they tried to determine the next
of kin. The closest kinsmen were Skeggi Gamlason from Melar
and Ospak, the son of Glum from Eyri in Bitra, who were
both tough and ambitious men. Thorodd was made to pay
compensation for the killing of Atli, the sum of two hundred
pieces of silver.

Then Snorri the Godi made a proposal: 'Would you people
from Hrutafjord agree to waive the compensation in return for
Grettir being cleared? I expect him to inflict a lot of suffering
for as long as he is an outlaw.'

Grettir's kinsmen agreed eagerly, saying they did not care
about money if he could be left to live in peace and freedom.
Thorodd said he knew he was in a difficult position and would
accept such a settlement for his part.

Snorri told them to find out first whether Thorir from Gard

would grant permission for Grettir to be cleared, but when Thorir heard this he flew into a rage and said Grettir would never be released from his outlawry or escape from it.

'And to give him even less chance of being cleared,' he said, 'a higher price will be put on his head than for any other outlaw.'

Since he rejected the idea so flatly, nothing was done about lifting Grettir's outlawry. Gamli and his men took the money into their safekeeping, but Thorodd Half-poem received no compensation for his brother Thorbjorn. He and Thorir then both put up a reward for capturing Grettir, three marks of silver each. This was considered an exceptional move, since no higher price than three marks had ever been put on a man's head before.[61] Snorri said it was unwise to go to such lengths to keep a man in outlawry who was capable of causing such trouble and many would pay the price for it. Then they all parted ways and rode home from the Althing.

52 | When Grettir had crossed the Thorskafjord moor and entered Langidal he helped himself to the crofters' belongings, taking whatever he needed. He took weapons from some of them and clothing from others. Some were more reluctant than others, but after he had gone they all said they had had no choice.

Vermund the Slender, Killer-Styr's brother, was living in Vatnsfjord at that time. He was married to Thorbjorg, the daughter of Olaf Hoskuldsson. She was nicknamed Thorbjorg the Stout.

At the time when Grettir was in Langidal, Vermund had ridden to the Althing. Grettir headed north over the ridge to Laugabol, where a man named Helgi lived, the leading farmer in the district. Grettir stole a fine horse that the farmer owned, then set off to Gervidal. A man named Thorkel lived there; he was fairly well off, but a petty character. Grettir took everything he wanted from Thorkel, who did not dare to complain or resist. From there, Grettir went to Eyri and along that side of the fjord, taking both food and clothing from everyone and dealing out much rough treatment, which most people suffered grudgingly.

Grettir grew bolder and ceased to be on his guard. He travelled on all the way to Vatnsfjardardal and spent many nights in a shieling there. He slept in the woods there and completely relaxed his guard.

When the shepherds realized this, they made the rounds of the farms and said that a great brute had arrived in the district whom they did not think would be easy to deal with. The farmers gathered up to form a band of thirty men and hid in the woods without Grettir knowing about them. The shepherds kept watch for a chance to capture Grettir, although they had no idea who the man was.

One day when Grettir was lying asleep the farmers approached. When they saw him there they made plans to capture him with the least risk to themselves and decided that ten of them would jump on him and others tie him by the feet. This was done and they threw themselves on top of him, but Grettir reacted so violently that they were thrown off him and he managed to get to his knees, which gave them the chance to throw ropes around his body and legs. Grettir gave two of them such a hard kick on the ears that they were knocked unconscious. Then they all piled on top of him and he thrashed around for a long time, but eventually they managed to overpower him and tie him up.

After that they discussed what to do with him. They asked Helgi from Laugabol to take charge of him until Vermund returned from the Thing.

Helgi replied, 'I have more important things to do than to let my farmhands keep guard over him, because my land is tough to work. I certainly won't take him with me.'

Then they asked Thorkel from Gervidal to take charge of him, saying that he had ample provisions.

Thorkel protested and said he had no chance of doing so – 'because I live on my farm by myself with my old wife, far away from everyone else. You're not going to land me with this problem.'

'Thoralf from Eyri, you should take Grettir then,' they said, 'and watch him for the duration of the Thing, or at least pass him on to the next farm and take responsibility for making sure he does not escape. Put him down as firmly tied up as he is now when you take him.'

Thoralf answered, 'I don't want to take Grettir, because I have neither the provisions nor the money to keep him. Nor was he captured on my land. There's more trouble than honour at stake in taking charge of him or doing anything with him. He'll never set foot in my house.'

Then they asked each farmer in turn, and they all refused. This conversation of theirs was the basis of the poem called 'Handing Grettir Around',[62] which witty men composed and embellished with humorous phrases for people's amusement.

After discussing the matter at length, they agreed not to let their good fortune become misfortune, so they set straight to work and put up a gallows right there in the woods. They planned to hang Grettir there and then and went about the task very boisterously.

Then they saw three people riding along the valley below. One of them was wearing brightly coloured clothes and they took it to be Thorbjorg, the wife of the farmer from Vatnsfjord, as in fact it turned out to be. She was going off to the shieling. She was a woman of firm character and foresight and she took charge of local affairs and decided everything when Vermund was away from home.

She rode up to the crowd and was helped down from her horse. The farmers welcomed her warmly.

Then she said, 'What sort of a meeting are you holding here? And who is that thick-necked man sitting tied up over there?'

Grettir said his name and greeted her.

She replied, 'Whatever drove you to want to come here and cause trouble to my thingmen, Grettir?'

'You can't provide for everything,' said Grettir. 'I had to be somewhere.'

'What bad fortune you have,' she said, 'letting these wretches capture you without being able to fight them off. And what do you farmers plan to do with him?'

The farmers told her they were going to string him up on the gallows for the trouble he had caused.

'Grettir may well have deserved this,' she replied, 'but executing Grettir will be more than you men of Isafjord can handle, because he is a man of renown and great family, even though Fortune does not favour him. What would you do to save your life, Grettir, if I have you spared?'

'What do you suggest?' he asked.

'You will swear an oath,' she replied, 'not to cause any trouble here in Isafjord. You will not take vengeance on any of the men who attacked you and captured you.'

Grettir said she should decide the terms. Then he was untied. He later said that he had never shown such control over his temper as when he did not go for them while they lorded it over him. Thorbjorg invited him to stay with her and provided him with a horse to ride there. He went back to Vatnsfjord with her and waited for Vermund to return. She treated him well and earned wide renown from this episode.

Vermund turned sullen when he returned home and found out Grettir was there. Thorbjorg told him about the entire incident with the people from Isafjord.

'What did he do to deserve your sparing his life?' asked Vermund.

'There were many reasons,' Thorbjorg replied. 'First of all, you will be considered a man of much greater stature, married to a woman who had the courage to do such a thing. And then, his kinswoman Hrefna would not expect me to allow him to be killed. Thirdly, he is a man of outstanding accomplishments in many respects.'

'You are a wise woman in most ways,' said Vermund. 'Thank you for doing this.'

Then he told Grettir, 'You did not put up much of a defence, a great warrior like you, to let those wretches capture you. But that's what always happens to troublemakers.'

Then Grettir spoke a verse:

39.
Great was my lack
of good fortune
in the midst
of the sea-roof's fjord   *sea-roof*: ice (Isafjord = Ice fjord)
when those old
hogs grabbed
a firm hold
on my head's bones.

'What did they plan to do with you once they had captured
you?' Vermund asked.

Grettir spoke a verse:

40.
Many said
that I deserved
the bridal   *Sigar*: semi-legendary king who punished
gift of Sigar – a noose.   Hagbard for courting his
Until they met   daughter, by having him hanged
the rowan branch   *rowan branch*: Thor once saved himself from
adorned with leaves   drowning by grabbing a rowan
and covered with praise.   branch; a play on Thorb + jorg,
                                                      'Thor's rescue'

Vermund asked him, 'Would they have hanged you if they had
been left to themselves to decide?'

Grettir spoke a verse:

41.
I would have stuck
my own head
in the baited snare
before its time,
if Thorbjorg,
woman so fair,
had not saved
this poet.

Vermund asked him, 'Did she invite you to stay with her?'

Grettir answered:

42.

She asked me to come
with her, the tree   *tree*: rowan tree (i.e. Thorbjorg, cf. verse 40)
that held out to Thor
a helping hand;
gave a fine horse
and granted peace
to the serpent who coils   *serpent*: Grettir is a snake's name
in the Thunderer's bed.   *Thunderer's bed*: Earth, the wife of Odin

'You will lead a great and difficult life,' said Vermund, 'and
now you have learnt to be on your guard against your enemies.
I have no mind to keep you here and incur the ill-will of many
powerful men. You are best advised to seek out your kinsmen,
for few men will be prepared to take you in if they can avoid
it. And you are not one who easily yields to another's bidding.'

Grettir spent some time in Vatnsfjord, then left for the West
Fjords. He called upon many men of great standing, but
invariably something happened to stop them taking him in.

53 | Towards the end of autumn Grettir headed back south
     and did not stop until he reached Ljarskogar, where his
kinsman Thorstein Kuggason welcomed him warmly. Thorstein
invited him to stay for the winter and Grettir accepted the offer.

Thorstein was an industrious man and a fine craftsman, and
made all his men work hard as well. Grettir did not care much
for physical labour and in this respect they did not get on
together. Thorstein had had a church built on his farm. He also
built a bridge from his farm, with great craftsmanship. The side
of the bridge, beneath the struts that supported it, was rigged
with rings and bells[63] which would peal if anyone crossed
it, and they could be heard two miles away at Skarfsstadir.
Thorstein had put a great deal of effort into making the bridge,
because he was a very skilful blacksmith. Grettir was energetic
at hammering the iron, though he could not always be bothered
to do it, but he kept himself under control through the winter

and no incidents happened. But when the people of Hrutafjord heard that Grettir was staying with Thorstein, they sent out a party as the spring arrived.

Thorstein, however, got word of this.

He told Grettir to find himself shelter somewhere else instead, 'For I can see that you're not prepared to work, and I don't have any use for men who don't make any effort.'

'Where do you suggest I go, then?' asked Grettir.

Thorstein told him to go south and see his kinsmen there – 'but call on me again if they fail you.'

Grettir did as he said and went down to Borgarfjord to see Grim Thorhallsson. He stayed with him until after the Althing, then Grim told him to go to Hjalli and stay with Skafti the Lawspeaker. Grettir continued south along the lower path over the moors, not stopping until he reached Tunga, the farm of Thorhall Asgrimsson, Ellida-Grim's grandson. He avoided travelling where there were farms. Thorhall knew who Grettir was from his ancestry, although his name was also well known all over Iceland because of his accomplishments. Thorhall was a wise man and treated Grettir well, but did not want him to stay there for long.

54 | Grettir went from Tunga up to Haukadal and from there he went north to Kjol. He stayed there for much of the summer and no one travelling north or south over Kjol could rest assured that he would not relieve them of their belongings, because he had little chance of picking up anything else there.

One day when Grettir was on Dufunefsskeid as usual, he saw a man riding along Kjol from the north. He was a big man, seated on a fine horse with a bridle studded with nails and embossed at the ears. He was leading another horse with bags on it. The man was wearing a wide-brimmed hat which concealed his face.

Taking a fancy to the man's horse and belongings, Grettir went up to him, greeted him and asked him his name.

He said his name was Loft: 'And I know your name, too.

You must be Grettir Asmundarson the Strong. Where are you heading?'

'I haven't chosen a place to go to yet,' answered Grettir, 'but my business with you was to find out if you want to hand over some of your belongings.'

Loft replied, 'Why should I let you have what is mine – what will you give me for it?'

'Haven't you heard that I'm not in the habit of paying for things,' answered Grettir, 'but I generally get what I want all the same?'

'You can offer other people those terms,' Loft said, 'but I won't hand over what's mine. Let's be going our separate ways.'

And he rode past Grettir, goading on his horse.

'Let's not part so hastily,' said Grettir as he snatched the horse's reins out of Loft's hands and held them.

'Be on your way,' Loft said to him. 'You won't take anything from me if I can stop you.'

'We'll put that to the test, then,' said Grettir.

Loft reached down past the leather cheek-patches of the bridle, grabbed the reins between the bit and where Grettir was holding them and tugged so hard that they slipped right out of Grettir's hands.

Grettir looked at his palms and realized that this man certainly had some power.

He looked at him and asked, 'Where are you heading now?'

Loft answered him with a verse:

43.

I am heading	
for the storm's frost-cauldron	*cauldron*: i.e. a cave
below the beetling	
expanse of ice;	*ice*: i.e. glacier (probably Balljokul, see verse 44)
there the snake,	*snake*: i.e. Grettir
salmon of the ground,	*salmon* (i.e. fish) *of the ground*: snake
may meet a pebble	*pebble*: Icel. *hall-*; *palm's land*: hand (Icel. *mund-*)
and the palm's land.	= a man named Hallmund

Grettir said, 'No one can be certain of finding where you live if you don't say it more plainly.'

Then Loft spoke a verse:

44.
I have trouble
hiding from you
if you are set
on seeking me out.
It is in the land
of Borgarfjord,
Balljokul by men
it is called.

Then they parted. When Grettir realized that he was no match in strength for that man, he spoke this verse:

45.
Seldom I would seek such a meeting,
with swift Illugi standing far
from my side, and Atli,
a staunch rain-maker with metal,   *rain-maker with metal*: warrior
as when that man, undaunted,
drew the reins from my hands.
The wise-eyed woman asks   *wise-eyed woman*: his mother, Asdis?
if I am awed by awful Loft.

After that, Grettir set off from Kjol for the south and rode to Hjalli, where he met Skafti and asked him for help.

Skafti replied, 'I'm told that you are causing rather a lot of trouble and have been robbing people of their belongings. That is not worthy of a man of such great kin. The matter would be easier to consider if you did not go around robbing people. But since I am supposed to be the Lawspeaker in this country, I am under obligation not to break the law by harbouring outlaws. I want you to go somewhere where you do not need to rob people of their possessions.'

Grettir said he gladly would, but added that he could hardly bear being alone for fear of the dark.

Skafti said Grettir was not free to act only as he chose – 'and you should never trust anyone enough to allow what happened to you in the West Fjords to repeat itself. Many people have lost their lives through overconfidence.'

Grettir thanked him for his advice and returned to Borgarfjord that autumn. He met his friend Grim Thorhallsson and told him about Skafti's suggestions. Grim told him to go north to Fiskivotn on the Arnarvatn moor, and he did so.

55 | Grettir went up on to the Arnarvatn moor and made himself a hut there, the ruins of which can still be seen. He settled in and since he wanted to do anything except rob people he took a net and boat and caught fish to live on. He found life on the mountain very dismal, because he was so afraid of the dark. But when other outlaws heard that Grettir had gone there, many were keen to find him for the security it would offer them.

There was a man from north Iceland named Grim, who was an outlaw. The people of Hrutafjord made a bargain with him to kill Grettir, promising him his freedom and a payment if he managed to do so. He went to see Grettir and asked him to take him in.

'I don't think you would be any safer even if you stayed with me,' Grettir replied. 'You outlaws are difficult to see through, but I dislike being alone if I can avoid it. I also only want someone to stay with me if he will do any kind of work that happens to need doing.'

Grim said he had not expected anything else and urged him to let him stay there. Grettir was won over in the end and took him in. He stayed there into the winter and waited for a chance to go for Grettir, but did not find it easy to attack him. Grettir was suspicious of him and kept his weapons by his side day and night, and Grim never dared to make a move against him while he was awake.

One morning Grim returned from fishing, entered the hut and stamped his feet to find out whether Grettir was asleep, but he lay there without stirring. Grettir's short-sword was hanging above his bed and Grim imagined he would never have a better chance. He made a great noise to try to make Grettir speak, but he said nothing. He felt sure Grettir was fast asleep, stole up to the bed, reached out for the short-sword, took it down and drew it.

Just as Grim raised the short-sword, Grettir leapt up and grabbed it, seized him by the shoulder with his other hand and dashed him to the floor so hard that he was dazed.

'So this is the way you treat me, for all the good impression you tried to make,' said Grettir.

He got the whole story out of Grim, then killed him. Now Grettir realized what taking in an outlaw involved. The winter passed and nothing caused Grettir more suffering than his fear of the dark.

56 | Thorir from Gard heard of Grettir's whereabouts and decided to hatch a plan to have him killed.

There was a man named Thorir Redbeard, a very stout man and a ferocious killer, which is why he had been outlawed throughout Iceland. Thorir from Gard called for him and when they met he asked Redbeard to undertake a mission for him and kill Grettir the Strong. Redbeard said that this would not be an easy task, since Grettir was a clever and cautious man.

Thorir asked him to try, 'For this is a noble deed for such a brave man as you. I will free you from outlawry and give you plenty of money as well.'

Redbeard accepted the offer and Thorir told him how to go about killing Grettir. Afterwards Redbeard headed for the east, because he thought that would create less suspicion about his movements. He arrived at Arnarvatn moor after Grettir had spent a year there, and when they met, Redbeard asked Grettir to take him in for the winter.

Grettir replied, 'I do not intend to let anyone else try the trick that smooth talker played on me last autumn. After he had been here for a while, he tried to take my life. I won't risk taking in outlaws any more.'

'You certainly cannot be blamed for distrusting outlaws,'

said Thorir Redbeard. 'You must have heard about all the killings and unjust acts I have been responsible for, but it has never been claimed that I would commit such a cowardly deed as to betray my master. It is bad to be a bad man, because a bad man is judged to be like even worse men. And I wouldn't have come here, either, if I'd had a better option, but I don't think there are many men who could overcome us if we support each other. Take a chance with me and see whether you get on with me, and send me away again if you sense anything deceitful about me.'

'I'll take one more chance on you,' replied Grettir, 'but you can be certain that if I suspect you of treachery it will cost you your life.'

Thorir agreed. So Grettir took him in and found that he had the strength of two men in everything he undertook. He was willing to do any job Grettir sent him to do. Grettir did not need to do a single chore and had never led such a comfortable life since he went into exile, yet he remained so firmly on his guard that Thorir Redbeard never saw a chance to attack him.

Thorir spent two years on the moor with Grettir. He began to grow bored with being there and pondered what plan he could adopt that Grettir would not see through.

One spring night a great storm got up while they were asleep. Grettir awoke and asked where their boat was. Thorir leapt out of bed and ran out to the boat, then smashed it to pieces and strewed them all over the place as if the wind had swept them there.

Afterwards he went back to the hut and said in a loud voice: 'We are in trouble, my friend. Our boat has been smashed to pieces and the nets are lying far out in the lake.'

'Go and fetch them, then,' said Grettir, 'because I think you are responsible for smashing the boat.'

'Of all the things I can do,' replied Thorir, 'swimming is the one I have least aptitude for. I feel confident about pitting myself against any other normal man at anything else. Surely you realize that I haven't intended you to do a stroke of work since I came to you. I wouldn't ask you to do this if I could do it myself.'

Grettir stood up, took his weapons and went to the lake. A point of land there juts out into the water with a large cove on one side. The water was very deep right up to the land and had undermined the bank.

Grettir said, 'Swim out and fetch the nets and let me see what kind of a man you are.'

'I told you before,' said Thorir, 'that I can't swim. I don't know what's happened to all your heroism and courage.'

'I'll retrieve the nets, then,' said Grettir. 'But don't betray my trust in you.'

'Do you really expect such deceit and cowardice from me?' Thorir replied.

Grettir said, 'You will prove for yourself what kind of a man you are.'

Then he threw off his clothes and weapons and dived in after the nets. He gathered them up, headed back to land and threw them up on to the bank. When he was about to go ashore, Thorir snatched up the short-sword and drew it quickly. He darted towards Grettir as he stepped up on to the bank and swung a blow at him. Grettir threw himself backwards into the water and sank like a stone. Thorir watched the water, planning to prevent him from landing when he resurfaced. Grettir swam underwater right underneath the bank out of Thorir's sight until he reached the cove behind him. He went ashore there, catching Thorir unawares. The next thing Thorir knew was when Grettir lifted him up above his head and dashed him to the ground so hard that he lost his grip on the short-sword. Grettir managed to grab it and without saying a word to him lopped off his head. Thorir's life came to an end there and then.

After that, Grettir flatly refused to take in outlaws, even though he could hardly bear being by himself.

57 | Thorir from Gard was at the Althing when he heard that Thorir Redbeard had been killed. Realizing that this was not a simple matter to handle, he decided to ride away from the Althing and travel west by the route over the lower moors. He took a band of almost eighty men with him and intended

to take Grettir's life. When Grim Thorhallsson found out, he sent word to Grettir and told him to keep on his guard; Grettir always kept an eye on people's movements.

One day he saw a large band of men riding up in the direction of where he was staying. He ran up to a pass between the cliffs, not wanting to flee because he had not caught sight of the whole party. Then Thorir arrived with all his men and told them to finish off Grettir for good, saying that the evil-doer would not put up much of a defence this time.

Grettir answered him: 'There's many a slip betwixt cup and lip. You've come a long way for this and some of you will earn a few scars before we part company.'

Thorir urged his men to attack. The pass was so narrow that Grettir could easily defend one side of it, but he was puzzled why no one ever dealt him a blow from behind. Some of Thorir's men were killed and others were wounded, but they could make no headway.

Then Thorir said, 'I had heard that Grettir was exceptionally strong and brave, but I never knew he was skilled in the magic arts until what I have seen now. Twice as many men are being killed while he keeps his back turned to them. I see now that we are dealing with a troll, not a man.'

He told his men to retreat and they did so. Grettir was puzzled by what was happening, for he was worn out. Thorir and his men turned round and rode off to the north and people said it had been a humiliating expedition; Thorir had lost eighteen men and many others were wounded. Grettir went up the pass and saw a huge man sitting up against a crag, badly wounded.

Grettir asked him his name and he said it was Hallmund – 'You'll recognize me if I tell you that you thought I held the reins rather tight when I met you on Kjol the other summer. I feel I have repaid you now.'

'I definitely think you have acted nobly towards me, whether or not I can repay you in turn.'

Hallmund said, 'I want you to come to where I live, because you must find life tedious up here on the moor.'

Grettir accepted gladly and they set off south together for the Balljokul glacier. Hallmund lived in a big cave there with his daughter, who was stout and very imposing. They treated Grettir well and she nursed their wounds. Grettir spent much of the summer there.

He composed a lay about Hallmund which contains this verse:

46.
High he steps and swaggers on,
Hallmund in his mountain hall.[64]

This verse is also in it:

47.
The battle-keen sword crawled
like a snake over tracks of wounds
when the stormy weather rained
weapons in wether fjord.   *wether fjord*: Hrutafjord (cf. verse 38)
Those staunch men from Kelda
had the chance to hold my wake,
but brave Hallmund from the cave
helped me escape unscathed.

It has been said that Grettir killed six men at the battle, and Hallmund twelve. As the summer wore on, Grettir grew eager to go back to the settlements to see his friends and kinsmen. Hallmund told him to call on him if he went south and Grettir promised he would.

He went west to Borgarfjord and from there to the valleys of Breidafjord to consult Thorstein Kuggason about where to go next.

Thorstein thought that Grettir's enemies were growing in number and few people would take him in.

'But you could go south to Myrar and see what is in store there,' he added.

That autumn, Grettir went south to Myrar.

58 | Bjorn, the Champion of the Hitardal people,[65] was living
     | at Holm then. He was the son of Arngeir and grandson
of Bersi the Godless whose father Balki had taken land in
Hrutafjord, as described earlier. Bjorn was a powerful chieftain
and a very forceful man and often harboured outlaws. When
Grettir arrived at Holm, Bjorn welcomed him warmly, because
their ancestors had been close friends. Grettir asked if he could
give him any help.

Bjorn told him that because Grettir had enemies all over the
country by now, people would avoid giving him protection, so
as not to incur outlawry themselves: 'But I could give you some
help if you leave the people under my protection in peace,
whatever you do to anyone else in this district.'

Grettir agreed to that.

Then Bjorn said, 'I have noticed that there is a good fortress
and hiding-place in the mountain beside the river at Hitara, if
you use your ingenuity. There is a hole right through the mountain that can be seen from the road, because the main path lies
below it, with a scree slope stretching up to it which hardly
anyone could scale if there was a strong man at the top to
defend the lair. I think the best plan you could consider is to
stay there, because you can go from there to Myrar and the sea
to provide for yourself.'

Grettir said he would accept any advice he had to offer. Then
he went off to Fagraskogarfjall and made himself a place to
stay there. He covered the mouth of the hole with grey homespun cloth, which gave the impression that the cave was still
open when seen from the path below. He went down into the
district to gather provisions and the people of Myrar regarded
Grettir as a terrible scourge.

Thord Kolbeinsson was living at Hitarnes then. He was a fine
poet. In those days he and Bjorn were great enemies and Bjorn
did not think it was entirely futile if Grettir were to cause
trouble to Thord's men or livestock.

Grettir always stayed with Bjorn and they challenged each
other at various feats. *The Saga of Bjorn* claims that they were
a match for each other in sports, but most people believe that

Grettir was the strongest man to have lived in Iceland since Orm Storolfsson and Thoralf Skolmsson stopped undertaking trials of strength. Grettir and Bjorn swam right down Hitara in one stretch, all the way from the lake to the sea. They put the stepping-stones in the river that have never moved since, even when it swelled or froze or filled with clumps of ice. Grettir stayed on Fagraskogarfjall mountain for a winter without being attacked, although many people suffered losses at his hands. They were unable to act against him because he could defend himself easily and was on friendly terms with the people who lived closest to him.

59 | There was a man named Gisli. He was the son of Thorstein, whom Snorri the Godi had had killed. Gisli was a big, strong man with a liking for impressive weapons and clothes; he thought very much of himself and was quite boastful. He was a merchant and made land at Hvita that summer, after Grettir had been on the mountain for the winter. Thord Kolbeinsson rode down to the ship. Gisli greeted him warmly and offered him any of his goods that he wanted. Thord accepted his offer and they started talking.

Gisli said, 'Is it true what I'm told, that you are at a loss for a way to rid yourself of this outlaw who has been causing you so much harm?'

Thord said, 'I have not tried yet, but many people think he is a difficult man to attack, as many a man has found out to his cost.'

'I am not surprised that you have trouble dealing with Bjorn when you can't rid yourself of the other one. Unfortunately I'll be too far away this winter to be able to put matters right for you.'

'Hearsay will be the safest way for you to handle him.'

'You don't need to go telling me about Grettir,' said Gisli. 'I faced tougher challenges when I went raiding with King Canute the Great and in Britain. I was said to have guarded my place on board ship then. And I feel confident about myself and my weapons, if I ever had the chance to fight Grettir.'

Thord replied that Gisli would not go unrewarded if he got rid of Grettir – 'And there's a higher price on his head than for any other outlaw. It was six marks of silver to start with and Thorir from Gard added another three this summer, but everyone agrees that whoever wins the reward will have earned a great deal.'

'Men will do anything for money,' said Gisli, 'not least merchants like me. But we should keep this to ourselves. He might be more on his guard if he finds out that I'm planning something with you. I'll be spending the winter out on Olduhrygg – is his lair on my way there? He'll be caught by surprise. I won't muster a big party to attack him.'

Thord was pleased with the plan. He rode home afterwards and let the matter rest there.

But this was a case of the saying, 'The woods have ears.' Some friends of Bjorn from Hitardal had overheard Gisli and Thord's conversation and told him about it in detail. Bjorn told Grettir when he met him and said they would see how he stood up to that test.

'It wouldn't exactly be a pity,' said Bjorn, 'if you were to rough him up a bit, but don't kill him if you can avoid it.'

Grettir grinned and made no comment.

Around the time of the autumn sheep round-up, Grettir went down to the Flysja district and stole some sheep. He managed to catch four wethers. The farmers became aware of his movements and went after him. He reached the slope only an instant before the farmers made it there. They tried to drive their sheep away from him, without attacking him with weapons. There were six of them and they blocked his path. Grettir flew into a rage at the thought of losing his sheep, grabbed two of the farmers and tossed them down the slope, knocking them unconscious. When the others saw this, they made a half-hearted attack. Grettir took the sheep, hooked them together by their horns, flung a pair over each of his shoulders and went up to his lair. The farmers went back, feeling they had come off the worse and more displeased with their lot than ever.

Gisli stayed at his ship that autumn until it was laid up. He was delayed for many reasons and only finished late. He rode off from the south just before the Winter Nights and stayed at Hraun, on the south side of the River Hitara.

The next morning, before he rode on, Gisli spoke to his companions: 'We'll wear brightly coloured clothes when we ride today,' he said, 'to let the outlaw see that we are not the ordinary sort of travellers who wander along here every day.'

There were three of them in all; they did as Gisli had said.

When they had crossed the river he spoke to them again: 'I'm told the outlaw is on top of these mountains here and it's not an easy place to approach,' he said. 'So wouldn't he be pleased to come and meet us and take a look at our belongings?'

They said he was accustomed to doing that.

That same morning, Grettir had got up early in his lair. The weather was cold and freezing and there had been a light snowfall. He saw three men riding over Hitara from the south, their elegant clothes and enamelled shields shimmering in the sunlight. It occurred to Grettir who they might be and he felt he really needed to relieve them of some of their belongings, and he was curious to meet such braggarts. He took his weapons and ran down the scree.

When Gisli heard the stones clattering he said, 'There's a big man coming down the slope there to meet us. We must act bravely, for there is a fine catch to be had.'

His companions said that the man wouldn't walk right into their hands unless he had some self-confidence – 'and it is fitting that he who begs will receive.'

Then they leapt down from their horses.

That moment, Grettir came up, took the bag of clothing that Gisli was carrying behind his saddle and said, 'I'll have this. I often stoop to trifles.'

Gisli replied, 'No, you won't! Don't you know who you're dealing with?'

'I can't exactly say I do,' Grettir told him, 'but since I'm asking for such a trifle, you can't expect special treatment from me.'

'Maybe you think it's a trifle,' said Gisli, 'but I'd sooner part with three thousand ells of homespun[66] than this. You're certainly an unjust character, and you don't try to hide it either. Attack him, men, and see what he's capable of.'

They went for Grettir, who backed off to a rock beside the path where he made his defence. The rock is known as Grettishaf (Grettir's Lift). Gisli urged his men to attack, but Grettir could see that he was not as brave as he pretended to be, because he always kept behind them. Grettir lost his patience then, swung his short-sword and dealt one of Gisli's companions his death blow, then leapt out from behind the rock and attacked so furiously that Gisli was driven back right along the side of the mountain. Then Gisli's other companion was killed.

'You don't show much sign of having done brave deeds far and wide,' said Grettir, 'and what a miserable way to part from your companions.'

Gisli replied, 'The fire seems hottest to a burned man. And it's a tough job to deal with a man of such fiendish strength.'

They exchanged a few blows before Gisli threw down his weapons and ran away along the foot of the mountain. Grettir gave him time to throw off anything he wanted, and whenever Gisli had the chance he shed some item of clothing. Grettir never quickened his pace to close the gap between them. Gisli ran the whole way over the mountain and right across Kaldardal valley, along the slopes at Aslaugarhlid and above Kolbeinsstadir, then out into the lava field at Borgarhraun. By then he was only wearing his underwear and was exhausted. Grettir followed and was always only an arm's length away. He snatched up a large branch. Gisli did not stop until he reached the River Haffjardara, which was swollen and difficult to cross. He was about to run out into the water when Grettir broke into a spurt, grabbed him and overpowered him.

Grettir threw him to the ground and said, 'Are you Gisli who wanted to meet Grettir Asmundarson?'

'I've found him now,' Gisli replied, 'but I don't know how we will part. Keep what you have taken from me and let me go free.'

'You won't understand what I say to you,' said Grettir. 'I must give you something to remember me by.' Then he pulled Gisli's undershirt over his head and thrashed him with the branch on his back and both sides. Gisli kept trying to wriggle out of the way, but Grettir flayed the skin off him before he set him free. Gisli thought he would sooner not learn anything from Grettir than take another flogging like that. Nor did he ever do anything else to earn such treatment.

When Gisli had got to his feet, he ran out to a great pool in the river and swam across it, reaching the farm named Hrossholt that night in a state of exhaustion. He lay in bed there for a week, his body covered in welts. After that, he returned to where he was staying.

Grettir went back, picked up the clothes that Gisli had cast off and took them home with him. Gisli never got them back.

Many people thought Gisli had been dealt a fitting punishment for all his bravado and boasting. Grettir composed this verse about their dealings:

48.
The horse that nibbles with its teeth
lightly when it ought to bite   *ought to bite*: i.e. during a horse-fight
saves its breath until the end
then runs off from the other horse.
From me that day at Myrar
ran interfering Gisli
farting like a carthorse,
stripped of fame and honour.

The following spring Gisli made his ship ready and strictly forbade that anything he owned should be transported by the route south past the mountain, saying that the Devil himself lived there. Gisli rode south around the coast all the way to his ship. He and Grettir never met again and he was completely discredited after that incident. He is now out of the story.

Matters continued to worsen between Thord Kolbeinsson and Grettir. Thord hatched many plans to have Grettir driven away or killed.

60 | When Grettir had been on Fagraskogarfjall for two years and his third winter there was beginning, he went south to Myrar, to the farm named Laekjarbug, where he took six wethers against the owner's will. From there he went down to Akrar and drove two bulls and many sheep off to slaughter, then went south to Hitara.

When the farmers became aware of his movements, they sent word to Thord at Hitarnes, asking him to do something to get rid of Grettir, but he declined. He answered their pleas by sending his son Arnor, who was later known as the Poet of Earls, to go with them, and told them not to let Grettir get away. Word was sent all over the district.

A man named Bjarni, who lived at Jorvi in the Flysja district, gathered a band of men from the west side of Hitara. The plan was to send parties in from either side of the river.

Grettir had two men with him. One was a brave man named Eyjolf, the son of the farmer from Fagriskog, and another man was with them.

Thorarin from Akrar and Thorfinn from Laekjarbug were the first to arrive, with a band of almost twenty men in all. Grettir wanted to cross the river, but Thorgeir, Arnor and Bjarni turned up on the west bank. A narrow point of land jutted out into the river on Grettir's side and when he saw the expedition arriving he drove the stolen animals there, because once he got his hands on anything he never wanted to let go of it again.

The people from Myrar attacked him boldly straight away. Grettir told his companions to guard his rear against attack. There was not room for many people to attack him at once. A tough battle ensued. Grettir swung to either side with his short-sword and they found it hard to move in close to him. Some of the people from Myrar were killed there and others wounded. The party moving in from the other side of the river arrived late, because the ford was not close by, and after only a short fight the attackers retreated. Thorarin from Akrar was a very old man, so he did not take part in the attack.

When the battle was over, Thorarin's son Thrand arrived, together with Thord's nephew Thorgils Ingjaldsson and Finnbogi, the son of Thorgeir Thorhallsson from Hitardal, and Steinolf Thorleifsson from Hraundal. They urged everyone to renew the attack and another fierce assault was mounted.

Grettir realized that there were only two options, to flee or stop at nothing. He advanced so furiously that no one could hold his ground, because there was such a crowd there that Grettir thought he had no chance of escaping and he wanted to do as much as he could before he was killed – he also wanted to face someone he considered a challenge. He ran for Steinolf from Hraundal and struck a blow at his head, splitting it down to his shoulders. Straight afterwards he dealt another blow which struck Thorgils Ingjaldsson in the middle and almost sliced him in half. Thrand tried to attack him and avenge his kinsman, but Grettir swung at him and hit him on the right thigh, slicing off the muscles and leaving him incapacitated. After that he dealt a great wound to Finnbogi.

Then Thorarin called out and told them to retreat – 'because the longer you fight him, the worse treatment he will deal out to you. He is picking you off one by one!'

They did as he said and turned away. Five men had been killed on the spot and five more were fatally wounded or maimed. Most of the men who had been in the encounter sustained some wounds. Grettir was exhausted, but only slightly wounded. The people from Myrar left, their ranks seriously depleted, because many brave men had been killed there.

The party from the west of the river made slow progress and did not arrive until the encounter was over. When they saw the routing their companions had been given, Arnor was unwilling to risk his own life and was severely criticized for it by his father and many others. People thought he had not acted like much of a warrior. The place where they fought is now called Grettisoddi (Grettir's Point).

Grettir and his men took some horses and rode up to the foot of the mountain, because they all had some wounds. When they reached Fagriskog, where Eyjolf stayed, the farmer's daughter was standing outside and asked them if there was any news.

Grettir gave her an account of the battle, and spoke this verse:

49.

Goddess who serves the ale horns,   *Goddess who serves the ale horns*:
the great gash on Steinolf's head   *woman*
will never manage to heal –
and more men died besides.
Bleak is Thorgils' future,
for his bones were all split open;
people say that eight
breakers of treasure are dead.   *breakers of treasure*: men

After that, Grettir went up to his lair and stayed there for the winter.

61 | The next time Bjorn met Grettir he told him he thought much had happened: 'And you won't be safe here much longer. You have killed my kinsmen and friends, but I won't abandon the promise I made to you for as long as you stay here.'

Grettir said he had been defending his own life and limbs – 'But it is unfortunate that you are displeased.'

Bjorn said that what was done was done. Soon afterwards, some men whose kinsmen had been killed by Grettir visited Bjorn and told him not to let that troublemaker stay there tormenting them any longer. Bjorn said it would be done as soon as the winter was over.

Thrand, the son of Thorarin from Akrar, recovered from his wounds. He became a worthy man. He married Steinunn, the daughter of Hrut from Kambsnes. Steinolf's father, Thorleif from Hraundal, was an important figure. The people of Hraundal are descended from him.

No other accounts are given of Grettir's dealings with the people of Myrar while he stayed on the mountain. Bjorn remained friends with him, although it cost him other friendships to allow Grettir to stay there, because the people were displeased not to receive compensation for their kinsmen.

Around the time the Thing was held, Grettir left Myrar. He went to Borgarfjord once again to see Grim Thorhallsson and consult him about what he should do. Grim said he did not have the means to keep him, so Grettir went to see his friend Hallmund and stayed with him until towards the end of summer.

In the autumn, Grettir went to Geitland and waited for the weather to clear. Then he went up on to the Geitlandsjokul glacier and headed towards the south-east, taking a cauldron and tinder-box with him. It is thought that Hallmund, who knew much of the country, gave him directions about where to go.

Grettir forged on until he found a long and fairly narrow valley[67] that was enclosed by the glacier on all sides and above. He found a place to descend and saw beautiful slopes with grass and brushwood growing on them. There were hot springs there, which Grettir presumed was the reason that the spot was not covered by the glacier. A small brook flowed through the valley with level spits on either side. The sun only shone in there for a short time each day. Grettir was astonished at how many sheep were in the valley, much finer and fatter than he had ever seen.

Grettir settled down there and made a hut from the wood he managed to find. Then he caught some sheep to eat; a single one yielded twice the meat of those from other places.

There was a dusky-brown ewe there whose size particularly impressed him. The ewe had a lamb with it that Grettir fancied eating, so he caught it and cut it up. There was half a weight of suet inside it and the meat was much better still. When the ewe began to pine for its lamb it went up to Grettir's hut every night and bleated so loudly that he could never sleep. He deeply regretted killing the lamb – on account of the disturbance it caused him.

At dusk every evening he would hear a voice calling farther up the valley and the sheep would all flock to the same fold.

Grettir said that a half-troll, a giant named Thorir, ruled over the valley and kept him under his protection. Grettir named the valley Thorisdal (Thorir's valley) after him. He said Thorir had some daughters that he had some fun with, and they took to it eagerly because visitors were rare. To observe the fasts, Grettir made a rule of eating only suet and liver during Lent.

Nothing eventful happened that winter. Grettir grew so bored that he was unable to stay any longer, so he left the valley, headed due south down over the glacier and descended it by the middle of Skjaldbreid. There he erected a slab of stone and made a hole in it, and it said that anyone who puts his eye to the hole can see into the gully that runs down from Thorisdal.

Then he went across the south of Iceland to the East Fjords. He spent the whole summer and winter travelling and went to see all the leading men, but he was turned away everywhere and could find neither food nor a place to sleep. Then he went back to the north, staying in various places.

62 | Shortly after Grettir had left the Arnarvatn moor a man named Grim arrived there, the son of the widow from Kropp. He had been outlawed for killing the son of Eid Skeggjason from As. He stayed in the place Grettir had been and caught plenty of fish from the lake. Hallmund resented Grim for taking Grettir's place and set his mind on making sure that Grim would not gain anything, no matter how much he fished.

One day Grim caught a hundred fish, carried them back to his hut and stacked them outside. But when he came out the next morning every single fish had gone.

Puzzled, he went to the lake and caught two hundred fish, brought them back and stacked them outside, but the same thing happened: they had all disappeared in the morning – and he began to suspect something.

On the third day he caught three hundred fish, carried them back and kept watch over his hut. Grim could see through a hole in the door if anyone came to the hut. Time passed and about a third of the way through the night he heard some rather heavy footsteps outside. When Grim heard this he took an axe which he had with him, a very sharp weapon. He wanted to find out what this man was doing. The stranger had a huge basket on his back, then put it down and looked around, but did not see anyone outside. He rummaged around in the fish approvingly, then heaped them all into his basket, filling it. The catch of fish was so big that Grim expected a horse could not carry more, but the stranger picked up the basket and bent down to lift it on to his back. Just as he was standing up, Grim ran out and swung his axe with both hands, sinking the whole of the blade into his neck. The stranger reacted quickly and made a rush for the mountain to the south with the basket on his back. Grim gave chase, wondering whether he had wounded him. They went all the way south to the foot of Balljokul glacier, where the man went into a cave. A bright fire was burning inside and a woman was sitting beside it, heftily built and imposing. Grim heard her greet the man as her father, calling him Hallmund. He threw down his load with a heavy sigh and she asked him why he was covered with blood.

He answered her with this verse:

50.
It is clear to me
that no man may
rely upon
his own strength,
for men's resolve
falls short
on their dying day
when their fortune fails.

She asked him in detail about the incident and he told her everything that had happened.

'You must listen now,' he said, 'as I relate all my exploits. I will recite a poem about them and want you to carve it out on a rune-stick.'

Then he recited the Lay of Hallmund, which contains these verses:

51.
I proved my worth
when I tugged Grettir
with full force
off those reins.
Then I saw him
stand and stare
a good while
into his palms.

52.
Next of all
came Thorir
to the moor
of Arnarvatn
and we two
made battle,
the play of swords,
with eighty men.

53.
Slashing blows
from Grettir's hand
seemed to strike
on their shields,
but I have heard
that men thought
the sword-tracks I left
were much greater.

54.
I made hands
and heads fly
from men's bodies
at Grettir's back,
so that one
and eighteen men
from Kelda
lay there to die.

55.
I have dealt giants
and their kind
and cliff-dwellers
harsh treatment,
beaten hard
many evil spirits
and brought death
to half-trolls,
brought trouble
to almost all
monstrous beings
and elves' kin.

Hallmund named many of his exploits in the poem, for he had been all over the country.

Then his daughter said, 'That man kept a tight grip on what was his – which wasn't surprising after the way you provoked him. But who will avenge you now?'

'I'm not sure the chance will ever arise,' answered Hallmund. 'I feel certain that Grettir would take vengeance if he had the opportunity, but it will be impossible to withstand the good fortune of that man who did this to me, because he will achieve great things.'

Hallmund's strength began to wane as he recited the poem and as soon as he finished it, he died. She was unable to contain herself and wept bitterly.

Then Grim entered the cave and told her to take heart – 'for no one lives beyond his fated day. And he brought it upon himself, because I could hardly stand there and watch him robbing me.'

She said there was much truth in what he said – 'and over-bearing reaps a bad reward.'

She cheered up somewhat as she talked to him, and Grim stayed in the cave for many nights and learned the poem. He and Hallmund's daughter got on well together.

Grim spent the winter on Arnarvatn moor[68] after Hallmund died. Thorkel Eyjolfsson confronted him on the moor later and they fought. Their duel ended when Grim had the chance to take Thorkel's life, but refused to kill him. In return, Thorkel took him into his house, arranged for him to go abroad and gave him plenty of valuables. It was thought a noble way for them to treat each other. Grim became a seafarer afterwards and a great many stories are told of his adventures.

63 | To return to Grettir. When he left the East Fjords he moved under cover and disguised himself in order to avoid meeting Thorir. He lived outdoors on Modrudal heath and various other places, and was sometimes on Reykir heath.

When Thorir heard that Grettir was on Reykir heath, he gathered a band of men and rode there, determined not to let him get away. Grettir hardly noticed them before they arrived. He was at a shieling with another man. When they saw the parties and had to act quickly, Grettir said they had to stun their horses and drag them into the shieling, which they did. Thorir and some men rode past them northwards over the moor, but they could not find their friend Grettir and they turned back.

When the party had ridden past them again, Grettir said: 'They'll have a disappointing journey if they don't find us. You keep an eye on the horses and I'll go out to meet them. It would be a good joke to play on them if they don't recognize me.'

Grettir's companion tried to dissuade him, but he set off all the same, wearing different clothes and a wide-brimmed hat covering his face, with a staff in his hand. Then he walked out into their path. They greeted him and asked whether he had seen some men riding across the moor.

'I must have seen the men you are looking for. You've just missed them, because they were here south of those marshes on the left.'

As soon as he told them this they galloped off for the marshes. The land was so marshy that they became bogged down and had to drag their horses through it, and spent much of the day floundering there. They cursed the beggar for playing such a trick on them.

Grettir went straight back to his companion and when he met him he spoke this verse:

56.

I did not ride to face the tenders	*tenders of swords*: warriors
of swords that strike terror into shields;	
I tread a solitary path, a life	
of tribulation is shaped for me.	
I would not meet the brave	
stormers of Odin's wall;	*Odin's wall*: shields
when Thorir musters men	
so many, I make for safety.	

Grettir and his companion rode at full gallop down from the western side of the moor and past the farm at Gard before Thorir returned with his men. As they approached the farm they were joined by a man who did not recognize them. They saw a young woman standing outside the farm, dressed in fine clothes. Grettir asked who she was and the newcomer said it was Thorir's daughter.

Then Grettir spoke a verse:

57.

Empty as my words may often be,	
you shall tell your father,	
wise Sun-goddess who guards	*goddess who guards gold*: woman
the gold where the serpent sits,	
how I ride past his grand farm,	
a jewel mounted on the horse	*prow's land*: sea; its *horse*: ship;
that gallops the prow's land,	*jewel*: seafarer
and two men with me.	

From this verse the newcomer realized who the others were and rode to the farm to say that Grettir had just ridden past.

When Thorir returned home, many people certainly thought Grettir had pulled the wool over their eyes. Thorir mounted spies to look out for Grettir wherever he might go. Grettir's answer was to send his companion to the west of the district with their horses while he went up to the mountains disguised in a cowl. Then he went north at the beginning of winter and no one recognized him.

Everyone said Thorir had been given the same treatment as ever, or even worse, in his dealings with Grettir.

64 | There was a priest named Stein who lived at Eyjardalsa in Bardardal. He was a good farmer and a wealthy man and had an energetic, grown-up son named Kjartan.

There was a man named Thorstein the White who lived at Sandhaugar south of Eyjardalsa. His wife, Steinvor, was young and cheerful. They had some children who were young at this time. Their farm was haunted by trolls.

Two years before Grettir arrived in the north, Steinvor had gone to Eyjardalsa for Christmas Mass as usual, while her husband stayed home. Everyone went to bed that evening and in the night a great crashing noise was heard in the main room, moving in the direction of the farmer's bed. No one dared get out of bed and find out what it was, because there were very few people there. When his wife came home in the morning the farmer had vanished and no one knew what had become of him. A year went by.

The following winter the farmer's wife wanted to go to Christmas Mass again and told her farmhand to stay at home. He was reluctant, but told her to do as she pleased. The same thing happened: the farmhand vanished, and everyone thought this was a strange occurrence. Seeing splashes of blood by the front door, they realized that evil beings must have taken them both. Word of this incident spread far and wide.

Grettir heard about it and because he was particularly skilful at putting an end to hauntings and ghosts he set off for Bardardal, arriving at Sandhaugar on Christmas Eve. He went in disguise and called himself Gest (Visitor). The farmer's wife could see that he was exceptionally powerfully built, but the other people who lived there were afraid of him. He asked to be allowed to stay there.

The farmer's wife said there was food for him – 'but you stay here at your own risk.'

He agreed.

'I will stay here,' he said, 'and you can go to Mass if you wish.'

She replied, 'You must be a brave man to dare to stay here.'

'I'm a man of many talents,' he said.

'I don't fancy staying here,' she said, 'but I cannot cross the river.'

'I'll take you across it,' he said.

Then she made herself ready to go to Mass, and so did her small daughter. There had been a heavy thaw and the river was swollen, with clumps of ice floating down it.

The farmer's wife said, 'Neither horses nor men can cross this river.'

'There are always places to ford,' said Gest. 'Don't be afraid.'

'Carry the girl over first,' said the farmer's wife. 'She's lighter than I am.'

'I can't be bothered to make two trips,' said Gest. 'I'll carry you both on my arm.'

She made the sign of the Cross and said, 'There's no way you'll ever make it. What will you do with the girl?'

'I'll find a way,' he said, snatching them up and seating the girl in her mother's lap. Then he carried them both on his left arm in order to leave his right arm free, and waded out into the river.

They were too scared even to scream. The river broke over his chest the moment he entered the water, then a huge clump of ice drifted towards him, but he thrust out his free hand and deflected it. Then the river became so deep that it broke over his shoulders. He waded on mightily until he reached the bank on the other side and set the women down on to land.

Then he turned back. It was dusk when he returned to Sandhaugar and he called out for his food. After eating his fill he told the people on the farm to go farther inside the main room, then he took the tables and spare timber and wedged them across the room to make a wall so high that none of them could get over it. No one dared to challenge what he was doing or utter a word of complaint. There was a door below the gable in the side wall to the room, with a platform by it. Gest lay down there without undressing. A light was left to burn in the room at the door, and Gest lay there well into the night.

When the farmer's wife arrived at Eyjardalsa for the Mass, everyone was astonished that she had managed to cross the river. She said she was not sure whether it was a man or a troll who had carried her across.

The priest said it was definitely a man, 'Although few are a match for him, and we'll keep quiet about this. He might be there to bring about a remedy to your troubles.'

The farmer's wife stayed there for the night.

65 | To return to Grettir. Towards midnight he heard a great noise, then a huge trollwoman entered the room. She was holding a trough in one hand and a big knife in the other. She looked around when she was inside and, seeing Gest lying there, rushed at him. He leapt up to confront her and they attacked each other ferociously and struggled for a long time in the room. She was stronger, but he dodged her cleverly. They smashed everything that was in their way, even the partition which divided the room crossways.

She dragged him out through the door and towards the front entrance, where he made a firm stand against her. She wanted to drag him outside the farmhouse, but could not manage it until they had broken down the entire door-frame and took it with them around their necks. Then she lugged him off down to the river, right up to the chasm. Gest was exhausted, but either had to brace himself or let her hurl him into it. They struggled all night and he felt he had never fought such a powerful beast before. She was pressing him so tightly to her body that he could do nothing with either of his arms except clutch at her waist. When they were on the edge of the chasm he lifted her off her feet and swung her off balance, freeing his right arm. At once he grabbed for the short-sword he was wearing, drew it, swung it at her shoulder and chopped off her right arm. He was released the moment she plunged into the chasm and under the waterfall.[69]

Gest the visitor was left stiff and exhausted and lay on the edge of the cliff for a long time. He went back at daybreak and lay down on the bed, swollen and bruised.

When the farmer's wife came back from the Mass she saw the mess in her house, went over to Gest and asked him what had happened there that everything was broken and smashed. He told her about the entire episode and she found it remarkable and asked him his name. He told her his real name and told her to fetch the priest, saying that he wanted to talk to him. This was done.

When Stein the priest arrived at Sandhaugar he realized at once that it was Grettir Asmundarson who called himself Gest. The priest asked him what he thought might have happened to the men who had vanished and Grettir said he assumed they had gone into the chasm. The priest said he could not believe his stories without seeing any proof, but Grettir said they would find out for sure later. Then the priest went home. Grettir lay in bed for many days, the farmer's wife treated him very well and Christmas came and went.

According to Grettir, the trollwoman plunged into the chasm when she received her wound, but the people of Bardardal claim she turned to stone at daybreak while they were wrestling and died when he chopped off her arm – and is still standing there on the cliff, as a rock in the shape of a woman.[70] The people who lived in the valley hid Grettir there that winter.

One day after Christmas Grettir went to Eyjardalsa and when he saw the priest he said to him: 'I notice that you don't have much faith in my account, so I want you to go down to the river with me and see how probable you think it is.'

The priest agreed. When they reached the waterfall they saw a cave in the cliff face, which was so sheer that no one could climb it and was almost ten fathoms down to the water. They had taken a rope with them.

The priest said, 'It looks way beyond what you can manage, to go down there.'

Grettir replied, 'There is a way, and all the greater for great men. I'll take a look at what's in the cave while you keep an eye on the rope.'

The priest said it was up to him, drove a peg into the top of the cliff and piled rocks around it.

66 | Next, Grettir looped the end of the rope around a rock and lowered it down to the water.

'How do you plan to get down there now?' asked the priest.

'I don't want to be tied to anything when I enter the waterfall,' said Grettir. 'I have an intuition.'

Afterwards he prepared himself to set off. He removed most of his clothes and girded on his short-sword, but did not take any other weapons. Then he leapt over the side of the cliff and down into the waterfall. The priest watched the soles of his feet disappear, then had no idea what had become of him. Grettir dived under the waterfall, which was no easy task because to avoid the swirling current he had to dive right down to the bottom before he could resurface on the other side. There was a ledge that he climbed on to. Behind the waterfall, where the river plunged over the side of the cliff, was a huge cave.

He entered the cave, where a great log fire was burning. Grettir saw a giant lying there, monstrous in size and terrible to behold. When Grettir approached it, the giant snatched up a pike and swung a blow at the intruder. Known as a shafted sword,[71] this pike was equally suited for striking or stabbing and had a wooden shaft. Grettir returned the blow with his short-sword, striking the shaft and chopping through it. The giant tried to reach behind him for a sword that was hanging on the wall of the cave, but as he did so Grettir struck him on the breast, slicing his lower ribs and belly straight off and sending his innards gushing out into the river where they were swept away.

The priest, sitting by the rope, saw some slimy, bloodstained strands floating in the current. He panicked, convinced that Grettir was dead, abandoned the rope and went home. It was evening by then. The priest said that Grettir was certainly dead and described it as a great loss.

To return to Grettir. He struck a few quick blows at the giant until he was dead, then went inside the cave. He lit a flame and looked around. It is not said how much treasure he found there, but people assume it was a great hoard. He stayed there into the night, found the bones of two men and put them into a bag. Then he made his way out of the cave, swam back to the rope and shook it, expecting the priest to be there. When he realized the priest had gone, he had to clamber up it with his hands and finally made it to the cliff top.

Then he headed back to Eyjardalsa, went to the church porch and left the bag there, which had the bones in it and a rune-stick beautifully carved with this verse:

58.

I entered the black chasm where
the plummeting rock face gaped
with its cold spraying mouth
at the maker of sword-showers.   *sword-showers*: battle
The plunging current pressed hard   *trollwoman's hall*: cave?
at my breast in the trollwoman's hall; *wife of the god of poets*: Idunn,
the wife of the god of poets   wife of Bragi; a concealed pun
burdened my shoulders with her hate.   on the word *ida*, 'eddy'

And also this one:

59.

The trollwoman's ugly lover
came at me from his cave,
made his long and bold
struggle with me, for certain.
I snapped his hard-edged pike
away from its shaft – my sword,
ablaze with battle, split
open his breast and black belly.

The runes also stated that Grettir had taken these bones from the cave. When the priest went to church the next morning he found the stick and all the rest, and read the runes. By then, Grettir had gone back to Sandhaugar.

67 | The next time the priest saw Grettir he asked him in detail
     | about the incident and Grettir told him the entire story of
his voyage, adding that the priest had not kept a very trustworthy hold on the rope, which the priest admitted. People
realized that these evil beings had been responsible for the
disappearances in the valley. No visitations or hauntings ever
occurred in the valley afterwards and Grettir was considered to
have rid the place of a great evil. The priest buried the bones in
the churchyard.

Grettir spent the winter at Sandhaugar, keeping a low profile.
But when Thorir from Gard heard a rumour that Grettir was
in Bardardal, he sent a party off to claim his life. People advised
Grettir to leave, so he set off westwards.

When he reached Gudmund the Powerful's[72] farm at Modruvellir, Grettir asked him for help, but Gudmund said it was
unsuitable to take him in.

'Your only option,' he said, 'is to settle down somewhere
where you do not need to live in fear of your life.'

Grettir said he did not know where that might be.

Gudmund said, 'There is an island in Skagafjord named
Drangey. It is a good place to mount a defence, because it can
only be ascended by ladder. If you could get up there I cannot
imagine anyone would ever hope to overcome you by weapons
or trickery, provided you keep a close watch over the ladders.'

'Let it be put to the test, then,' said Grettir. 'But I have grown
so afraid of the dark that I could not be alone even if my life
depended on it.'

Gudmund said, 'That may be, but never have greater faith in
anyone other than yourself. Many people are not all that they
seem.'

Grettir thanked him for his advice and left Modruvellir, not
stopping until he reached Bjarg. His mother welcomed him
warmly and so did Illugi. He spent a few nights there and heard
that Thorstein Kuggason had been killed in the autumn before
Grettir went to Bardardal. Now he felt his enemies were definitely beginning to close in on him.

Then Grettir rode south over Holtavarda heath, planning to take vengeance for Hallmund's death if he ran into Grim. But when he reached Nordurardal he heard that Grim had left two or three years previously, as described earlier. Grettir found out this news so late because he had spent two years in hiding and a third in Thorisdal and had not met anyone who would tell him any news.

Then he headed for the valleys of Breidafjord and waited in ambush for travellers crossing Brattabrekka. Once again he helped himself to the crofters' belongings. This was in midsummer.

Towards the end of that summer, Steinvor from Sandhaugar gave birth to a boy named Skeggi. At first he was said to be the son of Kjartan, the son of the priest at Eyjardalsa. Skeggi was distinguished from all his brothers and sisters by his strength and build. By the age of fifteen he was the strongest person in north Iceland, and then his paternity was attributed to Grettir. Everyone thought he would grow into an outstanding man, but he died at the age of sixteen and there are no stories about him.

68 | After Thorstein Kuggason was killed, Snorri the Godi grew very cold towards his own son Thorodd and Bork the Stout's son Sam.[73] The reason is not described, except that they had refused to carry out some great deed which Snorri had put to them. Snorri the Godi threw Thorodd out of his home and told him not to come back until he had killed an outlaw, and there the matter rested. Thorodd moved to the Dales.

There was a widow named Geirlaug who lived at Breidabolstad in Sokkolfsdal. She was harbouring a young man who had been outlawed for wounding someone, and put him to work as her shepherd. Snorri's son Thorodd heard this, rode over to Breidabolstad and asked where the shepherd was.

The widow said he was watching over the sheep. 'What do you want of him, anyway?'

'I want his life,' said Thorodd. 'He is an outlaw.'

She replied, 'You won't gain much prestige by killing a wretch like him. Since you have such a great opinion of your own bravery, I can point out a much greater feat to undertake if you really have a mind to put yourself to the test.'

'What's that?' he asked.

She replied, 'Grettir Asmundarson is hiding in the mountains up there. Take him on. That's much more your calibre.'

Thorodd welcomed the idea and said, 'I'll go and do that.'

He drove his spurs into his horse and rode up the valley. When he reached the hills below the River Austura, he saw a fawn horse with a saddle on it. He also saw a big man who had weapons with him, and went over to him. Grettir greeted him and asked him who he was.

Thorodd told him his name and asked, 'Why don't you ask what I'm here for, instead of my name?'

'Because it's bound to be some trifle,' said Grettir. 'Aren't you Snorri the Godi's son?'

'That I am,' said Thorodd. 'And now we will find out which of us is the stronger.'

'That's easy,' said Grettir. 'Haven't you heard that I don't bring much luck to most people who touch me?'

'I know that,' said Thorodd, 'but the time has come to risk it.'

He drew his sword and attacked furiously, while Grettir defended himself with his shield without raising his weapon against Thorodd. This went on for a while and Grettir did not sustain any wounds.

Then Grettir said, 'Let's put a stop to this game. You'll never take me on and win.'

Thorodd struck as hard as he could.

Grettir grew bored of dealing with Thorodd, grabbed hold of him, sat him down beside him and said, 'I can do exactly as I please with you and I'm not afraid of being killed by you, but I am afraid of that old grey-haired father of yours, Snorri the Godi, and his plans. They've brought about the downfall of many a man. You should choose yourself a task that you are up to. Fighting with me isn't child's play.'

When Thorodd saw that he was not making any headway he calmed down somewhat, and they went their separate ways.

Thorodd rode home to Tunga and told his father about what had passed between him and Grettir.

Snorri the Godi smiled and said, 'Many a man is blind to his own faults and this shows the great difference between the two of you. You struck blows at him and he could have done anything he wanted with you. But Grettir acted wisely by not killing you, because I would not have put up with your remaining unavenged. For my part, I will help him if I am present when his affairs are discussed.'

Snorri was moved that Grettir had treated Thorodd well and in all his plottings he proved to be Grettir's constant friend.

69 | Grettir rode north to Bjarg shortly after he and Thorodd parted, and remained there in hiding for a while. Then his fear of the dark became so intense that he did not dare go anywhere when it grew dark. His mother invited him to stay, but said she could see it would hardly help him, considering that he had people against him throughout the land.

Grettir told her she would not suffer any difficulties on his account: 'But I will not go on living, if the price is being alone,' he said.

His brother Illugi was fifteen years old at the time and highly accomplished. He was present at their conversation. Grettir told his mother what Gudmund the Powerful had advised him to do and said that he would try to find out if there was a chance of going to Drangey, but he would not be able to stay there unless he had a trustworthy man with him.

Then Illugi said, 'I will go with you, brother, but I do not know if my presence will be of any worth to you, apart from the fact that I'll be loyal to you and not run away for as long as you stand, and I will be fully aware of how you are getting on if I accompany you.'

Grettir replied, 'You are the man in whose company I am most cheerful, and if my mother does not object I would gladly have you come with me.'

Then Asdis said, 'I have come to the point where I am on the horns of a dilemma. I cannot lose Illugi, yet I know that Grettir is in such a predicament that some action has to be taken. Much as I regret seeing you both depart, my sons, this is what I want if it makes Grettir's lot better than before.'

Illugi was pleased at her words and looked forward to going with Grettir. She gave them a lot of money and they made preparations to leave.

Asdis led them off from the farm and before they parted she spoke these words: 'There you go, my two sons, and your deaths will be the saddest of all, but no one can avoid what is ordained. I will never see either of you again. Meet the same fate. I do not know what fortune you seek in Drangey, but you will both perish there and many people will begrudge your presence there. Be on your guard against treachery. You will be killed by weapons; I have had strange dreams. Be wary of sorcery; few things are mightier than black magic.'

After saying this, she burst into tears.

Then Grettir said, 'Do not weep, mother. If we are killed it will be said of you that you had sons, not daughters. Live well and in good health.'

After that, they parted.

Then they travelled north through the countryside and met their kinsmen. They stayed there for the autumn and into the winter. Then they headed for Skagafjord, went northwards through Vatnsskard and on to Reykjaskard, then down the slope at Saemundarhlid and on to Langholt. They reached Glaumbaer late in the day. Grettir kept his hood off, as he always did outdoors, whatever the weather.

After they had moved on a short way, a man came up to them from the opposite direction. He had a large head and was tall, slim and poorly dressed. He greeted them and asked them their names. They told him and he said he was named Thorbjorn. He was a vagrant who could not be bothered to work, and very boastful; people made great fun of him and some even played tricks on him. He tried to impress them and told them many stories about the local people. Grettir found him highly amusing.

He asked whether they needed someone to work for them.

'I'd like to go with you,' he said.

Then he talked them into letting him go along with them. The snow was drifting heavily and the weather was cold. Because he was boisterous and a great joker, he was nicknamed Glaum (Merrymaker).

'When you went around bareheaded in that storm,' said Glaum, 'the people at Glaumbaer were very curious about whether you are as strong as you are insensitive to the cold. There were two farmer's sons there, quite uncommonly strong, and the shepherd called them out to tend the sheep with him, but they claimed they were so cold they could hardly dress.'

Grettir said, 'I saw a young man in a doorway pulling on his gloves and another walking between the cattleshed and the compost heap. I could hardly be afraid of either of them.'

Then they went to Reynines and spent the night there. From there they went out to the shore to the farm named Reykir where a man named Thorvald lived, a good farmer. Grettir asked him for help and told him of his plans to go out to Drangey. The farmer said that the people in Skagafjord would not regard him as a friendly gift, and he refused to commit himself. Then Grettir took the money that his mother had let him have and gave it to the farmer. His brows lifted when he saw the money and then he ordered his farmhands to ferry them out at night, by moonlight. Reykir is the closest point on land to the island, four miles away.

When they reached the island Grettir was impressed by what he saw, because it was covered in grass but had cliffs that rose so steeply from the sea that they could not be ascended except by putting ladders up to them. If the upper ladder was then pulled up, it was impossible for anyone to land on the island. There was also a large bird colony on the cliffs in summer. Eighty sheep were kept on the island, too, owned by farmers from the mainland. They were mainly rams and ewes that were intended for slaughter. Grettir settled down there. By that time he had been an outlaw for fifteen or sixteen years,[74] according to Sturla Thordarson.

70 | These were the chieftains in the district of Skagafjord
     when Grettir arrived in Drangey: Hjalti who lived at Hof
in Hjaltadal, the son of Thord Hjaltason whose grandfather
was Thord Skalp. Hjalti was a chieftain, a very noble and
popular man. His brother was named Thorbjorn Hook, a big,
strong man, tough to deal with and ruthless. Their father,
Thord, had married late in life and his wife was not their
mother. She treated her stepchildren badly and Thorbjorn worst
of all, because he was difficult and brutal.

Once when Thorbjorn was sitting and playing a board game
using big pieces that fitted into the board on long pins, his
stepmother walked by and saw him playing the game. She
thought he was idling away his time, so she threw a few remarks
in his direction and he answered her back insolently. Then she
picked up one of the pieces and struck Thorbjorn on the cheek
with the peg on it, but it glanced off into his eye, gouging it out
on to his cheek. He leapt to his feet and gave her such a drubbing
that she was confined to bed by it and then died from the
beating. People said that she had been pregnant at the time.
After that, Thorbjorn became a great troublemaker. He took
his inheritance and lived at first in Vidvik.

Halldor, the son of Thorgeir and grandson of Thord from
Hofdi, lived at Hof on the Hofdi coast. He was married to
Thordis, the daughter of Thord and sister of Hjalti and
Thorbjorn Hook. Halldor was a worthy farmer and very
wealthy.

There was a man named Bjorn who lived at Haganes in Fljot.
He was a friend of Halldor from Hof and they supported each
other in every matter.

A man named Tungu-Stein lived at Steinsstadir. His father
was Bjorn, the son of Ofeig Thin-beard. Ofeig was the son of
Crow-Hreidar, to whose father Eirik from Goddalir gave the
tongue of land down from the marsh at Skalamyri. Stein was a
man of renown.

There was a man named Eirik, the son of Starri the Dueller
and grandson of Eirik from Goddalir, whose father was Hroald,

the son of Geirmund Stiff-beard. Eirik, Starri's son, lived at Hof in Goddalir. All these men were highly respected.

Two brothers lived at Breida in Slettahlid and they were both named Thord. They were men of great strength, yet peaceable.

All of these men owned a share in the island of Drangey. Some people say that no fewer than twenty men shared the island and that none of them would sell his share to any other. Thord's sons owned the largest shares, because they were the wealthiest.

71 | Time passed until the winter solstice when the farmers made ready to fetch their sheep from the island for slaughtering. They manned a boat and each of them took at least one person with him; some had two. When they approached the island they could see people moving around. This struck them as strange and they imagined that a ship had been wrecked and its crew had come ashore there. They rowed up to where the ladders were, but the people above pulled up the ladders. Puzzled by this, the farmers called out to them and asked who was there. Grettir told them his name and those of his companions. The farmers asked who had ferried him out to the island.

Grettir replied, 'Someone ferried me here who had a boat and a pair of hands and was more a friend of mine than yours.'

The farmers answered, 'Let us fetch our sheep and take them back to land with us and you can keep for nothing the sheep of ours that you've slaughtered.'

'That's a fine offer,' Grettir replied, 'but now each of us will keep what we already have. I'll tell you straight out that I won't leave here unless I'm dragged away dead. I'm not letting go of what I've got my hands on.'

The farmers fell silent, feeling that a great bringer of woe had come to Drangey. They offered him expensive gifts and fine promises, but Grettir refused them all and the farmers went away again, dissatisfied with their lot. They told the people of the district who this scavenger was who had gone to the island.

This news took them by surprise and they did not think any action could be taken. They talked the matter over during the winter and could not see a plan for removing Grettir from the island.

72 | Time went by until the Hegranes Assembly came around in the spring. There was a great gathering from all the districts that the assembly covered. They spent much of the spring engaged in both legal cases and festivities, because at that time there were many men in these districts who liked celebrating.

When Grettir heard that most of the local people had gone to the assembly he made plans with his friends, because he always remained on good terms with those who were closest to him and did not spare anything that he had acquired. He said that he wanted to fetch provisions from land, but that Illugi and Glaum should stay behind. Illugi thought this inadvisable, but let Grettir have his way. Grettir told them to guard the ladder, saying it was important. Then he went to the land and took what he thought he needed. He went everywhere secretly and no one realized he was on land. He heard that there were great festivities at the assembly and was curious to go there, so he took an old, rather shabby costume and arrived at the assembly as people were leaving the Law Council on their way back to their booths.

Some young men said that the weather was fine and pleasant, and that it would do them good to arrange wrestling matches and entertainment. Everyone agreed that this was a good idea and went to sit down near the booths. Thord's sons were largely in charge of the entertainment.

Thorbjorn Hook was a bossy character and organized the entertainment in a forceful way; everyone had to do what he wanted. He grabbed people by the shoulders and tossed them into the ring. The first to wrestle were the weakest, then each in turn, and everyone had great fun.

When most of the men had wrestled, except for the very strongest, the farmers talked over who would be prepared to wrestle with either of the brothers named Thord mentioned earlier, but no one was willing to. They went up to various men and challenged them, but the harder they were pressed, the more reluctant they became.

Then Thorbjorn Hook took a look around and noticed a heavily built man sitting there, but could not see his face clearly. Thorbjorn grabbed at him and tugged him, but he stayed where he was and did not budge.

Then Thorbjorn said, 'No one has held his ground as firmly as you today. Who is this man?'

Grettir replied, 'I'm called Gest (Visitor).'

'Surely you want to take part in the entertainment,' said Thorbjorn. 'You're a welcome guest.'

'I think that many things are quick to change,' said Gest. 'I won't jump to my feet and play a game with you, since I'm a complete stranger here.'

Many people said he would deserve to be treated well if he, a stranger, was willing to give them a little entertainment. He asked what they wanted of him, and they told him to wrestle with someone.

He said that he had given up brawling – 'but I used to enjoy it for a while.'

Since he did not refuse absolutely, they urged him all the more.

Then he said, 'If you set so much store by having me join in, you can have it your way if you guarantee my security here at the assembly and until I get back home.'

They all leapt to their feet and said they would gladly do so. There was a man named Haf who urged them most of all to guarantee the man his security. He was the son of Thorarin, whose father was named Haf and his grandfather Thord Knapp, who had taken the land from Stifla in Fljot to the River Tungua. Haf lived at Knappsstadir and was a great speaker. He proposed the pledge of safety with great conviction, and this is the opening of his speech:[75]

'I hereby proclaim safety among all men, in particular for the same Gest who is sitting here, including all godis and worthy farmers and every common man who is able to fight and bear weapons, and all other people of the district of the Hegranes

Assembly or wherever they come from, named or unnamed, let us pledge safety and full peace to this unknown visitor called Gest, in play and wrestling and all entertainment, for his stay here and journey home, whether he needs to go by sea or over land and by whatever means of transport. He will be safe in all places, named and unnamed, for as long as he needs to return home safe and sound, while these pledges hold. I proclaim this truce for us and our kinsmen, friends and relatives, for men as for women, bondswomen and slaves, servants and free men. Any man will be a truce-breaker who breaks this truce or violates this pledge, banished and cast out from God and good men, from heaven and from all holy men, unfit for the company of men and in all places driven out like an outlaw wherever truce-breakers drift or Christian men attend church or heathen men sacrifice in their temples, where flame burns, earth grows, an infant calls its mother and a mother bears a son, where man kindles fire, a ship sails, shields glint, the sun shines, snow settles, a Lapp skis, a fir-tree grows, the eagle flies for the whole spring day with a firm wind beneath both wings, the firmament arches, the world is settled and the wind carries water to the sea, slaves sow grain. He will be barred from churches and the company of Christian men, heathens, houses and caves, from every world except Hell. Let us now be in accord and agreement with each other and of good mind whether we meet on mountain or shore, ship or skis, earth or glacier, on the ocean or on horseback, like a man who meets his friend by water or his brother on a road, as reconciled with each other as a son with his father or a father with his son in all our dealings. Let us now join hands and keep this truce firmly and all words spoken in this pledge, witnessed by God and all good men and all those who hear my words or are present now.'

Many people remarked that these were great words.

Then Gest said, 'You have proclaimed and spoken well, if you do not break your word later. Now I will not hesitate to make my contribution.'

After that he threw off his cowl and stripped to the waist. All the men looked at each other with expressions of alarm. They realized that this was Grettir Asmundarson, because he surpassed all other men in physique and strength. Everyone fell silent and Haf realized he had acted rashly. The local people grouped into pairs and each accused the other, but most of all they blamed the man who had proposed the pledge of safety.

Then Grettir said, 'Tell me plainly what you are pondering, because I will not sit here unclothed for long. There is more at stake for you than for me, whether you keep the truce or break it.'

They said little in reply and sat down. Thord's sons and their brother-in-law Halldor began talking among themselves. Some of the people wanted to keep the truce, but others did not. They all nodded to each other.

Then Grettir spoke a verse:

> 60.
> I have gone unrecognized this morning
> by many necklace-bearers,   *necklace-bearers*: men
> stormers of shields in battle   *stormers of shields*: warriors, men
> do not know which face to wear.
> A challenging game has been offered
> to men of stinging speech,
> they waver in keeping their word:
> Haf's bombast has ebbed away.

Then Tungu-Stein said, 'Do you think that's the way it is, Grettir? What do you think the chieftains will decide to do? It's true that you're a man of outstanding strength. But can't you see the way they are putting their heads together?'

Then Grettir spoke a verse:

> 61.
> The lifters of valkyrie's drapes   *valkyrie's drapes*: shields
> are rubbing their noses together,
> trees that ram the war-goddess's wall   *war-goddess's wall*: shields
> are jousting with their beards.
> With harsh minds they team up,
> plunderers of the dragon's bed,   *dragon's bed*: gold
> regretting the truce
> that they proclaimed to me.

Then Thord's son Hjalti spoke: 'This will not be done. We will keep our pledge, even though we were not as wise as you. I don't want to set people an example by breaking the truce that we ourselves have declared and pledged. Grettir will be free to go where he wants and be safe until he returns from this journey. Then our pledges will be over, whatever happens between us.'

Everybody thanked him and felt he had acted nobly, considering the circumstances. While he spoke, Thorbjorn Hook fell silent.

Then it was suggested that one of the two Thords should wrestle with Grettir and he said it was up to them to decide. One of the brothers came forward. Grettir stood there firmly and Thord took a swift run at him, but he did not budge. Then Grettir reached over Thord's back, took hold of his breeches and lifted him off his feet, then threw him backwards over his head so that he landed on his shoulders, suffering a considerable fall. People said that both brothers should tackle him at once and they did so. A great tussle ensued and each gained the upper hand in turn. Grettir always managed to keep one of the brothers on the ground, but all three of them went down on their knees or were thrown down. They wrestled so hard that they were bruised and scratched all over. Everyone greatly enjoyed the match.

When they finished, everyone thanked them for the wrestling match and the spectators agreed that the two of them were no stronger than Grettir alone, even though they were each a match for two strong men. The brothers were so equal in strength that neither could outdo the other when they wrestled together.

Grettir did not stay at the assembly for long. The farmers told him to give up the island, but he refused and they could do nothing about it.

Grettir returned to Drangey and Illugi welcomed him gladly. They stayed there quietly and Grettir told the others about his journey. The summer went by.

Everybody felt the people of Skagafjord had acted very nobly by honouring their pledges so well. Considering the offence that Grettir had caused them, it can be seen what trustworthy men lived there then.

The less wealthy farmers agreed among themselves that there was little to be gained from owning small shares in Drangey and offered to sell them to Thord's sons, but Hjalti said he did not want to buy them. Moreover, the farmers made a condition that whoever wanted to buy their shares would either have to kill Grettir or drive him away from the island. Thorbjorn Hook said he would not flinch from leading an attack on Grettir if they would pay him to do so. Hjalti made over his share in the island to his brother Thorbjorn, who was the more ruthless of the two and an unpopular man. More farmers followed suit. Thorbjorn acquired a large share in the island for a small price and he undertook to drive Grettir away.[76]

73 | Late in the summer Thorbjorn Hook took a fully manned boat to Drangey, and Grettir and his men went to the edge of the cliff. They talked together and Thorbjorn asked Grettir to do him a favour and leave the island. Grettir said there was no hope of that.

Thorbjorn said, 'I might be able to lend you some assistance if you do so. Many of the farmers have made over their shares in the island to me now.'

Grettir replied, 'Now you have confirmed my resolution never to leave, by telling me that you own the greater part of this island. It's fitting for us to share the scurvy-grass here. It is true that I found it tough having the whole of Skagafjord against me, but in this case I will stop at nothing, because neither of us is smothered by popularity. You might as well stop coming here, because my mind is made up.'

'There is a time for everything,' said Thorbjorn, 'and you will come to grief.'

'I will take that risk,' said Grettir, and they parted.

Thorbjorn went back home.

74 | It is said that by the time Grettir, Illugi and Glaum had
     | spent two years on Drangey they had slaughtered almost
all the sheep that were there. But it is mentioned that they
spared the life of one ram, which had a grey belly and big horns.
They made a lot of fun of it, because it was so tame it would
wait outside for them and run after them wherever they went.
It would go back to their hut in the evening and rub its horns
against the door.

They enjoyed being on the island, because there was plenty
of food from birds and eggs. But firewood was in very short
supply. Grettir always made Glaum watch out for driftwood.
Wood was often washed ashore which he brought back for
firewood. The brothers had no work to do apart from catching
birds and gathering eggs on the cliffs when they felt like it.

Glaum began to grow very lazy about his work. He started
to complain about it and took less care than before. It was his
job to guard the fire every night and Grettir warned him firmly
about doing so, because they had no boat with them.

One night, the fire happened to go out. Grettir turned surly
and said that Glaum deserved to be thrashed. Glaum said his
life was a misery being stuck in exile and scolded and beaten if
anything went wrong. Grettir asked Illugi what they could do
and he said that as far as he could see they would have to wait
there until a boat came along.

Grettir said that was a hopeless approach – 'I would rather
risk trying to make it to land.'

'That seems a huge chance to take,' said Illugi, 'because we're
lost if anything happens to you.'

'I won't drown while I'm swimming,' Grettir said, 'but I'll
have much less faith in the slave in future, since so much was
at stake for us.'

The shortest route to land was four miles from the island.

75 | Grettir prepared for his swim by putting on a homespun cowl and breeches and having his fingers wrapped up together. The weather was good and he left the island late in the day. Illugi thought his voyage boded ill.

Grettir swam into the fjord with the current behind him and it was completely calm. He swam vigorously and reached Reykjanes when the sun had set, then went up to the farm at Reykir and bathed in the hot pool there, because he was quite cold. After a long bask in the pool that night, he went into the main room. It was very hot there, since the fire had been alight that evening and the room had hardly cooled down. He was very weary, fell fast asleep and lay there into the day.

In the morning, the people on the farm got up and two women were the first to enter the main room, a servant-woman and the farmer's daughter. Grettir was asleep and his clothes had slipped off on to the floor. They saw a man lying there whom they recognized.

Then the servant-woman said, 'Upon my word, sister, Grettir Asmundarson is here, lying naked. He looks big-framed to me all right, but I'm astonished to see how poorly endowed he is between his legs. It's not in proportion to the rest of him.'

The farmer's daughter answered, 'Why can't you ever keep your mouth shut? You're no ordinary idiot – just keep quiet.'

'I can't keep quiet about that, sister,' the servant-woman said. 'I'd never have believed it if anyone had told me.'

Then she went over to take a peek and ran back to the farmer's daughter every so often, roaring with laughter.

Grettir heard what she said. And when she ran across the floor once more he grabbed her and spoke a verse:

62.

That wench takes things too lightly:
Few invokers of spear-storms   *spear-storms*: battles;
have much choice about the sword   their *invokers*: warriors
that adorns their forest of hair.

I bet I have twice the balls
that other spear-thrusters boast,
even if their shafts
can outstretch mine.

He snatched her up on to the cross-bench and the farmer's
daughter ran out of the room. Then Grettir spoke a verse:

63.
The seamstress sitting at home,
short-sworded she calls me;
maybe the boastful hand-maiden
of ball-trunks is telling the truth.   *ball-trunks*: penises
But a young man like me
can expect sprouts to grow
in the groin-forest: get ready
for action, splay-legged goddess.

The servant-woman shouted at the top of her voice, but when
she left Grettir she did not taunt him again.

Soon afterwards he stood up, went over to Thorvald the
farmer, told him of his problem with the fire and asked him to
ferry him back. He did so, borrowed a boat and took him to
the island and Grettir thanked him for his noble gesture.

When word got around that Grettir had swum four miles,
everyone was full of admiration for his feats both on land and
at sea.

The people of Skagafjord criticized Thorbjorn Hook heavily
for not driving Grettir from Drangey and said they would take
back their shares in the island. He could not see any way out
of his problem, but asked them to be patient.

76 | That summer a ship arrived at the Gonguskard estuary
    | with a man named Haering on board. He was young and
so fit that he could climb any cliff. He went to stay with
Thorbjorn Hook and was there into the autumn. Haering urged
Thorbjorn to go to Drangey, saying he wanted to see whether
the cliff was so great that it could not be climbed in any place.

Thorbjorn said he would certainly not go unrewarded if he got on to the island and managed to wound Grettir or kill him. He made it all sound very feasible to Haering.

Afterwards they went to Drangey and put the Norwegian ashore somewhere. He was supposed to take Grettir and the others unawares if he managed to scale the cliff, while Thorbjorn and his men brought their boat to the ladder and started talking to Grettir. Thorbjorn asked whether he wasn't planning to leave the island, but Grettir replied that there was nothing he was more determined to do than stay put.

'You have played many tricks on us,' said Thorbjorn, 'even if we do manage to take revenge, and you do not seem to fear much for your safety.'

They went on like this for a long time and did not reach any agreement.

To return to Haering, he climbed back and forth on the cliff face and managed to scale it in a place where no man has succeeded either before or since. When he reached the top of the cliff he saw where Grettir and Illugi were standing with their backs turned to him. He thought of winning immediate wealth and renown. The brothers were unaware of his movements, because they thought the island was inaccessible except where the ladder was. Grettir was arguing with Thorbjorn and his men and there was no lack of threatening words on either side. Then Illugi happened to glance around and saw a man right behind them.

Illugi said, 'There's a man coming for us wielding his axe and he looks rather hostile to me.'

'Go and deal with him, then,' said Grettir, 'and I'll guard the ladder.'

Illugi went to face Haering and when the Norwegian saw him he ran off across the island. Illugi chased him the length of the island and when Haering reached the edge of the cliff he jumped off it, breaking every bone in his body. His life came to an end there. The place where he perished has been called Haeringshlaup (Haering's Leap) ever since.

Illugi went back and Grettir asked him how he had left the man he had been sent after.

'He wouldn't trust me to take care of him,' said Illugi, 'so he broke his neck for himself at the foot of the cliff. May the farmers pray for him as a dead man.'

When Thorbjorn Hook heard this, he told his men to cast off: 'I have made two expeditions against Grettir now and I won't be going a third time unless I am somehow the wiser. They seem likely to stay on Drangey, no matter what I can do about it. But I think Grettir will not stay here for as long as he has until now.'

Then they went home and this trip was considered even worse than the one before. Grettir spent the winter in Drangey and he and Thorbjorn did not meet again that winter.

At this time Skafti Thoroddsson the Lawspeaker died. This was a great setback to Grettir, since he had promised to advocate the commutation of Grettir's sentence when he had been in outlawry for twenty years. It was the nineteenth year of his outlawry when the events just described took place.

In the spring Snorri the Godi died and many incidents occurred at this time which do not come into this story.

77 | At the Althing that summer, Grettir's kinsmen discussed his outlawry at length. Some of them felt that he had completed his sentence,[77] since he was well into the twentieth year of it. However, the people who had brought charges against him would not accept this, claiming he had committed many deeds that deserved outlawry since then and therefore his sentence should be correspondingly longer. A new Lawspeaker had been appointed, Stein Thorgestsson, whose grandfather was Stein the Much-travelled, son of Thorir Autumn-darkness. Stein the Lawspeaker's mother was Arnora, the daughter of Thord Bellower. Stein was a wise man. He was asked to make a ruling and told them to check whether this was the twentieth summer since Grettir had been outlawed. This proved to be the case.

Then Thorir from Gard joined in and tried to find every possible objection. He managed to discover that Grettir had spent one year in Iceland when he was not an outlaw, meaning that he had been an outlaw for eighteen years.

The Lawspeaker said that no man should be an outlaw for more than twenty years, even if some years of his sentences overlapped – 'But before that time I will not deem to have anyone's outlawry lifted.'

Grettir's commutation from outlawry was ruled out on these grounds for the time being, but it seemed certain that the sentence would be lifted the following summer.

The people of Skagafjord were displeased by the prospect of Grettir's outlawry being lifted and asked Thorbjorn Hook either to hand back the island or kill Grettir. He found himself in a dilemma, since he did not know any way to overcome Grettir, but nevertheless wanted to keep the island. He sought all means of getting rid of Grettir, either with ruthless action or trickery or any other way he could bring it about.

78 | Thorbjorn Hook had a foster-mother named Thurid who was very old and not considered capable of doing much. She had been well versed in magic and knew many secret arts when she was young and people were heathen, but by this time it was thought she had lost all her powers. Yet although Christianity had been adopted in Iceland, many vestiges of paganism remained. It had been the law in Iceland that sacrifices and other black magic were not forbidden if they were practised in private, but were punishable by lesser outlawry if done publicly. For many people then it was true that a firm habit is hard to shake off and what is learnt in childhood becomes second nature. Since Thorbjorn was completely stumped he sought guidance where most people would have thought it least likely to be found, from his foster-mother, and asked her what advice she could give him.

She answered him, 'I think this goes to prove the old saying that many people go to the goat-shed looking for wool. What should I want less than to pretend to be greater than everyone else in this district and then turn out to be useless when it came to the test? But as far as I can see I cannot do any worse than you, almost bedridden as I am. If you want my advice, I must also decide how you should employ it.'

He agreed and said she had always offered him good counsel. Nothing else happened until hay-time.

One day the crone said to Thorbjorn, 'The weather is calm and clear today. I want you to go to Drangey and pick a quarrel with Grettir. I'll go with you and see how guarded he is in his speech. That will give me something tangible to work with when I see how Providence favours them and then I will make such words over them as I see fit.'

Hook answered, 'These trips to Drangey are becoming tedious, because when I go there I always return feeling worse.'

Then the crone said, 'I won't offer you any advice if you don't leave anything up to me to decide.'

'That won't happen, foster-mother,' he said, 'but I have said that I only want to go there a third time if I am in a better position.'

'You'll have to risk that,' the crone said. 'You'll have a lot of trouble before Grettir is laid low and the outcome for you will often seem uncertain. And you will pay the price for it in the end. But you have made such commitments that something has to be done.'

After that, Thorbjorn had a ten-oared boat launched and went aboard with eleven other men. The old woman was with them. They rowed out to Drangey and when Grettir and his brother saw them they went to the ladder and started discussing their affairs once again. Thorbjorn told Grettir that he had come yet again to find out if he would leave, saying that he would ignore what it had cost him and Grettir's stay on the island, if they parted with no harm done.

Grettir said he would not make or accept a compromise about leaving.

'I've told you that often enough and there's no need to discuss it with me,' he said. 'You can do as you please, but I'll stay here and take whatever comes.'

Realizing that he would not gain anything this time, Thorbjorn said, 'I think I know the sort of fiends I have to deal with here. A good few days are likely to pass before I come back again.'

'I won't consider it a great loss if you never come back,' Grettir replied.

The crone was lying in the stern of the boat, under some blankets.

Then she stirred and said, 'These men are brave, but Fortune does not go with them. There is a great difference between you. You have made them many fine offers, but they turn them all down and there are few more certain ways to court trouble than to refuse what is good. Now I curse you, Grettir, to be deprived of all favour, all endowments and fortune, all defence and wisdom, the more so the longer you live! I trust that you will have fewer days of happiness in the future than you have had until now!'

When Grettir heard this he was startled and said, 'What devil is that on the boat with them?'

Illugi replied, 'I think it's that old woman, Thorbjorn's foster-mother.'

'Curse the old witch!' said Grettir. 'That was the worst thing we could have expected. No words have ever unsettled me more than those that she spoke. I know that she and her sorcery will cause me harm. I'll give her something for visiting me,' and he grabbed a huge rock and hurled it down on to the boat, and it landed on the pile of blankets.

It was a longer throw than Thorbjorn imagined any man was capable of. A great shriek was heard. The rock had hit the old woman on her thigh and broken it.

Then Illugi said, 'I wish you hadn't done that.'

'Don't find fault with me for that,' Grettir said, 'but it disturbs me that it didn't hit her hard enough, because a crone's life wouldn't be too great a price to pay for both of ours.'

'How could she pay for us?' asked Illugi. 'That wouldn't make us worth much.'

Thorbjorn set off back home and they did not exchange farewells when they parted.

Then he said to the crone, 'It turned out as I expected: you did not earn much glory on your voyage to the island. You have been crippled and we are no closer to honour than before. We have to put up with not receiving compensation for one disgrace after another.'

She replied, 'This will be the beginning of their misfortune and I foresee that they will take a turn for the worse from now on. If I live to manage it, I do not fear being unable to take revenge for this incident they have brought upon me.'

'You speak like a woman of high courage, foster-mother,' said Thorbjorn.

They reached home and the old woman went to bed and was confined there for almost a month. By then her bad leg had set and she began getting about again.

People made great fun of their trip. They thought Thorbjorn had often been outwitted in his dealings with Grettir, first concerning the pledge of safety at the assembly, again when Haering perished and the third time when the old woman had her leg broken, without Thorbjorn being able to make any move against them in return. Thorbjorn Hook was greatly vexed by such comments.

79 | Autumn passed until three weeks were left until winter. Then the crone asked to be taken down to the sea. Thorbjorn asked her what she wanted to do.

'It's a trifling errand,' she said, 'but it may portend greater tidings.'

He did as she requested and when she reached the shore she hobbled along by the sea as if following directions until she came to a tree lying there, a stub with the roots on, big enough to have to be carried on a man's shoulders. She looked at the tree and asked the men to turn it over for her. The underside looked burnt and rubbed down. She made them scrape a flat surface where the tree had been rubbed, then took her knife and carved runes into the root, smeared them with her blood and recited spells. Then she walked backwards and wither-shins around it, and spoke many mighty pronouncements upon it.

After that she had the tree put to sea, pronouncing that it

should drift out to Drangey – 'and may it harm Grettir in every way.'

From there she went back home to Vidvik. Thorbjorn said he could not see the point of this, but the crone said he would certainly find out later. There was a wind blowing landwards along the fjord, but the crone's tree set off against the wind and did not seem to travel any the slower for it.

Grettir was still in Drangey, as mentioned before, with his companions, and they were all feeling contented with their lot. The day after the old woman had put her spell on the tree, Grettir and the others went down the cliff to look for firewood. When they reached the west side of the island they found the tree with its roots, washed ashore.

Illugi said, 'Here is plenty of firewood, kinsman. Let's carry it back.'

Grettir kicked at it with his foot.

'An evil tree by evil sent. We should find some other firewood,' he said, throwing it out to sea.

He told Illugi to take care not to carry it back – 'because it is sent to bring us bad fortune.'

After that they went back to their hut and did not mention the matter to Glaum. The following day they found the tree, closer to the ladder than before. Grettir put it back out to sea and said it should never be brought to where they lived. The night passed. A rainy gale got up and they did not feel like going outside, so they told Glaum to go and look for firewood. He complained at their cruelty in sending him out whenever the weather was bad. When he went down the ladder he found the old woman's tree and thinking he had done well for himself, he picked it up, struggled back to the hut and threw it down with a great thud.

When Grettir heard this he said, 'Glaum has found something. I'll go out and see what it is,' and he took his wood-axe and left.

Then Glaum said, 'Don't make a worse job of cutting it up than I did of bringing it back.'

Grettir lost his temper and swung his axe at the tree with

both hands, without bothering to see what tree it was. And the moment the axe struck the tree it slid flat and glanced off into Grettir's right leg above the knee, delivering a deep wound right to the bone.

Then he looked at the tree and said, 'The more evil intent has proved the more powerful, and this will not be the only time. This tree here is the one that I have twice thrown back to sea. You have caused us misfortune twice now, Glaum, once when you let our fire go out and now that you have brought back this tree of ill fortune. If you have a third mishap it will be the death of you and all of us.'

Illugi dressed Grettir's wound, which did not bleed much. Grettir slept well that night and three nights passed without the wound causing him any pain. When they undid the bandage, the cut had grown over so much that it was almost healed.

Then Illugi said, 'I don't expect that you will suffer from this wound very long.'

'That would be a good thing,' said Grettir, 'but this has been a strange incident, however it turns out, and I have an intuition that it will be otherwise.'

80 | They lay down to sleep that evening and in the middle of the night Grettir began thrashing about. Illugi asked him why he was restless.

Grettir told him that his leg was hurting – 'and more likely than not it has changed colour.'

They kindled a light and when they undid the bandage his leg looked swollen and black as coal, and the wound had split open and looked much nastier than before. It caused him such great pain that he could not keep still or sleep a wink.

Then Grettir said, 'This was only to be expected, for the sickness I have contracted is not without reason; it is the work of sorcery. The crone intends it to avenge the rock I threw at her.'

Illugi said, 'I told you that no good would come of that old crone.'

'Everything will end up the same way,' said Grettir, and he spoke five verses:[78]

64.

The sword's edge often
tipped the balance in battle,
when I fought off the harsh berserks
and held the birchwood house,
again when the gold-maid's champion,   *gold-maid's champion*:
Hjarrandi, lost his hands,   protector of woman, i.e. man
while Bjorn and Gunnar alike
lost their lives and peace of mind.

65.

Again I went out once
on board a wide ship
to Dyrholmar, a seasoned
seafaring wielder of spears.
Then Vebrand's fine heir,
dispatcher of heavy spears,
made his mighty challenge
to peace-loving Torfi.

66.

While many wrangled with weapons,
the brave fighter, a tree fenced in   *tree*: man
by the giant's walls of shields,
was split up from this poet.
He gave me a horse later
once the tree with oars for branches   *tree with oars for branches*:
had lost his life at Grettir's hands   seafarer
in the spattering surf of spears.

67.

I heard Thorfinn was little thought
strong in deeds of daring,
but that barbed tree Arnor's son   *barbed tree*: tree (man) with a
said he would cut my life short.   spear's point, i.e. warrior
The hard-headed spreader of gold   *spreader of gold*: generous man
from the snake's bed lost his nerve   *snake's bed*: i.e. hoard of gold
when he found me alone outdoors,
I was not that easy prey.

68.

I managed to guard my life
against the holders of spears,
it was not seldom that I needed
such faith when hemmed in.   *hag*: Thurid, Thorbjorn's foster-mother;
Now that tough hag, land of stones,   *stones*: jewels,
has wrought a spell on the tree   their *land*: woman (perhaps an
that sheds flaming battle-swords.   ironic reference to the rock Grettir
Fierce is the force of magic.   threw at her) *tree*: man, warrior

'We will be on our guard now,' said Grettir, 'because Thorbjorn Hook won't be planning this as the only move against us. Glaum, I want you to guard the ladder every day from now on and pull it up at night, and do this faithfully, for much is at stake. And if you betray us, you will soon suffer for it.'

Glaum promised to do it properly. Then the weather became rougher, a north-easterly wind got up and it grew colder. Every evening Grettir asked whether the ladder had been pulled up.

Glaum said, 'What a time to expect anyone to come. Would anyone be so set on taking your life that he would kill himself to do so? It's more than impossible to travel in this weather. I think your great courage has failed you if you expect everything to be the death of you two.'

'You will acquit yourself much worse than either of us,' said Grettir, 'whatever it is that has to be done. But you must guard the ladder, even if you have to be forced to do it.'

They made him go out every morning, and he disliked it.

The pain in Grettir's leg intensified; the whole of it swelled up and his upper and lower thigh began to fester. The infection spread all around the wound, so that Grettir was on the brink of death. Illugi sat nursing him day and night and paid no attention to anything else. This was during the second week after Grettir had cut himself.

81 | Thorbjorn Hook was staying at home in Vidvik, disgruntled about failing to get the better of Grettir.

A good week after the crone had cast the spell on the tree, she went up to Thorbjorn and asked him whether he was planning to visit Grettir.

He said there was nothing he was more determined to do.

'Do you want to see him, foster-mother?' he asked.

'I will not meet him,' said the crone. 'But I have sent him my greeting, which I expect will have reached him. I think the best course for you would be to act quickly and go to see him soon, otherwise you won't have the chance to overcome him.'

Thorbjorn replied, 'I have made so many disastrous voyages there that I will not go there now. It's ample reason that the storm is too fierce for travelling anywhere, however urgent the need.'

'You must be completely empty-headed if you can't see a way around that,' she replied. 'I'll give you some advice yet again. Go and gather some men first and ride over to your brother-in-law Halldor at Hof to ask his counsel. If I have any control over Grettir's health, would it be surprising if I didn't control the breeze that's playing there at the moment, too?'

Realizing that the crone could see further than he thought, Thorbjorn sent word around the district to muster a band of men. He was answered immediately that none of the men who had handed over their shares in Drangey was prepared to lend any help; they said that Thorbjorn should have both his share in the island and the job of attacking Grettir. But Tungu-Stein sent him two followers, Thorbjorn's brother Hjalti sent three and Eirik from Goddalir sent one. Thorbjorn took six men from his own farm and the party of twelve set off from Vidvik for Hof. Halldor invited them to stay and asked the purpose of their visit. Thorbjorn told him the whole story. Halldor asked whose idea it was and Thorbjorn told him that his foster-mother had urged him to do it.

'No good will come of this,' said Halldor, 'because she is a sorceress and that is forbidden now.'

'I can't provide for everything,' said Thorbjorn. 'But I will put an end to this somehow if I have my say. How will I go about getting on to the island?'

'I can tell that you are trusting in something,' said Halldor, 'although I don't know how good that is. If you want to go ahead with it, go over and see my friend Bjorn at Haganes in Fljot. He owns a good boat. Tell him that I have asked him to lend it to you. From there you can sail along the fjord to Drangey, but this voyage of yours looks rash unless Grettir is ill or injured. And you can be certain that if you don't overcome him honourably, he has plenty of people to seek redress. Don't kill Illugi if you can avoid it. And I can tell that some of this plan is not completely Christian.'

Halldor lent him six men for the trip. One was named Kar, another Thorleif and the third Brand, but the others are not named. The eighteen of them set off for Fljot, reached Haganes and gave Bjorn Halldor's message. He said it was his duty to do what they asked for Halldor's sake, but added that he did not owe Thorbjorn any favours and thought it was a fool's errand. He tried hard to discourage them. They could not be talked into turning back, but went to the shore and launched the boat, which was already rigged by the boat-shed. Then they made ready to set sail and everyone on land thought the weather was impossible for travelling.

When they hoisted the sail, the boat soon picked up great speed into the fjord, and after they reached the main part of the fjord where the water was deeper the gale died down so sharply that they never felt it was too windy. They arrived at Drangey after nightfall.

82 | To return to Grettir. He was so ill by now that he could not stand. Illugi sat beside him, while Glaum was supposed to keep guard. Once again he made a lot of complaints, saying that they seemed to think their lives would just drain away for no apparent reason. He went out of the hut very reluctantly.

When he reached the ladders he said to himself that he wasn't going to pull up the top one this time. He grew very sleepy, lay

down and slept the whole day, right up until the time Thorbjorn
reached the island. He and his men noticed that the ladder had
not been pulled up.

Then Thorbjorn said, 'Something unusual is going on here,
since no one is up and about, but their ladder is still down. Our
trip may well prove more eventful than we thought at first.
Let's hurry to the hut and not let our courage fail us. We can
be certain that if they are in good health, we will all have to do
the very best we can.'

Then they climbed up on to the top of the island, looked
around and saw someone lying a short way from the ladder,
snoring loudly.

Thorbjorn recognized Glaum, went up to him, hit him on
the ear with the hilt of his sword and told the wretch to wake
up: 'Any man whose life depends on your loyalty is certainly in
a poor position.'

Glaum sat up and said, 'There they go again. Do you think
it's too much freedom for me to lie out here in the cold?'

Hook said, 'Are you so stupid that you don't even realize
your enemies are here and will kill you all?'

Instead of saying anything, Glaum screamed with all his
might when he recognized the men.

'Either you shut up this instant,' said Hook, 'and tell us about
the layout of your hut or I'll kill you.'

Glaum said no more than if his head were being held under
water.

'Are the brothers in their hut?' asked Thorbjorn. 'Why aren't
they up and about?'

'It's impossible,' said Glaum, 'because Grettir is ill and at the
point of death and Illugi is watching over him.'

Hook asked about Grettir's health and what had happened,
and Glaum told him how his wound had come about.

Then Hook said with a laugh, 'This proves the old saying,
that old friendships are the last to break, and also, in your case,
that a slave makes a poor friend, Glaum. Bad as he may be,
you have betrayed your master shamefully.'

Many of the men abused him for his disloyalty, then beat
him so hard he was almost crippled by it, and left him lying

there. Then they went over to the hut and hammered on the door.

Illugi said, 'Grey-belly's knocking at the door, brother.'

'And knocks hard, too,' said Grettir, 'and ruthlessly,' and at that moment the door burst open.

Illugi leapt for his weapons and defended the door, blocking their entry. They attacked for a long time, but could only get the points of their spears inside and Illugi chopped them all off from the shafts. Seeing that they were making no headway, they leapt up on to the roof of the hut and tore it up. Then Grettir got to his feet, grabbed his spear and thrust it out between the rafters. It struck Kar, Halldor from Hof's farmhand, and went right through him.

Hook told them to proceed with caution and keep themselves covered – 'because we can defeat them if we act sensibly.'

Then they ripped the roof from the ends of the beam and forced against it until it broke. Grettir was unable to get up from his knees, but grabbed his short-sword Kar's Gift. At that moment the attackers jumped down into the hut and the two sides swapped blows fiercely. Grettir swung his short-sword at Hjalti Thordarson's follower Vikar, striking him on the left shoulder as he jumped down into the hut and cutting right through his shoulders and down his right side. The man was chopped clean in half and his body fell on top of Grettir in two pieces. Grettir could not raise his short-sword as quickly as he wanted, and at that moment Thorbjorn Hook lunged his spear between his shoulders, causing a great wound.

Then Grettir said, 'Bare is the back of a brotherless man.'[79]

Illugi threw a shield over Grettir and protected him so valiantly that everyone praised his defence.

Then Grettir asked Hook, 'Who showed you the way to the island?'

'Christ showed us the way,' Hook said.

'I would guess,' said Grettir, 'that wretched old crone, your foster-mother, showed you the way, because you have surely trusted in her advice.'

'Your fate will be the same, regardless of whom we have trusted,' said Hook.

They attacked fiercely, but Illugi defended them both vigorously. By now Grettir was completely put out of action by illness and wounds. Then Hook told his men to close in on Illugi with their shields – 'since I have never seen his like in a man of his age.'

They did so and hemmed him in so tightly with pieces of wood and weapons that he could not put up any defence, so that they managed to seize him and hold him. He had dealt wounds to most of the attackers and killed three of Hook's followers.

After that they went for Grettir. He had slumped forward and could not put up any defence, because he was already at the point of death from his leg injury. His thigh had festered all the way up to his groin. They dealt him so many wounds that there was little or no blood left to come out of each one. When they thought he must be dead, Hook grabbed for Grettir's short-sword, saying he had carried it long enough. But Grettir had clenched his fingers so tightly around the hilt that it would not come free. Many others joined in, but they could do nothing either. In the end eight of them tried and none of them could loosen his grip.

Then Hook said, 'Why should we show the outlaw any mercy? Put his hand over that beam.'

When they had done so, they chopped off Grettir's hand at the wrist and the fingers straightened out and released their grip on the hilt. Then Hook took the short-sword with both hands and chopped at Grettir's head. It was such a mighty blow that the sword could not withstand it and a piece broke off half-way down the edge. Thorbjorn's men watched and asked him why he had ruined such a fine weapon.

Hook replied, 'Then it will be easier to identify if anyone asks.'

They said there was no need, since the man was already dead.

'There's more to be done yet,' said Hook.

And he dealt two or three blows to Grettir's neck before the head came off.

'Now I know for certain that Grettir is dead,' Hook said.

It was in this way that Grettir lost his life, the most valiant man who has ever lived in Iceland, one year short of forty-five[80] when he was killed. He was fourteen when he killed Skeggi, which was his first killing, and everything went in his favour and to his advantage until he tackled the wretch Glam at the age of twenty. When he was sentenced to outlawry he was twenty-five. He spent more than nineteen years as an outlaw and often faced great ordeals – and kept his faith well, as far as he was able. He could foresee most events, but could do nothing about them.

'Here we have felled a great warrior,' said Thorbjorn. 'Let us take the head to land with us since I do not want to lose the price that has been put on it. Then there will be no mistaking that I killed him.'

The others said it was up to him, but were not impressed, because they all thought he had acted dishonourably.

Then Hook said to Illugi, 'It is a great shame that such a vigorous man as you should fall prey to the folly of joining this outlaw in his evil doings and condemn yourself to be killed without the right to compensation.'

Illugi answered, 'As soon as the Althing is over next summer, you will know who has been outlawed. But neither you nor that old woman, your foster-mother, will pass judgement on this case, because it was your sorcery and black magic that killed Grettir, yet you put him to the sword when he was at death's door anyway, and compounded your sorcery with this malicious deed.'

Then Hook said, 'You speak boldly, but it will not turn out like that. I want to show you that I think your life will be a great loss, so I will spare you if you swear an oath of loyalty not to take vengeance upon any man who has been on this expedition.'

Illugi said, 'That might have been worth considering if Grettir had been given the chance to defend himself and you had got the better of him by noble means and sheer strength. But now there is no chance that I will earn my life by acting as basely as you. I'll tell you straight out that no one will be a greater scourge to you than I will, if I live, because I'll be a long time forgetting the way you overcame Grettir. I much prefer to die.'

Thorbjorn discussed with his companions whether they should grant Illugi his life or not. They said he should decide on what action to take, because he was in charge of the expedition. Hook said he did not want to risk being dogged by a man who would not give them any promises.

And when Illugi realized they were going to kill him he said with a laugh, 'Now you've decided to do what was closer to my heart.'

They led him out to the east side of the island at daybreak[81] and beheaded him there, and all praised his courage and said he was unlike anyone of his age. Then they buried both the brothers in a shallow grave on the island, but kept Grettir's head and took it away with them, along with all the weapons and clothing that were of any value. Hook kept Grettir's fine short-sword for himself and carried it around with him for a long time afterwards.

They took Glaum with them and he complained bitterly. The storm abated that night and they rowed to land in the morning. Hook went ashore at the closest point and sent the boat on to Bjorn.

When they reached Osland, Glaum began complaining so bitterly that they could not be bothered to take him with them any farther and killed him there and then, and he cried at the top of his voice before he was beheaded.

Hook went back home to Vidvik, pleased with the outcome of his expedition. They kept Grettir's head in salt in an outhouse at Vidvik that became known as Grettir's Shed, and it lay there all winter. Hook was greatly despised for his deed when people realized that he had overcome Grettir with sorcery.

Hook stayed there until after Christmas, then rode off to see Thorir from Gard and told him about the killings, adding that he laid claim to the price that had been put on Grettir's head.

Thorir said he would not conceal the fact that he was responsible for Grettir's outlawry.

'I often received harsh treatment from him,' he said, 'but I never wanted to claim his life by acting like an evil-doer or sorcerer as you have done. I will not give you any money, since

in my view you have forfeited your right to live through your
magic and sorcery.'

Hook replied, 'I expect you are prompted more by miserliness
and meanness than by any concern about the way Grettir was
killed.'

Thorir said the obvious thing for them to do was to wait for
the Althing and accept what the Lawspeaker deemed right. And
Thorir and Thorbjorn Hook parted in complete animosity.

83 | Grettir and Illugi's kinsmen were furious when they heard
     | about the killings and took the view that Hook had com-
mitted a malicious deed by killing a dying man, and doubly
so by using sorcery. They consulted the wisest men, who all
condemned Hook's behaviour.

Four weeks into the summer, Thorbjorn rode west to
Midfjord. When word of his travels spread, Asdis summoned
people to her, including many of her friends: her sons-in-law
Gamli and Glum and their sons Skeggi, who was called the
Short-handed, and Ospak, who was mentioned earlier. Asdis
was so popular that everyone in Midfjord took her side, even
those who had been Grettir's enemies before. The first to do so
was Thorodd Half-poem, along with most of the people of
Hrutafjord.

Then Hook arrived at Bjarg with a band of twenty men,
bringing Grettir's head with them. Not all the men who had
promised Asdis their support had arrived by then. Thorbjorn
and his men went into the main room with the head and put it
down on the floor. Asdis was in the room along with many
other people. They did not exchange greetings.

Then Hook spoke a verse:

69.

From the island I have carried
Grettir's insatiable head,
the brooch-goddess is forced   *brooch-goddess*: woman
to mourn the red-haired man.

> Here on the floor you can see
> the peace-breaker's head; it will rot
> before the goddess of the golden flame   *flame from waves*: gold;
> from waves, unless she salts it.   its *goddess*: woman

Asdis remained quiet while he spoke the verse. After that, she spoke a verse:

> 70.
> No less than sheep fleeing a wolf
> you would have jumped into the sea,   *sow*: Freyja, the fertility goddess;
> men of golden sow's droppings,   her *droppings*: gold (but the image
> laughing-stock of the north,   of a sow's droppings is also insulting)
> had the battle-tree stood upright   *battle-tree*: warrior
> on the island, had Grettir
> the war-bringer been sound.   *I make light of your praise*: i.e. I am
> I make light of your praise.   liberal with it, or mocking

Many people said it was not surprising that she had such brave sons, considering how brave she was herself, after all she had suffered.

Ospak was outside and talked to those of Hook's men who had not gone indoors. He asked about the killings and they all praised Illugi's defence. Then they described how tightly Grettir had held on to the short-sword when he was dead, which everyone thought was remarkable.

A large band of men was seen riding up from the west. They were many of Asdis's friends, including Gamli and Skeggi from Melar. Thorbjorn Hook had planned to hold a confiscation court for all of Illugi's possessions, but when the party arrived he saw he was helpless to act. Ospak and Gamli were very agitated and wanted to attack Hook, but the wiser people in the band told them to follow the advice of their kinsman Thorvald and other chieftains, saying that the more wise men who handled Hook's case, the worse it would be regarded.

They were kept apart and Hook rode away and took Grettir's head with him, intending to take it to the Althing. He rode home thinking the outlook was grim, because almost all the chieftains in the country were related to Grettir and Illugi either by blood or marriage.

That summer Skeggi the Short-handed married Valgerd, the daughter of Thorodd Half-poem, and Thorodd then joined in the proceedings with Grettir's kinsmen.

84 | The men rode to the Althing and Hook had fewer supporters than he had expected, because his action was so widely condemned. Halldor asked whether they ought to take Grettir's head to the Althing and Hook indicated that he intended to have it with him.

'That is inadvisable,' Halldor said, 'because you will have enough opponents anyway, even if you don't prompt people into remembering their grief.'

They were already on their way, heading south across Sand. Hook took the head and had it buried in a mound of sand which is now called Grettir's Mound.

A large crowd attended the Althing. Hook presented his case and praised his own deeds highly, saying that he had killed the greatest outlaw in the country, and claimed the reward that had been put on Grettir's head. Thorir gave him the same answer as before. The Lawspeaker was asked for his ruling. He said he wanted to hear if there were any arguments against Hook receiving the reward for killing Grettir, otherwise he would be entitled to the price that had been put on his head.

Then Thorvald Asgeirsson summoned Short-hand to bring the counter-charge. He countered by accusing Thorbjorn Hook firstly of magic and sorcery that led to Grettir's death and secondly of killing him when he was already dying, and demanded outlawry as punishment.

The men at the Althing took sides and few of them supported Thorbjorn. Things turned out differently from what Thorbjorn had expected, since Thorvald and his son-in-law Isleif claimed that anyone who brought about a man's death by sorcery deserved to forfeit his own life. At the suggestion of wise men it was concluded that Thorbjorn should sail abroad the same summer and never return to Iceland for as long as anyone remained alive who had a claim against him for killing Grettir and Illugi. It was also made law that all practitioners of black magic should be outlawed.

Thorbjorn realized the position he was in and left the Thing, expecting Grettir's kinsmen to mount an attack on him. Nor did he receive any of the reward that had been placed on Grettir's head, because Stein the Lawspeaker did not want it to be paid for such a malicious deed. No compensation was paid for the men who were killed when they went with Thorbjorn to Drangey, which was cancelled out against the killing of Illugi, although Illugi's kinsmen disapproved strongly of this ruling.

Everyone rode home from the Thing and all the charges that had been made against Grettir were waived.

Grettir's nephew Skeggi, who was Gamli's son and Thorodd Half-poem's son-in-law, went north to Skagafjord at the instigation of Thorvald Asgeirsson and his son-in-law Isleif, who later became Bishop of Skalholt, and with everyone's approval. He took a boat and went to Drangey to fetch Grettir and Illugi's bodies and took them to Reykir on Reykjastrond where they were buried at the church.[82] As proof that Grettir is buried there, when the church at Reykir was moved in the days of the Sturlung clan, his bones were dug up and everyone thought they were huge and strong. Illugi's bones were then buried north of the church and Grettir's head by the church on the farm at Bjarg.

Asdis stayed at Bjarg and was so popular that no one ever caused her any trouble, not even when Grettir was in outlawry.

Skeggi the Short-handed took over the farm at Bjarg when Asdis died and he became an important man. His son Gamli was the father of Skeggi from Skarfsstadir and Asdis, who was the mother of Odd the Monk.[83] A great line is descended from her.

85 | Thorbjorn Hook joined a ship at Gasar and took all the
   | belongings that he could with him, while his brother Hjalti
took over his lands. Hook gave him Drangey, too. Hjalti
became a great chieftain, but is not mentioned further in this
saga.

Hook went to Norway and continued to swagger. He claimed
to have done a great deed in killing Grettir, and so it seemed
too to many people who were unfamiliar with the circumstances. But many knew what a renowned man Grettir was.
Hook mentioned only the part of their dealings that was to his
credit and left out all that was less praiseworthy.

The story reached Tunsberg in the autumn and when
Thorstein Dromund heard about the killings he turned very
sullen, because he had been told that Hook was very tough and
ruthless. Thorstein recalled the comments he had made about
his arms[84] when he and Grettir talked together long before.

Thorstein stayed on the alert as to Hook's whereabouts. They
both spent the winter in Norway; Thorbjorn was in the north
and Thorstein in Tunsberg and they had never seen each other
before. However, when Thorbjorn found out that Grettir had
a brother in Norway he thought this would be a dangerous
contingency in a foreign country, so he sought advice about
where he should go.

In those days many Norwegians went to Constantinople to
serve as mercenaries. Thorbjorn was attracted by the idea of
going there to earn fame and fortune and of keeping away from
Scandinavia and Grettir's kinsmen. He made preparations to
leave Norway and set off, not stopping until he reached Constantinople where he became a mercenary.

86 | Thorstein Dromund was a wealthy and highly respected
   | man. When he heard that Thorbjorn Hook had left the
country and gone to Constantinople, he quickly entrusted his
property to his kinsmen and set off in search of him, following
close behind wherever he went. Hook was not even aware of
his movements.

Thorstein Dromund arrived in Constantinople shortly after Hook and wanted to kill him at all costs, but they did not know each other by sight. They both asked to join the Varangian Guard and were welcomed when it was known that they were from Norway. Michael Catalactus[85] was the Byzantine emperor at that time.

Thorstein Dromund kept watch to see if he could identify Hook, but did not manage to because there were so many people there. He could not sleep and was very displeased with his lot, feeling that he had suffered a great loss.

The next thing that happened was that the Varangian Guard was supposed to go on a mission to quell fighting in the country. It was their custom and law to hold a Weapon Taking before they left, and they did so this time too. When the Weapon Taking was made, all the Varangians were obliged to assemble with any others who intended to go on the mission with them, to display their weapons. Both Thorstein and Hook turned up. Thorbjorn was the first of the two to show his weapon; he had the short-sword Grettir's Gift with him. When he showed it to the others, many people admired it and said it was a fine weapon, but that the chip on the edge was a great flaw, and asked how it had come about.

Hook said this was a tale worth the telling.

'The first thing that happened was that out in Iceland,' he said, 'I killed a warrior called Grettir the Strong, who was the toughest and bravest man there. No one could defeat him until I appeared. Because I was fated to defeat him I managed to overcome him, even though he had many times the might that I did. When I chopped off his head with the sword, a chip broke from the edge.'

The people standing nearby said he must have had a hard head and showed the sword to each other. Thorstein realized from this which man was Hook and asked to see the short-sword like the others. Hook passed it over, since most of them praised his courage and exploits and he thought that this man would do so too, naturally unaware that Thorstein or any of Grettir's kinsmen were present.

Dromund took hold of the sword and immediately wielded

it and struck at Hook. The blow hit him on the head with such force that it sank down to his jaws. Thorbjorn Hook dropped down dead to the ground, ignobly.

Everyone was dumbfounded. The emperor's treasurer seized Thorstein at once and asked for an explanation as to why he had committed such an atrocity at a sacred assembly.

Thorstein said he was Grettir the Strong's brother, adding that he had never managed to take revenge for him until then. Many of the Varangians agreed that this strong man must have been important, considering that Thorstein had travelled so far across the world to avenge him. The emperor's officers thought this was a likely explanation, but there was no one there to corroborate Thorstein's story and it was the Varangians' law that any man who killed another should pay with nothing less than his own life. Thorstein was given a quick, harsh sentence: he was to be confined to a dark cell in a dungeon and await execution there if no one paid a ransom to free him.

A man was already in the dungeon when Thorstein was put in it. He had been there a long time and was on the verge of death from deprivation. It was both foul-smelling and cold there.

Thorstein said to the man, 'What do you think about your life?'

'It is awful,' the man replied, 'because no one wants to help me and I have no kinsmen to pay my ransom.'

'Many things cannot be foretold,' said Thorstein. 'Let us be cheerful and find something to keep our spirits high.'

The man said there was nothing that could keep his spirits high.

'Let us try all the same,' said Thorstein, and he began to sing songs.

He had such a mighty voice that hardly anyone could compare with him, and he did not spare it. There was a public street a short way from the dungeon. Thorstein sang so loud that the walls resounded and the other man, who had been close to death before, took great joy in it. Thorstein went on singing into the evening.

87 | There was a noble lady named Spes who lived in the city,
     | very rich and of a good family. Her husband was named
Sigurd. He was wealthy, but of lesser family than hers and she had
married him for money. There was little love between them and
she felt she had married beneath her. She was proud and obtrusive.

It happened that while Thorstein was keeping his spirits high
by singing that evening, Spes strolled along the street near the
dungeon and heard a voice so beautiful that she said she had
never heard the like before. She was out with a large group of
servants and told them to go and find out who had such a fine
voice. They asked who had been incarcerated there. Thorstein
told them his name.

Then Spes asked, 'Are you as accomplished in other things
as you are at singing?'

He said there was not much evidence of that.

'What wrong have you done,' she asked, 'to warrant being
tormented in there?'

He told her he had killed a man in order to avenge his brother.

'But I couldn't produce witnesses to prove it,' he added, 'so
I was put in here, unless someone would pay my ransom to free
me. But I don't think there is any chance of that, because I have
no kinsmen here.'

'It will be a great loss if you are killed,' said Spes. 'Was the
brother that you avenged such a famous man?'

He said he was more than twice his own worth and she asked
him what proof there was of that.

Then Thorstein spoke a verse:

71.

Eight callers of the sword-meet	*callers of the sword-meet*: warriors
could not remove the sword	
from hardy Grettir's hand,	
high woman heaped with rings,	
until the firm-handed	
strappers of the scabbard	*strappers of the scabbard*: swordsmen, warriors
chopped the shoulder-leg	*shoulder-leg*: arm
from the wave-horse's rider.	*wave-horse*: ship; its *rider*: seafarer

'What great qualities,' said the ones who could understand the verse.

Once Spes heard this she said, 'Will you accept your life from me, if there is the chance?'

'Gladly I will,' said Thorstein, 'if my companion who is sitting in here with me is released too. Otherwise we'll stay here together.'

She replied, 'I expect you are more worth paying for than he is.'

'Be that as it may,' said Thorstein, 'either we leave here together or not at all.'

Then she went to where the Varangians were staying and asked for Thorstein to be released, offering the money for it. They were willing to do so, and through her influence and wealth she had both men released.[86] When Thorstein came out of the dungeon he went to see Spes. She took him into her household and kept him there in secret. Sometimes he went on missions with the Varangians and proved to be a man of outstanding courage in all their exploits.

88 | In those days Harald Sigurdarson was in Constantinople and Thorstein became friends with him. Thorstein was considered a man of great standing now, since Spes made sure he had plenty of money. Spes was impressed by his accomplishments and they fell in love. She began to run very short of money, because she entertained her friends lavishly. Her husband, too, noticed a change in her and in many aspects of her behaviour, particularly in the amount she spent. He found out that gold and treasures which were in her keeping had gone missing.

Once her husband Sigurd talked to her about it, saying that she had started behaving very strangely: 'You pay no heed to our wealth and squander it left and right. You look as if you are going around in a trance and are always avoiding me. I know for certain that something is going on.'

She replied, 'I told you and my kinsmen when we were married that I wanted to be independent and free with all things

THE SAGA OF GRETTIR THE STRONG

which are seemly, which is why I am open-handed with your money. Or were you hinting at other things which might be shameful for me?'

He answered, 'I'm not completely free of the suspicion that you have someone whom you prefer to me.'

'I don't know that you have any grounds for that,' she said, 'and I think you're saying all this without any justification. There is no point in us talking to each other if you make such insinuations about me.'

Then he dropped the subject for the time being.

Spes and Thorstein went on as before and paid no heed to malicious gossip, because she trusted in her shrewdness and popularity. They would often sit talking together and enjoying themselves.

One evening when they were sitting in one of the upstairs rooms where her valuables were kept, she asked Thorstein to sing something, thinking that her husband was sitting drinking as usual. She locked the door. After he had been singing for a while, someone knocked at the door and called out to her to open it; her husband was there with many servants. Spes had opened up a large chest to show Thorstein her valuables, and when she realized who was there she refused to open the door.

'I have a quick plan,' she said to Thorstein. 'Jump into the chest and keep quiet.'

He did so and she bolted the chest and sat down on top of it. Just at that moment her husband entered the room, after he and his men had broken down the door.

'Why are you making such a commotion?' said Spes. 'Are some troublemakers chasing you?'

Her husband replied, 'It's about time that you reveal the sort of woman you really are. Where is the man whose voice was booming just now? I expect you think he sounds better than I do.'

She said, 'No one is a total fool if he knows when to hold his tongue. And the same goes for you. You imagine you are so cunning and expect your lies will stick to me, but they will be put to the test now. If you're telling the truth, then take the man, because he won't get out through the walls or the rafters.'

He searched the house and found nothing.

'Why don't you take him then,' she said, 'if you're so sure that he's here?'

Then he fell silent and was unable to work out what trick was being played on him. He asked his men whether they hadn't heard it too. But when they saw that Spes disapproved, they would not corroborate anything, saying that sounds could easily be mistaken. Her husband left then, convinced that he was right even though he could not find the man. After that he stopped spying on his wife and her doings for a long while.

Another time much later, Thorstein and Spes were sitting in the room where her husband kept his clothes; there was both cut and uncut cloth in it. She showed Thorstein many cloths and they spread them out. When they were not on their guard, her husband came along with many men and broke down the door. While they were breaking in, she bundled the cloths on top of Thorstein and was leaning up against the pile when the others entered.

'Are you still going to deny that there's a man here with you?' said her husband. 'Here are some people who saw you both.'

She told them not to be so excited: 'You will not fail to find what is here, but leave me alone and do not push me around.'

They searched the building, found nothing, and eventually gave up.

Then Spes said, 'It is always good to exceed people's expectations. Obviously you could not hope to find what was not here. Won't you admit your folly, my husband, and retract your slanders against me?'

He replied, 'Far from it, because I am convinced that you are genuinely guilty of the accusations I have made against you. And if you think you can clear your name, you will have to prove it.'

She said she did not mind that and they dropped the subject.

After that, Thorstein was generally with the Varangians. People say he sought advice from Harald Sigurdarson and that he and Spes would never have found a solution without the benefit of his wisdom.

Time went by and Spes's husband Sigurd announced that he

would be going away on some errand. His wife did not discourage him. When her husband had left, Thorstein moved in with Spes and they spent all their time together. Her house was built projecting over the sea and several rooms had the sea below them. Spes and Thorstein always sat together there. There was a little hatch in the floor, unknown to anyone except the two of them, and they left it open in case they needed to act quickly.

As for her husband, he did not leave at all, but went into hiding with the idea of spying on his wife. And one evening when they least suspected, they happened to be sitting enjoying themselves in the room above the sea when her husband suddenly took them by surprise with a large band of people with him. He posted several men at a window in the house and told them to see whether what he said was right. Everyone said he was telling the truth and must have been earlier, too, and they stormed the room.

When they heard the noise, Spes told Thorstein, 'You must go down here at all costs. Give me a signal if you manage to get clear of the buildings.'

He said yes and dived out through the hole in the floor, then Spes kicked the hatch down and it fell into place, so that there was no sign that the floor had been tampered with.

Then her husband and his men entered the room. They went around searching it, but found nothing, as was to be expected. The room was empty and there was nothing inside except the smooth floor and some cross-benches. His wife sat there toying with the rings on her fingers; she ignored the men and acted as if this were none of her business. Her husband was perplexed and asked his men whether they hadn't seen the man. They said they definitely had.

Then Spes said, 'This goes to prove the old saying that all things happen in threes. The same has happened to you too, Sigurd. As I see it, you have burst in on me three times, but are you any the wiser than you were in the beginning?'

'I'm not the only one to tell the tale this time,' said her husband. 'You will be given a chance to prove your innocence in the whole matter, because there is no way that I will accept such a disgrace without recompense.'

'I think you are asking the very thing I wanted to offer,' she said, 'since I welcome the chance of clearing my name of these slanders. They have been spread so far that I will suffer disgrace if I do not clear myself of them.'

'You will likewise have to deny that you have given away our money or treasures,' he said.

Spes replied, 'When I undertake to prove my innocence, I will likewise clear myself on all the counts you have levelled against me. But think what the outcome will be. I will go to see the bishop straight away tomorrow and he can state how I can prove my complete innocence of all the slanderous words you have spoken against me.'

Her husband was satisfied with this answer and left with his men.

To return to Thorstein. He swam clear of the buildings and went ashore where he thought it was suitable. He took a burning log and held it up, so that it could be seen from Spes's house. She spent a long time outdoors that evening and night, wanting to know if Thorstein had made it to land. And when she saw the flame she realized that he had made it ashore, because they had agreed upon this signal.

The next morning Spes invited her husband to go and discuss their situation with the bishop, and he readily agreed. They went before the bishop and her husband made the same accusations about her. The bishop asked whether she had ever been accused of such things before, but no one said they had heard anything. Then he asked about the grounds on which Sigurd made these accusations, and he produced some men who had seen her sitting in a locked room with a man whom he suspected of seducing her. The bishop said she was welcome to try to prove her innocence of these accusations if she wished.

She said she would gladly do so.

'I believe,' said Spes, 'that I can find plenty of women who will recommend that I may be allowed to swear to my innocence in this matter.'

Then the oath was stated to her and the day decided when it should be sworn. She went home afterwards, contented, and met Thorstein to make their plans.

89 | That day passed and the day appointed for Spes to swear her oath came around. She invited all her friends and kinsmen and presented herself in the finest clothes that she owned. Many elegant women went with her. The weather was very rainy, the road was wet and there was a big ditch that had to be crossed on the way to the church. And when Spes and her party reached the ditch a great crowd was waiting there, including many poor people who asked for alms, since this was a public street.

All the people felt obliged to greet her as warmly as they could and wished her well since she had often helped them kindly. Among the poor people was a beggar with a stick, a large man with a long beard.

The woman stopped by the ditch, because the people of the court thought they would get dirty crossing it.

Seeing that this woman was more elegantly adorned than the other women, this huge beggar spoke to her.

'Good lady,' he said, 'please condescend to allow me to carry you across this fen, because we beggars are obliged to serve you in such a way as we can.'

'How well can you carry me,' she said, 'since you can't even support yourself?'

'It would be a proof of your humility,' he said, 'and I cannot offer you more than I have. Everything will turn out better for you if you do not humiliate a poor man.'

'You can be sure,' she said, 'that if you do not carry me properly it will cost you a flogging or even some greater disgrace.'

'I will gladly risk that,' he replied and ambled out into the ditch.

She gave the impression that she expected him to carry her badly, but climbed on to his back all the same. He stumbled along slowly, walking with two crutches.

When he reached the middle of the ditch, he began to wobble to all sides.

She told him to make more effort – 'This will be the worst journey you have ever made if you drop me here.'

The wretched character plodded on and picked up strength, and made the utmost effort and came close to the other side. Then he stumbled and shot forwards, throwing her on to the bank, but falling into the ditch himself right up to the armpits. As he lay there he grabbed at the lady, but because he could not get a grip on her clothes he put his muddy hand on her knee and all over her bare thigh.

She leapt up cursing him, saying that evil beggars always caused trouble – 'You really deserve to be left lying there for dead, if it were not beneath my dignity to deal with such a wretched creature.'

He replied, 'How differently fortune favours people. I thought I was treating you well and hoped for alms from you, but all I earn is curses and abuse and nothing of any use,' and he gave the impression of being very upset.

Many people pitied him, but she said he was just a conniving old man. But when many of them pleaded on his behalf, she took out her pouch which was full of gold coins.

She shook out the coins and said, 'Take this, old man. It would never be right if you were not paid in full for the way I have abused you. We will part on the terms that you deserve.'

He picked up the gold and thanked her for her kindness. Spes went to the church, where a large crowd was waiting. Sigurd launched into her and told her to prove herself innocent of the accusations he had made against her.

She replied, 'I pay no heed to your accusations. What man do you claim to have seen in the room with me? I always need men of worth near me and I do not consider that shameful. But I swear that I have not given any man gold and been defiled by him apart from my husband and that wicked begger who put his muddy hand on my thigh when he carried me over the ditch today.'

Many people agreed that this was a full oath and that it was no flaw on her character just because an old man had unexpectedly taken a liberty with her. She said that she had to include everything that happened to her.

Afterwards she swore to the oath as it now was stated. Many people said that she was proving the saying that 'An oath should leave few things unsworn.' She replied that she expected wise men would consider that it had dispelled all suspicion.

Then her kinsmen declared that it was a great torment for women of standing to be slandered in such a way without recompense, since a woman was liable to be punished by death if she was found to have committed adultery. Spes then asked the bishop to grant her a divorce from Sigurd, saying that she did not want to put up with his slanders. Her kinsmen presented the request, and through their agency and gifts of money the divorce was granted. Sigurd received little of their wealth and was banished from the country. In this case, as in others, the weaker was forced to yield. He did not manage to have his way even though he was in the right.

Spes took charge of all their money and was considered a very forceful woman.

On closer scrutiny her oath seemed suspect and it was assumed the terms had been laid down for her by clever men. It was discovered that the beggar who had carried her over the ditch was Thorstein Dromund, but Sigurd did not manage to win redress in the matter.

90 | Thorstein Dromund was with the Varangian Guard while this episode was on everyone's lips. He won such renown that it was felt that hardly any man of such accomplishments had ever been there. He earned great honour from Harald Sigurdarson, who respected their kinship,[87] and it is thought that Thorstein followed his advice.

Shortly after Sigurd was banished from the country, Thorstein made a proposal of marriage to Spes. She answered him favourably, but referred the matter to her kinsmen. They held meetings about it and it was decided to leave the choice to her. With her kinsmen's approval they made the settlement and remained happily married with plenty of money. Thorstein was regarded as a man of good fortune for the way he had solved his problems. They spent two years together in Constantinople.

After that, Thorstein told his wife that he wanted to go back to Norway to reclaim his property there and she said the

decision was his to make. He sold the property he owned and
realized a good sum of money from it. Then they set off on
their journey with a fine group of people and travelled all the
way until they reached Norway. Thorstein's kinsmen welcomed
them both very warmly and were quick to realize how generous
and magnanimous Spes was. She soon became extremely popular. They had children and stayed on their property in Norway,
contented with their lot.

Magnus the Good was king of Norway then. Thorstein soon
went to meet him and was well received, because of the great
renown he had earned for avenging Grettir the Strong. Apart
from Grettir Asmundarson, scarcely any instance is known of
an Icelander being avenged in Constantinople.

Thorstein is said to have become one of King Magnus the
Good's men. He stayed in Norway for nine years after he
arrived there and both he and his wife were held in high regard.
Then King Harald Sigurdarson left Constantinople and King
Magnus gave him a half-share in the kingdom of Norway. They
were joint rulers of Norway for a while.

Many of the people who had been friends with King Magnus
were discontented after his death. They had all liked him, but
found it difficult to secure the favour of King Harald, who was
harsh and vindictive.

Thorstein Dromund began to show his age then, although he
remained very vigorous. By that time, sixteen years had passed
since the killing of Grettir Asmundarson.

91 | Many people urged Thorstein to meet King Harald and
    | enter his service, but he would not agree.

Then Spes said, 'I don't want you to go and see King Harald,
Thorstein, because we owe a greater debt to another king and
need to consider that. We are both growing old and are past
our prime and have acted more on our own inclinations than
on Christian teachings or the principles of righteousness. I know
that this debt of ours cannot be paid either by our families or
with our own wealth, but that we must give account of it
ourselves. Now I want us to change our way of life and leave

this country to go and see the Pope in Rome, because I believe that my matters can be settled there.'

Thorstein replied, 'I am equally aware of the things you mention. It is right and appropriate for you to decide, after you let me decide when the outlook was far less promising; we will act exactly as you prescribe.'

Their decision took everyone by surprise. By now, Thorstein was two years short of sixty-five, but still very able-bodied. He summoned all his kinsmen and relatives by marriage and revealed his plans to them. Wise men approved, but felt their departure would be a great loss.

Thorstein said that it was not certain whether they would return.

'I want to thank you all,' he said, 'for how well you safe-guarded my wealth the last time I was out of the country. Now I want to invite you and ask you to take charge of my children and their inheritance, and bring them up as your qualities allow you to, since I have reached the age where I am equally likely to come back or not, even if I live. Provide for everything I leave behind here just as if I would never return to Norway.'

They answered that the arrangement would be capably man-aged, 'If Thorstein's wife stays behind to look after everything.'

Then Spes said, 'I travelled abroad from Constantinople with Thorstein, leaving behind both kinsmen and wealth, because I wanted both of us to meet the same fate. I have enjoyed staying here, but I am not tempted to spend a long time here in Norway or in the northern countries if he leaves. We have always been compatible and nothing has ever come between us. Now we will go together, because we share the knowledge of what has happened from the time we first met.'

When they had made those arrangements, Thorstein asked some respected men to divide up his wealth into two halves. Thorstein's kinsmen took charge of the half that was intended for his children, who were brought up with their father's family and developed into people of great character. A large family is descended from them in Vik. Thorstein and Spes divided up one share of their wealth and donated some to churches for the benefit of their souls, and took the rest with them. Then they set off for Rome and many people prayed for their well-being.

92 | They travelled all the way until they reached Rome. When they appeared before the man who was appointed to hear confessions, they gave a true account of all that had happened and the clever device they had employed to contrive their marriage. They meekly offered to undertake any penitence and atonement that he wished to impose on them, but because they had made up their minds to atone for their shortcomings without any compulsion or enmity on the part of men of the Church, they were released from all imposition as far as was possible and were kindly asked to provide wisely for their souls and live pure lives thereafter, once they had been granted total absolution. They were felt to have conducted themselves wisely.

Then Spes said, 'At last I think that all our affairs have been well handled and concluded. Now we have not shared only misfortune. Since foolish men may follow the example we set earlier in our lives, we will end them in a way that good men may emulate. Let us hire men who are gifted at working in stone, to make a stone cell for each of us so that we may atone for our transgressions against God.'

Thorstein paid to have a stone cell built for each of them and provide whatever else they needed to live. When the stone cells had been built, at an appropriate time and when everything was completed, they gave up their secular life together of their own free will, in order to enjoy instead eternal life together in the world to come. They went to separate cells and lived for as long as God allotted them, and thus they ended their lives.

Most people regarded Thorstein Dromund and his wife Spes as the most fortunate of people, considering the situation they found themselves in. None of his children or descendants is known to have ever come to Iceland.

93 | Sturla the Lawspeaker has said[88] that he does not consider
   | any outlaw to have been as distinguished as Grettir the
Strong, and justifies this on three grounds. First, he regards him
as the wisest, since he spent the longest time in outlawry of any
man and was never overcome for as long as he kept his health.
Second, he was the strongest man in Iceland among his contemporaries, and more capable than others at laying ghosts and
visitations to rest. The third reason was that, unlike any other
Icelander, he was avenged in Constantinople and what is more,
the man who avenged him, Thorstein Dromund, became so
exceptionally favoured by fortune in the last years of his life.

Here ends the Saga of Grettir Asmundarson, our fellow
countryman. Thanks be to those who have listened, but few to
him who has scrawled this saga. Here is the end of this work
and may we all be delivered unto God.

Amen.

Notes

1. *Ofeig Hobbler*: The Icelandic *burlufótur* probably refers to someone who either walks clumsily or stomps. Like other sagas, *The Saga of Grettir the Strong* is extant in a number of manuscripts with variations in wording. In one manuscript, Ofeig is called 'Club-foot'. For the 'feet and legs' theme, see Introduction.

2. *Kjarval*: (Irish *Cearbhall*) An Irish king (d. 887 or 888), named in several Sagas of Icelanders as the ancestor of many leading settlers of Iceland. Among them is his grandson Helgi the Lean, who gives land to Asmund the son of Ondott Crow, in chapter 8.

3. *the battle*: i.e. the battle of Havsfjord (*c.*885). Although this battle in Norway is mentioned in many Kings' Sagas and Sagas of Icelanders, the precise site has not been identified.

4. *Wolf-skins*: Sagas occasionally make a distinction between 'Wolf-skins', who clad themselves in pelts instead of armour, and berserks, who wore conventional armour.

5. *Olvir the Child-sparer*: According to *The Book of Settlements* he earned his nickname by refusing to take part in the alleged Viking custom of throwing children into the air and impaling them on spears.

6. *prepared to accept farms in Norway as being of any value*: Since Harald Tangle-hair (later known as Harald Fair-hair) confiscated land all over Norway from those who refused to swear loyalty to him, the lands of those who fled from him were worthless. Similarly, he assumed the right to inherit from all foreigners who died in his realm.

7. *Thorvald from Drangar*: The father of Eirik the Red, founder of the Viking settlement in Greenland, and grandfather of Leif Eiriksson the Lucky, the first European to visit North America.

8. *there was little left to settle*: *The Book of the Icelanders* by Ari Thorgilsson the Learned and other medieval sources state that Iceland was settled over a period of roughly sixty years, from

874–930. According to the chronology of *Grettir*, Onund Tree-leg arrives in Iceland around 900, when little remaining good land is to be had.

9. *Aud the Deep-minded*: As the author points out later, the characters in this chapter feature in *The Saga of the People of Laxardal*. Aud the Deep-minded is one of the great women characters of the sagas. She is the widow of Olaf the White, the Viking king of Dublin, mother of King Thorstein of Scotland and matriarch of noble families in Orkney and the Faroe Islands. In Iceland she was the head of an important family, a settler who claimed a large area of rich land and shared it out among not only her relatives but also her workers and slaves, the foremother of great men and the heroes of *The Saga of the People of Laxardal*. Olaf's byname Feilan is probably an Icelandic form of the Irish name *Faelan*, 'wolf cub'.

10. *Kjalarnes Assembly*: The first local assembly – a forerunner of the Althing – was set up at Kjalarnes in south-west Iceland by Thorstein, the son of the first settler, Ingolf Arnarson, and father of the Lawspeaker Thorkel Moon.

11. *Kari the Singed*: Kari Solmundarson was the only person to escape from the burning in *Njal's Saga*, and avenged the deaths of Njal and his family.

12. *He found a whale beached*: Beached whales were a great 'windfall', especially in times of hardship, and the clashes occasioned by disputes over boundaries or beached whales in common land are described in a number of sagas. Another beached whale prompts a battle later in this saga, involving the 'Sworn Brothers' Thormod and Thorgeir.

13. *Ingolf*: i.e. Arnarson, the first settler of Iceland.

14. *the means to travel abroad*: Goods, often homespun or tallow, which Icelanders would take abroad to sell and cover their costs of travelling. It is a widespread motif in the Sagas of Icelanders for budding heroes to ask their fathers for 'the means to travel abroad' at the age of twelve, be refused and leave anyway with little means of support. Norway was generally their first destination.

15. *Dromund*: A type of galleon, generally explained as a loan-word from Old French: *dromont, dromunz*. One manuscript of *Grettir* says that Thorstein and his wife Spes bought themselves a 'dromund' when they left Constantinople for Norway.

16. *red-haired*: Grettir shares this and other characteristics with the strong god Thor, who repeatedly defended the realm of the gods from attacks by giants.

17. *Vinlander*: i.e. a traveller to Vinland (North America).
18. *did not lounge around in the fire hall*: Grettir was therefore not the archetypal 'coal-biter' or 'male Cinderella' found in some sagas.
19. *Bersi . . . Thorgils*: According to Snorri Sturluson's *Heimskringla*, Bersi, Torfa the Poetess's son, was aforeships with Earl Svein at the battle of Nes (1015), then captured by King Olaf Haraldsson, to whom he later composed a eulogy of which three verses survive. Kormak is conceivably the eponymous hero of *Kormak's Saga*, although according to other sources he and his brother would have been dead by this time.
20. *Only a slave . . . a coward never*: A proverb. The terms are in fact ambiguous, since the word for 'slave' could also mean 'wretch' (as used to describe the ghost of Glam in chapters 33 and 35), while the word used for 'coward' has homosexual connotations. The double sense could be rendered by the rather more awkward 'Only those who are base take revenge at once, and the unmanly never.' See also chapter 28.
21. *handle my legal duties*: i.e. sit on the panels which passed judgements.
22. *Grettishaf (Grettir's Lift)*: Two other rocks in the saga bear this name, see chapters 30 and 59.
23. *sword . . . Vatnsdal clan*: Jokul and the Vatnsdal clan are described in chapter 13 and in *The Saga of the People of Vatnsdal*. This sword is presumably the heirloom Aettartangi acquired from Jokul's father Ingimund the Old.
24. *Life has changed . . . land-hugging seas*: In its preserved form at least, this verse is too obscure to sound better 'if you look closely at it, but is none too pretty on first impression'. The intended ambiguity would seem to lie in whether the kenning is read as meaning something like 'lounging around eating stodgy food on board' or 'doing battle with the waves'. Like many other episodes in the saga, this scene and Grettir's subsequent 'awakening to action' is a 'set piece' of dissembling with an almost theatrical quality.
25. *sewing up Grettir's shirt-sleeves*: Sleeves were sewn together or fastened at the wrist in some other way after people had dressed.
26. *warship (karfi)*: A special type of light craft used for coastal sailing, smaller than the longship and knorr.
27. *the glow of a treasure hoard*: This belief, accompanied by breaking of a mound to win the treasure, is a common motif in the saga tradition as well as folklore. Horses, riches and other

necessities for the afterlife were often placed in graves according to Viking burial custom. Mound-breaking episodes tend to be highly stereotyped: the hero enters the mound by a rope, collects the valuables and generally finds good weapons there, then does battle with the mound-dweller and wins; meanwhile, his accomplice runs away from the rope before knowing the outcome. The description here is paralleled when Grettir tackles the monster in Bardardal (chapter 66).

28. *He placed the head up against the mound-dweller's buttocks*: Ghosts in the sagas have physical substance and several instances are recorded of ritually placing a ghost's head between its buttocks to 'kill' it. Grettir does the same with the ghost of Glam in chapter 35.

29. *Then the earl went abroad, as described in his saga*: The Saga of Earl Eirik is unknown apart from this and one other passing reference.

30. *Their bodies . . . in a shallow grave*: The berserks are buried on the littoral, i.e. the land which is flooded at high tide. The medieval Norwegian *Gulathing* legal code prescribes that evildoers should be 'buried at the shoreline where the sea and green turf meet'.

31. *my namesake*: The name Bjorn means 'bear'.

32. *He said later*: Grettir's own account of events is cited in five places (chapters 21, 35, 52, 61 and 65) and in one instance his account is quoted to qualify other sources. In citing the hero as a direct source, *The Saga of Grettir the Strong* is unique in the genre. This device serves to lend an exceptional degree of credibility to the narrative and also elevates the author in status, bringing the saga closer to the approach of modern biography and the 'documentary novel'.

33. *He also took the piece of the paw that he had cut off*: Heroes wrestle with ferocious bears in several other sagas. Here, the author puns upon the motif: Grettir wrestles with two bears at once, one of them human (Bjorn). The human bear Bjorn is shallow but arrogant; the animal is sensible and methodical, as they tend to be in stories. A third bear may be identified in the form of the fur cloak which Bjorn throws into the den and Grettir reclaims.

34. *carry his brother's life around in his purse*: Accept money instead of making a revenge killing of his brother's killer.

35. *five men, while one escaped*: An inconsistency in numbers from the preceding sentence.

36. *Isleif, who later became bishop of Skalholt*: Isleif Gizurarson was
     the first bishop of Iceland, from 1056–80.

37. *Thorgils Masson*: Thorgils is named Maksson (son of Mak) in
     The Saga of Grettir the Strong, but in *The Saga of the Sworn
     Brothers* his father's name is Mar (giving the patronymic
     Masson), which has been used in this translation for consistency's
     sake. The incidents that follow – the clash over flensing the
     whale, Thorgils' killing and the settlements made for it – are also
     described in chapters 7–8 of *The Saga of the Sworn Brothers*.

38. *outer Almenningar*: A far-flung part of the north-west coast of
     Iceland. Almenningar means 'common land', as is referred to
     later in the defence for the claim to the whale.

39. *Thorgeir Havarsson and Thormod Kolbrun's Poet*: The fearsome
     heroes of *The Saga of the Sworn Brothers* return to this saga
     when Grettir spends the winter in their company at Reykjaholar,
     on which he commented afterwards: 'When I was there the most
     enjoyable part of my meal was being around to eat it in the first
     place' (chapter 50). Verse 25 in chapter 27 is one of the fifteen
     from Thormod's elegy on Thorgeir preserved in their saga. The
     casual reference to the killings mentioned in it suggests that the
     author of *The Saga of Grettir* assumed his audience was familiar
     with them. Where this saga differs in its account of the settlement
     is in highlighting Asmund's role in the defence, as if to elevate
     him in stature before Grettir returns from Norway.

40. *Asgeir Scatter-brain, who was Asmund Grey-locks' uncle on his
     father's side*: According to *The Saga of the People of Laxardal*
     he has five children, including Hrefna (who is described as
     Grettir's kinswoman in chapter 52 and was the wife of Kjartan
     Olafsson, the main hero of *The Saga of the People of Laxardal*)
     and the brothers Kalf and Thorvald (who appear in some parts
     of this saga and became the leading men in Midfjord after the
     death of Thorkel Scratcher from the Vatnsdal clan).

41. *Skafti*: Skafti Thoroddsson was Lawspeaker (the highest office in
     the Icelandic Commonwealth) for twenty-seven years (1004–30)
     and is frequently mentioned in the sagas. He appears to have
     been favourably disposed towards Grettir.

42. *Bardi*: Bardi Gudmundarson was the main hero of *The Saga of
     the Slayings on the Heath*, which reaches its climax when Bardi
     leads a band of men from north Iceland to take revenge on the
     people of Borgarfjord for the death of his brother Hall, ending
     in a mighty battle where many lives are lost.

43. *killings at Fagrabrekka*: Described in *The Book of Settlements*

and *The Tale of Hromund the Lame*. Sleitu-Helgi was a Norwegian who arrived in Iceland with eleven companions, all unruly Vikings. They stayed with Thorir Thorkelsson and eventually Sleitu-Helgi married his daughter. Sleitu-Helgi and his men stole horses from Hromund the Lame, who brought charges against them, but they responded by attacking him at his home, Fagrabrekka. Most of the Vikings, and Hromund, were killed in the battle. Again, with this passing reference the author appears to assume his readers are familiar with the story.

44. *the Slayings on the Heath*: One of the best-known battles under the Icelandic Commonwealth, described in the saga of the same name, the first part of which is preserved only in a retelling from the first half of the eighteenth century.

45. *Forsaeludal*: A short, narrow valley leading up from Vatnsdal, the home of Grettir's mother's family. Near the ruins of the farm at Thorhallsstadir are a large gully and chasm with many beautiful waterfalls in it, including Skessufoss ('Ogress Falls'), which could have been a suitable home for the evil beings Glam was sent to exterminate.

46. *Sylgsdalir in Sweden*: This place is unidentified; Sweden often features as the remote home of giants and pagans, on the border of civilization. 'Glam' is a rare name in medieval Icelandic literature, although it is borne by giants in *Bard's Saga* and Snorri Sturluson's mythological *Prose Edda*. Originally this was a poetic name for the moon, but when used of giants it probably meant 'starer, gazer', which well fits in with Glam's 'wide blue eyes' and ability to paralyse Grettir merely by looking at him.

47. *black as hell and bloated to the size of a bull*: The same phrase is used to describe another merciless ghost, that of Thorolf Hobbler in *The Saga of the People of Eyri*. In its wording, the description of the fate met by the shepherd Thorgaut in the next chapter echoes that of *The Saga of the People of Eyri* and may be modelled on it.

48. *straddling the roof*: Sitting across the ridge of the roof and kicking against the sides is a distinctive trait of Icelandic ghosts, which in many cases seem to take a delight in causing disturbance and damage as much as scaring people by their very presence.

49. *Thorgaut caused no one harm afterwards*: i.e. his spirit rested in peace.

50. *he is different from any human form*: Ghosts in folktales and sagas were frequently bloated beyond their human proportions, sometimes becoming gigantic in shape as appears to be the case

with Glam. This may equally be a reference to Glam's mysterious origin, paganism and magical gifts, even an implication that he was not 'human' even before being killed by the monster that haunted Forsaeludal, but rather an 'evil spirit', as Thorhall calls him.

51. *Glam was endowed ... ghosts*: Such a curse imposed by a ghost is not found in any other saga. One unique feature of *The Saga of Grettir the Strong* is that the hero in effect loses to the opponent he vanquishes. Even though Grettir kills Glam, he is haunted by loneliness and fear of the dark during his long outlawry and ceases to develop his full potential. Grettir's life from this point on might be described as prolonged death throes which do not come to an end until he is finally overcome on Drangey.

52. *battle of Nes*: King Olaf Haraldsson (later Saint Olaf) ascended to the Norwegian throne in 1014 and shared the crown with Earl Svein Hakonarson. He defeated Svein at Nes (now named Brunalanes) in Oslo Fjord on 3 April 1015 and was sole ruler until he died in the battle of Stiklestad in 1030.

53. *Thorir*: Thorir Skeggjason from Gard became Grettir's chief adversary during his exile, putting large sums of money on his head and opposing all attempts to remit his sentence.

54. *carry hot iron*: A medieval ordeal supposedly allowing the accused to prove his innocence. The accused would take several steps holding glowing iron in his hand. Afterwards his hand would be bound and if it proved to be undamaged when the bandages were removed three days later, he would be declared innocent.

55. *his kinship with King Olaf*: Grettir and King Olaf were cousins three times removed, with a common ancestor four generations back in Ofeig Hobbler, as stated in chapter 1.

56. *demand that man back and forbid him to work for you*: According to the 'Grey Goose' law code, Thorbjorn is legally entitled to make such a demand; the penalty was a fine of three marks.

57. *the Saddle-head Verses*: These have not been preserved outside those exchanged here and could be a popular 'spin-off' dramatization from the tradition of Grettir the outlaw, in which he is portrayed as a glorified companion and champion of the common people.

58. *Sturla Thordarson ... some accounts say that he was killed in Midfitjar*: Sturla Thordarson (1214–84) was an important chieftain, poet, historian (author of the longest saga in the compilation *Sturlunga Saga*, sagas of later kings of Norway and one of

the main versions of *The Book of Settlements*) and Lawspeaker
(1272–82). He has even been considered the author of the original version of *The Saga of Grettir the Strong*, mainly based on
four references to him and the events of his time in the saga, but
they may be devices of a later author to lend authenticity. That
the spear was not found 'until the days that people still alive
today can remember ... towards the end of Sturla Thordarson
the Lawspeaker's life' has also been read as evidence that the
saga was written when people born around 1270 had reached
old age, namely 1320–50. However, this statement alone is
inconclusive evidence for dating the saga. The reference to other
accounts in which Thorbjorn Ox is killed in Midfitjar suggests
that the author of *The Saga of Grettir* is drawing on a wide
variety of sources.

59. *Snorri the Godi*: The main character in *The Saga of the People
of Eyri*, Snorri the Godi features widely in other sagas as a
shrewd leader and man of authority. Later, Grettir wisely avoids
incurring Snorri's wrath by refusing to fight his hot-headed son.

60. *You can stay here if you want*: In *The Saga of the Sworn Brothers*
Grettir is mentioned as spending the winter with Thorgils, Thorgeir and Thormod, but the (mock-)heroic episodes which follow
are not recounted there.

61. *no higher price than three marks had ever been put on a man's
head before*: It was not uncommon for wronged parties to put a
price on the head of outlaws; the standard reward was one mark
of tender (= 48 ells of homespun) and three marks of tender were
offered in the case of major criminals. Here the reward of three
marks of silver is eight times the going rate. Outlaws were also
promised their freedom in return for killing other outlaws, cf.
the two attempts in later scenes when Grettir is in hiding on the
Arnarvatn moor.

62. *'Handing Grettir Around'*: This 400-line poem is attached to the
oldest manuscript of the saga, but has been badly damaged by
attempts to erase its highly pornographic content from the calf-
skin. For a discussion of its origins see the Introduction.

63. *was rigged with rings and bells*: This bridge with its built-in
alarm system is unique in the Sagas of Icelanders, but has parallels
in Continental-influenced saga Romances.

64. *High he steps ... mountain hall*: This refrain is echoed in *The
Tale of the Mountain-Dweller*, in a completely different context.

65. *Bjorn, the Champion of the Hitardal people*: In *The Saga of
Bjorn, Champion of the People of Hitardal*, Grettir's presence

only warrants a passing mention. Orm Storolfsson and Thoralf
Skolmsson were renowned strongmen from the earliest generation of settlers in Iceland. In *Bard's Saga*, Thoralf Skolmsson
wrestles with Hallmund from Balljokul, who appears in *The Saga
of Grettir the Strong*, and 'they are nearly matched'.

66. *three thousand ells of homespun*: Roughly the price of forty
cows.

67. *long and fairly narrow valley*: Thorisdal is mentioned in many
Icelandic folktales from later centuries, and is always described
in a similar fashion, as a concealed valley in the wilderness where
outlaws took sanctuary.

68. *Grim spent the winter on Arnarvatn moor*: This account seems
to draw on another in *The Saga of the People of Laxardal*, where
the same Grim has a similar encounter with Thorkel to that
described with Hallmund here, though it does not end in a killing.

69. *waterfall*: The topography of Bardardal is difficult to reconcile
with the description here, especially since there is no waterfall in
the River Eyjardalsa to match the one that Grettir swims under.
Interestingly, there are many waterfalls near Thorhallsstadir
in Forsaeludal, where Grettir wrestled with Glam, which are
much closer to this description, including one named Skessufoss
('Ogress Falls').

70. *a rock in the shape of a woman*: According to folklore, trolls are
creatures of darkness and turn to stone if caught by the rays of
daylight. Many natural rock formations with semi-human shapes
are explained in this way.

71. *shafted sword*: The Icelandic term *heftisax*, found only here,
mirrors the *hæftmece* which Beowulf uses to dispatch Grendel's
mother.

72. *Gudmund the Powerful*: Gudmund Eyjolfsson the Powerful was
one of the leading chieftains of his time and was famed for his
generosity. He is the main character of *The Saga of the People
of Ljosavatn* and features in many others.

73. *After Thorstein Kuggason was killed . . . Thorodd and Bork the
Stout's son Sam*: Although Thorstein Kuggason is mentioned in
many sagas, none of them relates how he died (in the year 1027,
according to annals). A rather more favourable portrait of
Thorodd Snorrason is presented in other accounts (such as *The
Saga of the People of Eyri* and *The Saga of King Olaf the Saint*),
and the reason for his dispute with his father is unknown. Bork
the Stout, Snorri the Godi's paternal uncle, is one of the main
characters in *Gisli Sursson's Saga*.

74. *fifteen or sixteen years*: This calculation is consistent with the chronology of the saga itself, if Grettir's first (lesser) outlawry at the age of fifteen is included.

75. *the opening of his speech*: This long and eloquent pledge of a truce closely resembles the one delivered in *The Saga of the Slayings on the Heath* and also a passage in the 'Grey Goose' law code.

76. *he undertook to drive Grettir away*: Although Drangey is an isolated island where Grettir would appear to be likely to do least harm, with its vast bird population and its scurvy-grass it served as a source of food for much of the community living along the fjord (hence the references to Grettir as a scavenger). The roles are reversed: instead of ridding the ordinary people of monsters, he has become one.

77. *Some of them felt that he had completed his sentence*: Despite the promise made by Stein Thorgestsson (who was Lawspeaker from 1031–3), no legal grounds are known for commuting sentences of outlawry after twenty years have been served.

78. *five verses*: The incidents alluded to in verses 65, 66 and 67 are not related in the saga itself. The encounter in verse 67 is mentioned in *The Saga of the People of Ljosavatn*, but it is stated there that they did not fight.

79. *Bare is the back of a brotherless man*: This proverb is also found in *Njal's Saga*, used ironically by Kari.

80. *one year short of forty-five*: This chronology is inconsistent with the saga itself and is not in some manuscripts.

81. *at daybreak*: Killing at night was considered murderous and despicable.

82. *buried at the church*: The 'Grey Goose' law code prescribes that outlaws should not be buried in church ground without the approval of the bishop of the quarter.

83. *Odd the Monk*: Odd Snorrason was a monk at Thingeyri monastery, in the Hunavatn district where *Grettir* is set, in the second half of the twelfth century. Around 1190 he wrote a Latin life of King Olaf Tryggvason, now only preserved in an Icelandic translation from the thirteenth century.

84. *the comments he had made about his arms*: In Chapter 41 Grettir says, 'I don't think I've ever seen another pair of tongs like those arms of yours. I can't imagine you even have the strength of a woman.' 'That may be true,' replies Thorstein, 'but you should know that if these skinny arms don't avenge your death, nothing ever will.'

85. *Michael Catalactus*: Michael IV became emperor of Byzantium (1034–41) after marrying the empress dowager Zoë. It was under his rule in particular that the Varangian Guard flourished, with its strong contingent of mercenary warriors from Scandinavia.

86. *she had both men released*: One version of *The Saga of King Harald the Stern* (who was king of Norway from 1046–66 and died at the battle of Stamford Bridge, days before the Battle of Hastings) contains a similar episode in a 'black dungeon' in Constantinople, where Harald is released by a mystical woman inspired by the spirit of his half-brother, King Olaf the Saint. Furthermore, Thorstein's later courtship of Spes and his ingenious avoidance of her suspicious husband echo the description of Harald's love affair with Maria, niece of the empress Zoë. Although the events in Constantinople are strongly influenced by Continental Romance and are 'Eastern' fantasies, the historical presence of Harald and other northerners there is corroborated by Greek historians.

87. *their kinship*: As mentioned in chapter 1 and pointed out by Grettir to King Olaf in chapter 39, they have a common forebear in Ofeig Hobbler.

88. *Sturla the Lawspeaker has said*: The citation of the Lawspeaker's judgement on Grettir has been interpreted as meaning that he composed at least an early version of the saga, although this may be simply a formal literary device; similarly the author of *The Saga of Hord and the People of Holm* also concludes by listing three qualities of his hero.

THE STRUCTURE OF
THE SAGA OF GRETTIR THE STRONG

Part I
Onund Tree-leg
(chs. 1–13)

Part II
The Life of Grettir
(chs. 14–85)

Part III
Thorstein Dromund and Spes
(chs. 86–93)

Act I
Childhood
(chs. 14–16)

Act II
First trip to Norway
(chs. 17–24)

Act III
Glam
(chs. 28–37)

Act IV
Second trip to Norway
(chs. 37–45)

Act V
Outlawry
(chs. 46–85)

Grettir returns and avenges Atli
(chs. 46–8)

Grettir in the West Fjords and Kjol
(chs. 49–54)

Grettir on Arnarvatn moor and in Hallmund's cave
(chs. 55–7)

Grettir in the West and in Thorisdal
(chs. 58–61)

Grettir in the East Fjords and the North
(chs. 61–8)

Last stand on Drangey, Aftermath
(chs. 69–85)

Plot Summary

The Saga of Grettir the Strong is divided into three sections, dealing with Grettir's great-grandfather, Onund Tree-leg, Grettir himself, and his half-brother Thorstein Dromund and his wife Spes.

Readers are also advised to consult the maps, because localized episodes are an exceptionally strong feature of this saga.

Part I: Onund Tree-leg (chs. 1–13)

The story of Onund Tree-leg forms a prelude to the main story, and like the opening of so many Sagas of Icelanders it focuses on events in Norway which led to the settlement of Iceland in the late ninth and early tenth centuries. This section is based on the thirteenth-century *Book of Settlements*, which is a detailed account of the different places in Iceland claimed by the voyagers who arrived from Norway and the Viking settlements of Britain over the period 870–930.

There is something in the punchy immediacy of the style in this section that suggests the heathen belief in man above all else, living solely by his own strength and dying with a satisfied smile on his lips. Although it is not long, this prelude forms a necessary part of the whole. Unlike Grettir, Onund remains in Fortune's favour, even when Providence restricts his physical prowess. A leg wound does not bring Onund to his death, as it will Grettir; instead, he becomes 'the bravest and nimblest one-legged man ever to live in Iceland' (ch. 11). Onund regrets swapping his rich ancestral heritage in Norway for 'this cold-backed mountain', but he and other members of his pioneering generation settle down to a peaceful existence.

The next generation – the first to be born and bred in Iceland – is beset by quarrels, yet lacks the epic stature of the settlers. The splendid account of the battle over the beached whale verges on the mock-heroic (ch. 12). The prelude ends by introducing Grettir's father Asmund as a young man, unappealingly lazy and moody as his own son will also be (much to Asmund's irritation). The difference, however, is that Asmund goes abroad, returns a rich man and becomes a worthy farmer, while Grettir comes back from his voyage (his first exile) with a reputation for strength, but also for temper, rashness and excessive ambition. While abroad, Asmund also begets Grettir's half-brother Thorstein Dromund, who waits behind the scenes in Norway for the chance to resolve the action by avenging Grettir in Constantinople in the closing chapters.

The action in this opening section jumps more swiftly between characters and scenes than the main story. It is summarized in the table below.

Ch.	Action
1	Onund introduced. Onund, Balki, Orm and Hallvard defeat King Kjarval and spend three summers raiding Ireland and Scotland, then go to Norway.
2	Ascent of Harald Tangle-hair (later King Harald Fair-hair) in Norway. Onund joins the allies against him, but they are defeated in the Battle of Havsfjord, where Onund loses a leg and gains the nickname Tree-leg.
3	Onund and Thrand go to the Hebrides. Ofeig Grettir and Thormod join them. Onund is betrothed to Ofeig's daughter Aesa and Thrand to Thormod's daughter.
4	Battle with the Vikings Vigbjod and Vestmar.
5	Balki and Hallvard settle in Iceland. Thrand and Onund make peace with Eyvind, son-in-law of Kjarval, in Ireland.
6	Ofeig Grettir and Thormod settle in Iceland. Eyvind and Thrand quarrel over their paternal inheritance. Thrand and Onund go to Norway to collect the inheritance, then Thrand goes to Iceland.
7	Onund kills Harek, who has taken over his property in Norway. Grim kills Ondott Crow for selling land from Bjorn's inheritance. Onund and Ondott's sons burn him to death, fight the local people, and stay with Eirik. Slaying of Asgrim.
8	Onund and Ondott's son Asmund sail to Iceland.
9	Onund settles in Strandir, farming at Kaldbak and Reykjarfjord.
10	Ofeig Grettir is killed by Thorbjorn, Champion of Earls, at Grettisgeil. Olaf Feilan marries Alfdis from Barra, a kinswoman of Onund's wife Aesa.
11	Onund and Aesa have two sons, Thorgeir Bottle-back and Ofeig Grettir. When Aesa dies, Onund marries Thordis. Their son is

Ch. Action

Thorgrim Grey-head, Grettir the Strong's grandfather. When Onund dies, Thordis marries Audun Shaft. Their son is Asgeir from Asgeirsa. Quarrels over land and rights in Strandir (see map on p. 258).

12 Battle of Rifsker over beached whale.

13 Thorgrim moves to Bjarg in Midfjord. His and Thordis's son Asmund Grey-locks grows up and sails abroad. He marries Rannveig in Norway; their son is Thorstein Dromund. Asmund returns to Iceland, marries Asdis and takes over the farm at Bjarg on his father's death.

Part II: The Life of Grettir (chs. 14–85)

In chapter 14 the central action of the saga begins: the life of Grettir Asmundarson the Strong. Since the 'Life of Grettir' is both complex in structure and wide in scope, it is summarized here in the form of five separate acts. Grettir's outlawry in Act V is subdivided further into six independent regional episodes. This is a convenient approach for summarizing the plot and illustrating the way that the main themes develop, and should also help the reader to distinguish between similar incidents and characters with similar names – the use of echoes and parallels is a distinct feature of this saga, as illustrated in the table on pp. 236–7.

There is an apparent inconsistency between the chronology of the saga and various statements by the author, mainly because Grettir does not seem to be an outlaw in Iceland for nearly twenty winters after his second sentence. However, if we count his outlawry as beginning with his first sentence (three years in Norway), followed by a winter in Iceland and another in Norway (making a total of five), then he appears to be entering the fifteenth year of his second sentence of greater outlawry (making a total of twenty) at the age of 35, when he dies on Drangey.

Act I (chs. 14–16)
Portrait of the Outlaw as an Unruly Child

Ch.	Action	Grettir's age	Time according to the saga	Outlawry	Year
14	Grettir the menace	10	autumn–winter		1006
15	Ball game on the ice in Midfjord	14	winter		1010
16	Thorkel Scratcher's prophecy about Asmund's sons	15	spring		1011
	Trip to the Assembly – Grettir kills Skeggi First sentence of outlawry		summer (June)		

The child Grettir is introduced as a very sharply drawn character with conflicting traits that remain with him for the rest of his life: he is overbearing, taciturn and rough, mischievous in both word and deed, short-tempered, unheedful, unruly, obstinate and a troublemaker. This negative picture is compounded by Grettir's ill-treatment of the farm animals, which is unparalleled in the sagas. While all these tendencies hint at a difficult adult life, Grettir also displays other qualities that could serve a good-tempered man well – and they earn him renown in individual episodes. Some of his qualities are marred by corresponding flaws: intelligent/impatient; cunning/malicious; chooses his words well/surly; poetic gift/love of lampoons; large and strong/lazy.

The contrast is heightened by the character of Grettir's brother Atli, who is their father's favourite and a promising farmer. Grettir and Asmund do not get on (as ch. 14 shows), although this friction is also an ironic comment on Asmund's disagreements with his own father. Like Egil Skallagrimsson and other heroes, Grettir is the apple of his mother's eye. Asdis comes from a high-born family, sides with Grettir in his rebellion against his father, instils him with ancient heroic ethics and gives him a fine sword to take on his first journey from home. This is by no means the only instance in the Sagas of Icelanders where women of strong character are more aware of the old heroic values than are their husbands, who have settled down to farm the land in peaceful coexistence with God and men.

Act I ends with Grettir being sentenced to three years' outlawry for his first slaying.

Act II (chs. 17–24)
Trials of Strength and Spirit

Ch.	Action	Grettir's age	Time according to the saga	Outlawry	Year
17	Sails to Norway with Haflidi	15	late summer		1011
18	With Thorfinn on Haramsoy		autumn–winter	(1)	1011–12
	Enters the mound		before Yule		
19	Kills the berserks		Yule		
20	Leaves Haramsoy	16	spring		
	Summer at Vagen		summer		
	With Thorkel at Salten		autumn–winter early	(2)	1012–13
21	Kills the bear		winter		
22	Leaves Salten	17	spring		
	At Vagen		autumn		
	– kills Bjorn				
23	Steinkjer in Trondheim		autumn–winter	(3)	1013–14
	– kills Hjarrandi				
24	With Thorfinn on Haramsoy	18	spring		
	Tunsberg – kills Gunnar				
	Returns to Iceland		summer		1014

In Act II Grettir undergoes his first ordeals as a fully formed hero. After lazing around on the ship leaving Iceland, he bails it out and saves a seemingly hopeless situation for the first of many times. His string of triumphant tests of strength continues when they reach land, bringing him renown and honour: he retrieves weapons and treasure from Kar's mound, defeats twelve berserks and wrestles with a bear. The motifs of these 'Herculean labours' are paralleled in other sagas, particularly the legendary ones. Yet the portrayal of Grettir's ascendancy to a heroic role has a slapstick colouring. On board ship bound for Norway, Grettir's great achievement of bailing out the ship faster than the rest of the crew is rather Chaplinesque; he kills the bear to retrieve a bearskin thrown there by its namesake (Bjorn); and he dispatches the berserks less by physical strength than with verbal skills and dissemblance – yet he deludes the helpless and innocent women as much as the villains. But his rise to grandeur comes to an end when he takes offence at a slight and kills three brothers. Then Grettir is no longer safe in Norway and returns to Iceland, his outlawry over; but in a sense another outlawry, from his roots in Norway and society's values, has begun.

Act III (chs. 28–37)
Fighting Evil

Ch.	Action	Grettir's age	Time according to the saga	Outlawry	Year
28	Grettir arrives in Skagafjord, wrestles with Audun, quarrels with Bardi	18	summer		1014
29	Horse-fight at Langafit				
30	Battle at Grettishaf				
31	Low profile The Slayings on the Heath; Grettir and Bardi meet		August		
32–33	Hauntings in Forsaeludal				
34–35	Grettir kills Glam, incurs his curse Grettir stays at home		Winter Nights winter		1014–15

Ch.	Action	Grettir's age	Time according to the saga	Outlawry	Year
36	Thorbjorn Traveller slanders Grettir		autumn		1014
37	Grettir at Gasar – kills Thorbjorn Traveller Second trip abroad	19	spring		1015

This section opens with a short diversion (chs. 25–27) describing the most infamous pair of troublemakers in all the sagas: the sworn brothers Thorgeir and Thormod Kolbrun's Poet (cf. *The Saga of the Sworn Brothers*). Grettir's father Asmund rises in social status as a farmer and worthy citizen with the settlement he engineers at the Althing for the slaying of Thorgils Masson after another dispute over a beached whale – in which law rather than brute force is brought to prevail over Thorgeir. Meanwhile, Grettir becomes increasingly impatient and rash, provoking quarrels and eager to test his strength against anything, seemingly compelled by a self-destructive force.

The story digresses to describe a succession of hauntings in Forsaeludal, which will set the scene for the turning point in Grettir's life – and ultimately his downfall. The shepherd Glam is brought in to rid a farmer, Thorhall, of a ghost with trollish characteristics, but Glam dies while doing so and his ghost returns to haunt the farm with redoubled vigour. A worthy adversary has been found for Grettir and their battle is described with an almost a cinematic quality. And while Grettir is victorious, Glam's curse 'caps' his strength and makes him afraid of the dark: finally, limits have been imposed on Grettir's heroism.

Act IV (chs. 37–45)
All Out of Luck

Ch.	Action	Grettir's age	Time according to the saga	Outlawry	Year
37	Arrives in Norway	19	late summer		1015

Ch.	Action	Grettir's age	Time according to the saga	Outlawry	Year
38	Travels north Accidentally burns Thorir's sons to death Goes to see the king in Trondheim	19	early winter winter		
39	His short temper costs him the chance to prove his innocence by an ordeal				
40	Goes to Jaeren 'around Yule'; kills Snaekoll the berserk		Christmas		1015
41	Goes to Tunsberg after Yule, stays there until spring Returns to Iceland	20	spring summer		1016
42–5	Thorbjorn Ox kills Atli				

Grettir goes to Norway for a second time, and Glam's curse is already beginning to work. These episodes strike a sharp contrast with Grettir's previous, triumphant journey through Norway. Even when he tries to perform a good deed by swimming to fetch fire for his shipwrecked companions, he accidentally burns to death the sons of a powerful Icelander, Thorir from Gard, for which he will later be declared an outlaw. Grettir's temper gets the better of him and he forfeits the chance to prove his innocence with an ordeal by fire. Grettir's half-brother Thorstein, who lives in Norway, is reintroduced before the scene switches to trace the remainder of the tragic hero's life in Iceland; Thorstein will return at the end of the story to take revenge and allow a Christian moral to be drawn.

Act V (chs. 46–85)
Journey around an Island

Act V is the longest and most complex, a sprawling succession of
encounters in the worlds of men and beings, which culminates in
Grettir's exile and death on Drangey. While the scenes are structured
to alternate between the comic and the serious, enhancing the tragic
undertone, they can be divided into geographical sections (see map on
pp. 262–3).

1. Grettir returns and avenges Atli (chs. 46–8)

Ch.	Action	Grettir's age	Time according to the saga	Outlawry	Year
46	Declared an outlaw at the Althing	20	June		1016
47	Returns to Iceland Saddle-head Verses Stays at Bjarg		August		
48	Slays Thorbjorn Ox and Arnor Stays at Ljarskogar		autumn		

2. Grettir in the West Fjords and Kjol (chs. 49–54)

Ch.	Action	Grettir's age	Time according to the saga	Outlawry	Year
49	Goes to Tunga, then Reykjanes	20	winter nights		1016
50	Arrives at Reykjaholar and spends the winter there with the sworn brothers		winter	1	1016–17

Ch.	Action	Grettir's age	Time according to the saga	Outlawry	Year
51	In the West Fjords, captured by farmers,	21	spring–summer		
52	saved by Thorbjorg				
53	Stays with Thorstein in Ljarskogar	22	winter–spring	2	1017–18
	Stays with Grim until after the Althing		summer		
54	On Kjol		summer		
	Seeks advice from Skafti and Grim				
	Goes to the Arnarvatn moor		autumn		

Grettir's 'grand tour' of Iceland allows him to meet the heroes of a number of other important sagas, in which he is mentioned summarily. Some of these scenes are written from a comic or ironic viewpoint, such as his uneasy truce with the sworn brothers.

3. Grettir on Arnarvatn moor and in Hallmund's cave (chs. 55–57)

Ch.	Action	Grettir's age	Time according to the saga	Outlawry	Year
55	First winter on Arnarvatn moor, with the treacherous outlaw Grim	23	winter	3	1018–19
56	Second and third winters on Arnarvatn	24–5	summer–winter	4	1019–20
	moor, with the treacherous outlaw Thorir Red-beard	25	summer–winter	5	1020–21

Ch.	Action	Grettir's age	Time according to the saga	Outlawry	Year
57	Battle at Hamraskard, goes to join his rescuer Hallmund		summer		
	Goes to West Iceland		autumn		

For the first time, Grettir follows the advice of Skafti the Lawspeaker and avoids preying on farmers to survive. Although his fear of the darkness intensifies, he is fated to live in solitude and should learn to trust no other outcasts from society after his encounters with two deceitful outlaws. In the last part of his exile, however, he will break this commandment by allowing the lazy slave Glaum to join him on Drangey – which leads to his downfall.

4. Grettir in the West and in Thorisdal (chs. 58–61)

Ch.	Action	Grettir's age	Time according to the saga	Outlawry	Year
58	First winter in the mountainside lair on Fagraskogarfjall	26	winter	6	1021–22
59	Episode with the boastful Gisli		autumn		
	Second winter in the lair	27	winter	7	1022–23
60	In the lair; battle with local farmers at 'Grettir's Point'		summer–autumn		1023
	Third winter in the lair	28	winter	8	1023–24
61	Seeks advice from Grim, stays with Hallmund		June (Althing) summer		1024
	In Thorisdal between the glaciers	29	winter	9	1024–25

Grettir returns to the world of men, apparently in less danger there than he was in the wilderness. He is protected by the hero of another saga, Bjorn, the Champion of the People of Hitardal, but takes no direct part in that saga's action; rather, he seems to be in the role of comic punisher of the arrogant, in the humiliation he deals out to the dandyish Gisli.

Thorisdal is a hidden valley on the edge of the wilderness where outlaws seek refuge under the protection of trolls. The valley was the setting for folktales and stories of outlaws in later centuries, which seem to draw heavily on the description in *The Saga of Grettir*. A striking feature of this scene is that the source for this passage appears to be Grettir himself: it describes what he saw and felt, and even cites him as an authority. In the world of giants and trolls he is free from Glam's curse and no longer fears the dark. It seems that the only reason he leaves the valley is that he is bored there.

5. Grettir in the East Fjords and the North (chs. 61–68)

Ch.	Action	Grettir's age	Time according to the saga	Outlawry	Year
61	'Fool's errand' to the East Fjords, seeking support	30	summer–winter	10	1025–27
62	Death of Hallmund				
63	Stays on the heaths between the east and the north		summer		1027
	Heads north		early winter		
64	Arrives in Bardardal just before Christmas,				
65–66	fights the trolls and stays in the valley	31	winter	11	1127–28

Ch.	Action	Grettir's age	Time according to the saga	Outlawry	Year
67	Seeks advice from Gudmund the Powerful, goes to Bjarg		spring	11	1028
	Ambushes travellers crossing Brattabrekka		mid-summer		
68	Challenged by Thorodd, son of Snorri the Godi		summer		

Again, Grettir is untroubled by Glam's curse in Bardardal. The battle with the monster there is his second great feat in ridding a community of a pest from another world, but unlike the encounter with Glam he reaps only glory from it. While the scene has clear parallels with Beowulf's fight with Grendel's mother in the Old English poem, the author has probably slotted Grettir into an international folktale motif rather than drawn directly on a specific and possibly written source. Other literary links are provided with the death of Grettir's friend, the giant Hallmund, which echoes a passage in *The Saga of the People of Laxardal*, and a meeting with the son of Snorri the Godi, the main character of *The Saga of the People of Eyri*.

6. Last stand on Drangey, aftermath (chs. 69–85)

Ch.	Action	Grettir's age	Time according to the saga	Outlawry	Year
69	Illugi and Grettir travel through the northern countryside	31	summer	11	1028
	They head for Drangey		autumn		
70	Chieftains in Skagafjord				

Ch.	Action	Grettir's age	Time according to the saga	Outlawry	Year
71	Farmers meet Grettir		winter solstice		
	First winter on Drangey	32	winter	12	1028–29
72	Hegranes Assembly, wrestling match		spring		1029
73	Thorbjorn Hook's first expedition to Drangey		late summer		
74	Second winter on Drangey	33	winter	13	1029–30
75	Grettir swims to fetch fire		(spring)		1030
76	Thorbjorn Hook's second expedition to Drangey Haering climbs the cliff		autumn		
	Third winter on Drangey	34	winter	14	1030–31
	Death of Snorri the Godi		spring		1031
77	Length of Grettir's outlawry disputed at the Althing		June		
78	Thorbjorn Hook's third expedition to Drangey, with Thurid the crone. Grettir and Thurid swap insults, he injures her with a rock		August		

Ch.	Action	Grettir's age	Time according to the saga	Outlawry	Year
79	Thurid sends the cursed tree-stump to Drangey Grettir injures his leg	34	three weeks before winter	14	1031
80	Grettir's wound turns gangrenous; bad weather				
81	Thorbjorn Hook gathers forces, fourth expedition to Drangey				
82	Attack on Drangey, Grettir and Illugi killed	35	winter	(15)	1031

The closing chapters of Grettir's self-imposed exile are fairly self-explanatory. Drama is gradually built up when Thorbjorn Hook manages, after several failed attempts and with the help of his foster-mother Thurid's sorcery, to scale the island. Grettir and his brother Illugi die heroic deaths, fighting to the last against insurmountable odds. In the aftermath, chapters 83–86, the tone of the saga changes. Thorbjorn Hook's killing of Grettir earns him condemnation from the viewpoints of both the heroic ethic and Christian morality.

Part III: The 'Tale' of Thorstein Dromund and Spes (chs. 86–92)

In the third and final main section, the scene and atmosphere change, from the harsh, exposed rocky stronghold of Drangey in the far north to the colourful court of the Byzantine emperor in Constantinople, a world of romance. Thorstein Dromund is the hero of this section, making up for what he lacks in brawn with the more 'sophisticated' accomplishments of cunning and musicality. Equally, the real hero might be seen as Spes, the first female to play a leading, active role in the saga. She frees Thorstein from imprisonment in the dungeon, plots to meet him when he becomes her lover, and leads the saga to its monastic conclusion with a learned disquisition.

While this section is clearly influenced by the fashionable Continental Romances of the thirteenth and fourteenth centuries, especially in its cuckoldry theme, it also draws heavily on a branch of Icelandic tradition, with clear parallels in *The Saga of King Harald the Stern* (in the compilation *Morkinskinna*).

Parallels

One of the challenges in following the plot of *The Saga of Grettir the Strong* is the deliberate use of parallels in the action – in some cases the same or similar names occur in scenes that reflect on, reinforce or contrast with each other. These devices may be summarized as follows:

Paired	Tripled (and quadrupled)
Grettir and Audun fight	Atli, Grettir and Illugi (and Thorstein Dromund)
Grettir fetches treasure from a mound (Haramsoy) or a cave (Bardardal)	Grettir's tests in childhood
	Grettir lifts rocks
Grettir's travels to Norway	Grettir kills three brothers in Norway (Bjorn, Hjarrandi and Gunnar)
Grettir fights berserks	
Outlaws stay with Grettir on Arnarvatn heath	Three of his main adversaries are called Thorbjorn (Ox, Traveller and Hook) (and Glaum on Drangey)
Grettir, in disguise, calls himself Gest	
Grettir and Thorir from Gard meet	Grettir fights evil spirits (Haramsoy, Forsaeludal and Bardardal) (and called a scavenger on Drangey and killed by Thorbjorn Hook)
Grettir swims to fetch fire (Norway and Drangey)	
	Grettir's longest stays in the wilderness (Arnarvatn moor, Thorisdal and Drangey)
	Three years in three places (Arnarvatn heath, Fagraskogarfjall and Drangey)

Paired	Tripled (and quadrupled)
	Valleys (Forsaeludal, Thorisdal and Bardardal)
	Hallmund steals fish from Grim on Arnarvatn moor three times
	Grettir's women (the wife of Bard the crewman, (possibly) the wife of Thorfinn from Haramsoy, and the mother of his son, Steinvor at Sandhaugar) (and the servant-woman at Reykir)
	Thorbjorn Hook's unsuccessful trips to Drangey
	Grettir tricks Hook
	Thurid's cursed tree-stump comes ashore on Drangey
	Glaum's accidents (fire, tree and ladder)
	Thorstein and Spes meet secretly and Sigurd makes three unsuccessful attempts to find him
	Sturla Thordarson states three reasons why Grettir is the most distinguished of all outlaws

ONUND TREE-LEG (CHS. 1–13)

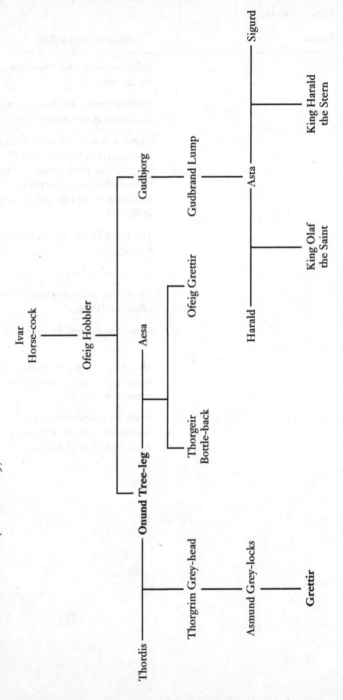

THORGRIM GREY-HEAD

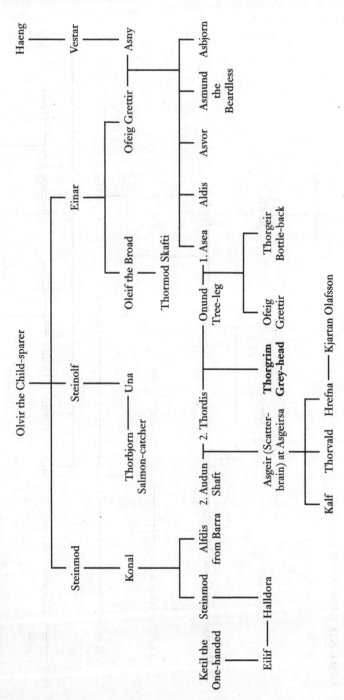

ASMUND AND ASDIS

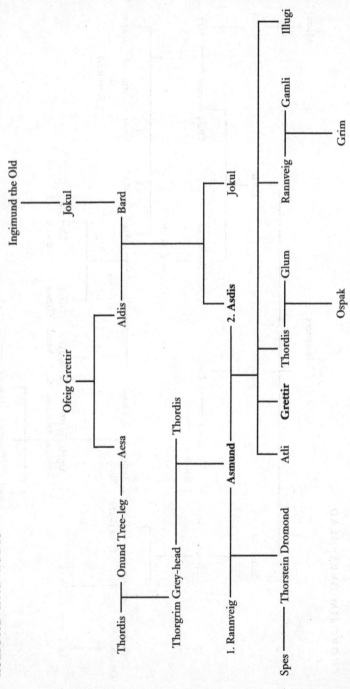

Social, Political and Legal Structure

The notion of kinship is central to the sense of honour and duty in the sagas. It essentially involves a sense of belonging not unlike that underlying the Celtic clan systems. The Icelandic word for kin or clan (*ætt*) is cognate with other words meaning 'to own' and 'direction' – it could be described as a 'social compass'.

Establishing kinship is one of the justifications for the long genealogies, which tend to strike non-Icelandic readers as idiosyncratic detours, and also for the preludes in Norway before the main saga action begins. Members of the modern nuclear family or close relatives are only part of the picture, since kinsmen are all those who are linked through a common ancestor – preferably one of high birth and high repute – as far back as five or six generations or even more.

Marriage ties, sworn brotherhood and other bonds could create conflicting loyalties with respect to the duty of revenge, of course, although in *The Saga of Grettir the Strong* there are no such crises. Most characters seem to want to avoid direct involvement, suggesting that the vendetta ethic had outlived its function. A strict order stipulated who was to take revenge within the immediate family, with a 'multiplier effect' if those seeking vengeance were killed in the process. The obligation to take revenge was inherited, just like wealth, property and claims.

The system was patriarchal, although there are notable exceptions. Likewise, the duty of revenge fell only upon males, but women were often responsible for instigating it, either by urging a husband or brother to action by suggesting they are cowards or by bringing up their sons with a strong sense of vengeance and even supplying them with old weapons that are family heirlooms.

Iceland was unique among European societies in the tenth to thirteenth centuries in two distinct respects: it had no king and no executive

power to follow through the pronouncements of its highly sophisticated legislative and judicial institutions. This lack of an executive
power meant that there was no way of preventing men from taking
the law into their own hands, which gave rise to many memorable
conflicts recorded in the sagas, but also led to the gradual disinte-
gration of the Commonwealth in the thirteenth century.

The Althing (established 930 at Thingvellir) served not only as a
general or national assembly (which is what its name means), but also
as the main festival and social gathering of the year, where people exchanged stories and news and renewed acquaintances with old friends
and relatives. Originally it was inaugurated (with a pagan ceremony)
by the leading chieftain or godi (*allsherjargoði*), a descendant of the
first settler, Ingolf Arnarson, in the tenth week of summer. Early in
the eleventh century the opening day was changed to the Thursday of
the eleventh week of summer (June 18–24). Legislative authority at
the Althing was in the hands of the Law Council, while there were
two levels of judiciary, the Quarter Courts and the Fifth Court.

The Law Council originally comprised the thirty-six godis, along
with two thingmen for each, and the Lawspeaker, who was the highest
authority in the Commonwealth, elected by the Law Council for a
term of three years. It was the duty of the Lawspeaker to recite the
entire procedures of the assembly and one-third of the laws of the
country every year. He presided over the meetings of the Law Council
and ruled on points of legal interpretation.

Quarter Courts, established at the Althing around 965, evolved
from earlier regional Spring Assemblies, probably panels of nine men,
that had dealt with cases involving people from the same quarter.
Three new godords (the office or authority of a godi) were created in
the north when the Quarter Courts were set up. The godis appointed
thirty-six men to the Quarter Court and their decisions had to be
unanimous.

Around 1005 a Fifth Court was established as a kind of court of
appeal to hear cases which were unresolved by the Quarter Courts.
The godis appointed forty-eight members to the Fifth Court and the
two sides in each case were allowed to reject six each. A simple
majority among the remaining thirty-six then decided the outcome
and lots were drawn in the event of a tie. With the creation of the
Fifth Court, the number of godis was increased correspondingly and
with their two thingmen each and the Lawspeaker, the Law Council
then comprised 145 people in all.

Legal disputes feature prominently in the Sagas of Icelanders and the
prosecution and defence of a case followed clearly defined procedures.

Cases were prepared locally some time before the Thing and could be dismissed there if they were technically flawed. Preparation generally took one of two forms. A panel of 'neighbours' could be called, comprised of five or nine people who lived near the scene of the incident or the home of the accused, to testify to what had happened. Alternatively, a party could go to the home of the accused to summon him during the Summons Days, two weeks before the Spring Assembly, but three or four weeks before the Althing.

The accused generally did not attend the Thing, but was defended by someone else, who called witnesses and was entitled to disqualify members of the panel. Panels did not testify to the details and facts of the case in the modern sense, but determined whether the incident had taken place. The case was then summed up and a ruling passed on it by the Quarter Court.

Cases were often settled without going through the complex court procedure, either by arbitration, a ruling from a third party who was accepted by both sides, or by self-judgement by either of the parties involved in the case. Duelling was another method for settling disputes, but was formally banned in Iceland in 1006.

Penalties depended upon the seriousness of the case and took the form of either monetary compensation or outlawry. A confiscation court would seize the belongings of a person outlawed for three years or life. Two types of outlawry were applied, depending upon the seriousness of the offence: lesser outlawry (*fjörbaugsgarður*) and full outlawry (*skóggangur*). According to the legal code *Grágás*, a lesser outlaw enjoyed sanctuary in three homes in Iceland, no more than one day's passage from each other, and safe passage along a direct route between them, but was obliged to leave the country as soon as possible for three years' exile. A formal request for passage abroad also had to be made on his behalf; thus, in *The Saga of Grettir the Strong*, Asmund asks his friend Haflidi to take Grettir to Norway after his first sentence of outlawry at the age of fifteen (ch. 17). A fine of one mark was also levied on the outlaw – *fjörbaugsgarður* means literally 'life-ring enclosure' and the penalty was originally a silver ring to be paid to the godi in charge of the court, as a token to save the offender's life, while the enclosure was his safe route into exile. A sentence of lesser outlawry was converted to full outlawry if he returned to Iceland before three years, if no passage was requested on his behalf, or if he could not arrange to leave the country within three summers after sentence was passed on him. While Grettir accepts his lesser outlawry and goes to Norway where he wins fame and renown, a hero's refusal to leave is also crucial to the drama of some sagas, the best-known example being Gunnar Hamundarson in *Njal's Saga*, who consciously chooses to face certain death at home.

Full outlawry meant that a man lost all his goods and rights and was not to be fed, helped on his way or sheltered – it was tantamount to a death sentence. The full outlaw often had no recourse but to live in the wilds – as the term for him, *skógarmaður* ('forest man'), implies. Grettir spends long periods in the inhabited wilderness, but also enjoyed the unlawful protection of chieftains such as Bjorn, Champion of the People of Hitardal (ch. 58). Powerful local leaders sometimes pitted outlaws against each other in their running feuds:

> One winter it was said that Bjorn had some full outlaws living with him, and got them to build a fortification around his farm. And for this same harbouring of outlaws Thord prosecuted Bjorn, hoping to get redress, if he could, for Bjorn's invalidation of the last case against him. He expected that this time he would be more successful in his suit. It happened sometime later that Thord Kolbeinsson sheltered two full outlaws and got them lodgings in Hraundal . . .
>
> (*The Saga of Bjorn, Champion of the People of Hitardal*, ch. 22)

Some of the more infamous outlaws, such as Gisli Sursson and Grettir the Strong, however, were simply considered 'too hot to handle' by most chieftains:

> Then he [Gisli] spent another three winters journeying around Iceland, meeting up with various chieftains and trying to elicit their support. As a result of Thorgrim Nef's evil arts, and the magic rite and spells he had performed, Gisli had no success in attempting to persuade these chieftains to ally themselves with him; although their support sometimes seemed almost forthcoming, something always obstructed its course.
>
> (*Gisli Sursson's Saga*, ch. 21)

> Then he [Grettir] went across the south of Iceland to the East Fjords. He spent the whole summer and winter travelling and went to see all the leading men, but he was turned away everywhere and could find neither food nor a place to sleep.
>
> (*The Saga of Grettir the Strong*, ch. 61)

A full outlaw could be rightfully slain wherever he was found – in Iceland or abroad – but the killer did not always earn much renown from doing so (for example Eyjolf the Grey in *Gisli Sursson's Saga* and Thorbjorn Hook in *The Saga of Grettir*) and sometimes ultimately paid with his life in revenge. Exclusion from society did not end with the outlaw's death, since he was not to be buried in hallowed ground, although this was sometimes done later. Grettir's head and body are buried in separate plots:

> Grettir's nephew Skeggi, who was Gamli's son and Thorodd Half-poem's son-in-law, went north to Skagafjord at the instigation of Thorvald Asgeirsson and his son-in-law Isleif, who later became Bishop of Skalholt, and with everyone's approval. He took a boat and went to Drangey to fetch Grettir and Illugi's bodies and took them to Reykir on Reykjastrond where they were buried at the church. As proof that Grettir is buried there, when the church at Reykir was moved in the days of the Sturlung clan, his bones were dug up and everyone thought they were huge and strong. Illugi's bones were then buried north of the church and Grettir's head by the church on the farm at Bjarg.
>
> (ch. 84)

It was common to put a bounty on an outlaw's head. This was generally one mark (48 ells of homespun), but was raised to three in the case of serious threats to society such as Grettir. Outlaws could have their sentences reduced or commuted if they killed other outlaws – Grettir narrowly escapes plots by two who try to befriend him (chs. 55–6). This appears to be the only way in which an outlaw could free himself from the life sentence, despite the claim in *The Saga of Grettir* that the maximum penalty is twenty years:

> At this time Skafti Thoroddsson the Lawspeaker died. This was a great setback to Grettir, since he had promised to advocate the commutation of Grettir's sentence when he had been in outlawry for twenty years. It was the nineteenth year of his outlawry when the events just described took place. [. . .] At the Althing that summer, Grettir's kinsmen discussed his outlawry at length. Some of them felt that he had completed his sentence, since he was well into the twentieth year of it. However, the people who had brought charges against him would not accept this, claiming he had committed many deeds that deserved outlawry since then and therefore his sentence should be correspondingly longer. A new Lawspeaker had been appointed, Stein Thorgestsson [. . .] He was asked to make a ruling and told them to check whether this was the twentieth summer since Grettir had been outlawed. This proved to be the case.
>
> Then Thorir from Gard joined in and tried to find every possible objection. He managed to discover that Grettir had spent one year in

Iceland when he was not an outlaw, meaning that he had been an outlaw for eighteen years.

The Lawspeaker said that no man should be an outlaw for more than twenty years, even if some years of his sentences overlapped – 'But before that time I will not deem to have anyone's outlawry lifted.'

Grettir's commutation from outlawry was ruled out on these grounds for the time being, but it seemed certain that the sentence would be lifted the following summer.

(chs. 76–77)

No justification for this claim can be found in *Grágás* or other collections of the old law. It is a legal fabrication and a purely dramatic device inserted by an author who lived more than a century after the laws of the Commonwealth were supplanted by those of the kingdom of Norway, and outlawry replaced by more 'modern' forms of punishment.

Glossary

The Icelandic term is printed in italics, with modern spelling

Althing *alþingi*: General assembly (see Social, Political and Legal Structure).

assembly *þing*: See Social, Political and Legal Structure.

ball game *knattleikur*: A game played with a hard ball and a bat, possibly similar to the Gaelic game known as hurling (which is still played in Scotland and Ireland), only with two players instead of two teams. The rules are uncertain, but the object appears to have been to knock the ball over the opponent's goal line. Ball games are a common motif in the sagas and quarrels over them often lead to lasting and fatal conflicts.

bed closet *hvílugólf, lokrekkja, lokhvíla, lokrekkjugólf*: A private sleeping area used for the heads of better-off households. The closet was usually partitioned off from the rest of the house and had a door that was secured from the inside.

berserk *berserkur* (literally 'bear-shirt'): A warrior who could assume the might of a bear during a kind of induced trance in battle, which made him apparently immune to blows from weapons. In his *Heimskringla* (History of the Kings of Norway), Snorri Sturluson attributes this power to a blessing by Odin, the chief god of the pagan pantheon: 'Odin knew how to make his enemies in battle blind or deaf or full of fear, and their weapons would bite no more than sticks, while his own men went without armour and were as crazed as dogs or wolves, biting at their shields, and as strong as bears or bulls. They killed people, but were impervious to both fire and iron. This is called "going berserk".' By the time of the sagas, berserks had lost all religious dignity and tended to be cast in the role of brutal but simple-minded villains; when heroes do away with them, there is usually little regret and a great deal of local relief.

Closely related to the original concept of the berserk (implied by its literal meaning) are the shape-shifters.

bloody wound *áverki*: Almost always used in a legal sense, that is, with regard to a visible, most likely bloody wound, which could result in legal actions for compensation or some more drastic proceedings like the taking of revenge.

board game *tafl*: Probably refers to chess, which had plainly reached Scandinavia before the twelfth century. However, in certain cases it might also refer to another board game known as *hnefatafl*. The rules of *hnefatafl* are uncertain, even though we know what the boards looked like.

booth *búð*: A temporary dwelling used by those who attended the various assemblies. Structurally, it seems to have involved permanent walls covered by a tent-like roof, probably made from cloth.

compensation *manngjöld, bætur*: Penalties imposed by the courts were of three main kinds: awards of compensation in cash; sentences of lesser outlawry, which could be lessened or dropped by paying compensation; and sentences of full outlawry with no chance of being moderated. In certain cases a man's right to immediate vengeance was recognized, but for many offences compensation was the fixed legal penalty and the injured party had little choice but to accept the settlement offered by the court, an arbitrator or a man who had been given the right to self-judgement (*sjálfdæmi*). It was certainly legal to put pressure on the guilty party to pay. Neither court verdicts nor legislation, nor even the constitutional arrangements, had any coercive power behind them other than the free initiative of individual chieftains with their armed following.

confiscation court *féránsdómur*: See Social, Political and Legal Structure.

cross-bench *pallur, þverpallur*: A raised platform or bench at the inner end of the main room, where women were usually seated.

directions *austur/vestur/norður/suður* (east/west/north/south): These directions are used in a very broad sense in the sagas. They are largely dependent on context and they cannot always be trusted to reflect compass directions. Internationally, 'the east' generally refers to those countries to the east and south-east of Iceland, and although 'easterner' usually means a Norwegian, it can also apply to a Swede (especially since the concept of nationality was still not entirely clear when the sagas were being written), and might even be used for a person who has picked up Russian habits. 'The west' or to 'go west' tends to refer to Ireland and what is now the United Kingdom, but might even refer to lands farther afield; the point of orientation is west of Norway. When confined to Iceland, directions sometimes refer to the quarter to which a person is travelling, for example a man going to the Althing from the east of the country might be said to be going 'south' rather than 'west', and a person going home to the West Fjords from the Althing is said to be going 'west' rather than 'north'.

dowry *heimanfylgja* (literally 'that which accompanies the bride from her home'): This was the amount of money (or land) that a bride's father contributed at her wedding. Like the bride-price, it was legally her property. However, the husband controlled their financial affairs and was responsible for the use to which both these assets were put.

drapa *drápa*: A heroic, laudatory poem, usually in the complicated metre preferred by the Icelandic poets. Such poems were in fashion between the tenth and thirteenth centuries. They were usually composed in honour of kings, earls and other prominent men, living or dead. Occasionally they were addressed to a loved one or made in praise of pagan or Christian religious figures. A drapa usually consisted of three parts: an introduction, a middle section including one or more refrains, and a conclusion. It was clearly distinguished from the *flokk*, which tended to be shorter, less laudatory and without refrains.

duel *hólmganga* (literally 'going to the island'): Used for a formally organized duel, probably because the area prescribed for the fight formed a small island with clearly defined boundaries that separated the action from the outside world; it might also refer to the fact that small islands were originally favoured sites for duels. The rules included that the two duellists slashed at each other alternately, the seconds protecting the principal fighters with shields. Shields hacked to pieces could be replaced by up to three shields on each side. If blood was shed, the fight could be ended and the wounded man could buy himself off with a ransom of three marks of silver, either on the spot or later. The rules are stated in detail in *Kormak's Saga*:

> The duelling laws had it that the cloak was to be five ells square, with loops at the corners, and pegs had to be put down there of the kind that had a head at one end. They were called tarses and he who made the preparations was to approach the tarses in such a way that he could see the sky between his legs while grasping his ear lobes, with the invocation that has since been used again in the sacrifice known as the tarse-sacrifice. There were to be three spaces marked out all round the cloak, each a foot in breadth, and outside the marked spaces there should be four strings, named hazel poles; what you had was a

hazel-poled stretch of ground, when that was done. You were supposed to have three shields, but when they were used up, you were to go on to the cloak, even if you had withdrawn from it before, and from then on you were supposed to protect yourself with weapons. He who was challenged had to strike. If one of the two was wounded in such a way that blood fell on to the cloak, there was no obligation to continue fighting. If someone stepped with just one foot outside the hazel poles he was said to be retreating or to be running if he did so with both. There would be a man to hold the shield for each one of the two fighting. He who was the more wounded of the two was to release himself by paying duel ransom, to the tune of three marks of silver.

(ch.10)

The duel was formally banned by law in Iceland in 1006, six years after the Icelanders had accepted Christianity.

earl *jarl*: A title generally restricted to men of high rank in northern countries (though not in Iceland), who could be independent rulers or subordinate to a king. The title could be inherited or it could be conferred by a king on a prominent supporter or leader of military forces. The Earls of Lade who appear in a number of sagas and tales ruled large sections of northern Norway (and often many southerly areas as well) for several centuries. Another prominent, almost independent, earldom was that of Orkney and Shetland.

east *austur*: See 'directions'.

fire hall *eldaskáli*: In literal terms, the fire hall was a room or special building (as perhaps at Jarlshof in Shetland) containing a fire and its primary function was that of a kitchen. Such a definition, however, would be too limited, since the fire hall was also used for eating, working and sleeping. Indeed, in many cases the word *eldaskáli* seems to have been synonymous with the word *skáli*, meaning the hall of a farm.

foster- *fóstur-, fóstri, fóstra*: Children during the saga period were often brought up by foster-parents, who received either payment or support from the real parents. Being fostered was therefore somewhat different from being adopted: it was essentially a legal agreement and, more importantly, a form of alliance. Nonetheless, emotionally and in some cases legally, fostered children were seen as being part of the family circle. Relationships and loyalties between foster-kindred could be very strong. Note that the expressions *fóstri/fóstra* were also used for people who had the function of looking after, bringing up and teaching the children on the farm.

freed slave *lausingi, leysingi*: A slave could be set free or his freedom bought, and thus acquire the general status of a free man, although this status was lowly, since if he (or she) died with no heir, his (or her) inheritance would return to the original owner. The children of freed slaves, however, were completely free.

full outlawry *skóggangur*: Outlawry for life. See Social, Political and Legal Structure.

games *leikar*: The word *leikur* (sing.) in Icelandic had the same breadth of meaning as 'game' in English. The games meetings described in the sagas would probably have included a whole range of 'play' activities. Essentially, they involved men's sports, such as wrestling, ball games, 'skin-throwing games', 'scraper games' and horse-fights. These games took place whenever people came together and they seem to have been a regular feature of assemblies and other gatherings (including the Althing) and religious festivals such as the Winter Nights. Sometimes prominent men invited people together specifically to take part in games.

ghosts/spirits *draugar*, *afturgöngur*, *haugbúar*: Ghosts in medieval Scandinavia were seen as being corporeal and therefore capable of wrestling or fighting in other ways with opponents. This idea is naturally associated with the ancient pagan belief in Scandinavia and elsewhere that the dead should be buried with the possessions that they were going to need in the next life, such as ships, horses and weapons. The suggestion was that in some way the body was going to live again and need these items. There are many examples in the sagas of people encountering or seeing 'living ghosts' inside grave mounds. These spirits were called *haugbúar* (literally 'mound-dwellers'). Because of the fear of spirits walking again and disturbing the living, various measures could be taken to ensure some degree of peace and quiet for the living. See, for example, *Gisli Sursson's Saga* (chs. 14 and 17).

godi *goði*: This word was little known outside Iceland in early Christian times and seems to refer to a particularly Icelandic concept. A godi was a local chieftain who had legal and administrative responsibilities in Iceland. The name seems to have originally meant 'priest' or at least a person having a special relationship with gods or supernatural powers, and thus shows an early connection between religious and secular power. As time went on, however, the chief function of a godi came to be secular. The first godis were chosen from the leading families who settled Iceland in *c.*870–930. See Social, Political and Legal Structure.

hall *skáli*: *Skáli* was used both for large halls such as those used by kings, and for the main farmhouse on the typical Icelandic farm.

hayfield *tún*: An enclosed field for hay cultivation close to or surrounding a farmhouse. This was the only 'cultivated' part of a farm and produced the best hay. Other hay, generally of lesser quality, came from the meadows, which could be some distance from the farm.

hayfield wall *túngarður*: A wall of stones surrounding the hayfield to protect it from grazing livestock.

hersir *hersir*: A local leader in western and northern Norway; his rank was hereditary. The original hersirs were probably those who took command when the men of the district were called to arms.

high seat *öndvegi*: The central section of one bench in the hall (at the inner end or in the middle of the 'senior' side, to the right as one entered) was the rightful high seat of the owner of the farm. Even though it is usually referred to in English as the 'high seat', this position was not necessarily higher in elevation, only in honour. Opposite the owner sat the guest of honour.

homespun (cloth) *vaðmál*: For centuries wool and woollen products were Iceland's chief exports, especially in the form of strong and durable homespun cloth. It could be bought and sold in bolts or made up into items such as homespun cloaks. There were strict regulations on homespun, as it was used as a standard exchange product and often referred to in ounces, meaning its equivalent value expressed as a weight in silver. One ounce could equal three to six ells of homespun, one ell being roughly 50 centimetres.

horse-fight *hestaat/hestavíg*: A popular sport among the Icelanders, which seems to have taken place especially in the autumn, particularly at autumn meetings. Two horses were goaded to fight against each other, until one was killed or ran away. Understandably, emotions ran high, and horse-fights commonly led to feuds.

hundred *hundrað*: A 'long hundred' or 120. However, it rarely refers to an accurate number, rather a generalized 'round' figure.

judgement circle *dómhringur*: The courts of heathen times appear to have been surrounded by a judgement circle, marked out with hazel poles and ropes, where judgements were made or announced. The circle was sacrosanct and weapons were not allowed inside it – nor was violence.

knorr *knörr*: An ocean-going cargo vessel.

lesser outlawry *fjörbaugsgarður*: Outlawry for three years. See Social, Political and Legal Structure.

longship *langskip*: The largest warship.

main room *stofa*: A room off the hall of a farmhouse.

mark *mörk*: A measurement of weight, eight ounces, approximately 214 grams.

Moving Days *fardagar*: Four successive days in the seventh week of 'summer' (in May) during which householders in Iceland could change their abode.

north *norður*: See 'directions'.

outlawry *útlegð, skóggangur, fjörbaugsgarður*: See Social, Political and Legal Structure.

quarter *fjórðungur*: Administratively, Iceland was divided into four quarters based on the four cardinal directions.

sacrifice, sacrificial feast *blót*: There is great uncertainty about the nature of pagan worship and cults in Scandinavia, and just as the theology and mythology of the Nordic peoples seem to have varied according to area, it is highly questionable whether any standardized rules of ritual practice ever existed there. It should also be remembered that the population of Iceland came from all over Scandinavia, as well as from Ireland and the islands off Scotland. Religion was very much an individual matter and practices varied. The few references to sacrifices in the sagas are somewhat vague, but these sometimes seem to have involved the ritual slaughter of animals.

shieling *sel*: A roughly constructed hut in the highland grazing pastures away from the farm, where shepherds and cowherds lived during the summer. Milking and the preparation of various dairy products took place here, as did other important farm activities like the collection of peat and charcoal burning (depending on the surroundings). This arrangement was well known throughout the Scandinavian countries from the earliest times.

slave *þræll*: Slavery was quite an important aspect of Viking Age trade. A large number of slaves were taken from the Baltic nations and the western European countries that were raided and invaded by Scandinavians between the eighth and eleventh centuries. In addition, the Scandinavians had few scruples against taking slaves from other Nordic countries. Judging from their names and appearance a large number of the slaves mentioned in the sagas seem to have come from Ireland and Scotland. Stereotypically they are presented as being stupid and lazy. By law, slaves had hardly any rights and they and their families could only gain freedom if their owners chose to free them or somebody else bought their freedom (see 'freed slave'). In the Icelandic Commonwealth, a slave who was wounded was entitled to a third of the compensation money; the rest went to his owner.

south *suður*: See 'directions'.

spirits See 'ghosts'.

Spring Assembly *vorþing*: The local assembly, held each spring. The first regular assemblies in Iceland were held at thirteen sites, lasted four to seven days between 7 and 27 May and were jointly supervised by three godis. The Spring Assembly had a dual legal and economic function. It consisted of a court of thirty-six men, twelve appointed by each of the godis, where local legal actions were heard, while major cases and those which could not be resolved locally were sent on to the Althing. In its other function it was a forum for settling debts, deciding prices and the like. Godis probably used the Spring Assembly to urge their followers to ride to the Althing; those who remained behind paid the costs of those who went. See Social, Political and Legal Structure.

sworn brotherhood *fóstbrœðralag*: An oath undertaken by two or more men to face the same fate or that whoever survives the other will take vengeance. Oaths were sworn with a ritual described in *The Saga of the Sworn Brothers* (ch. 2):

> It had become a tradition among men of renown to become bound to each other by a law which stated that whoever outlived the other would undertake to avenge his death. They had to walk beneath a triple arch of raised turf, and this signified their oath. The arch was made by scoring out three lengths of turf and leaving them attached to the ground at both ends, then raising them to a height whereby it was possible to walk underneath them.

Blood oaths were also common.

temple *hof*: In spite of the elaborate description of the 'temple' at Hofstadir (literally 'Temple Place') in *The Saga of the People of Eyri* (ch. 4), and other temples mentioned in the sagas, there is no certainty that buildings erected for the sole purpose of pagan worship ever existed in Iceland or the other Scandinavian countries. To date, no such building has been found in archaeological excavations. In all likelihood, pagan rituals and sacrifices took place outdoors or in a specified area in certain large farmhouses belonging to priests, where the idols of the gods would also have been kept.

Thing *alþingi*: See 'Althing'.

thingman/men *þingmaður/þingmenn*: Every free man and landowner was required to serve as a thingman ('assembly man') by aligning himself with a godi. He would either accompany the godi to assemblies and other functions or pay a tax supposed to cover the godi's costs of attending them.

troll *tröll*: Trolls in the minds of the Icelanders were not the huge,

stupid figures that we read about in later Scandinavian tales and
legends. At the time of the sagas they were essentially evil nature
spirits, a little like large dark elves. It is only in later times that they
came to blend with the image of the Scandinavian giants.

Viking *víkingur*: This word normally has an unfavourable sense in the
Sagas of Icelanders, referring to violent seafaring raiders, especially
of the pagan period. It can also denote general bullies and villains.

weight *vætt*: The equivalent of 160 marks or about 40 kilos.

west *vestur*: See 'directions'.

Winter Nights *veturnætur*: The period of two days when winter begins,
around the middle of October. In the pagan era this was a particularly holy time of the year when sacrifices were made to the female
guardian spirits and social activities such as games meetings and
weddings often took place. It was also the time when animals were
slaughtered so that their meat could be stored over the winter.

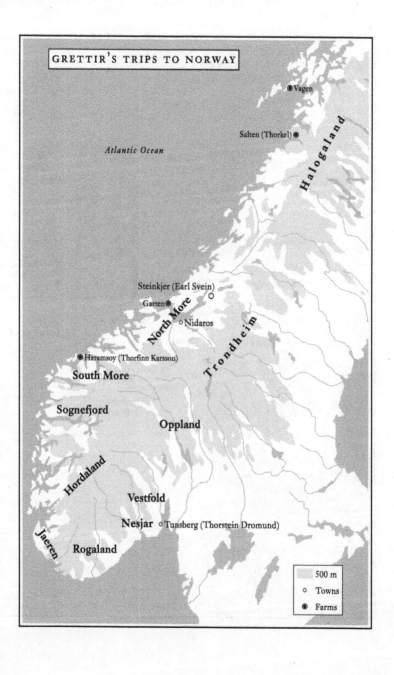

GRETTIR'S TRIPS TO NORWAY

Atlantic Ocean

Halogaland

⊛Vagen

Salten (Thorkel) ⊛

Steinkjer (Earl Svein) ○
Garten⊛
North More
○Nidaros

Trondheim

⊛Haramsoy (Thorfinn Karsson)

South More

Sognefjord

Oppland

Hordaland

Vestfold

Nesjar   ○Tunsberg (Thorstein Dromund)

Jaeren

Rogaland

500 m
○ Towns
⊛ Farms

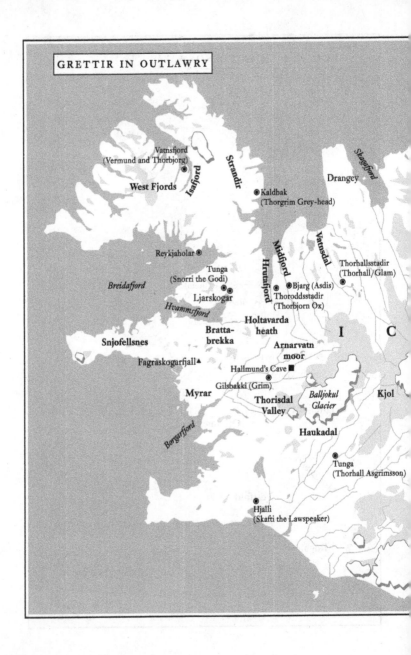

GRETTIR IN OUTLAWRY

Vatnsfjord
(Vermund and Thorbjorg)

Strandir

Drangey

West Fjords

Isafjord

Kaldbak
(Thorgrim Grey-head)

Midfjord

Vatnsdal

Reykjaholar

Tunga
(Snorri the Godi)

Hrutafjord

Thorhallsstadir
(Thorhall/Glam)

Breidafjord

Ljarskogar

Bjarg (Asdis)

Thoroddsstadir
(Thorbjorn Ox)

Hvammsfjord

Holtavarda
heath

I   C

Bratta-
brekka

Snjofellsnes

Arnarvatn
moor

Fagraskogarfjall▲

Hallmund's Cave ■

Gilsbakki (Grim)

Balljokul
Glacier

Kjol

Myrar

Thorisdal
Valley

Borgarfjord

Haukadal

Tunga
(Thorhall Asgrimsson)

Hjalli
(Skafti the Lawspeaker)

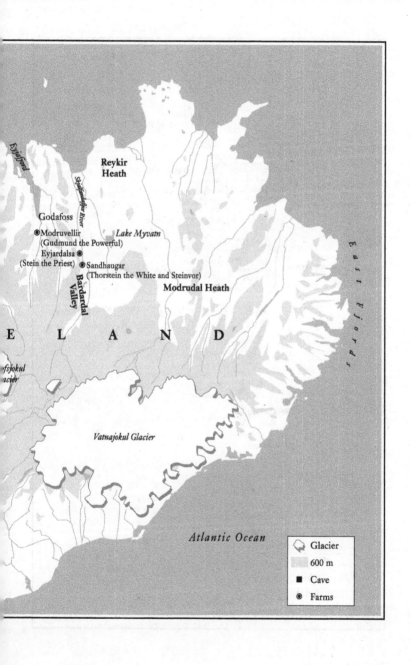

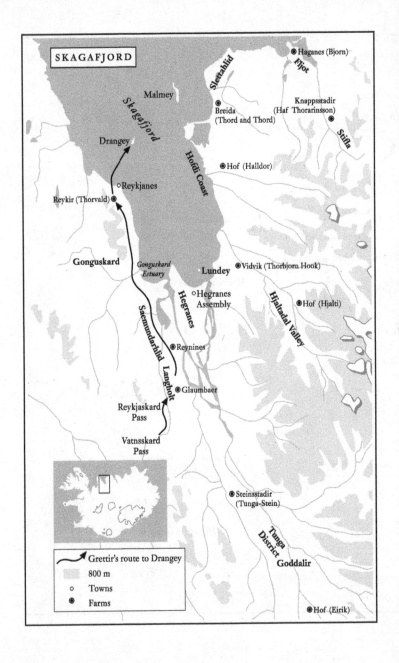

SKAGAFJORD

Haganes (Bjorn)

Fljot

Slettahlid

Malmey

Knappsstadir
(Haf Thorarinsson)

Breida
(Thord and Thord)

Sfifla

Drangey

Skagafjord

Hofdi Coast

Hof (Halldor)

Reykjanes

Reykir (Thorvald)

Gonguskard
Estuary

Lundey

Vidvik (Thorbjorn Hook)

Gonguskard

Hegranes
Assembly

Hegranes

Hof (Hjalti)

Hjaltadal Valley

Saemundarhlid

Langholt

Reynines

Glaumbaer

Reykjaskard
Pass

Vatnsskard
Pass

Steinsstadir
(Tunga-Stein)

Tunga
District

Goddalir

Hof (Eirik)

Grettir's route to Drangey

800 m

○   Towns

◉   Farms

Index of Characters

READ MORE IN PENGUIN

In every corner of the world, on every subject under the sun, Penguin represents quality and variety – the very best in publishing today.

For complete information about books available from Penguin – including Puffins, Penguin Classics and Arkana – and how to order them, write to us at the appropriate address below. Please note that for copyright reasons the selection of books varies from country to country.

In the United Kingdom: Please write to *Dept. EP, Penguin Books Ltd, Bath Road, Harmondsworth, West Drayton, Middlesex UB7 0DA*

In the United States: Please write to *Consumer Services, Penguin Putnam Inc., 405 Murray Hill Parkway, East Rutherford, New Jersey 07073-2136.* VISA and MasterCard holders call 1-800-631-8571 to order Penguin titles

In Canada: Please write to *Penguin Books Canada Ltd, 10 Alcorn Avenue, Suite 300, Toronto, Ontario M4V 3B2*

In Australia: Please write to *Penguin Books Australia Ltd, 487 Maroondah Highway, Ringwood, Victoria 3134*

In New Zealand: Please write to *Penguin Books (NZ) Ltd, Private Bag 102902, North Shore Mail Centre, Auckland 10*

In India: Please write to *Penguin Books India Pvt Ltd, 11 Community Centre, Panchsheel Park, New Delhi 110017*

In the Netherlands: Please write to *Penguin Books Netherlands bv, Postbus 3507, NL-1001 AH Amsterdam*

In Germany: Please write to *Penguin Books Deutschland GmbH, Metzlerstrasse 26, 60594 Frankfurt am Main*

In Spain: Please write to *Penguin Books S. A., Bravo Murillo 19, 1°B, 28015 Madrid*

In Italy: Please write to *Penguin Italia s.r.l., Via Vittorio Emanuele 45/a, 20094 Corsico, Milano*

In France: Please write to *Penguin France, 12, Rue Prosper Ferradou, 31700 Blagnac*

In Japan: Please write to *Penguin Books Japan Ltd, Iidabashi KM-Bldg, 2-23-9 Koraku, Bunkyo-Ku, Tokyo 112-0004*

In South Africa: Please write to *Penguin Books South Africa (Pty) Ltd, P.O. Box 751093, Gardenview, 2047 Johannesburg*

PENGUIN CLASSICS

THE PROSE EDDA
SNORRI STURLSON

'What was the beginning, or how did things start? What was there before?'

The Prose Edda is the most renowned of all works of Scandinavian literature and our most extensive source for Norse mythology. Written in Iceland a century after the close of the Viking Age, it tells ancient stories of the Norse creation epic and recounts the battles that follow as gods, giants, dwarves and elves struggle for survival. It also preserves the oral memory of heroes, warrior kings and queens. In clear prose interspersed with powerful verse, the *Edda* provides unparalleled insight into the gods' tragic realization that the future holds one final cataclysmic battle, Ragnarok, when the world will be destroyed. These tales from the pagan era have proved to be among the most influential of all myths and legends, inspiring modern works as diverse as Wagner's *Ring* cycle and Tolkien's *The Lord of the Rings*.

This new translation by Jesse Byock captures the strength and subtlety of the original, while his introduction sets the tales fully in the context of Norse mythology. This edition includes also detailed notes and appendices.

Translated with an introduction, glossary and notes by Jesse Byock

Penguin Classics

EGIL'S SAGA

'The sea-goddess has ruffled me,
stripped me bare of my loved ones'

Egil's Saga tells the story of the long and brutal life of the tenth-century warrior-poet and farmer Egil Skallagrimsson: a psychologically ambiguous character who was at once the composer of intricately beautiful poetry and a physical grotesque capable of staggering brutality. This Icelandic saga recounts Egil's progression from youthful savagery to mature wisdom as he struggles to defend his honour in a running feud against the Norwegian King Erik Blood-axe, fights for the English King Athelstan in his battles against Scotland and embarks on colourful Viking raids across Europe. Exploring issues as diverse as the question of loyalty, the power of poetry and the relationship between two brothers who love the same woman, *Egil's Saga* is a fascinating depiction of a deeply human character, and one of the true masterpieces of medieval literature.

This new translation by Bernard Scudder fully conveys the poetic style of the original. It also contains a new introduction by Svanhildur Óskarsdóttir, placing the saga in historical context, a detailed chronology, a chart of Egil's ancestors and family, maps and notes.

Translated by Bernard Scudder

Edited by Ornulfur Thorsson

PENGUIN CLASSICS

THE EPIC OF GILGAMESH

'Surpassing all other kings, heroic in stature,
brave scion of Uruk, wild bull on the rampage!
Gilgamesh the tall, magnificent and terrible'

Miraculously preserved on clay tablets dating back as much as four thousand years, the poem of Gilgamesh, king of Uruk, is the world's oldest epic, predating Homer by many centuries. The story tells of Gilgamesh's adventures with the wild man Enkidu, and of his arduous journey to the ends of the earth in quest of the Babylonian Noah and the secret of immortality. Alongside its themes of family, friendship and the duties of kings, *The Epic of Gilgamesh* is, above all, about mankind's eternal struggle with the fear of death.

The Babylonian version has been known for over a century, but linguists are still deciphering new fragments in Akkadian and Sumerian. Andrew George's gripping translation brilliantly combines these into a fluent narrative and will long rank as the definitive English *Gilgamesh*.

'This masterly new verse translation' *The Times*

Translated with an introduction by Andrew George

PENGUIN CLASSICS

GISLI SURSSON'S SAGA *AND* THE SAGA OF THE PEOPLE OF EYRI

'Fate must find someone to speak through. Whatever is meant to happen will happen'

Based on oral tales that originated from historical events in tenth-century Iceland, these two sagas follow the fate of a powerful Viking family across two generations, from its Norwegian ancestry through fierce battles to defend its honour. *Gisli Sursson's Saga* is a story of forbidden love and divided loyalties, in which the heroic Gisli vows to avenge the murder of his 'sworn brother' and sets in motion a chain of bloody events that culminate in tragedy. *The Saga of the People of Eyri* continues the story with Snorri, a cunning leader of the next generation, who uses his intellect to restore social order. Blending gripping narrative, humour, the supernatural and shrewd observation, these tales reveal the richness of the saga tradition and present a vivid record of a society moving from individualism to a Christian ethic of reconciliation and order.

These clear, contemporary translations are accompanied by an introduction giving historical and literary background to the sagas. This edition also includes appendices, maps, notes on the texts, a glossary and an index of characters.

Translated by Martin S. Regal and Judy Quinn
Edited with an introduction by Vésteinn Ólason